Ranjit Ratnaike was born in Sri Lanka and lives in Adelaide, Australia where he is a physician. He has lived in the Himalayan foothills training women as health workers, and worked on various health projects in Asia and the western Pacific region.

His interests include music and cooking.

Blog address: www.ranjitratnaike.com

SARADASI

THE PROPHECY

RANJIT RATNAIKE

SILK ROAD

This edition published in 2012 by:
Silk Road Publishing Company Pty. Ltd.
35 The Annie Watt Circuit
West Lakes Shore, South Australia, 5020
Australia.

www.silkroadpublishingco.com
Email: publisher@silkroadpublishingco.com

First published in 2009 by alto books pty. ltd., Australia.

ISBN: 978-0-9873097-0-9

National Library of Australia Cataloguing-in-Publication entry

Author:	Ratnaike, Ranjit N.
Title:	Saradasi : the prophecy / Ranjit Ratnaike
ISBN:	9780987309709 (pbk.)
Dewey Number:	A823.4

Cover concept by Dileep Ratnaike
Cover design and illustrations by Myke Mollard
Designed by Massimo Matteotti
Author photograph by Basil Popowycz
Printed and bound in the United States of America

The book is dedicated to my parents.

Cyril Hector Ratnaike
Irene Mildred Ratnaike

Acknowledgements

Writing Saradasi –The Prophecy was an interesting experience. I wrote most of the manuscript during long evenings working for an international organisation in places as diverse as a freezing hotel in Ulaanbaatar, Mongolia; in my narrow cell-like room in the Ginza Mitsui Urban hotel, Tokyo and in an apartment in Manila, Philippines where my spirited neighbours worked only at night.

I am grateful, at the end of this journey to members of my family and many friends for their help.

My son Dileep suggested that I should write a science fiction book. The basic cover concept was his and his comments on the first draft were invaluable. Stephanie, my wonderful wife, tirelessly and with great patience and insight read my many revisions, making excellent suggestions, as did my daughter Alinta and my younger son Christen.

David Petrie my friend and brother-in-law, a voracious and discerning reader, kindly read the initial draft. Committed to honest opinions, his verdict provided the encouragement to continue. I am most indebted to him.

I thank Austin Milton and David Newble who helped in various ways. I also thank Angela Barbour, Mary Denys, Alison Hodgetts, Ann Jenkins, and Bronwyn Petrie for their help. It was a pleasure working with my editor James Beckingham whose skill and intelligence I admire.

Four Hundred Years Ago:
The Beginning

They were at their favourite meeting place, a narrow valley, desolate and beautiful, surrounded by mountains on mountains heavy with snow. Three rivers flowed across the valley to a star-shaped lake surrounding a rock. A white flame rose hundreds of feet from the centre of the rock, a silver line across the lake, not flickering despite the screaming gusts of wind from mountain gorges and ravines.

The Astral Lords of the East, the West and the South, dressed in white robes sat cross-legged on the rock, their eyes closed, their auras brighter than the flame.

From another world, the Nereima Galaxy, the small spacecraft with three passengers they sent for, sped towards them and hovered, settling on the lake.

Grand Sound Master Hiransa from the planet Droha Major, tall and stooped, his grey hair swirling in the wind, stepped through the open hatch on the flame reflected on the water. The second passenger, the Great Khan of the planet Asurat, his green bushy eyebrows across his forehead quivering, joined the Grand Sound Master. A High Priest from the planet Astharia followed him smiling, his baldhead shining in the glow of the flame. He tilted his head back looking at the rock above them.

The Sound Master heard the snow falling on the valley and wondered why none fell on the lake. Walking on the water towards the rock they heard the three Astral Lords chanting.

In an instant, they rose above the water and stood by the flame facing the Astral Lords.

The oldest Astral Lord welcomed them. 'I am the Lord of the West,' he said. 'We will tell you about the final battle for the

Nereima Galaxy. In every universe there are two forces in battle. We represent the Forces of Good trying to defeat the Forces of Evil which destroy persons, nations and entire worlds.'

The female Astral Lord spoke to the Great Khan. 'You are the Great Khan of a planet in the Saradasi Empire in the Nereima Galaxy. You are also the head of your race the Suxt-Sux, the greatest actors in the Galaxy. They could mimic our voices and mannerisms flawlessly and wearing a facemask impersonate us as Astral Lords.'

'We would not dare.'

'Make certain you and succeeding Great Khans nurture the skills of the Suxt-Sux nation which must help defeat the evil one, Prince Vira who commands the Forces of Evil.' She looked at the smiling High Priest. 'The High Priests from your planet have the great gift to foresee the future. Your descendant, Midi78 using this gift, will help in a great search to win the battle.'

'I am the Lord of the East,' the younger male said gazing across the lake. 'Pay attention. Lord Gaima, commander of the Forces of Good, who is our superior, has fought Prince Vira to bring goodness to the Nereima Galaxy for many thousand years. Because both armies are weary, they search for a new way to decide the fate of the Nereima Galaxy.'

A hush fell over the valley. The two voices echoed around them like the rumble of thunder.

***

Prince Vira: My Lord Gaima, controlling the Nereima Galaxy is of little importance to my Master. He talked of handing it over to you.

Lord Gaima: The Nereima Galaxy is not his to give or to keep.

Prince Vira: No. I am being playful.

Lord Gaima: Continue, please.

Prince Vira: My Master agrees with our preliminary discussions to a contest between two small teams to decide who will control the Nereima Galaxy.

Lord Gaima: I agree.

Prince Vira: I will select a team of two to represent the Forces of Evil.

Lord Gaima: Two?

Prince Vira: Two.

Lord Gaima: Please continue.

Prince Vira: I will give you a choice. You may select two to represent you, or you may have four. No! Make it five.

Lord Gaima: Five against two?

Prince Vira: Yes. Five if I select them for you.

Lord Gaima: Yes.

Prince Vira: Let us make this battle interesting. Let the battle be in the future. Looking into the future I will select your team.

Lord Gaima: Why is the battle in the future and not immediately?

Prince Vira: I want to help you. My team of two is in a locus of evil, *The Place*. Your team of five needs one weapon. With this one weapon they can enter *The Place* and destroy my team.

Lord Gaima: The weapon?

Prince Vira: A favourite of yours. Goodness.

Lord Gaima: Goodness?

Prince Vira: Yes. If your team enters *The Place* with enough goodness they will automatically destroy my team.

Lord Gaima: Who are on my team?

Prince Vira: Whoever they are, you can increase their goodness.

Lord Gaima: How will I do that?

Prince Vira: The contest is in the future. You have boasted that you can transflux genes of goodness into living beings. Here is your opportunity. Transflux goodness into your team's genes in their cycles of rebirth over four hundred years.

Lord Gaima: Who is on my team?

Prince Vira: We must decide on a starting date. Let us say in four hundred years, and the duration one year.

Lord Gaima: I agree.

Prince Vira: We must not interfere with our teams when the battle begins.

Lord Gaima: I agree. Should all five enter *The Place*?

Prince Vira: Yes. Their power lies in their total goodness.

Lord Gaima: Who is on my team?

Prince Vira: Saradasi. Five Saradasi.

Lord Gaima: Saradasi? Saradasi? Five Saradasi?

Prince Vira: Yes, my Lord Gaima. Saradasi. Saradasi who brutally rule four planets in the Nereima Galaxy, hated by billions.

Lord Gaima: What are their names?

A roar of thunder drowned his reply.

***

The sun rose turning the white mountains shades of pink and red.

Grand Sound Master Hiransa, seated by the flame sprang up. 'Saradasi? Saradasi? The Nereima Galaxy is lost!'

'Mark well the date the battle begins,' the Lord of the East said. 'The clocks, all ten thousand eight hundred and ninety nine will strike in glorious harmony.'

The High Priest frowned. 'Where?' he asked, 'will there be ten thousand eight hundred and ninety nine clocks?'

The Lord of the East turned to the Sound Master. 'During the battle the Sound Master helping the Saradasi team will travel on the *Wave*. He will be your direct descendent.'

'Lord, my descendent? I have no partner.'

The Lord of the East's eyes narrowed. 'Listen when I speak to you. His name will be Master Glance.'

'Glance?'

Grand Sound Master Hiransa looked away when the Lord of the East stared at him.

'Go now. What you have seen and heard today is *The Prophecy*. Tell your people to pass on *The Prophecy* from generation to generation. Do as we say and remember we are astral Lords, not astral fools.'

***

The three visitors looked around them. There was no rock, lake, rivers or mountains.

The sun beat down on them.

Their spaceship sat on a hot, treeless desert, its engines purring.

Emblazoned across it was a single word, *Wave.*

Three small animals with bulging eyes looked at them and waddled away.

The Archives - A Note

By

Midi78, High Priest from Astharia, a planet
in the Saradasi Empire

My friend, let me tell you about the archives you will read in this exciting story. As you know an archive is a collection of historical records about a place, an institution, a person or a group of people.

The archives are hundreds of years old, and mention the names of many people, long dead, to give life to them; but you need not remember their names. Instead, please carry in your mind their actions which bridge important past events to the present.

As the story unfolds you must remember a few names. They are: Shanaz the young female High Chancellor of the Empire, Seelawathie-Ap her devoted body guard, Lord Wynan her lover, Fariyal her much-loved cousin, Lord Rasalis the Chancellor of Security and his enigmatic friend Lord Medaris.

The gifted Sound Master Glance and his son Breve travel with me on the *Wave* to fulfil *The Prophecy*.

Long after I am gone, the names I mentioned will shine in myth and legend in the Nereima Galaxy and live in your memory.

ONE

The chimes of ten thousand eight hundred and seventy six clocks swept through ZenFah, a glowing, diamond shaped space station deep in the Nereima Galaxy. Midi78, the clock team leader on Level 480, grimaced at the disharmonious sound, while a security guard, new to the station, hurried past to the lavatories with his hands over his ears. He strode out frowning.

'When will this noise stop?' he groaned.

'Be patient,' Midi78 replied. 'When all the clocks chime in glorious harmony *The Prophecy* will be fulfilled.'

'If these clocks ever chime together we will not hear them because we will be deaf.'

'My friend,' Midi78 said, rubbing his bald head with his palms, 'let me tell you more about the clocks and *The Prophecy*.'

'I hear about *The Prophecy* every day,' the guard said. 'When the clocks strike together the predictions in *The Prophecy* will come to pass and the battle for the Nereima Galaxy will begin.'

'Then you should remember it is an honour to work here,' Midi78 said with a smile. He watched a platoon of guards run past, weapons drawn, to the theatre at the end of the mirrored corridor. 'Why are there so many guards?' he asked.

'We are on triple alert. I cannot tell you the reason,' the guard said striding towards the theatre.

Across the busy corridor Midi78 saw the male Merran seated in a recreation area, glancing at him as he had all morning. When the crowd thinned, Midi78 crossed over to the recreation area, approaching the Merran slowly.

'Good wishes to you!' Midi78 said. 'I see you are from the Island of Darkness on the planet Merr.'

The Merran rose, tottering on his feet, a dazzling figure in a high collared silver robe and wide brimmed silver hat, steadying himself with his arms spread out. He pressed his airflow mask to his face, sucking in air, adjusting the keys on the breathing apparatus buckled on his waist. The green tinge left his face.

The Merran raised his right arm in greeting and bent, stroking Midi78's cheek. 'You are from the planet Astharia,' he said.

'I am, my friend. I saw you watching me. May I help you?'

'You are a clock team leader,' the Merran said, turning away from three guards nearby. 'Tell me about *The Prophecy*.'

'It's no secret, my friend,' Midi78 replied. '*The Prophecy* tells of the battle for the Nereima Galaxy in which five Saradasi will represent the Forces of Good. When the clocks chime in harmony, the battle will begin. The five Saradasi have one year to defeat the Forces of Evil in *The Place* and their sole weapon is their goodness.'

'Saradasi with goodness?' the Merran scoffed.

Midi78 stood on his toes placing his hand over the Merran's mouth. 'Please, my friend, it is dangerous voicing such opinions. Some may hear what you say. Please be cautious, we are in a dangerous place.'

The Merran pointed to the mural on the wall opposite them, with *'Saradasi Empire, the Nereima Galaxy'* blazoned across it. The planet, Saradasi, shone bright red, the colonised planets, Astharia, Asurat, Califra and Merr glowed blue and the planet Natashi, a lifeless black.

'The Saradasi will not rule Natashi because they cannot reach it,' the Merran said, his mouth against Midi78's ear. 'The Nereima Galaxy is not the Saradasi Empire because Natashi will never be under vile Saradasi rule.'

Midi78 wiped his head. 'Please, my friend, you must not mention the Saradasi.'

The Merran spoke loudly over the jarring chimes of the clocks. 'You said the team of five Saradasi must reach *The Place* to defeat the Forces of Evil. Where is *The Place*?'

'Nobody knows, though people have talked of this evil place for thousands of years,' Midi78 replied. 'Explorers and scientists have spent their lifetime seeking *The Place* which the Saradasi team must find.'

The Merran coughed, his fingers moving over the keys of his breathing apparatus. 'You are a Gootamundra from the clan of High Priests,' he said. 'You must have seen a vision or received a revelation.'

2

'I have not. We believe *The Place* is in one of the seven universes.'

'One of the seven?' the Merran laughed. 'The Saradasi could not reach Natashi in this universe. How will they travel to another universe?'

'My friend, please think before you talk about the Saradasi and consider what you say. You place yourself in grave danger. I am also in danger.' Midi78 greeted a clock repair team on their zeeter, gliding above the crowds streaming towards the theatre.

A group of scruffy, wild-eyed Craxxian merchants left the crowd and surrounded Midi78 and the Merran. The merchants shouted, describing their mechanical toys. One thrust a yelping, multi-legged gooshe onto Midi78's shoulder praising it as an excellent pet.

'No, thank you,' Midi78 said, pulling at the gooshe crawling up his neck.

'One solar.'

'No thank you.'

'A bargain for just one solar.'

'No thank you, my friend, no.'

The merchant yanked the gooshe off Midi78's bald head while others thrust their toys at him. He turned to speak to the Merran. 'Where is my friend?' he asked.

Forcing his way through the Craxxian merchants he searched the corridor and hurried to the theatre. Why, he wondered, was the Merran interested in *The Prophecy*? Why ask him, a clock team leader? *The Prophecy* was not a secret and its details were available in libraries on the space station and throughout the Saradasi Empire.

'My friend, have you seen a tall Merran come in dressed in silver with an air mask covering his face?' Midi78 asked a guard at the entrance to the theatre.

'No.'

'Are you sure?'

'Yes, Midi78, a Merran has not entered the theatre. Go inside.'

Inside the crowded theatre, the audience from across the Saradasi Empire applauded loudly. Children shrieked with laughter as a bumbling magician fell off the stage. The bearded magician's multicoloured eyebrows fanning across his forehead quivered when every trick he performed ended in a catastrophe. The magician belonged to a race of hereditary actors, the Suxt–Sux, recognised even by the Saradasi as the most talented in the Empire.

Midi78 left the theatre and worked on the clocks that chimed out of tune. He stopped working when a loud musical tone rang through the station. A harsh recorded voice drowned the noise in the corridor.

'Attention all visitors to Space Station ZenFah. All travellers except Saradasi must seek permission for travel beyond ZenFah within the Saradasi Empire. The penalty for unauthorised travel is severe. Note well. Even those with a travel certificate cannot enter the Exclusion Zone surrounding the planet Saradasi. Death is the penalty for disobeying Saradasi travel rules.'

Sitting in the recreation area, Midi78 listened to a space station guide from his home planet Astharia talking to her tour group. 'Over three centuries have passed since the Saradasi built this space station, a monument to their engineering genius. It is a huge floating city, with thousands of shops and markets, where you can buy anything from a spacecraft to a new face. We are now on Level 480. We cannot visit the eight levels above us.'

'Good,' a member of the group said, yawning. 'The reason is?'

'The Saradasi use those floors.'

'Are there clocks there, to make the Saradasi deaf?'

'Be silent,' the guide warned. 'Recall my instructions to you.'

She shook two tour group members awake. 'Quick. Watch the screen. You will see a Saradasi.'

The lights dimmed.

A Saradasi female with a high-bridged nose and large violet eyes appeared on the screen above them, brushing aside a strand of curly hair from her forehead. 'We Saradasi are beginning our three hour fast for the day,' she said. 'During this time no food or drink will be available for sale. We forbid you to eat or drink in public. If you disobey this order we will punish you and expel you from Space Station ZenFah and debar you from future entry. Obey. The fast begins now.'

A member of the tour group said, gazing at the screen, 'Is it correct, Guide, that the Saradasi are the most beautiful living beings in the Saradasi Empire?'

'Yes. Everything beautiful is in the divine ratio of 1:1.68. The Saradasi face follows this ratio,' the guide said.

Midi78 returned and sat at his workstation, thinking about the Merran and his disappearance. He watched a platoon of grim faced guards patrol the corridor.

O

The Administrator of Space Station ZenFah and her assistants sat watching the bank of screens in the Command Centre.

'Greetings, Archduke Pirantha-Los from Terumana. I am Maxianusa,' the Administrator said in InterWord, the language the Saradasi created for communication within their Empire. 'Saradasi Space Control grants your squadron entry permission. Deactivate your weaponry now and we will scan and immobilise your spaceships when you dock.'

She glanced at a screen. 'You Terumana are confined to your ships except for the twenty most senior officers. I repeat twenty officers, no more, may leave their ships. After Stage One entry procedures, you will undergo bacterial, viral and parasitic sterilisation. Report for metabolic stabilisation. When your metabolism is stable, board the transport vehicle reserved for you. Alight at the perfumery on Level 103. If after visiting the perfumery you have a bad smell, you must employ perfumers to accompany you to all public areas. Be warned, you are now within the Saradasi Empire.'

Maxianusa, a non-Saradasi, knew the Archduke Pirantha-Los well from his previous visits to the space station. He was from Terumana, a planet in an eastern dwarf galaxy, whose inhabitants hated and feared the Saradasi. She watched two hundred Terumana spacecraft dock, each ship resembling an animal from Terumana, painted with a snarling mouth and bloody teeth. The Archduke Pirantha-Los and nineteen Terumana officers disembarked, dressed in orange vests and flared skirts. Metal sheaths with spikes covered their arms and coloured feathers adorned their helmets showing their rank. She watched them reluctantly submitting to the strict entry procedures and leave the medical chamber, each Terumana with a metabolic stabiliser flask connected to his neck. They boarded the transport vessel and on Level 103 pushed their way to the perfumery. The perfumers, their heads enclosed in clear helmets connected by tubes to a portable air supply, sat in sullen groups.

'The usual charge is five solars,' the Archduke argued.

'Not for Terumana,' a perfumer one-third the size of a Terumana, shouted back through her amplifier. 'Fifty solars. The next price is fifty five solars because you are wasting our time.'

'What is good is not cheap. What is cheap is not good!' a Terumana commander shouted to his colleagues. With a roar of agreement they paid the fee and entered the perfumery.

When the Terumana swaggered into the Command Centre, Maxianusa sat on a platform examining her feet. Glowering, red teeth bared, knotted green hair reaching their waists, they pounded the floor with their thick metal-soled boots. They leered and lunged at the perfumers spraying the Command Centre.

'Terumana, wear the voice-boxes you were given round your throat,' Maxianusa ordered. 'We now broadcast all conversations in the Command Centre. The voice-boxes will convert your language to InterWord.'

A Terumana lifted one leg and roared, 'I speak for the luminescent Archduke Pirantha-Los, the fearless one, the bravest of the brave, the incandescent one, attack squadron leader extraordinaire, worthy of being the Lord Admiral of the Terumana fleet, though not yet.'

Maxianusa clapped her hands. The perfumers sprayed more perfume.

'I agree,' a Terumana officer bellowed, leaping into the air and striking the floor with his feet, the sound like a thunderclap. He jumped, higher. Missing his footing, he fell and slithered along the floor, colliding with the Archduke who kicked him. Clutching his right ankle he rose to his feet, shouting, 'Terumana alive and dead admire our Archduke Pirantha-Los.' The Archduke kicked him again on his swelling ankle.

'I demand an apology,' the Archduke snarled. 'The Sector 1 Controller refused to let us travel in Sector 1 tonight. Why?'

'Because I told him to,' Maxianusa said. 'The traffic in Sector 1 is hostile to you.'

'Hostile to me? One ship of my squadron can destroy an entire fleet from anywhere.'

'This is a single ship,' Maxianusa said.

'One ship? You are refusing Sector 1 access to my entire fleet because of *one* ship? It may fit in my ship.'

The Terumana guffawed, stamping their boots.

'Yes, it is a small ship that will fit in your ship,' Maxianusa agreed.

'Your Luminescence, we should capture this ship,' a Terumana officer suggested. 'It can decorate your lavatory.'

'A grand idea. Perhaps my water will sink the ship and drown its passengers.'

The Terumana hooted with laughter.

'Others, beyond this Command Centre are listening to you,' Maxianusa warned.

'Why are you not laughing?' Archduke Pirantha Los asked, baring his teeth at Maxianusa. 'Is my suggestion not amusing?'

'No, it is not amusing,' Maxianusa said. 'The two passengers on the ship will also not find your suggestion amusing.'

'Why not?'

'The craft,' Maxianusa said, 'is Saradasi.'

'Saradasi? Saradasi?' the Archduke stammered. 'Are you sure?' He stumbled back, staring at Maxianusa.

The silence grew.

Maxianusa stepped from the platform and walked towards the Archduke. 'Yes, the craft you want to pass your water on and drown its passengers is the *Mithras Ennab* with Lord Wynan, who is the new High Chancellor's General. The other occupant is Commander Fariyal, the High Chancellor's cousin. They are travelling home to Saradasi.'

The Terumana sat on the floor with the Archduke talking among themselves, their voices hushed.

Returning to her seat, Maxianusa peered at her jewelled toes. An aide ran to her and whispered and she pressed a key on her control panel. Space Station ZenFah glowed purple.

'I am Maxianusa, Administrator of Space Station ZenFah,' she announced. 'Listen to me all staff and visitors. Space Station ZenFah is on purple alert due to an emergency and only Saradasi craft may leave the space station. Saradasi Space Control cannot locate the *Mithras Ennab* in Sector 1 and if you have any knowledge of the *Mithras Ennab*, inform me immediately. The penalty for withholding information is death.'

Maxianusa snapped her fingers at the Archduke. 'You demanded to use Sector 1. Why? Why Sector 1? Were there other Terumana craft in Sector 1? What have you Terumana done to the *Mithras Ennab*?'

'There are no Terumana craft in Sector 1. I knew of no Saradasi craft in Sector 1. I asked to use Sector 1 to reach our destination faster.'

Maxianusa snapped her fingers again. Two platoons of guards filled the Command Centre, surrounding the Archduke and his advisers.

Maxianusa bent her head, listening to an aide and ran her tongue over the rings on her lip. 'I want the truth,' she said. 'We are unable to monitor Sector 1 because a severe electron storm in Sector 1 has disabled our equipment. You Terumana have damaged our equipment. Who taught you Terumana to create an electron storm? I repeat where is the *Mithras Ennab*? Where are the other Terumana?'

'There are no Terumana in Sector 1,' Pirantha-Los insisted. 'The Terumana are innocent. This is a Saradasi plot to extract a penalty from us.'

'You Terumana have caused more problems. The electron storm in Sector 1 must have stranded and endangered the *Gaina*. We cannot locate it as well.'

'What is the *Gaina*?' the Archduke asked.

'It is the largest water carrier in the Nereima Galaxy, bringing water to this station. The guards will take you to your quarters.'

The Archduke Pirantha Los staggered out, leaving behind him a puddle on the floor and a trail of large footprints.

O

Midi78 sat at his workstation thinking about the *Mithras Ennab*. The tour guide from Astharia beckoned him and they walked into the recreation room.

'In the next few moments,' the guide said, 'you must not appear surprised and draw attention to us. Preserve your serene look.'

'I will,' Midi78 replied.

'I am Faris, the Suxt-Sux actor,' the guide said.

'Faris? The most famous actor in the Saradasi Empire?'

'Yes. And we meet again,' Faris said.

'So, my friend, you were the Merran I met this morning and the magician on the stage in the theatre.'

'Yes.'

'Were the Craxxian toy merchants, who surrounded us and helped you leave for the theatre, Suxt-Sux actors in your tour group?' Midi78 asked.

'Yes. I left you disguised as a Craxxian toy merchant. My silver clothes are hidden in your workstation.'

'Why all these disguises? There must have been an easier way to talk to me,' Midi78 said.

'We Suxt-Sux are constantly acting and developing our skills every moment we are awake. Great acting is like a plant and needs constant care, water and nourishment. I go to sleep at night in disguise, not as a Suxt-Sux. When I awake the next morning, for that day I am the person whose disguise I adopted.'

'I am a Gootamundra and I read minds,' Midi78 said. 'I think, my friend, there is another reason for all your actions.'

'Yes,' Faris agreed. 'My life is in great danger. I am therefore cautious.'

'Danger? Here in the space station?'

Faris pointed to the guards near the recreation room.

On the screen above them, Maxianusa, her face taut announced: 'Shanaz, the High Chancellor of the Saradasi Empire, will speak to the citizens of the Empire.'

The face of the recently elected young High Chancellor filled the screen. 'Saradasi Space Control cannot find the *Mithras Ennab,*' she said. 'The Saradasi Empire will hunt those responsible for its loss to the ends of our Nereima Galaxy and beyond. We will punish them, their families and seven future generations. The Saradasi Empire is on purple alert. Saradasi Space Control restricts travel within the Empire except for Saradasi and other approved craft.'

Midi78 saw fear on the face of a Saradasi, the bravest race in the galaxy. He shook his head. 'Who,' he asked, 'would dare attack a Saradasi craft?'

'Not Terumana,' Faris said. 'They fear the Saradasi more than any other race. The Saradasi know of every Terumana plan because one in fifty Terumana military officers spy for the Saradasi.'

'How could a Saradasi craft travelling within the Saradasi Empire disappear?' Midi78 asked.

'It seems like a magician's trick in space,' Faris said.

9

TWO

The spaceship *Wave* cruised in the Nereima Galaxy with Sound Master Glance and its crewmember Breve asleep in their cabins.

Breve woke when the message alarm rang.

'*Wave*, this is Saradasi Space Control. You are approaching the western zone of the Nereima Galaxy. Reconfirm your destination.'

'This is Breve on board the *Wave*. We have authority to travel to the Western Galaxy.'

'You will dock immediately at Security Station 105 in north-eastern Merr.'

'Thank you,' Breve replied, keying in the co-ordinates.

When they docked, a Saradasi Space Control Superintendent waved her assistants to another ship while she inspected the *Wave*, examining its rusty, crudely repaired hull.

'We should ban this vehicle from the Nereima Galaxy,' she said. 'The state of disrepair of your ship disgusts me.' Speaking softly, she added, 'Meet me at noon. I am expecting a message for you.' She left to inspect a soil and gravel tanker.

The three indigo-haired travellers sitting on the quay opposite the *Wave* greeted Master Glance and Breve.

'We are from Astharia,' one of them said in InterWord. He increased his voice amplifier when Master Glance cupped his hands behind his ears. 'Sir, we wonder how your craft travels. It is old and in great disrepair and we fear for your safety.'

Master Glance touched the *Wave* lovingly. 'We trust in good fortune,' he replied.

'You are not from our Nereima Galaxy?'

'No. We live in the Western Galaxy, beyond the Starlizz Galaxy. I am Master Glance and this is Breve.'

'You are lucky to have travelled safely over such a long distance,' another Astharian marvelled.

The third Astharian squinted at the *Wave*. 'I think it is dangerous to travel in it.'

'Though we fear for our lives, we must return home. We come from a sad place,' Master Glance answered, brushing his long hair from his face.

'Sad?'

'Our planet Droha Major is dying because our sun is dying. Snow and ice are strangling our beautiful home,' Master Glance explained, stroking his beard.

The Astharians held their heads in their hands.

'Have you enough food and drink on your craft? By our laws we must share what we have with you. Have you money? We can give you some solars,' an Astharian said.

'Thank you. You are most kind,' Master Glance replied. 'We have enough supplies. Thank you.'

The Astharians embraced Master Glance and Breve and sat on their seats, hands on their bowed heads, their perfume lingering in the air. Master Glance and Breve listened to the harsh sounds from the *Wave* while walking away.

'The *Wave* sounds too healthy,' Master Glance murmured. Breve reached for the control panel slung round his neck and increased the pitch and volume of the pre-recorded thudding sound from the *Wave's* air purification unit. They passed through the decontamination chamber to the space mall to spend time until Saradasi Space Control allowed them to leave.

Master Glance sat on a seat and, grimacing, drank his morning dose of medicine, which Breve gave him. He thanked him and wondered what message the Superintendent had for him. It would be from Lord Rasalis, the Chancellor of Security of the Saradasi Empire he thought.

○

The *Wave* left Security Station 105 before nightfall, cleared to leave the Nereima Galaxy with a reminder of the severe penalty if the *Wave* entered the Exclusion Zone of the planet Saradasi. During dinner Master Glance surprised Breve by telling him the friendly Astharians who offered them help were Saradasi spies, Suxt-Sux actors from the planet Asurat in disguise, not Astharians.

In his cramped cabin on deck two Master Glance lay on his bunk thinking about his meeting with Grand Master Ashe, the head of the Assembly of Sound Masters, who often said, 'Life is short, and precious and therefore, conciseness is essential.'

The *Wave* arrived late at night in Aloka, the capital of Droha Major, shrouded in darkness. The once majestic city with its broad avenues, elegant buildings and lush gardens, lay in decay. The grand city squares were empty, the fountains silent. The city's sparse population, cast in gloom and icy coldness, survived narrowly on the meagre energy the Saradasi supplied grudgingly.

In the chill of dawn Master Glance rose from his bed, wished his wife goodbye and left home in his warmest robe to meet Grand Master Ashe. The dying sun cast a faint morning glow through the mist as he crossed the streets wet with snow to climb the trail through the woods; the once green trees were blighted with the scaly greyness of death.

He stopped at a small clearing with stunted trees and looked at the jagged blue line of snow-covered mountains. He heard a giggle. Two children ran up to him, grabbed his hands, pointing to their kite.

'Think, children,' Master Glance said smiling, untangling the red kite flapping in the wind from a branch and tousling their hair.

The wind picked up, swirling the snow from the trees. Listening to the snow crunch beneath his boots he walked to the park below. Once a jewel of the city, it lay dead. He continued up a flight of steps cracked and overgrown with weeds, to the school of wind music, its walls streaked and dull.

Despite the cold, a young female music teacher sat on a bench beneath a tree her head bent listening to a child playing a reed instrument. She said, 'Play with your heart, not just with your fingers.' She jumped to her feet when she saw Master Glance and greeted him warmly.

'Please, Master Glance, you must not smile! You are encouraging poor intonation.'

'Intonation is the key to great music,' he said when the child joined them.

The child nodded, sitting on the bench with them and laying her instrument on her lap.

'It is not enough to play the notes,' Master Glance explained. 'You must pitch the notes at the correct frequency relating to the other notes.

This is what intonation is. Intonation is more powerful than nimble fingers. When you play with others you must listen to them, and also listen carefully to your own playing.' He patted her head. 'Remember, the silence between notes is as important as the notes themselves. Think about what I have told you.'

'Thank you, Master Glance,' the child said smiling shyly.

'A piece of music is like a bunch of five beautiful flowers. The five flowers are the melody, the harmony, the rhythm, the volume and the unique sound of each instrument. When you play, enjoy yourself and think about the five flowers.'

When she left, he asked the teacher, 'Is it too cold to play in the open?'

'No. If she plays well in the cold, she will play better when her fingers are not cold.'

Master Glance left the park and followed a path winding up a hill. The Grand Master's house was on the crest of the hill, the curved green roof splattered with snow. After half an hour's walk he passed through the wooden gate to the patio surrounding the house. Bright pillars supported the roof.

In the centuries old house, Grand Master Ashe lived alone. He sat wrapped in a blanket, on a high backed chair on the patio. A decanter with wine and two goblets were on the table in front of him. He motioned Master Glance to sit next to him. The scent from a grove of trees below blew towards them.

'Welcome home. I have missed you and Breve. How are you and how is your health?' he said, stroking his short beard.

'My health is improving,' Master Glance replied.

'Are you sure? How is Breve?'

'He is well, and will see you this evening.'

They talked of the past and of their dying planet; of the future and its hopelessness unless the Saradasi increase their energy supply. As always they spoke of a new home, perhaps in another galaxy.

'We must talk about *The Prophecy* and *The Place*,' Grand Master Ashe said. 'I will summarise what people in the Nereima Galaxy say about *The Prophecy*. The Nereima Galaxy is the new battlefield in the war between good and evil. If Prince Vira's Forces of Evil defeat the Forces of Good, they will destroy the Nereima Galaxy. The battle for the Galaxy will begin soon.'

14

He sipped his wine and continued. 'Many hundreds of years ago, our ancestor Grand Master Hiransa obeyed the instructions he received in a vision. He travelled with Sx'Tillah, the Great Khan of the planet Asurat, and Midi73, the Gootamundra High Priest from the planet Astharia to meet three Astral Lords: the Lord of the North, the Lord of the South and the Lord of the East. Sitting with these Astral Lords they heard a conversation between the Astral Lord Gaima and the evil Prince Vira about the battle for the Nereima Galaxy. They said their Forces of Good and Evil have battled since the beginning of time. Because their armies were exhausted each agreed to field a small team to decide the fate of the Nereima Galaxy.'

The trees rustled again. They looked up at the sky darkening above them, thick with clouds wreathing the mountains. Skeins of mist rose from the moorland below them. They heard a group of musicians play and smelt the smoky fragrance of fires warming freezing homes.

'How are you aware of these details?' Master Glance asked.

'Prince Vira proposed a team of two,' the Grand Master went on, 'Brother Red and Brother Green, who live in a locus of evil, *The Place*. What is curious is, he offered Lord Gaima a team of five provided he, Prince Vira, selected them.'

'Those who are evil are never generous,' Master Glance said.

'Surprisingly, Lord Gaima agreed. They set a date in the future for the battle to begin, in three hundred and seventy seven years from that day.'

'It is a Fibonacci number.'

'Yes. Looking into the future Prince Vira chose five Saradasi to represent Lord Gaima. He said the single weapon they needed to destroy his team was their goodness. He must have meant compassion, morality, kindness and a sense of justice. The five Saradasi must destroy his team of two before one of them wins the game they are playing. The winner's prize is the Nereima Galaxy, his to destroy.'

'I am confused why Lord Gaima agreed,' Master Glance said.

'There lies a great and deep mystery, which I am not allowed to reveal until Lord Gaima's team enters *The Place*,' Grand Master Ashe said.

The sound of a bell ringing reached them from across the valley. The bell rang thrice, and the echo faded.

'The tone of the bell is harsher,' Master Glance said. 'There is a small crack at the base.'

Grand Master Ashe nodded and sipped his wine. 'Lord Rasalis the Saradasi Chancellor of Security, informs me the battle will begin in days.

The Saradasi face two great problems. First, where is *The Place*? Second, are there five Saradasi with enough goodness to overcome the two brothers?'

'The second problem would be solved if goodness was for sale,' Master Glance replied. 'Their lack of goodness is a problem without a solution.'

'There may be a solution,' the Grand Master replied. 'Over lunch, I will tell you about a vast and brilliant plan involving hundreds of people Lord Rasalis has devised to help the five Saradasi. You asked how I knew the details of what Lord Gaima and Prince Vira said to each other.' He drained his wine and placed the goblet on the table.

'I can guess,' Master Glance said. 'Our ancestor Grand Master Hiransa recorded the conversation, and you have heard the recording.'

'Tell me what you know of reincarnation,' the Grand Master said.

'Some races on Merr and Califra and in our own Western Galaxy believe in reincarnation. They believe a person is born with a soul and a physical body. The body, not the soul, dies many times. The soul is re-born in a different physical body. At a certain point both the body and the soul die. The soul is born once and dies once.'

'I have never believed in reincarnation because there is no evidence. Why does this cycle of rebirth occur?' Grand Master Ashe asked.

'This cycle of birth and death and rebirth occurs for the soul to learn during each lifetime.'

'Is there a memory of the previous life?'

'People have no memory of their past life. Perhaps the soul remembers. When after a sufficient period of learning, the soul dies, the cycle ends. Re-birth no longer occurs.'

'Is there proof of all this?' Grand Master Ashe said.

'None. There are many events in life we accept which we cannot prove,' Master Glance said.

'Tell me, what happened on the *Wave*.'

'We were in the Nereima galaxy and unexpectedly a strong field of ionised plasma trapped the *Wave*.'

'Ionised plasma?'

'Ionised plasma is like a cloud of gas. Shall I explain this?'

'No.'

'We lost control of the *Wave* and were drifting dangerously when I thought we found *The Place*. We could not fix the coordinates because every instrument on the *Wave* failed. Breve and I were sick with nausea, vomiting and severe dizziness.'

'Can you guess where you were?'

'Perhaps we strayed into another universe or perhaps we entered a gap-hole or a portal between two universes. The astrologers and astronomers on Merr believe *The Place* is a circular area in another universe with great evil at its centre.'

Grand Master Ashe refilled his goblet and breathed in the aroma of the wine. 'Why did you state in your report you might have found *The Place*?'

'I heard four words, "Your game, Brother Red," spoken in InterWord.'

Grand Master Ashe re-arranged his blanket. 'There may be thousands of brothers playing a game.'

'Perhaps. We know *The Prophecy* says Red is the name of one of the brothers in Prince Vira's team.'

'Your problem is how to retrace your movements and search for *The Place*. I have arranged for four Sound Masters to help you. Our honour binds us to help the Saradasi find *The Place* whether we like them or not. And our routine work, spying on others, a task we despise, will continue.'

'For a pittance of energy,' Master Glance added.

The Grand Master grimaced. 'Please ask Breve to visit the Vault tomorrow to meet Master Retrion and learn about the complex Saradasi. Master Retrion will also teach him to access our Sound Master Archives and the Saradasi Archives, when you are on the *Wave*. Have you told Breve we illegally hold copies of the Saradasi Archives?'

'No.' Master Glance pushed aside his goblet of wine. 'We are fortunate we have two sources of audiovisual archives dating back thousands of years.'

'We are very fortunate. Eat with me. I will tell you about Lord Rasalis's grand plan to save the Nereima Galaxy.'

○

When the first glimmer of light crept over the mountain peaks, Breve left home on the long walk to the Vault wearing two warm robes, his head bent against the wind. He crossed 'The Field of Berries,' now a wasteland, and hurried to the end of a valley. Here he paused, his head back, and looking up, thought how the vault appeared to float in the air. The main building, a fluted triangle of glass eighteen storeys high, was on a stone ledge protruding from the mountainside. A waterfall, fed by a thermal spring, cascaded down one side of the vault like a veil of foam.

Breve climbed the steps to the entrance hall where the Master of the Vault, Master Retrion greeted him with an embrace. They walked through the cold building to a small room.

'Has your father's health improved?'

'Yes, Master Retrion.'

'I have the material the Grand Master wants you to view. In secret we keep copies of the Saradasi Archives, so precious to them. This is most illegal,' Master Retrion said warming his hands over a brazier. 'The Saradasi believe in the power of information. They record their Archives using an extensive surveillance apparatus and have thousands of informers on every planet. Has your father told you how the Saradasi make their audio-visual Archives?' Master Retrion asked pushing the brazier closer to Breve.

'No.'

'The Saradasi have a talent for miniaturisation. They use minute audio-visual recorders, the majority no larger than a grain of sand and therefore difficult to detect. Their agents hide these in public and private places, trees and rocks, and in vehicles. Many informants carry them. Cleverly disguised mechanical birds which Saradasi Security control, carry larger appliances. The Saradasi Archives also contain closely guarded particulars about themselves to pass onto their descendants. I cannot tell you how we get copies of these Archives which we store in our Vault.'

Master Retrion warmed his hands and rubbed his face. 'Our Sound Master Archives are different. As you know, Breve, we Sound Masters once recorded only sound. During the last few hundred years we record sight and sound using the sophisticated machines on our spaceships. We are skilled, mobile, audiovisual information gatherers for the Saradasi, travelling across the Nereima Galaxy and sometimes beyond. All this work is for our survival. You are aware the Saradasi forbid us from recording conversations between themselves anywhere in the Nereima Galaxy. Here in the Vault, Sound Masters analyse and evaluate two sets of information: what we collect and what Saradasi Security may send us. After analysis, we relay what we think is important to Saradasi Security. We have the easy task. The Saradasi have the difficult task, deciding how to use what we give them.'

'They must trust us,' Breve said.

'Yes.'

'Breve, use the control panel on the armrest of your chair to view the Archives the Grand Master selected for you. You should begin with QF 987. I will return soon.'

Sound Master Archive QF 987
Sound Only
Part 1: The Saradasi
Narrator: Grand Master Belaria

Who are the Saradasi? Where did they come from? These are difficult questions to answer when the Saradasi themselves deliberately promote contradictory versions of their origins.

One story tells of a King who banished his youngest son and his followers because of riotous living and lawlessness. These exiles wandered their galaxy for years and reached the planet Saradasi, whose name is a distortion of the Prince's own name, Saradas.

Another legend is of an Emperor who commissioned a genetic engineer to create a colony of warriors for his army. The engineer created the perfect warrior, intelligent and curious, with unparalleled mental and physical skills and fled his home with his creation. The engineer's name was Saradas, and his creation the Saradasi.

The most popular account is the Saradasi are from planet lightyears from the Nereima Galaxy, which was engulfed by greed, hatred and war. None heeded the warnings of the few who prophesied a cataclysmic end to life on their planet.

Seven mysterious teachers gathered a group of seven hundred people in a remote settlement and taught them for nine months. They returned to their countries to change the thought patterns destroying their planet. They failed. Accused of suffering from paranoid delusions, the authorities institutionalised them for life.

Epidemics of infectious diseases occurred, many incurable, caused by mutations of organisms due to temperature change. Environmental exploitation led to severe pollution of the atmosphere, soil and water. Rivers ran dry and millions died of thirst, and wars over water raged. Fluxes in atmospheric pressure caused more deaths.

The planet lay in its death throes, strangled by the greed, neglect and stupidity of its people.

The seven teachers returned and transported one thousand five hundred and ninety seven inhabitants from their planet to a planet in the Nereima Galaxy they called Saradasi.

Here the Saradasi thrived.

End of Archive

Sound Master Archive QF 987
Sound Only
Part 2: Saradasi Religious Beliefs
Narrator: Grand Master Belaria

During the early years of nationhood, spirituality dominated Saradasi life. The Saradasi were obsessed with achieving everlasting life in a geographically unknown place, they called Nevaeh. Saradasi theologians pondered over Nevaeh and its location and were unanimous that Nevaeh was a place reserved for the Saradasi. They accepted there would be everlasting life for other races in less sophisticated locations, separate from theirs.

In Nevaeh, they claimed, an identical twin existed in suspended animation for each Saradasi. Each meritorious act of an individual would contribute towards awakening the twin. When a Saradasi dies with enough merit, he or she will awaken the twin and spend eternity in Nevaeh. This simple, comfortable and comforting idea formed the core of Saradasi religious thought.

Since no Saradasi knew the extent of merit necessary to activate their twin, they performed an excess of what they considered good deeds. Their noblest deeds were converting non-Saradasi races in the Nereima Galaxy to their spiritual beliefs.

Thus, Saradasi sanctified colonialism to satisfy their unquenchable greed to amass good deeds. This evangelical fervour led to forming The Inter Planetary Evangelistic Society, governed by a First Warden and seven Wardens elected by the members, the evangelists. The Society entwined itself around the minds and lives of the Saradasi like a rapacious parasite, spreading its political and religious influence.

Bitter quarrels rose among rival groups of evangelists vying for power. Based on minutiae of dogma they banded themselves as factions of the left, the right, the centre right, and inexplicably the left right centre.

Flocks of Saradasi evangelists, ravenous for good deeds, descended on billions of people in the Nereima Galaxy, dismembering their societal structure, scorning their culture, belittling their religious beliefs, and deriding their values. Most importantly the evangelists, by devaluing the lives, and worth of the non-Saradasi justified stealing their freedom from them.

End of Archive

Breve paced the room briskly, watching gusts of wind fling sheets of steaming water against the tall windows. He sat again, drawing the brazier closer.

Sound Master Archive QF 988
Sound Only
The Saradasi Empire
Narrator: Grand Master Belaria

None except Saradasi live on the home planet, Saradasi. The Saradasi High Council, which governs the Saradasi Empire, restricts non-Saradasi from visiting the planet and has set an Exclusion Zone of many million miles beyond it.

From this mysterious planet the Saradasi rule their Empire consisting of the planets Astharia, Asurat, Califra and Merr.

The Saradasi, as a rule, appoint non-Saradasi females from Merr, to the powerful positions of Planet Governor and Province Governor. In the Empire, a Planet Governor administers each vassal planet except the desert planet Asurat, where the Great Khan, a member of the Suxt-Sux race of renowned actors, is the Planet Governor. The Planet Governors belong to an exclusive, pampered, well-paid coterie with great prestige and power.

The Saradasi divided each planet in the Empire, irrespective of its size, into twelve provinces numbered one to twelve. Female Province Governors, supervised by the Planet Governor, administer the Provinces. Each Planet and Province Governor lives in a splendid residence, similar in size and shape throughout the Empire. The residence dominates the landscape, signalling Saradasi presence and power.

In the cities in the Empire, public squares where large crowds could gather, are not a feature. Streets and roads are not straight, preventing rapid travel. Mechanisms exist to cantilever sections of roads to block and sequester parts of the city. The Saradasi military control water, energy and food supplies. The Saradasi ban student gatherings, and regard as treason public or private criticism of individual Saradasi or employees of the Saradasi Empire.

Rebellion and uprisings against Saradasi rule are rare. Retribution is swift and terrible, and extends to immediate and extended families of the accused.

End of Archive

Breve left the room and joined Master Retrion.

'The water is not as hot as before,' Master Retrion remarked, pointing at the plumes of steam rising from a spray of water on a Vault wall. 'Has Grand Master Ashe told you of Lord Rasalis 's plan for the Nereima Galaxy?'

'No. My grandfather said I would hear about it. He mentioned the actors of the Suxt-Sux race. How will they help the Saradasi?'

'Patience, Breve,' Master Retrion said, patting his nephew's head. 'Therein lies the genius of Lord Rasalis.'

○

The *Wave* left Droha Major a day later for the Nereima Galaxy and Space Station ZenFah. Master Glance checked his sound machines named 'Eavesdroppers,' hoping for information on *The Place*, while Breve sat in the recreation room replaying the final portion of an archive.

They continued with their routine tasks on the *Wave*. Master Glance was priming his machines to sound an alarm if they captured the words 'Brother Red,' 'Brother Green,' 'game,' 'score,' or words about winning or losing. He spent the evenings refining a machine that would automatically link a voice captured on the *Wave* with a person's image, location and other intimate details, stored in the Saradasi data banks.

Time passed. The day before they entered the Nereima Galaxy, Master Glance and Breve sat in the recreation room discussing the meeting they would have with Faris, the Suxt-Sux actor from Asurat, and Midi78, the priest from Astharia, when they reached Space Station ZenFah. When Breve left the recreation room to check the navigation signal from Space Station ZenFah, Master Glance went to his cabin after taking his evening dose of medicine.

In the late hours of the night Breve tapped Master Glance on his shoulder. 'Father, Grand Master Ashe.'

The communication screen on the flight deck brightened. Grand Master Ashe sat on the windswept patio of his home, a thick quilt across his shoulders. Small clumps of snow lay on the ground.

His piercing gaze bore through the screen when he spoke on the most secure frequency Sound Masters used. 'You must not communicate with me till I give you permission. Go directly to Space Station ZenFah and let nothing distract you. Anything you see or hear is not your concern and you must not communicate with me or anyone else. Confirm.'

'Yes,' Master Glance said.

'Switch off your recording instruments immediately. Travel safely and carefully.' He smiled at Master Glance and said, 'go back to sleep.'

Later that night, Breve performed a routine check of the defence and assault systems on the *Wave* and increased the sensitivity of the outer perimeter intruder alert. He frowned when he saw the navigation screen and checked the movement log of all Saradasi spacecraft, automatically copied to Sound Masters travelling in the Nereima Galaxy. He ran to the lower deck and shook Master Glance awake in his cabin.

On the flight deck, Breve pointed to the movement log and the navigation screen. 'It is the *Mithras Ennab* and it is not on course to Saradasi. Should we inform Saradasi Space Control?'

'No. Remember what the Grand Master said? What we see or hear must not concern us, Breve. We must obey our instructions.' Master Glance leaned back in his seat and rubbed the sleep from his eyes.

'Father, it is the *Mithras Ennab*. The passengers listed on the movement log are Lord Wynan and Commander Fariyal, the High Chancellor's cousin.'

'We must follow our orders,' Master Glance said, looking at the navigation screen clouded by a deepening haze. He touched a switch and listened.

'Breve, identify the other sound we are hearing.'

'Father, a second vessel is drawing near the Mithras Ennab.'

'Is it the sound pattern of the water carrier, *Gaina*?'

Breve nodded.

THREE

Dawn was breaking over the Upper City in Saradas, the capital of the home planet Saradasi, with sunlight creeping over the few houses on the hills facing the bay.

The small two-storied house of wood and glass with graceful lines nestled in a grove of trees separate from the others. The transparent western wall looked out across the bay to the old wharves and to the sea beyond. The north wall framed the snow-streaked Mirellar Mountains. Here, on the second floor of her home, Shanaz, the youngest High Chancellor of the Saradasi Empire, sat staring across the bay, ash blue and calm in the light filtering through the clearing mist.

Except for a handful, most Saradasi lived twelve miles below the surface of the planet in the magnificent Lower City, the centre of the Saradasi Empire. Built on a square grid across artificial valleys and mountains, rivers and streams flowed across lush green meadows, and waterfalls swept into blue lakes teeming with fish. Birds of a thousand colours stalked their prey. Terraced, vivid flower gardens and long reflecting canals adorned the Lower City.

Shanaz heard the moan of the wind. The promise of a glowing day faded, the sky becoming dark and brooding. The wind rose to a howl. The bay churned into a cauldron of white foam and snow beat against Tarich's Tavern by the old wharves.

It was thirty-two days since the Saradasi nation elected her High Chancellor. She regretted accepting a job she disliked, after her father's recent mysterious death. The *Cayetana,* the personal spacecraft of the High Chancellor, Lord Laramis, her father, left Saradas with an unidentified passenger. The *Cayetana* never arrived at its destination.

Lord Rasalis, the Chancellor of Security himself supervised the search, which he abandoned after a few weeks, saying, 'we will need many years to comb the inaccessible, rugged, terrain.' The purpose of the High Chancellor's visit was puzzling. None believed Lord Laramis

25

wished to relax in the thermal springs with healing properties in Ancore South. Shanaz knew her father rarely sought relaxation; nor was he ill. Why was there no record of the route coordinates? Who was the other passenger? Why were teams of searchers unable to find what remained of the *Cayetana*?

She went to her command post on the ground floor, bare except for a table, a console, a seat, and a large screen. Sitting at the console she punched a button. A middle-aged female Saradasi appeared on the screen and showed her wristband with the insignia of a senior communications coordinator.

'Yorens Wer, why is there no information on the *Mithras Ennab*?' Shanaz demanded.

'We have no new information.'

'I asked you a question. Questions need answers. If you are not competent to answer, tell me who can. You are harassing me.'

Yorens Wer was silent.

'What is the latest report?'

'Saradasi Space Control has not found the *Mithras Ennab*. There is no evidence of an accident.'

Shanaz felt fear clasping her. Another Saradasi ship had disappeared mysteriously, like her father's, despite the *Mithras Ennab* unlike the *Cayetana*, carrying a tracking sensor linked to Saradasi Space Control, recording its functions, movements and on board activities. Saradasi Space Control would automatically detect a problem on the spaceship. Why, she wondered, was the *Mithras Ennab* elusive? Why had Saradasi Space Control and its master computer Keptron failed?

Shanaz said angrily, 'Saradasi Space Control has not found the *Mithras Ennab*? Not found? Stop using comfortable words. Say instead its two occupants have fled the Nereima Galaxy.'

'It is unlikely,' Yorens replied.

'They have fled the Empire,' Shanaz insisted. 'They are traitors who fled to humiliate me.'

'Why should they flee?' Yorens asked. 'Why would two senior officers of the Saradasi military flee? Fariyal is your cousin and Lord Wynan is the High Chancellor's General, your General.'

Shanaz slammed her palm on the console. She scowled at the distorted screen and muttered, 'You hate me too, Yorens.' She kicked her seat aside and ran to her living quarters. She lay on her bed looking at the Mirellar Mountains in the distance, thinking of Wynan, as she rubbed her eyes drowsily.

When she awoke, she smiled at Senior Communications Coordinator Yorens Wer who sat by her, stroking her hair. 'Only you love me, no one else does. Are you angry with me?' Shanaz asked squeezing the older woman's hand. 'I am sorry I was rude to you.'

'Shanaz, I am not angry because I know you are frustrated. I understand how you think and feel because I have looked after you since you were two years old and love you as much as your mother.'

'My mother never loved me and you know that. She was selfish and could not share her love for herself with anyone else.'

'Shanaz, you have been angry since we lost track of the *Mithras Ennab*. Can you recall what I taught you about anger?'

'Yes.'

'Say it aloud.'

'Anger is the result of a threat, fear or frustration.'

'Or?'

'A loss, even an emotional loss.'

'Say it again, please.'

'You are bullying me, as you have all my life. Anger is the result of a threat, fear, frustration or a loss.'

'Tell me, why you are angry?'

'I am angry because the *Mithras Ennab* is lost with Fariyal and Wynan on board, and because I hate being the High Chancellor, and because as High Chancellor I fear the threat facing the Saradasi Empire.'

'And?'

'I am angry because Fariyal may not return and Wynan may not return.'

'And?' Yorens Wer asked.

'I cannot control my anger because of what has happened.'

'Yes you can, Shanaz. Remember what I taught you about imagination? It is one of the most powerful forces in our universe. Use the power of imagination. Paint a picture in your mind of the *Mithras Ennab* in the green-blue skies of Saradasi. Close your eyes. Focus on the *Mithras Ennab* racing home. Shanaz, great surprises occur through mental imagery.'

Yorens Wer arranged the food she brought for Shanaz on a table and said, 'I must report for duty.'

'I love you,' Shanaz said, hugging her.

'I love you too, Shanaz.'

Shanaz watched the wind clawing at the trees in her garden, whipping their branches, swirling up the leaves into coloured spirals. The bay frothed, the waves hurled themselves against the dark stones of the wharves and the seawalls. She picked at the food and went to bed forcing herself not to think of Lord Wynan on the *Mithras Ennab* or of her visit as High Chancellor to Merr the next day.

She fell asleep and woke up from an uneasy dream. Rensoolar 67 Phange, the Province Governor of Province 6 on Merr, sat on a throne holding her in her palm, sneering at her, before swallowing her in a noisy gulp.

○

Shanaz left Saradasi the next morning for Flowia Valley, the capital of Province 6 on Merr to fulfil a visit her father planned when he was High Chancellor, to interview the Province Governor, Rensoolar 67 Phange for promotion to Planet Governor. Shanaz knew and disliked Rensoolar 67 Phange. Before she was elected High Chancellor, as a colonel in IV Army, she was Liaison Officer to the Province Governor in Flowia Valley. She remembered her superior, Sub-Commander Mandrias, cautioning her about the frequent criticism she made of Rensoolar 67 Phange and recalled a conversation with him.

'Here we are in this beautiful Flowia valley,' she had said. 'Unfortunately the valley is spoiled by the physical appearance of the Province Governor.'

'Rensoolar 67 Phange is from a small continent on southern Merr,' Sub-Commander Mandrias had replied. 'Like others of her race, she is intelligent and competent. That is why the Saradasi Empire employs members of her race in important administrative posts.'

She retorted the Governor did not look intelligent, and ridiculed her name because it had numbers. Mandrias explained the sophisticated method of naming the Governor's race adopts. 'A person's name,' he told her, 'provides immediate information on ancestry over generations, preventing intermarriage.'

She recalled criticizing Rensoolar 67 Phange's head as too large for her body. She said her jaw protruded and her was mouth too wide and like a slit. Her eyes bulge abnormally, she complained, predicting they would fall to the ground.

Sub-Commander Mandrias' gentle voice rang in her ears. 'Shanaz, remember a person's beauty is not in their appearance.'

On the day the *Cayetana* with her father disappeared, Sub-Commander Mandrias wished her well before she left for home, saying, 'I am relieved you are leaving. All you say about the Province Governor reaches her. She hates you.'

As High Chancellor of the Saradasi Empire, just over a month later, she was returning to Merr, and Rensoolar 67 Phange. The Planet Governor's residence shone in the sun as the Saradasi Battle Cruiser she was in descended.

Declining to rest, dismissing her security detail, Shanaz entered the gates of the large garden surrounding the Planet Governor's residence. She passed through the body scanners at the gate and sauntered up the stone drive with its colonnade of shady trees. When she neared the residence, she glimpsed Rensoolar 67 Phange at a window in the audience hall, watching her. Shanaz stopped, fussed over a shrub and examined a flowerbed closely. She sat on the grass verge and removed her boots, peered inside them and shook them.

She continued towards the entrance with slow, small steps. At the entrance foyer she grinned at the two guards, a Califran and a Merran. Each ran their handheld sensor over her wristband and unlocked the barrier for her to enter.

'I remember you,' Shanaz said. 'Have you forgotten me? No body search today? How are the two Astharian guards who said in Astharian, they enjoyed searching me? Where are your two friends?'

The Califran looked away. The Merran said, 'They are patrolling the south western border of the Kountacy desert.'

'Are they? It is the worst posting in the Empire and the temperature must remind them of me. I am told water boils there without a fire.' Walking along a passageway she recalled the letter she wrote when she was IV Army Liaison Officer to the governor.

Provincial Governor Rensoolar 67 Phange,

Since arriving here I have noted with interest you wear black when you are not in uniform.

I am interested in colours. If you wear black, all the clothes must be in the same shade of black. The exception is if the items of clothing are of different fabrics. This is important to remember.

My advice to you is, you must not wear black. Trying to match black is difficult.
Those who try, but not succeed look stupid. You will look gorgeous in bright yellow.
May I mention perfumes should not dull the senses of your visitors?

Your friend,

Colonel Shanaz.

Shanaz entered a long hall and strolled along a corridor, its walls painted with scenes from each planet in the Empire. She climbed the spiral staircase and stepped into the sunlit audience hall. A dark haired female of the Dost race from the planet Califra, approached her in military uniform, with her sword, in her language called a *kaduwa*, slung on her back.

'I am one of the Planet Governor's aides.' She spoke in faltering Saradasi. 'The Governor is sad.'

'Sad?' Shanaz asked.

'Yes. There is an emergency and therefore she asks you to please excuse her for a few minutes. She apologises. '

Ignoring Rensoolar 67 Phange sitting at her silver desk listening to a visitor, Shanaz followed the Dost to the far end of the hall and sat on a chair by a tall window overlooking the east garden. Why, she wondered, is a Dost in the Saradasi military, posted as a governor's aide? Shanaz moved her chair, her back to Rensoolar 67 Phange, and placed her boots on the polished window architrave.

Reflected in the window she saw the visitor leave. In single file, seven females entered the audience hall, their faces daubed in white, their heads covered in black scarves, wearing crimson gowns tied at the waist with a yellow sash fanning on the floor behind them. Rensoolar 67 Phange rose to greet them, placing her hands on each visitor's shoulders. They sat at a table on high stools. Another aide, a curly haired Merran came up and spoke softly to the Provincial Governor.

The Dost drew a chair next to Shanaz and sat facing the Province Governor.

'No,' Shanaz said when the Dost placed her voice-box on her throat. 'You are in the Saradasi military and should speak InterWord. You must not use a voice-box to translate your language to Saradasi or InterWord. Have you forgotten the rules of the Empire?'

The Dost placed the voice-box on her lap. Pointing to the females talking to Rensoolar 67 Phange, she said, 'They are a delegation from the village of Extral North.'

'Should their presence here interest me, Dost?' Shanaz asked, staring at the garden through the window.

'With you directly, nothing.'

Shanaz recalled the communication style the Dost employed and sighed.

'Are you tired?' the Dost inquired.

'No.'

She left, returning with a tray of refreshments.

'Thank you,' Shanaz said, selecting a drink.

'I am, as you can see, a Dost. I am from an island called Nuwara, in Province 4 on Califra. My home is a village seven thousand five hundred and one feet above sea level. We grow spices about which I can educate you.'

'I am happy to sit here alone and in silence,' Shanaz said.

Her face animated, the Dost described the fourteen varieties of spices her people grew, describing each plant, its use and market prices. 'Some spices are bark, some leaves and others roots,' she explained.

'I have no interest in spices. Go away, Dost.'

'I have to stay with you.'

Rensoolar 67 Phange coughed.

'The Governor has coughed,' the Dost said. 'She is not sick with the cough. Perhaps it is her gentle signal to me telling me I talk too much.'

'I had not noticed,' Shanaz said.

'I have been here two days,' the Dost went on, rocking on her chair, gazing at Shanaz. 'Look,' she said. She inhaled deeply and exhaled a green mist through her nose. Shanaz pushed her chair away.

'It is just a conjurer's trick which the Dost perform. May I teach it to you?'

'I can show you a famous Saradasi trick, though not as clever as yours,' Shanaz said, moving her chair and facing the Dost.

'Please teach me.'

'Keep still,' Shanaz said. 'The trick is this. My hands are not moving and I have targeted you with my firing-belt under my cloak. I have locked one sensor on your chest, another on your head. If you move, two laser beams will kill you. I need not use my hands. Move and you are dead.'

'What is the trick?' The Dost asked, not moving.

'I can also alter your state of consciousness with my firing-belt. I can take you and lock you in a glass cage I will have built for you. I will teach you to blow green air from all your body openings, at the same time.'

'I can practice and succeed,' the Dost said earnestly, 'but only for your eyes.'

Her laugh was infectious and Shanaz joined her. 'You can move, Dost,' Shanaz said. She saw the Dost tense and lean forwards, the hilt of the sword on her back no longer against the chair she sat on.

'On guard,' she whispered. 'Be alert. Trust me.'

Rensoolar 67 Phange called, and the Dost went across the room. She returned and said, 'Please come with me.' She mouthed, 'Be careful.'

Rensoolar 67 Phange rose from her seat. The seven female visitors moved towards the entrance door.

'I apologise for the delay,' she said, speaking in Saradasi. 'Please forgive me, High Chancellor. Before we begin our meeting I must tell you there has been an accident. These honourable elders from Extral North told me a group of school children, numbering one hundred and twelve has not returned from an expedition into the mountains. Their parents and friends have searched the mountains and have not found them. The Saradasi Military Commander here refused to use the life-form recognition equipment to find the children. High Chancellor, will you help?'

'I will not help. Neither the Saradasi military nor its equipment is here for non-military use.' She walked to the wall and looked attentively at a jewelled wall hanging.

Shanaz faced the delegation, 'The life or death of a group of children is of no concern to me or the Saradasi military and least of all to the Saradasi Empire.'

Rensoolar 67 Phange's shoulders drooped when she interpreted what Shanaz said to the Elders. 'Please,' she said to Shanaz, 'they are poor people. Their greatest treasure is their family. Please help them.'

'I will not,' Shanaz said. 'Searching for lost children is not the task of the Saradasi military. Who sent the children there? Who were the fools who looked after them?'

'You are a beast with no compassion,' Rensoolar 67 Phange said, flecks of spittle at the corners of her mouth.

Like the hum of an angry bird, the knife flew towards Shanaz. The Dost swung to her right, shielding Shanaz. The knife plunged into her left shoulder. Pushing Shanaz to one side, she drew her *kaduwa* and in two smooth movements she leaped across the floor, a trail of blood behind her.

Within a sword reach of the delegation, arching her body back she swung her *kaduwa* in a left to right upward arc. A short female slumped to the floor with a scream, her abdominal cavity gaping, intestines clutched in her hands, blood spurting and seeping across the floor.

'Assassins!' The Dost's scream filled the audience hall.

Each elder held a long knife. The Dost swung her *kaduwa* beheading another member of the delegation and gashing the neck of the one next to her.

'Dost,' Shanaz shouted, crouching behind a table. 'Dost, flat on the floor! I am firing.' The laser from the forward tubes of the firing-belt tore through the four delegates standing. The smell of blood and burning flesh filled the room.

Rensoolar 67 Phange leaned against a pillar, her face shining with perspiration, her hands behind her back staring at Shanaz.

'You are a traitor,' Shanaz said.

'No. I serve the Empire. I am not responsible for the actions of others.'

'They each carried a weapon,' Shanaz said. 'I am certain the guards scanned them. You gave them the knives to kill me.'

'I loathe all Saradasi, especially you,' Rensoolar 67 Phange said, glowering at Shanaz. 'You think I am a freak. I see you as a hideous animal with no compassion who should have died. I will kill you myself.'

Rensoolar 67 Phange holding a rapier in her hand, side-stepped when the Dost lunged at her.

She swung her free arm across the Dost's chest, pulled her towards her, and held the point of the rapier to her throat.

The sound was deafening. Forty members of the IV Army Strike Force smashed their way into the audience hall. Rensoolar 67 Phange drew her rapier across the Dost's throat before falling to the floor, killed by laser fire.

'Quick help the Dost,' Shanaz said.

A Strike Force Physician knelt resuscitating the Dost, pale and sweaty, slipping into unconsciousness. Air hissed in and out of her throat. The physician inserted a tube through her mouth to her windpipe and ventilated her. A medical aid pumped artificial blood into two veins.

Shanaz knelt by the Dost, her hand stroking her forehead, whispering, 'Thank you for saving my life.'

'It is unlikely she will live,' the physician said to Shanaz.

Shanaz watched the members of the medical team carrying the Dost in a capsule.

The Saradasi officer in the Strike Force greeted her.

'Thank you for coming here,' Shanaz said. 'A Saradasi is never alone.'

'Not if we follow orders to activate the communications channel on our wristband when we are on duty.'

'Why is a Dost here with a Planet Governor? Dost work in the military. Who is she? Shanaz asked.

'I cannot reveal this information.'

'You cannot reveal this information to me, the High Chancellor?'

'I am sorry. I am following my orders,' he replied, smoothing his hair.

'Two people tried to kill me. The Dost saved my life twice and is dying. You are stubbornly following your orders. What is your name?'

'Santana, Commander Santana, High Chancellor.'

'Have we met before, Commander?'

'We may have,' he said, looking at a female Califran captain. 'I cannot recall meeting you.' He swayed on his heels, smiling at the Califran captain.

'I will complain about you to your superior,' Shanaz said.

'For not remembering if I met you?'

'No, for your impertinence. I assume, from your arrogance and attitude, you are from Saradasi Security.'

'I am.'

'I once considered a career in Security,' Shanaz said. 'I changed my mind because it carried the frustrating burden of working with stupid colleagues. The two attempts on my life because of inadequate security, and meeting you, confirms my view.'

'I am sorry,' Commander Santana said. 'We misjudged the danger to you.'

'Stupidity often manifests as poor judgement. Please tell Lord Rasalis, our Chancellor of Security, what I said. Tell him he failed me, the Dost and the Empire. Even his large body may be overburdened with the humiliation he will have to bear.' She paused, adding, 'You may wish to help him with his guilt and shame.'

Shanaz walked out of the audience hall.

Later in the day after sharing a meal with Sub-Commander Mandrias and his family at IV Army Headquarters, she sat with his young son in the garden listening to him play the flute.

'I wanted to be a musician,' Shanaz said. 'I joined the military instead, to serve the Empire. You play beautifully. Your teachers and others will tell you how to interpret a piece of music. But be brave and let your heart interpret the music because the heart interprets music better than the brain.'

After he left, she sat watching the fish in a pond. Flowers bloomed in the gardens sloping towards a stream; a gardener picked fallen leaves from a rock garden. She was pleased the Saradasi insisted on creating a beautiful external environment wherever they worked, throughout the Empire. She bent looking at the fish in the pond when she heard a noise on the gravel path behind her. She rolled off the bench, crouching on the grass, her force-sword in her hand, the firing-belt activated.

Commander Santana speaking into his wristband ran towards her with a squad of soldiers.

'Are you trying to kill me too? Shanaz asked.

She saw the fear on his face when he said, 'No. Lord Rasalis wants to speak with you urgently. Please come with me to the communications centre. Your life may be in great danger even here in IV Army Headquarters.' He pointed to the sky. 'We have increased security.' A fleet of Saradasi Hunters and Interceptors darkened the sky. Two Saradasi Battle Cruiser sat above IV Army Headquarters.

In the underground communications centre Lord Rasalis, his face grim and haggard, filled the largest screen, while Commander Santana spoke into his wristband.

'Shanaz, I failed you,' Lord Rasalis said. 'I am now convinced you are in great danger and I will tell you more when I meet you. You must leave Merr now.'

'Who was the Dost who saved my life?' Shanaz asked.

'Her name is Seelawathie-Ap from Califra. I will take good care of her. She works for me in Saradasi Security. Shanaz, Commander Santana will escort you home with a VIII Army Protective Escort. Follow the instructions Santana gives you. A lethal toxin may have contaminated your clothes when you were at the Governor's residence. Wear the clothes Santana gives you and accept food and drink only from Santana. Trust only Santana. You must leave Merr immediately.'

FOUR

It was a gloomy day in the Upper City on Saradasi. The bay swirled. Mounds of melting snow lay against the trees lining the narrow cobbled streets. Shanaz sat in her home half listening to Lord Rasalis asking her to step aside from the problem of the *Mithras Ennab*. He reminded her that the burden was his to bear as Chancellor of Security of the Saradasi Empire.

'The High Council must find out what happened, how it happened, who was responsible and what action to take. I accept the responsibility and the blame is mine,' he said.

'Wynan and Fariyal will never return,' Shanaz said wearily. 'They are traitors. I have said this to you twice and you pretend to not hear me.'

Lord Rasalis saw the tears welling in her eyes and walked to the transparent western wall to watch three merchant ships inching their way to the wharves. 'Shanaz, we have no evidence of a criminal act. Be patient.'

'I am.'

'Think also,' Lord Rasalis said, 'of their closeness to you.'

Shanaz wiped her tears with the back of her hand. 'It is so hurtful because of their closeness to me.'

'I know how much you love Wynan. Be patient.'

'He does not love me.'

'I am sure he loves you.'

'You are sure? Does he confide in you? Or have your spies, informers and Sound Masters told you Wynan loves me? I know what you think about our relationship.'

Shanaz joined Lord Rasalis, watching the ships make fast to the south wharf. 'You too have ruined my life,' she said, with no anger in her voice. 'You secretly prevented me from joining a combat unit. You had me shunted from one safe, stupid job to another. Admit it.'

'Yes, I did. If not, you would not be here today.'

'What do you mean?'

'You know what I mean, Shanaz.'

'To die in combat would have been better than all this.'

'Because you want to die?'

'Yes! I wanted to die in combat because it is a shame for a Saradasi to commit suicide.' The words rushed out, 'Yes, to die in combat because I did not want to take my life and shame my father, my family and the military.'

Shanaz paused and said sobbing, 'And I did not want to dishonour you.'

'Shanaz, we are all proud of you,' Lord Rasalis said reaching out and holding her hands. 'I am so proud of you. In the short time you have been High Chancellor think of what you have achieved. In the Empire, from north to south and east to west, every citizen, though they may hate us Saradasi, respects the court system you argued for and implemented in such a short time.'

Shanaz shook her head. 'Do you see the paradox? Should I be proud of a good justice system in a sea of injustice?'

'You sound tired. Rest now,' he said and left her.

○

Shanaz woke when hailstones pounded the western wall of her home. She saw her uniform folded neatly on a chair. She admired the Saradasi military and the Saradasi Empire for not making a distinction between the uniform of a general and a cadet. The colonel's insignia on her wristband shone. She was pleased because she gained every promotion through merit alone. Shanaz passed her hand over the control panel above her head. The wall opposite her changed colour. She sat up in bed and watched the blurred images of Lord Wynan on the screen sharpen when she wiped her eyes.

'Where is he and Fariyal and the *Mithras Ennab*?' she wondered. If the *Mithras Ennab* was in the Nereima Galaxy, she reasoned, there was only one place it could be. She switched on a hologram of the *Nereima Galaxy*. Beneath the caption the *Saradasi Empire*, the small home planet, Saradasi, shone red. The colonised planets Astharia, Asurat, Califra and Merr glowed blue; Natashi, the planet not yet colonised, glimmered black.

Shanaz spoke into her wristband. 'Lord Rasalis, could the *Mithras Ennab* be in an area Saradasi Space Control does not monitor?'

'Where?'

'Around the planet Natashi which we have never reached.' She heard a sharp intake of breath.

'A clever thought,' Lord Rasalis said quickly. 'Shanaz, if we Saradasi have not succeeded in reaching Natashi, despite trying for hundreds of years, how will the *Mithras Ennab* reach there and why?'

'I will think about it,' Shanaz answered. 'I may surprise both of us when I find the answer. You, more than I, because my intuition tells me you know more about all this.'

'Shanaz, trust me,' he said.

'Should I?' she asked noticing his drawn face, despite the small image on her wristband.

FIVE

SARADASI MILITARY ACADEMY ON ASURAT—EIGHT YEARS AGO

Shanaz stepped on to the beach from the spacecraft on the island, Isia, on the desert planet, Asurat. Dense jungle surrounded the island, its centre described as a cauldron of fire. High velocity winds frequently changed its sandy contours. Here the Virtan Military Academy survived in proud, hot and humid isolation for two hundred and seventy years. Some said the Saradasi High Council set up Virtan to weed out the 'soft' and 'effete' from entering the Saradasi military. Many branded Virtan, because of its location, the anus of Saradasi military academies. Surviving Virtan was a badge of honour.

Shanaz began the long journey to Virtan from the spaceport on Saradas on the *Gaviota*, a cargo craft with accommodation for twelve passengers. When she left, her father, Lord Laramis, the High Chancellor was on Califra, and her mother said she was ill. Her friend, companion and cousin, Fariyal, who would have come, was posted on Merr. Lord Rasalis was the lone figure wishing her a safe journey. During the long stopover on Califra, two Astharians replaced the Saradasi flight crew.

When the *Gaviota* reached Isia, though curious, she did not question the captain when he said his orders were to set her down on the beach near the Virtan Military Academy and not at the spaceport. He assured her an officer from the academy would meet her.

The blue bay with white sand, fringed by dense green jungle was desolate. Clusters of tall rocks were half buried in the sand. She walked along the beach to a small sign that read, *Virtan Military Academy* with an arrow pointing to a path leading into the jungle. She sat in a clump of trees facing the *Gaviota* and placed her wristband to her ear, rotating her forearm until she heard the conversation on the flight deck. 'Anuras,' the soft spoken Astharian captain said, 'I told you to leave her alone.'

'I only waved goodbye.'

'There may be people watching us. Concentrate on your duties, Anuras. I want to leave as quickly as we can, please.'

'She is so beautiful. Who is she?' Anuras asked.

'Someone closely watched,' the captain said, busying himself.

'Is she in any danger? Will she be safe? Captain, please let me check the co-ordinates Saradasi Space Control gave us to set her down.'

'You do that, Anuras.'

'Sir, there are no co-ordinates to check because the record of this journey on the navigation log has been erased after we landed.'

Shanaz heard the captain grunt as he powered the *Gaviota* into the clouds. She walked to the water's edge, scanning the trees. Sitting on a rock, she removed her boots and dangled her feet in the warm water. She searched the treetops and decided the captain was teasing Anuras about being watched. The humid breeze carried the smells of the sea. A wave swept towards her, breaking around her knees and she caught a strand of seaweed between her toes and flung it back into the water. The beach was deserted. Squelching the warm sand with her toes, she looked up at the trees when a bird called, answered by another. Glancing at the trees she went to the sign, squatting to read the small letters written beneath *Virtan Military Academy,* "*Trespassers will be killed.*"

Wiping the sand from her feet she put her boots on and stepped on the path. She wondered why the access to a large military academy was along a path, dusty and uneven, wide enough for two people to walk abreast, with branches from trees and shrubs encroaching on it. She skirted puddles of muddy water, annoyed no one from the academy met her. A few hundred feet ahead the path turned to the right. Why such a sharp bend? The terrain was flat, the shortest distance between two points a straight line.

She left the path, pushing her way quietly through the trees. She walked parallel to the path, pausing to inspect the massive trees, some with trunks a hundred feet wide. Few leaves were on the ground beneath the trees despite their dense foliage.

'Interesting,' Shanaz thought. She picked a leaf and tried tearing it. Drawing her force-sword, she switched it to maximum power and struck the trunk of a tree. The clang of metal striking metal echoed and a cascade of blue sparks surrounded her. Tendrils of smoke rose from the white bark of the tree.

She adjusted the controls on her firing-belt, sheathed her force-sword and unclasping her cloak tucked it in her backpack. Changing direction often, she moved more silently. Her wristband showed the temperature rising. Perspiration dripped from her body, drenching her uniform. Shanaz re-tied her hair into a knot on top her head and glanced at the path on her right.

She heard a whistling sound behind her and flung herself on the ground. Moments later a smoke grenade exploded spewing thick, blinding, choking, pungent smoke. She began rising and dropped to the ground when a metal noose flew above her head. The smoke became denser when another grenade exploded. Bending low, she ran across the path, the noise ringing in her ears. Breathless, she squatted by a grove of shrubs and crawled behind the nearest large tree. A scorching flash of light shot over her left shoulder and she smelled burning metal when a small tree behind her ignited and crumbled. Shanaz fired her firing-belt upwards in a sweeping arc. Clusters of small sight and sound surveillance detectors exploded, scattering on the ground.

Alert for the glint of a detector, she made her way through the trees towards the sound of the surf, breaking into a zigzag run when she saw the sea. She stopped, sheltering within a dense clump of reeds on the beach. She remembered her mind master saying, 'Discipline is one of seven jewels adorning a true leader.' She forced herself to relax.

After counting down from five thousand, she crawled to a larger patch of reeds and ran across the beach into the water. A sleek amphibi-ous craft shot though the trees, skimmed across the beach and landed with a thud on the water, roaring towards her as she dived under. Seven light skinned Lesdians from Merr, their weapons drawn, ran onto the beach.

Shanaz surfaced some yards from the craft. On it, two armed Lesdians crouched by the harnessed pilot. The taller said in InterWord, 'Welcome! I am an officer from the academy. Please board the craft.'

Treading water, Shanaz shook the water from her hair. The Lesdians on the beach waded into the sea, standing waist deep, their weapons pointed at her.

'Get on board,' the Lesdian shouted. Shanaz shook her head. She pointed to her ears and shook her head again, moving towards the craft.

'Is she deaf?' he asked, beckoning her.

Shanaz moved to the side of the vessel, her hands cupped behind her ears, shaking her head. The Lesdian, yelling at her, leaned forwards, his long face close to hers.

'Are you deaf?' he roared, reaching out to grab her.

Shanaz swung her right arm behind his neck; her left hand grabbed his hair, and jerked his head over the side of the boat. Her left knee smashed into the angle of his jaw, crushing bone, tearing muscles, blood vessels and nerves. She pulled him into the water. Moving him aside, her arm round his neck, Shanaz bent back. Laser fire from her firing-belt tore through the craft and its two occupants.

Shanaz faced the seven Lesdians in the water, clasping the screaming Lesdian, her arm choking him, the anterior tubes of her firing-belt hard against his back. 'You are alive, and not dead because I want you to tell me why you are trying to kill me.'

The Lesdian moaned, his head limp.

'What I just did to you,' she whispered, 'we call the *Chinnadi manoeuvre*. There is another manoeuvre, but I think you will die before I show you what it is.'

'I am Saradasi,' she shouted to the Lesdians in the water. 'I may not kill all of you, but I will die trying. If any of you survive, Saradasi Hunter ships will hunt you till the end of your lives and after killing you, they will destroy your families.'

'Hunt us? Kill us?' a Lesdian shouted back, 'for what reason? We are from the Saradasi military, from VI Army and I am an officer. We are obeying our orders.'

'What orders?' Shanaz asked.

'To test a robot with a strong defence capability without destroying it.'

'All of you against one robot who looks like a female in a Saradasi military uniform?'

'Yes.'

'You lie.'

'I do not,' the officer replied, his face mottled.

A Saradasi Hunter landed on the beach and a Saradasi military officer ran into the water towards Shanaz. 'Please come with me.'

'I am going to kill you too,' Shanaz said.

He showed her the insignia on his wristband. 'This is an experiment gone wrong to test a robot. You were never in any danger and no injury would have occurred. Please come with me to the academy.'

'Who,' Shanaz asked, 'said I was a robot?'

The Commander gave her a friendly grin. 'Please ask General Varsana, the head of the academy. He may know.'

'Where are you from?' Shanaz asked.

'Saradasi Security.'

'You work, no doubt, with Lord Rasalis,' she said.

○

Later that evening, Shanaz stood before the Principal of the Virtan Military Academy, his protuberant teeth resting comfortably on his lower lip. He regarded her with neither interest nor indifference and was bored, Shanaz thought.

General Varsana left the room, moving down the steps to the pond in a garden enclosed by a wall with a gate. He motioned Shanaz to join him. 'Please,' he said, 'indulge an old man. Please count the number of fish in my pond. I will join you later.'

He started to walk, stopped, and said, 'I was going to say you resemble your mother, but I am not sure. I am happy to have you here.'

'Life is full of dangerous occurrences,' General Varsana remarked gloomily, his chin on his clasped hands.

She counted the fish, wondering why he mentioned her mother and why she was counting fish in a pond. 'Comply and then complain,' she mouthed kneeling over the pond.

She felt proud to be at Virtan, having resisted the pressure to enrol at the most renowned military academy in the Empire, the Ursan Military Academy on Saradasi. 'Why,' she had said repeatedly, 'should I enter an academy reserved for Saradasi when the military employs people from all nationalities?'

It was Lord Rasalis who suggested Virtan.

When General Varsana joined her, he asked, 'How many fish are there?'

'Thirty six, sir.'

'Thirty six? This morning there were thirty nine. Why, I wonder?'

'My count is wrong or three fish may have died since morning. I assume the fish do not eat one another. If so, there would perhaps be one big fat one.'

'Did you count them a second time?'

'No. Someone outside the wall threw a handful of pebbles into the pond. It was therefore difficult to count the fish again.'

'There are mischievous people who disturb my fish,' General Varsana said sadly. He led her back to his office, pointing to a single seat. When Shanaz sat, he said, 'let us see what happened.'

The visual recording Shanaz and General Varsana watched ended, showing the deserted beach, white caps on a rough, blue sea, and the branches of the trees bordering the beach bending in the wind.

'What do you think happened?'

'I thought there were two possibilities,' Shanaz answered. 'Either someone was trying to kill me or it was a dangerous test designed by a dangerous person to allegedly test a robot.'

'Life is full of dangerous occurrences,' General Varsana remarked gloomily, his chin on his clasped hands.

General Varsana looked at the walled garden. 'Your expected date of arrival is tomorrow,' he said, 'not today and *not* at this place on the beach. You should have arrived at the spaceport tomorrow. Not on the beach. Irregular. The *Gaviota* set you down on our counter-terrorist testing ground. We expected the robot on the beach today.'

'And did I do what the robot would have done, sir?'

'Yes, and very well.'

'And I could have died, sir.'

'No. We received strict orders to not damage the robot. It is a sophisticated multiple function battle robot, still a prototype and expensive. We were to test the robot's responses.'

'Sir, I am not a robot. I may have stumbled and injured myself or I may have drowned in the sea.'

'I agree. A waste of a good brain. A loss to the Empire.'

'Sir, may I please ask who told you I was due tomorrow and the robot today?'

'Lord Rasalis.'

'Would it seem strange, sir, that the Chancellor of Security of the mighty Saradasi Empire would concern himself with me and a robot?'

'Most strange. Odd,' General Varsana agreed, peering at her. 'In fact this matter will keep me awake tonight.'

'Sir, this matter will keep me awake for many nights.'

'Please forget this incident. We Saradasi are complex people and our Lord Rasalis is more complex than most.'

'You are correct, sir, and I appreciate your honesty. I came to this academy because of you, sir.'

'Thank you. Was coming here to Virtan always your aim?'

'No, Sir. Lord Rasalis told me about you and Virtan.'

'Lord Rasalis is too kind,' General Varsana murmured.

'There is such a rumour, sir, though unconfirmed.'

General Varsana coughed. 'I too have heard of this slender rumour. You will find, as time passes, Lord Rasalis is kinder beyond belief. Now go to bed. I am delighted you are here.'

'Sir, may I please speak of a small concern?' Shanaz said when she rose to leave.

General Varsana raised his eyelids.

'Sir, I refer to the interest Lord Rasalis has in me. Lord Rasalis as Chancellor of Security is, I am sure, interested in many people. I am uncertain if those who capture his interest are led to an inferno, as I was today, with their lives at risk, or led to paradise.'

'Being in a paradise or an inferno depends on what you make of your life,' General Varsana said. 'Both exist here in our world and not, after we die, in another world as our evangelists preach and indoctrinate us. You control your mind, unless you cannot, because of a mental illness. Paradise or an inferno, sadness and joy, are all interpretations of our mind. Remember, a cluttered confused mind is easier to control by others. Lord Rasalis does not rule your mind. He never can, though it may be his wish. You, and you alone, rule your mind.'

'Sir, what clutters and confuses our minds the most?' Shanaz asked.

'Greed.'

'Sir, you may have just taught me all I need to learn in my life.' Shanaz thanked him and left the room.

When she stepped into the garden, General Varsana, said, 'You wore a firing-belt when you arrived. Did you not know the military academy allows cadets to wear only their force-sword?'

'On the *Gaviota,* the co-pilot said I was to arm myself for an exercise and gave me a firing-belt.'

'Interesting,' General Varsana remarked.

'Sir, may I see the robot?'

'I am so sorry. Krenz V, as you know designed by your cousin Fariyal, never arrived here.'

○

Life at Virtan was lonely though never dull. Shanaz neither sought nor received favours because she was the High Chancellor's daughter. She worked hard, seeking respect, not affection from her teachers and colleagues, who treated her with uncertainty. She made no friends through choice.

The day of the final examination interview arrived. In the garden of the academy Shanaz sat on the grass, facing General Varsana and the external examiner, General Teras, a Saradasi, from VIII Army. The sun shone on them, the sea rumbled behind them, and fragrance from the trees scented the air.

'Why do flowers have unique fragrances?' General Teras asked. They discussed which factors determine the nature of the fragrance. Was fragrance a tool of seduction to help propagate the species? Why fragrance and not honey or colour as the enticement? What was the role of colour in the propagation of the species and to what extent did minerals in the soil, soil acidity and alkalinity influence colour? Why do some plants have coloured leaves and not flowers?

The interview was a formality, and meandered on.

A dining room steward placed a tray in front of them with plates of food elaborately arranged, and drinks, each with its serving measure.

'We must eviscerate this cadet's mind,' General Teras said, sternly. 'What is your greatest ambition?'

Shanaz hesitated. She saw General Teras frown. Candidates devoted much time to prepare an original answer to this inevitable question. She sat relaxed, smiling at the two generals. General Teras cocked his head expectantly. Shanaz leaned forward. General Varsana leaned forward, pressing his teeth on his lower lip.

'Sir,' Shanaz said softly, 'I mean no disrespect. My greatest ambition is to preserve the privacy of my ambitions.'

Shanaz looked at General Teras. Her thoughts slipped back to her childhood. She remembered him playing with her when she was a child and walking along the quiet path, the snow frozen, through a mountain pass to a beautiful place, Sirglin, from her home in VIII Army Headquarters. Lord Rasalis, never fit, panted beside them. Her father, Lord Laramis, Commander-in-Chief of VIII Army walked silently ahead. One of the officers behind them spoke, and another replied, 'Yes, we are all dreaming a dream with Lord Laramis.' She remembered she had never asked about the dream.

General Teras questioned her about deploying hologram armies as a ruse to mislead enemies. 'The interview is over. You have passed,' he announced after General Varsana nodded to him.

'Thank you, sir. General Varsana, may I please ask you about the fish.'

'In my pond?'

'Yes, sir, in your pond.'

'Fish to eat?' General Teras asked

'No, sir, fish to count,' Shanaz replied. 'General Varsana often asked me to count the fish in his pond. Strangely the number was never the same.'

'He puts them in and takes them out,' General Teras suggested.

'No, sir. He is very honest,' Shanaz said.

'Are new fish born?' General Teras ventured.

'General Varsana,' Shanaz said, 'I think you are very clever. Sir, last night I found the connection between the pond, leading to another pond, well camouflaged.'

'Why did you not look into this before? General Teras asked.

'Sir, it is foolish for a student to be as clever as the principal of her academy until she has graduated.' Shanaz reached into her pocket and opened her fist. 'Sir, I found this chain with a pendant among the water plants.'

General Varsana picked up the chain and Shanaz saw his eyes mist. 'This belonged to my late wife, who wore it once. It was a present from a merchant in Merr she helped. We Saradasi can have compassion.'

'It is beautiful,' Shanaz said.

'I would like you to have it please,' General Varsana said.

'Sir, I must refuse the gift. There will be someone more deserving than I to wear this.'

'No,' General Varsana said.

'Sir, you must be patient. The person who deserves this gift will meet you one day.'

'About Varsana's fish,' General Teras said, 'because you found the connection to the second pond he has lost a bet with a friend.'

'Why is Lord Rasalis never wrong about you?' General Varsana complained.

'Because, General Varsana, he knows me well. I am a toy he plays with to amuse himself and sometimes others.'

○

General Teras sat with General Varsana in his quarters.

'She could be the jewel in our crown,' General Varsana said. 'But, my observation during her time here is that she lacks compassion. At present, the rules of the Empire and nothing else guide her.'

'In the years ahead we must help strip off the hard layer that suffo-cates her goodness,' General Teras said.

General Varsana rested his chin on his hand. 'It will not be easy and we may fail. I assume Shanaz must know about *The Prophecy*, though she does not know her destiny yet. When she came here I placed her under the most intrusive surveillance. I have watched her every action and lis-tened to each word she spoke at Virtan. When the battle for the Nereima Galaxy begins, *if* she is on Lord Gaima's team, she must lead the team.'

'It depends how her destiny unfolds,' General Teras said. 'We have had years to think about *The Prophecy* and *The Place*. Are there five Saradasi with great goodness, who can be on the team to save the Nereima Galaxy?'

'I do not know. Time will tell,' General Varsana said. 'Have faith in Rasalis.'

General Teras shrugged. 'Shanaz has finished her training. What are your plans now? Are you going on home leave?'

'No. Rasalis wants me to help him with his plan, which you know about. He has placed his faith in the Great Khan. Would you trust him?'

'The Great Khan? No. Would you?'

'No, though Rasalis is not a fool.'

'Nor is the Great Khan,' General Teras replied. 'Why should the Great Khan help the Saradasi?'

'Because he enjoys ruling Asurat. He therefore, does not want the Nereima Galaxy destroyed by the Forces of Evil.'

'What will be the fate of the Nereima Galaxy?' General Varsana asked.

'I am not living in hope,' General Teras said.

SIX

At Space Station ZenFah the feared security guards were never far from Faris, the renowned Suxt-Sux race actor from Asurat. In his quarters on Level 70 he re-painted his eyebrows, spreading across his forehead, and checked his tasks for the day. Faris felt pleased that Midi78 had not recognised him in his disguises as a Merran, as a Craxxian toy merchant, or in the theatre playing the crazed, bumbling magician. He knew if he could deceive Midi78, a mind reader, he was indeed the greatest actor and master of disguise in the Nereima Galaxy. After viewing each of his fourteen new facemasks in the mirror, he crossed the room to the window overlooking Recreation Area 28. The swordsmen he sent for from Merr were not there yet.

He no longer strolled through the space station malls and markets buying items, small and large, and placing whispered orders, with the guards hovering near him. He had purchased all he needed for Lord Rasalis's plan.

His Great Khan warned him before he left Asurat, 'Always remember the space station is not a safe place despite Saradasi control and the thousands of guards. The Saradasi envoy of Lord Rasalis who visits me insists you must be alert. He said Lord Rasalis calls you his "treasure." Remember, though, the preciousness of a treasure may change in the mind of the owner. Therefore beware of treachery.'

Faris was disappointed he will no longer act in the vast theatres across the Nereima Galaxy, enjoying the applause of thousands. Soon he hoped, he and his cousin, the Great Khan, would complete and take part in the elaborate plan of Lord Rasalis to help the five Saradasi win the battle for the Nereima Galaxy. Though he hated the Saradasi for ruling his planet Asurat and for their arrogance and ruthlessness, he accepted that he and the Great Khan must honour their ancestor Sx'Tillah's promise to the three divine Astral Lords, almost four hundred years ago, to help the Saradasi save the Nereima Galaxy.

When he was a child, at sunrise and sunset, his parents and elders reminded him of Sx'Tillah's promise. His father would say in his sonorous actor's voice as if he were on a stage, 'Faris, my son, believe in *The Prophecy* and bring honour to this house.' He would pause, steal a look at Faris and say, 'We have not met a divine Astral Lord. Nevertheless, we believe what our forefathers told us.'

As he grew up, the previous Great Khan, the present Great Khan's father, would take him to watch the wonderful performances of his people, the Suxt-Sux, in theatres and in town squares and village greens in the Suxt-Sux nation. Every play he saw was exciting and mysterious, though what he enjoyed most was meeting the actors after the play. He once said to the Great Khan, 'My uncle, surely that ferocious giant must be from the planet Ezztrax Minor. He is twice our size!'

After the performance, in a well-guarded tent, the giant revealed himself as a Suxt-Sux boy actor. The Great Khan said, 'The genius of a Suxt-Sux actor is that he or she can be anyone anywhere.'

Faris smiled. He was at the centre of the great plan to save the Nereima Galaxy. For four years he shuttled between his home on Asurat to Space Station ZenFah; to distant cities in the Nereima Galaxy, and even beyond, to the elliptical blue galaxy. He spent the vast sums of money Lord Rasalis gave the Great Khan, slavishly keeping an account of every solar spent.

'Lord Rasalis has no trust in me though I trust you, Faris,' the Great Khan would grumble when they went through the expenses. 'Why should a solar here or there matter to Lord Rasalis?' he demanded.

'My seraphic Khan,' Faris had replied, 'let us not make Lord Rasalis angry. I save money by skimping on my food and lodging.' He recalled the Great Khan saying between mouthfuls of food, while he altered the accounts, 'You are too kind to your poor cousin who is destitute.'

O

After his first meeting with Midi78 on the space station, they met at night in his quarters, talking about *The Prophecy* and the mystery surrounding *The Place* where Prince Vira's team lived.

'My friend,' Midi78 would say, 'let me tell you about spells that can stop a wild beast in its tracks.' He spoke of the healing power of colours, specific notes and chords of music.

'Healed by music?' Faris marvelled.

'Yes, my friend. Even by the sound of the single correct musical note played near the patient's heart.'

Faris twitched his painted eyebrows. 'I am told you Gootamundra from Astharia cast horoscopes. They sound mysterious.'

'They are not mysterious,' Midi78 replied. 'A horoscope is a chart noting the location of the planetary bodies in a solar system, when a person is born. Astrologers analyse and interpret the influence of these heavenly bodies on the person's life. Skilled astrologers can predict, for example, the number and sex of your children. There is a Gootamundra here who can cast your horoscope if you give me the exact date, time, and place of your birth.'

'It is an astounding science,' Faris said.

When they met a day later Midi78 said to Faris, 'My friend, are you sure the particulars you gave us are correct.'

'I made no mistake,' Faris assured him.

'The horoscope has not revealed that you, the most famous actor in our galaxy, will be an entertainer. It foretells you will carry out great deeds and place your life at risk. We will talk more another day,' Midi78 said.

On another night Midi78 spoke of the notion of fate and pre-destiny and reincarnation. He said after death, the soul enters another physical body and perhaps many more, until it is released when the cycle of rebirth ends.

'What happens to the soul when it is released?' Faris asked.

'My friend, it depends on the life one led. Those who led lives with great compassion for others become Astral Lords. The Astral world has eight tiers.'

Late one night, while Faris sat working in his quarters, he received a message to accompany a troop of guards. They led him to Level 33, reserved for Saradasi craft. Rows of guards, their weapons drawn, lined the corridors leading to the docking bays.

The Great Khan's spacecraft, the *Lanoisia*, from Asurat, was on Pier 4, its interior lights dimmed. The forward door of the *Lanoisia* slid open and a uniformed figure, his eyebrows painted purple and ochre strode out.

'Faris, I greet you and wish you good health. Our lord, the Great Khan sends warm greetings. My instruction is we can talk freely here, not on the craft. We must be silent on board.'

'I understand. It is a most sensible precaution.'

'I have an urgent message from the Great Khan. The Saradasi envoy of Lord Rasalis awaits you.'

'Are the preparations complete at the secret location?'

'Yes. The stages and the actors and everything else you asked for awaits you.'

The *Lanoisia* left the space station on a direct route to Asurat with eight Saradasi Hunters and an Interceptor following it.

O

In Samsara, the summer capital of the Great Khan, Faris, refreshed after a nights sleep, walked along the seashore to the summer palace. A breeze from the orchards nearby blew across the beach. Above him, Samsara, a many tiered white city with silver spires, rose from the eastern shore of the Arianz Sea. That morning, the Great Khan's white palace reflected the rose red of the sky. Faris washed and wiped his feet and entered the courtyard of the unguarded palace and walked along the carpeted corridors to the foyer outside the assembly room. A courtier in bright green from headdress to embroidered cloth slippers greeted Faris, ushering him in. The Great Khan, once ruler of the small Suxt-Sux race, now Planet Governor of all Asurat, reclined on cushions on an octagonal golden dais. On either side of him two artists crouched, lovingly painting a complex design on his eyebrows. His favourite chef squatted by him, feeding him with a long spoon.

'Greetings, Faris. I was awake when you arrived last night, but I wanted you to rest. I therefore did not send for you.'

'My gracious Lord, I am at your service, night or day, night and day,' Faris murmured. 'My Khan, I am the dust under your precious feet.'

Faris sat on the carpeted floor, below the dais, near the bare feet of the Great Khan.

'Faris, it is a blessing to see you. I have news the battle for the Nereima Galaxy will begin soon, perhaps today, perhaps in a few days. We must all be ready.' The Great Khan opened his mouth to receive a spoonful of food. 'My sustainer!' he cooed, squeezing the cheeks of the chef feeding him. 'The Divine One in his or her mercy sent you to nourish me to health and vigour.'

The chef beamed, his cheeks aflame.

The Great Khan wrung his hands. 'Faris, Lord Rasalis's envoy is here in Samsara,' he said in a mournful voice. 'He reminded me of your important role in the battle. Would I forget? Is he suggesting I have a problem with my memory? His eyes bore into me when he speaks to me. His stare impales me. When I answer, he looks away. He upsets me. He intimidates me.'

The Great Khan sneezed. Three courtiers ran up to him. He sipped a drink and went on, 'This envoy of Lord Rasalis speaks unusually softly. He speaks deliberately softly and I strain to hear him. I move towards him to hear what he whispers and he moves back. Is this not harassment? He makes me, the Great Khan, feel inferior when he forces me to lean towards him when he speaks.'

'Indeed it is disturbing,' Faris agreed.

'He said you met the Gootamundra priest Midi78 at Space Station ZenFah, in the guise of a Merran on Level 480 opposite Recreation Area 202. He said you slipped into the crowd while you were with Midi78, disguised as a toy merchant and you acted on the stage as a mad magician. Why did he give me these details?'

'Light of my life, the facts you mentioned are correct and indeed, they have watched me with great attention. He wants to show you, because he is a Saradasi, he knows everything.'

The Great Khan rose with eight courtiers helping him onto the carpeted floor.

'Come,' he said, panting.

They left by a side door and climbed a flight of steps to a cupola above the assembly room. The Great Khan drew Faris into a dark, small cubicle draped on all sides with thick cloth. Inside, he lit a lamp and opened a box with white powder. Picking up a quill, he wrote, grinding his teeth, 'I hate the Saradasi. They are fornicators and thieves who stole our country. Their spies are everywhere and their cursed hidden machines, which we cannot find, record our every word and deed, even when we pass wind. Above us in the skies, the Sound Masters from Droha Major who we respect, gather and feed them facts, figures, intelligence, gossip and rumours for the small amount of energy for their planet's survival.'

Faris erased the writing with the block of wood by the side of the box. 'Wise of the wisest,' he wrote in a cramped hand, 'that is correct,' and smoothed the sand.

55

They left the cubicle and sat on a cool marble bench in the sunlight, on a balcony. A butler ran up to them with two waiters pushing a trolley heavy with food. The Great Khan thanked them and began eating. Seven courtyards spread below them, adorned with flower gardens, shrubs, fountains, and clusters of fruit trees. In each courtyard, gaily dressed crowds sat in neat rows, watching the actors performing on the stage in front of them.

The Great Khan swept his arms across the seven courtyards. 'See how diligently our people are practising. You have trained them well, Faris. Glory be to the Divine One for the great talents granted to us. The handsome Saradasi envoy of Lord Rasalis awaits us, Faris. We meet him today. He spends his time alone, thinking.' The Great Khan dabbed his face with a green handkerchief. 'I, the Great Khan, felt an icy hand grasp me when I met him last night on his Battle Cruiser. I said I was sorry to hear the *Mithras Ennab* was lost.'

'An apt condolence, light of my life,' Faris agreed. 'His response?'

'He replied in a whisper, his eyes locked on mine. He said, "Great Khan of Asurat, you are most kind to ask, though unkind if you have not told us the location of the *Mithras Ennab*."'

Faris sucked in his breath.

The Great Khan mopped his face. 'When I swore we have no knowledge of the *Mithras Ennab*, his eyes like chunks of ice frosted over. "Please," he whispered, "you must not call me Excellency. I hate titles, Great Khan."'

'What is the name of Lord Rasalis's envoy?' Faris inquired.

The Great Khan wiped his face. 'This is the first occasion he told me his name. He is Lord Medaris.'

'I know the name,' Faris said and sucked his breath in again.

'Yesterday,' the Great Khan said, 'he told me of the entire plan, cunning and brilliant like its architect, Lord Rasalis. I am to tell you the details. Listen well, Faris, he will question you when we meet him.'

Faris listened closely.

'Faris, what a wonderful role you have in Lord Rasalis's plan to help the five Saradasi on Lord Gaima's team. You will act in many roles and direct hundreds of actors mimicking many races. I look forward to my role, and, of course, helping you. Our tasks are immense.'

Faris bowed his head and touched the Great Khan's toes with his fingertips. 'My Khan, you are the sunrise and sunset of my life. No words can express my excitement to direct and act in this great enterprise. The Lord Rasalis is more than a genius. We actors will be his arms and legs and body and mouth and eyes to carry out his plan.'

'The envoy speaks of vast distances we have to travel,' the Great Khan said. 'He talks of strange places, of deserts and of snow-covered mountains.'

Below them, the crowd applauded the actors on a stage.

'The location of this great enterprise is a secret. I wonder why,' the Great Khan said. Holding Faris's hand he led him into the draped cubicle. He wrote, 'Why is Lord Rasalis secretive about the location?'

Faris answered, writing smoothly, 'He feels powerful by withholding information from us.'

'He has great and frightening power,' the Great Khan wrote.

'He needs more power to increase his self-esteem, which he considers inadequate,' Faris wrote.

Baring his teeth the Great Khan wrote in bold letters, 'I loathe the Saradasi. Can we slit their throats and survive?'

'That,' Faris wrote, 'is unwise. Where would we flee to?'

The Great Khan wrote, laughing, 'I fancy their planet, Saradasi. Faris, do you think Rasalis and Medaris know I am heavily disguised?'

'The disguise must indeed weigh heavily on you,' Faris wrote smiling, and drew his hand across, smoothing what they wrote.

The Great Khan giggled, leaving the cupola arm in arm with Faris.

O

That night Saradasi Space Control ordered the Great Khan to send Faris back to Space Station ZenFah on a commercial spacecraft with twenty guards, disguised as Samatalese jewellery merchants, with their wares strung across their bodies. They arrived a week later at the space station. From a deserted landing dock, Faris hurried to his quarters after completing the entry procedures and processes. He requested a guard to ask Midi78 to meet him at the perfumery on Level 103.

Faris met Midi78 disguised as a pregnant mother from north Astharia dressed in a bulky flared skirt, and a headdress made of shrunken trees. They wandered through the perfumery looking at the perfumes displayed, tier on tier, pausing to smell a few. Faris led Midi78 to a hall crammed with containers of liquids, tablets and powders.

'We can we speak freely here,' Faris said.

Leaving the perfumery, they sat in Recreation Room 65. When they finished their meal, Faris glanced at a clock. 'The Droha Major Sound Master Glance and his son, Breve, will arrive within the hour on the *Wave*. May we please meet in my quarters? It is a safe place to meet.'

'Why have we met here today and not in your quarters?' Midi78 asked.

'It is an order from the Saradasi' Faris said. 'When the *Wave* docks, guards will escort you from your quarters to mine.'

They left, wishing each other good health. In his quarters Faris logged into the Flight Information System. The *Wave* was entering Space Station ZenFah and assigned a berth on Level 18. He switched off the screen and lay on a couch, drifting into sleep.

He awoke when the signal at the entrance door sounded, and picked up the small disc inside the room, slipped under the heavy metal door. Striding out to the window he watched twelve guards patrol Recreation Area 28. The clocks chimed harshly for several minutes while he decoded the contents of the disc and swallowed it, remembering not to consume food or drink for half an hour. His digestive enzymes would break down the disc to low molecular weight proteins for his intestine to absorb.

Faris felt excited. He exclaimed to himself, 'Here? Here? Hidden here at Space Station ZenFah? How wise. Lord Rasalis is a genius.' His eyebrows quivered.

O

The controller on Level 18 spoke sternly, ordering the *Wave* to keep up with the flow of traffic. The pre-recorded sound of an engine needing urgent repair blared through the hidden speakers in the hull of the *Wave* as it slipped into to its berth. Master Glance and Breve disembarked and stopped to look at the *Erg,* a twenty-decked Daresian energy vendor docked opposite them. The captain of the *Erg* leered at Breve who tore his gaze from her when Master Glance tugged his sleeve. They passed through the entry processing chamber, the scanning chamber and the bubble shaped decontamination and sterilisation unit.

Their skin and clothes sterilised, their bodies minutely examined, their cell structure and contents categorised and checked against a database, Master Glance and Breve followed the guard who signalled them. They reached Recreation Area 28 where the guard pointed to a brightly lit corridor. The clocks in Recreation Area 28 chimed neither together or in harmony.

'The smell detector is at work,' Master Glance explained, inhaling the aroma at the end of the corridor. 'The smell of our bodies interferes with this smell. The detector recognises the change and sounds an alarm.'

'Come,' a voice called in InterWord. The door slid up. They entered a perfumed room with flowers, tables laden with food, and decanters of liquid and long stemmed chalices.

The tall, erect figure said, smoothing his coloured eyebrows and wriggling them when Breve stared at him, 'Some have difficulty with long names. I am therefore called Faris.'

'I am Midi78,' the smiling bald headed male, sitting on a chair, said.

'We greet you both. Faris, thank you for inviting us to your personal quarters,' Master Glance said. 'My son, Breve, and I, Sound Master Glance are honoured to meet you. We are from Droha Major, the cold planet in the Western Galaxy. Faris, we have seen your wonderful acting on many occasions, and Midi78, we know of you and your great powers to predict the future and even control spirits.'

Master Glance sat with his long fingers clasped on his lap.

'I am also honoured,' Faris said. 'My Great Khan and I, and all our Suxt-Sux people respect the Sound Masters of Droha Major. We know Sound Masters do not enjoy exchanging information for energy. If only we can give your planet some of the burning heat from our planet Asurat.'

'I am happy to meet you both,' Midi78 said. 'Master Glance, the honesty of your people is admired by my people and many others.'

Master Glance smiled his thanks. 'Our planet, Droha Major in the Western Galaxy, is dying, though our honour and dignity give us some warmth. Our self-esteem is eroding because of our work, but we continue to fear no one.' He moved to the window overlooking Recreation Area 28. The guards drove two drunken travellers who were singing, out of the area.

'Master Glance,' Midi78 asked, 'is there news of the *Mithras Ennab?*'

'No. We Sound Masters have no knowledge of what occurred to it,' he said watching the guards pace back and forth in Recreation Area 28.

'It is a great mystery how a Saradasi ship can disappear in the Saradasi Empire,' Midi78 said. He related what happened at the space

59

station between the Station Administrator Maxianusa and the Terumana Archduke Pirantha Los when he demanded to travel in Sector 1.

'Nobody I have met believes the Terumana were responsible for the loss of the *Mithras Ennab*,' Faris said.

'Nor do I,' Midi78 agreed.

'We live in strange times,' Master Glance remarked, looking into Recreation Area 28. 'Are we safe here?' he asked Faris.

'Yes,' Faris said, serving his guests the famous, bubbling Suxt-Sux drink, saa.

Master Glance thanked him. 'My orders are to meet you and leave Space Station ZenFah with Midi78. My destination is unknown. I will receive my travel orders from my Grand Master. I must mention, Lord Rasalis asked us to find the Dost Seelawathie-Ap who was injured protecting the High Chancellor, Shanaz. Neither I, on the *Wave*, or the other Sound Masters, have found her. It is most puzzling. We have failed despite Lord Rasalis giving us her voice patterns.'

'Please tell me, why is Seelawathie-Ap so important?' Faris asked.

'She is a Dost, like all the guards here, from an island on the planet Califra,' Master Glance explained. 'The Saradasi trained her to protect Shanaz. Unlike other Dost she has unusual powers which her village elders conferred on her. She can change her physical form.'

'May I inquire why the village elders gave her these powers and how her ability to change her form will help the Saradasi?' Faris asked.

'We can guess,' Master Glance answered. 'There is a rumour of an association between her ancestors, many generations ago, and the Saradasi. Her people may want to help the Saradasi find *The Place*. When she changes form, she can travel to other worlds and Lord Rasalis hopes she can take the five Saradasi on Lord Gaima's team to *The Place*, perhaps in another universe.'

Master Glance told them about Brother Red and of the single sentence, "Your game, Brother Red", the laughter, and the music he and Breve heard, which he believed was from *The Place*, and of the field of ionised plasma which trapped the *Wave*.

'Master Glance,' Midi78 said, 'you may have picked up the words, "Your game, Brother Red", from another universe.'

'Perhaps. I think we recorded this sentence within the Nereima Galaxy though we could not locate the source. We lost control of the *Wave* for a long period, and are fortunate to be alive. I agree we may have entered another universe, or gap-hole or portal to another universe.'

Midi78 sank back in his seat. He wiped the perspiration on his forehead with the back of his hand. 'Is this area well protected?' he asked.

'Yes,' Faris said beckoning Midi78 and pointing to the guards in Area 28.

The chimes struck with a shuddering noise.

'It is time to eat,' Midi78 said rising to his feet.

When Master Glance and Breve rose to leave, Midi78 looked questioningly at Faris. 'My friend, you must come with us,' he said.

'No. I am sorry, I cannot,' Faris said. 'I have many tasks to complete. Please go for your evening meal without me. I recommend Dining Room 10. When I am hungry I will send for some food.'

○

Master Glance, Breve and Midi78 sat in Dining Room 10, with its rotating ceiling and twenty adjustable tables and seats for diners. They listened to spacecraft crew exchange travel stories of increasing improbability. The arrival screens showed Pier 4 on Level 18 reconfigured and enlarged for the nine massive water transport craft belonging to the merchants Tsew, Naiderem and Gnik. A sign by the tenth berth, which was unoccupied, read, '*Reserved for Gaina.*'

'The Gaina?' Breve asked Master Glance.

'It is the largest water carrier in the Nereima Galaxy,' he said quickly, quietly tapping Breve's knee.

Midi78 pointed to the nine water carriers. 'Where are they from?'

'Their home planet is Lahin in the Starlizz galaxy,' Master Glance said.

They sat deciding on their meal, with diners at adjoining tables suggesting items on the wall menu, when a security guard ran up to them and whispered, 'An attempt was made to kill Faris. Please come with me.'

'Is he injured? How did this happen with so many guards near his quarters?' Master Glance asked hurrying to the exit.

'He is unconscious. A poisonous gas was pumped into his quarters through a hole drilled into the wall near Recreation Room 28.'

'Who could drill a hole in such a busy place with so many guards watching his quarters?' Master Glance asked.

'The guards are unconscious. We think someone poisoned them too.'

'I cannot believe this,' Master Glance said, frowning.

'Believe what you will. Saradasi Space Control wants you to leave Space Station ZenFah with Faris immediately,' the guard said urgently.

'With Faris? But why? Why should we leave with an unconscious person? There is excellent medical care here,' Master Glance said, staring at the guard.

'My troop leader will speak to you. It is dangerous for Faris to remain here and dangerous for you too.'

'Where is Faris now?' Midi78 asked

'Guards are taking him to the *Wave*.'

On Level 18, at the entrance to Pier 4 a Dost troop leader strode up to Master Glance. 'Master Glance? You must leave immediately, with Faris on board the Wave. Your Grand Master will confirm this order and give you travel instructions. Saradasi Space Control has contacted him.'

'Who ordered us to leave with Faris?'

'The orders are not mine,' the troop leader said curtly. 'Saradasi Space Control relayed an order from Saradasi Security from Lord Rasalis. Have you any other questions? If not, come with me.' Six guards carrying a capsule, surrounded by ten others, ran onto Pier 4.

'He is seriously ill,' the troop leader said.

Master Glance peered anxiously at the body in the clouded capsule connected to three gas cylinders. They carried the capsule on board the *Wave* where Master Glance led them to a cabin on the lower deck. He watched the troop leader secure and seal the entrance to the cabin. An engineer with him installed three valves for the gas to enter the cabin from the cylinders secured outside.

'I find all this most irregular,' Master Glance said shaking his head.

'Enter the cabin when your Grand Master orders you, not before,' the troop leader said. He gave Master Glance twelve gas cylinders which he said were curative gases to treat Faris, instructing him on the quantity, the frequency and duration of their release into the cabin.

'How will the gases once inside the cabin enter the capsule?' Breve asked.

'They will,' the troop leader snapped. 'Hurry.'

On the *Wave* Master Glance and Breve sat on the flight deck with Midi78 seated behind them waiting for clearance to leave the space station. The message alarm sounded. Sound Master Retrion appeared on the screen.

'The Grand Master confirms you must leave at once with Faris. Here are your travel orders,' he said as Breve them keyed in.

'I thought I have other urgent tasks,' Master Glance said. 'There are medical facilities here. I should be searching for The Place, and Seelawathie-Ap.' He muttered, 'I am a sound master not a gas master.'

The space station controller was relaying their clearance when the sound drowned her voice.

Master Glance said, 'Listen.'

All the ten thousand eight hundred and seventy six clocks on Space Station ZenFah chimed as one, in perfect harmony.

'So,' Master Glance said, 'the battle for the Nereima Galaxy has begun.'

SEVEN

On the spacecraft *Mithras Ennab,* its two passengers, Lord Wynan, the High Chancellor's General, and Fariyal, recently promoted from sub-commander to commander, were in their cabins. They were returning home to Saradasi from Merr, where Fariyal worked with Lord Wynan to set up Visual Disinformation Centres and promote the use of the battle robot she designed, Krenz V.

The *Mithras Ennab* carried the ostentatious markings of the Saradasi Empire: two crossed hands, an open book in one, and a sword in the other. At low altitude, the markings warned of the danger of interfering with or hindering the passage of a Saradasi spacecraft. Less prominently the *Mithras Ennab* bore the crest of the High Chancellor's General, a single silver bolt of lightning in a red circle.

The *Mithras Ennab* belonged to the Herk class of Interceptor space vehicles. When he worked briefly for the Master of the Fleet, Lord Wynan, at a Herk officers' meeting boasted about the Interceptor's automation linked to the Saradasi Space Control master computer Keptron. 'You, the crew,' he said, 'have to decide what food to eat, though some of you will starve, unable to decide.'

The *Mithras Ennab* bore the name of General Mithras Ennab who took no prisoners and accepted no surrender. He argued that surrender should occur before battle, and valueless at any other time. He famously said, 'If you are stupid enough to battle Saradasi, fight until you die. If not, you are a coward. If I capture you, I will teach you salutary lessons.' These lessons included castrating male prisoners or sterilizing female prisoners and releasing them, remarking, 'You will not breed fools to fight the Saradasi.'

On the *Mithras Ennab* Fariyal lay awake on her bunk, a slender figure with dark eyes and short hair. Her cabin mood-scanner altered the music, lighting and fragrance of the cabin. She stepped out of her bunk and opened the door of her cabin. Across the narrow passage in the larger cabin Lord Wynan snored. As the High Chancellor's General, his task was to liaise between the High Chancellor and the Saradasi military. Fariyal recalled how a year ago, the Saradasi military with the majority abstaining, elected him the High Chancellor's General after Lord Medaris twice declined the nomination. As the High Chancellor's General he was a member of the High Council.

Slim, and broad shouldered, Lord Wynan slept wearing the blue military uniform, a tunic with loose sleeves and ankle length trousers made of material impermeable to both heat and cold. The Saradasi military uniform bore no external insignia of rank.

Like all Saradasi military officers, Lord Wynan wore a wristband with a small communicator, a temperature and direction scanner, and a small insignia showing rank. On the floor beside his soft army issue boots, lay the famous Saradasi force-sword, two feet long, an inch wide, pointed, and double-edged. Though in appearance no different from other swords that cut, slashed or impaled an enemy, its primary purpose was to cause death by electrocution. Many hundred years before, Saradasi engineers and bio-technicians harnessed, and then increased the electricity created by the body, essential for brain, heart and muscle function. They channelled this minute electrical charge coursing through the body to a micro transformer in the handle of the sword, which generated a lethal voltage. Heightened mental and physical activity during a sword fight, significantly amplified the charge. The user could switch the charge on or off.

Fariyal stepped back, activated the intruder alarm, locked the door of her cabin after it slid shut and walked back to her bunk.

○

Fariyal woke to the soft sound from her wristband

It was a recorded message from her friend, Commander Giola, on Saradas in Saradasi, speaking in her husky voice.

'Fariyal, I have news for you. Something odd happened. This evening we celebrated my promotion to Commander at Tarich's Tavern. Shanaz, looking more beautiful than any of us there, walked in with Lord Rasalis and sat at a table opposite us. Much later, Lord Medaris came in with General Varitaa. He nodded briefly when he walked past Shanaz and Lord Rasalis and sat at a corner table on the terrace despite the wind.

'I watched Shanaz. Her eyes followed Lord Medaris until he sat. In a few moments she seemed a different person with her shoulders drooping and her face pale. She was not listening to Lord Rasalis. Shortly afterwards, she pushed her plate aside and left alone.'

Fariyal listened again to what Giola said, and thought about Shanaz, and the wonderful days they spent together as children.

She listened to the report she asked Giola, working in Saradasi Security, to send her.

Saradasi Security Report on Lord Wynan
Confidential to Lord Rasalis, Chancellor of Security
Author: Name Suppressed

'Lord Wynan, is the son of General Venias Appas who sat on the High Council, aspiring to be the High Chancellor of the Saradasi Empire. Many said exhaustion from trying to fulfil an ambition beyond his aptitude, and incompatible with his intellect caused his premature death.

In his career, Wynan always prospered over more deserving colleagues. Born on Asurat, he spent his childhood and youth there, when his father was a general in III Army. He enrolled at the Ursan Military Academy on Saradasi where he spent five undistinguished years. He survived academically by lavishing gifts on his colleagues, which rose in value as the complexity of his studies grew and the examinations became more taxing, or when his helpers' zeal wavered. None of his teachers described him as brilliant, hardworking, or talented except when his father questioned them. In private, even sycophants of his father described Wynan as 'average.' Honest teachers scorned their colleagues' poor judgement.

At his graduation, unlike in previous years, the academy did not publish the graduates ranking, claiming a technical problem erased the academic records of the graduates.

After graduation, Wynan studied his father conscientiously. He learned to use the talents of others and rifle their minds for ideas for his own betterment. He became adept with words, a wily flatterer and a smooth manipulator. He gave his superiors a connoisseur's blend of respect, attentiveness, humility and servility. He steadfastly remained a selfish braggart to his friends, insolent to those of no use to him and a bully to subordinates. He left a trail of abandoned friends he no longer needed. Many argued whether Wynan's worst character flaw was amorality or cowardice.

Those who feared his father or sought his patronage sheltered Wynan from failure. He thrived in the Saradasi military, provided with subordinate officers more brilliant than him, docile, and willing to deflect credit to him. His detractors muttered he would stroll through life in great grandeur, the voyage greased with charm and guile. His undoing, they predicted, would be his constant delusional state about his great worthiness.

Conclusion: He is most unsuitable to join Saradasi Security. I strongly recommend you reject his application.

Observation: He lacks the ability and intelligence to be even a poor administrative officer. Why does he want to join Saradasi Security?

Comment by Lord Rasalis: Because, stupidity and insight rarely converge in a brain challenged beyond its capacity.

After a meal in her cabin, Fariyal switched on the wall screen and dimmed the lights to watch the audiovisual military report on Wynan's posting in Kersia that Lord Rasalis asked her to prepare for him when she was a sub-commander. She compiled her report from the Saradasi Archives and Sound Master Archives which he provided. He insisted he wanted an audiovisual report with her as narrator, and not a written or verbal report.

'You are one of the few I trust, even above those closest to me,' he had confided when he visited her at her quarters in the Lower City late one night. 'Be honest in your views. The report is restricted.'

Military Report on Lord Wynan in Kersia.
To: Lord Rasalis, Chancellor of Security
From: Sub-Commander Fariyal
Narrator: Sub-Commander Fariyal.
The power of the Saradasi Military has not thwarted the spirit of freedom in some conquered people. Pockets of males and females exist like annoying burrs in the body of the Saradasi Empire.

The High Council asked Wynan to deal with what they called the nuisance in Kersia on Califra. This was when some members of the High Council, despite opposition, especially from his father, wanted the image of the Saradasi Empire to soften. They urged that conciliation and, or duplicity, replace violence. The nuisance in Kersia was a euphemism for a rebellion against Saradasi rule in south eastern Califra, which supplied food to many provinces of the Empire. Here Saradasi robots and their machines constantly ploughed, fertilised and reaped rich harvests. Because the area boasted the highest yield per unit of cultivated land, the High Council was reluctant to wage a battle that would destroy an asset.

The first opposition to Saradasi rule occurred in Province 8 and spread. A group of rebel leaders hidden in the northern mountains led the uprising. Enraged by the rebellion, the High Council dismissed three consecutive Planet Governors, and fined and dismissed twelve Province Governors. Transfer of Saradasi Military personnel, demotions, and cashiering of non-Saradasi military officers occurred regularly.

The rebellion spread and flourished.

General Salween, a respected Saradasi officer, commanded II Army, garrisoned in Kersia. In his debriefing he said the High Council conveyed its constant displeasure for not speedily resolving the problem. The High Council hinted at 'poor military leadership, grave ineptitude, irresolute decision making, a worrying lack of focus, and gross underestimation of the enemy capability.' He said he felt the High Council was goading him to resign, to not dismiss him, because of his popularity.

He lived alone on the Army Base with an elderly Kersian housekeeper who he treated graciously.

Medical reports state he was severely depressed: he rarely ate, showed no interest in his work or surroundings, woke abnormally early in the morning and was often tearful.

Saradasi Security at the Army Base reported General Salween spent his evenings in his garden with his collection of orchids. Months after the rebellion, Saradasi Security obtained information that he received his favourite plant as an anonymous gift. They learned from a rebel prisoner how teams of rebels scoured the mountains for this rare plant. The elusive young rebel leader was the grandnephew of General Salween's housekeeper.

In the fourteenth month of the worsening rebellion, unannounced, a military negotiator arrived to assist General Salween.

'He is a brainless tree trunk,' General Salween had declared, alluding to the negotiator's great size which slowed his movements. 'Single-handed,' General Salween predicted, 'he will create chaos here.'

The rebels murdered the negotiator. They said they liked neither the negotiator's appearance nor his attitude or aptitude. They displayed his body in a manner identical with that of two recently executed rebels. This act of faithful mimicry incensed the Saradasi High Council.

The next day the High Council recalled General Salween to Saradasi to undertake a task they claimed he would carry out with great distinction. On the day he left, General Wynan, not yet a Lord, took command of II Army to solve the problem in Kersia. He launched a series of actions on his father's advice.

Day One

Five hundred battle units of II Army withdrew from country garrisons in Kersia to the cities under aerial cover of Saradasi Battle Cruisers.

Day Two

Eighty battle units from military bases at Leura-Hltrym, and Htrep-Anudec withdrew. At dusk the last of the Saradasi military vehicles, the heavily armed Battle Cruiser Marius, left its base on Sader-Hytr to assume Califra zero orbit, at an altitude of three thousand feet. General Wynan set up his command post on the Marius.

Day Three

Thousands of rebels left their inaccessible lairs in the mountains flocking to the city of Ulman-Abbase to celebrate the Saradasi withdrawal. After a few hours of jubilation, the rebel high command pondered why the Saradasi forces left, becoming suspicious when their alcoholic stupor subsided.

Day Four

Paralysis from the waist to the feet occurred in 2.5 million Kersians.

Day Five

Paralysis occurred in 3.0 million people.

Day Six

The paralysis extended upwards. After weakness in the arms, muscle paralysis spread causing disturbances in speech, eye movements, swallowing and breathing.

The young and the elderly, who were most severely affected, died in their thousands.

Day Seven

General Wynan offered the rebel leaders an antitoxin to treat those alive, if the rebels surrendered.

Day Eight

The rebel leaders sent a message to General Wynan inquiring whether he would prefer the appendage of the enormous six legged Driconthyrus rammed down his throat or up another aperture below his waist.

General Wynan directed Commander Aricent, seconded from Saradasi Security, to respond to the message. He retired to his cabin, and sampled a variety of wines till he fell into an intoxicated sleep.

Day Nine

General Wynan broadcast a message asking one non-rebel Kersian civic leader to bring a severely affected person he or she knew to meet him on board the Marius. Military personnel carried a terrified, partially paralysed adult Kersian and a child with four paralysed limbs on board the Marius. General Wynan greeted them warmly.

'You are my guests,' he gushed, peering at the child, her face paralysed and distorted. She shrank back. He led the way to the reception room a deck below, walking slowly in the centre of the corridors, glancing at the cameras on board which beamed his every act and word throughout Califra. He explained the many benefits the Kersians enjoyed because of Saradasi rule. He looked closely at the civic leader, Merchant Armiaas.

'Considering what we Saradasi provide, is it unreasonable for me to ask you personally for your loyalty?' General Wynan asked Merchant Armiaas.

Since boarding the Marius, Merchant Armiaas's speech had worsened because of increasing vocal cord paralysis. He made a gurgling sound and blinked one eye.

General Wynan gestured to an officer to increase the illumination in the treatment room of the medical suite when Merchant Armiaas and the child received a dose of antitoxin. He smoothed his hair and walked to the centre of the room and declared, 'They have recovered! Let none say we Saradasi have no concern or affection for our subjects. The crimes of the rebels have affected these and other innocent people. The rebels have caused great suffering. I am happy I helped these innocent people to recover from the atrocities the rebels inflicted on them.' He looked sternly at the cameras.

That evening, the two visitors dined with General Wynan and the ship's officers to celebrate their recovery, the table laden with food and drinks never seen before on Califra. The waiters plied Merchant Armiaas with expensive wine. As the evening turned to night, Merchant Armiaas's hatred of the Saradasi decreased while his anger towards the rebels mounted. General Wynan repeatedly pointed out that it was the rebels who caused the problems. Merchant Armiaas and his host, both intoxicated, laughed loudly and often. Commander Aricent, leaning over, pointed to the cameras. Wynan pressed more wine on his guest and faced the camera smoothing his hair.

The next morning Merchant Armiaas and the child, with gifts and vials of anti-toxin to treat five thousand people, left the Marius with a promise that more antitoxin would be available when the rebels surrendered. General Wynan sent them both to the capital of Province 8, where the rebellion started. During the long journey back to their homes in Province 11 he knew Merchant Armiaas and the child would damage the rebel cause. Now wealthy beyond belief, Merchant Armiaas blessed the generous Saradasi general. He carried a specific suggestion to the Kersian people from General Wynan.

The rebels surrendered, pressured by the people, and were crucified in town squares.

Planet Governor Cxxdi-Cxxdi hosted a banquet in honour of General Wynan and during the dinner she asked, 'Is your work now complete?'

'I am disappointed with the outcome.'

'Disappointed? Because of the large number of deaths?'

'The deaths?' he asked surprised. 'Deaths are irrelevant. Orderly rule needs great sacrifices. The death of a single person or a million should not concern us. It is the Empire that matters.'

He congratulated Planet Governor Cxxdi-Cxxdi on the food and wine and praised her good looks.

It is recorded she declined his repeated requests to join him on the Marius.

On his return to Saradasi, a grateful nation elected General Wynan a Lord of the Saradasi Empire.

○

Fariyal awoke when the interior of her cabin throbbed with a purple light. She ran to the flight deck calling out to Lord Wynan to join her. When she entered the flight deck its normal hum was absent and the screens dark. The *Mithras Ennab* was motionless.

The face of a female appeared on every screen, her aura increasing, and the screens incandescent.

She spoke softly in Saradasi. 'Fariyal, I want to talk to you,' she said. 'I need your help. I am on an Ashanti-Ishtana craft with a child who is dying. I ask your permission to cross the Nereima Galaxy to Res-IV on the planet Tarasunaz in the Western Galaxy to seek urgent medical treatment. I know you have the authority to give me this permission.'

'How are you on our screens?'

'Can you give me permission to seek help to save the life of a child?'

Fariyal did not hesitate. 'I will not grant your request. The Saradasi Empire allows no traffic within its boundaries unless travelling for the Empire or with the authority of the officers of the Empire.'

'You are an officer,' the female pointed out. 'You can give me the authority.'

'I refuse. Who are you?'

'The child is dying. Please give me permission to take her to the nearest health post on Merr. Will you allow that?'

'No. You should have obtained clearance at Space Station ZenFah. You should know that.'

'ZenFah is beyond Merr. Are you asking me to return to Space Station ZenFah for permission and risk the child's life?'

'You are here illegally. Saradasi Space Control did not inform me of a craft in this sector. They should have destroyed your craft. Why are you on my screens?'

'Fariyal, you have sophisticated medical apparatus on board and you can ask for medical advice. Can you help us?'

'No. The life or death of a child is of no concern to me or to the Saradasi Empire,' Fariyal answered. 'You are here illegally. Saradasi Space Control will punish you.'

Lord Wynan entered the flight deck and sat scowling at the screens. He listened to the female and shouted, 'I am Lord Wynan. I am the High Chancellor's General. I order you to get out of our airspace.'

'Both your Empire and you have to learn the preciousness of life,' the female said. 'You have to learn that life is more valuable than rules. '

The *Mithras Ennab* shuddered. Its interior filled with darkness and Fariyal shivered as the temperature fell while she groped for the emergency button under her seat. Despite the drowsiness creeping over her she looked at Wynan whimpering, his head thrown back.

'Fariyal,' the voice of the female, now fading said, 'I will try to help you and the Nereima Galaxy. Come with me. Close your eyes, Fariyal.'

Fariyal heard a soothing gurgling sound and the he voice whispering, 'You killed an unborn child long ago. You killed a Maranti child on Asurat. Can you remember the Quartet? Can you remember the pregnant member of the Quartet who lost her unborn child and her life because of you?'

'Does it matter?' Fariyal asked drowsily. She tried to turn to look at Wynan, to ask whom he was talking to because she heard a male in the background. Her head drooped.

'Yes, Fariyal, you are committing the same crime again. You have to learn the value of life before you can save the Nereima Galaxy. Come with me.'

EIGHT

SHANAZ: MILITARY DUTY FIVE YEARS AGO

Shanaz met General Wynan in her second year after graduation. She received the routine postings to appreciate the power and genius of the Saradasi military. She learned of war though not of peace. Her teachers insisted the conquered must never rise to threaten the Saradasi Empire.

Shanaz served as an analyst in one of seven intelligence teams, each working separately with identical data to provide separate views to their superiors. She was posted at Eastern Command Headquarters in Province 8 on Merr, under the command of Lord Alexandris, a portly, jovial Saradasi of ferocious cunning. Shanaz developed the skills of deviousness, becoming adept and comfortable in the use of guile, threats and false promises to achieve the goals of the Saradasi Empire.

Shanaz met General Wynan when he arrived at Eastern Command Headquarters after a victory over King Eefoce, of Rias on Merr whose plan to fight the Saradasi was doomed. He was unaware that his beloved Queen, his twenty-two devoted concubines and the Commander in Chief of his army were communicating with Saradasi agents and gathering great wealth.

When a triumphant General Wynan arrived at Eastern Command, Lord Alexandris organised a lavish reception to welcome him and celebrate his victory over King Eefoce. Guests thronged the banquet hall in the Province Governor's residence, the high arched transparent roof letting in the warm afternoon sun. General Wynan sat on the dais with Lord Alexandris. Shanaz was with a group of colleagues on the gallery opposite the dais. She gazed at General Wynan, smiling and nodding to the crowd before him. After a brief speech of welcome and appreciation Lord Alexandris invited General Wynan to speak a few words.

Shanaz listened, enchanted by General Wynan's good looks and humility. 'My Lord Alexandris, my colleagues and friends. The Empire is victorious again. The victory is not mine. Our army is like a well functioning body in which I am a small part. My Lord Alexandris is the head.'

He paused, the timing perfect. He hesitated a moment as if searching for words in the speech written for him, the pauses marked, which he memorised with difficulty. 'I am,' he said, 'a single finger.'

Lord Alexandris and General Wynan circulated among the guests. Her mouth was dry when they approached her. Panic glued her lips and tongue. Her heart thudded. She knew she must control her rapid breathing.

'We met before, somewhere,' Wynan said. Taking her hand, he looked at her wristband. 'I see you are a Force-Sword Master,' he said. 'We should practice together, I am rusty.' She felt excited by his voice, his looks, his whole being. She feared what she wanted to say, 'Yes, General Wynan, I am honoured' would sound like a croak. She knew she had not met him, and he may have made a mistake. If he lied, it was to make her feel comfortable in his presence.

When they left, a Califran major tapped her on her arm. 'Greetings,' he said. 'How are you? We met at Reme, on Astharia.'

Shanaz waved him away, saying, 'We have not met. You may leave now.'

The major joined a group of friends and she heard him say, 'I won my bet. Pay up. You were right. She is a beautiful, vicious animal. A heavenly being will have to protect whoever she lives with.' Unconcerned, Shanaz walked downstairs to return to her quarters. She passed a small alcove, heard voices and paused to listen. Entering an adjacent room, she climbed on a chair and peered through a grill. A general and a battle commander she did not recognised sat across a low table.

General: Wynan is a silver-tongued fraud. We lead, we fight, we take the risks, and what is his contribution?

Battle Commander: He relishes the victory! He is not concerned how many lives we lose in battle. Though we are soldiers we should act responsibly and have compassion when death strikes. He has none. He was drunk the night before and during the battle, safe and comfortable in his Battle Cruiser.

General: I remember the night in Krimia when someone spoke admiringly of Medaris, how his face swelled with resentment. I wish there were more Saradasi like Medaris, humble and decent, unlike this vain pompous fool.

Battle Commander: He spends his time trying to win supporters because he aspires to be the High Chancellor's General.

General: Wynan? Wynan, the High Chancellor's General?'

Battle Commander: Yes and I predict he will succeed because the military will vote for him.

General: Why would they?

Battle Commander: Because eighty percent of people are stupid irrespective of what planet they live on.

Shanaz watched them saunter, laughing, to the banquet hall.

'They are jealous of him,' she said to herself returning to her quarters to be alone.

O

Three days later Shanaz heard of General Wynan's transfer to V Army. She masked her disappointment, not allowing it to interfere with her duties. Early one afternoon her immediate superior, sent for her.

'I have received orders of your promotion,' he said, not looking at her. 'Report to V Army, Military Base, Retuor, Califra.'

'V Army?' Shanaz asked.

The General continued with his work.

Shanaz left that night on the long trip to Retuor in Province 3 on Califra. After reporting to the duty officer at the military base, V Army, she went to her quarters, a small-detached wooden building among tall trees some distance from the main buildings, consisting of a combined living and sleeping area, a sophisticated workstation, bathroom and lavatory. In the army dining room, which provided the same meals to all personnel irrespective of race or rank, she picked at her food, annoyed because the menu was Eastern Califran.

A messenger brought her orders to her quarters. She was adjutant to General Wynan and she should report to him the next morning. Excited, unable to sleep, she tossed in bed, fretting for dawn and the opportunity to meet Wynan.

O

Shanaz entered General Wynan's office. He looked up briefly, nodded and pointed to a seat in front of him. She sat, hiding her disappointment at not receiving a warmer welcome. Behind General Wynan and to his right, a fat, ruddy-faced officer sat, his cloak over his shoulders, a mournful expression on his face, staring at his boots. His presence diluted her pleasure of being with Wynan.

'Tell me about yourself,' Wynan said.

Shanaz remained silent. They were the recipients of information and she the provider. She would play the tune and decide on the tempo. The fat officer shifted in his seat and looked at her. She gave him a well-practised stare, with the condemnation a stern teacher would level at a fidgety child. She remained silent. They looked at her. Shanaz drew out a sheaf of papers from her tunic pocket and offered them to General Wynan.

'To not waste time, I have written some important facts about myself.'

He took the three sheets of closely written paper and passed them to the officer beside him who placed them untidily on the floor.

'Thank you. I want you to tell me about yourself,' Wynan said.

Her throat constricted. She knew he was looking at her adoringly, covertly. These, she knew, would be his cherished memories of their first long conversation.

She knew he wanted to hear her speak. He may be a person enchanted by the voice of a person. Shanaz remembered the young voice master who was too close to her when he coached her. What did the fool say about her voice? 'Heavenly. Melodious'. Her pronunciation, he said, was perfect. The consonants clear and crisp like sharply struck bells. He praised the beguiling cadence when she spoke. A beguiling cadence! Can one ask for more?

Gazing at Wynan, she spoke about herself. He leaned forwards. She knew he wanted to see her more closely. She must concentrate on what she was saying. Now exhilarated, she felt sorry for the officer seated next to Wynan. How humiliated he must feel, excluded by Wynan and her from their conversation. She glanced at him. He sat hunched, asleep. She noticed Wynan breached etiquette when he said, 'tell *me*' and not *us*. She understood '*me*' carried a coded message. How else could he signal his feelings towards her? Shanaz recalled a friend say how cunning and devious people became when they were in love.

General Wynan cleared his throat and said, 'I can't hear you.' Shanaz giggled silently, flashing him the subtlest of conspiratorial glances. He looked up past her. A colonel walked in and spoke to him.

She gazed at Wynan, his head close to the colonel's. She knew it was Wynan's destiny and hers to be together and she would help fulfil his glorious destiny. It was not only her mother, who she knew never loved her, whose partner would be a Lord and then High Chancellor of the

Saradasi Empire. With her as a partner Wynan would be High Chancellor. What would her mother say? Shanaz smiled.

The hum of conversation ended. Wynan left the room.

'General Wynan has urgent work. Your interview will continue with General Ghais,' the colonel said.

'Tell me about yourself,' General Ghais said. 'Start from the beginning. I was not listening when you spoke to General Wynan. Tell me, what is the difference between the words start and begin, wide and broad? If I fall asleep, wake me.'

O

General Ghais, Chief Psychological Assessor in Saradasi Security, spoke to Lord Rasalis in his home in the Upper City on the home planet.

'Greetings, Rasalis,' he said. 'I agree with you about her.'

'Good!'

'I am not yet deaf,' General Ghais said.

'How is her stomach pain?' Rasalis asked.

'Abdominal pain,' Ghais corrected. 'The stomach is one organ within the abdominal cavity.'

'What do specialists of the mind know about the abdomen?'

'They are keenly aware of the abdomen and the organs within it, when a toxin added to someone's food results in nausea, diarrhoea, and severe abdominal pain.'

'The dining room steward who added the toxin to her food is one of my officers. She is skilled in her work,' Lord Rasalis said.

'At dawn, before the interview with Wynan, Shanaz was ordered to join a group for combat drill. She asked to be excused thrice for very short periods to visit the lavatory, and continued the strenuous exercise. Though ill she performed well. She *never* complained. That is what is important. She did not complain and completed the exercise. Three others withdrew because of fatigue, all males. You are right about her.'

'I am rarely wrong,' Lord Rasalis said. 'We may have a problem because of her attraction to Wynan. It is completely unacceptable. I will think of a solution.'

'I am very concerned about her safety,' Ghais said.

'We are protecting her,' Lord Rasalis answered.

'I mean protecting her from herself.'

'Explain what you mean.'

'I believe she is at great risk of taking her own life.'

'Are you certain?'

'Rasalis, like you, I too am rarely wrong. She is acutely depressed and, therefore, is in greatest danger from herself. Increase your vigilance, she may be suicidal. The decision to take one's own life often occurs on impulse. '

○

Shanaz knew her relentless, covert pursuit, and feints of intermittent disinterest attracted General Wynan to her. Inexplicably, despite her love for him and the conviction he loved her, she recognised the familiar sadness lurking in her life. Tiredness, like a pervasive illness, consumed her. She lost her taste for food and knew she was losing weight. Falling asleep at night and early morning awakening became a problem. The bouts of weeping were more frequent. She felt drained of energy, willpower and purpose, losing interest in life and recognised the symptoms of acute depression. Shanaz grappled with the perplexing nightmare of being in love.

'Why must a hundred fears hound and torment me?' she wondered. The despair she felt enraged her.

She knew her thinking was muddled. Doubt gripped her every thought. Sometimes clear crisp, soothing understanding shone within her, giving her hope, happiness and peace. Like a cycle of ill fate, the black shroud of depression would replace the ecstasy of her love for Wynan. She would brood, the same questions recurring. Why would Wynan love her? Why should this godlike person love her? Gods should love gods. Slowly, like a contagion, new conflicts arose and consumed her.

'Perhaps,' she argued, 'Wynan does not love me. It is pretence. Perhaps he loves me because I am the daughter of Lord Laramis, High Chancellor of the Saradasi Empire.'

In the dark loneliness of the night she would lie awake, and sob herself to sleep.

○

The V Army granted her six days home leave.

Shanaz decided her cousin Fariyal, her only friend, could lead her out of the maze she was lost in. Fariyal and she grew up as children, sharing their toys, joys, and hurts. Fariyal was older, protective towards her, tolerating her tempestuousness, impatience, rudeness and occasional selfishness. She would say sorry to Fariyal, tousle her short hair, hug her, and all would be forgiven. Fariyal never believed her when she said how beautiful she was and how much she loved her. It was Fariyal who knew she felt like an orphan, unloved, uncared for, and unaccepted even by her parents.

Shanaz met Fariyal on Saradasi, in Saradas. They spent four days together following the same routine, leaving the military barracks in the Lower City to have breakfast at Tarich's Tavern in the Upper City, stroll along the beach and cut across to the trail leading to the Mirellar Mountains. At noon they would sit on the grassy banks of Lake Tiaret to have their lunch with a bottle of Restian wine.

After listening to Shanaz talk about General Wynan, Fariyal asked, 'Does he love you?'

'I am not sure,' Shanaz answered.

'Shanaz, are you in love with him?'

'I am not sure.'

'What did you come to talk to me about, Shanaz?'

'You never help me,' Shanaz said angrily. 'You cloud every issue with questions. Not even you love me. Nobody loves me, and stop sighing when I speak.'

'Shanaz, why are you insisting nobody loves you?'

'Because, Fariyal, nobody loves me.' Shanaz looked across the green water of the lake. Two birds, a dazzling orange, flew close together, barely a feather apart. In the water a shoal of silver scaled fish swam past. A bird called.

'Fariyal, I feel lonely and afraid.'

'What about, Shanaz?'

'I am not sure. I am confused.'

'Shanaz, ask for a transfer.'

They walked back home to Saradas arm in arm. Shanaz searched the trees. Where was her arrogant looking Tumut in royal blue feathers with its unflinching gaze? She heard the high-pitched whistling sound and looked up, and swore the Tumut winked at her

○

On a sunless morning, the day after she returned to V Army Military Base in Retuor, Califra, and the air heavy with the threat of rain, General Wynan sent for her.

'I have some tasks to attend to. We leave tomorrow.'

They set out the next morning. After a desultory inspection of a forward battle position, half a day's journey brought them to the twisting blue Menur River. They set out on foot through a green meadow sloping to wooded hills. She wanted Wynan to hold her in his arms and hear him say how much he loved her. They sat beneath a clump of trees with scented leaves rustling in the wind rising from the gully below them.

Wynan held her to him. Shanaz leaned against his shoulder, placing her hand over his. She tried calming her mind. She looked at the mountains across the valley, with dark patches of trees against the snow.

'I want to spend the rest of my life with you,' she said.

She searched his face when he said, 'You are beautiful,' and saw the lust in his eyes. He tipped her face up to his and as his lips sought hers, she pushed him away and saw the surprise on his face. Her heart racing, she wondered why she felt afraid of someone she worshipped. He continued to caress her hair and bent to kiss her again.

'I need time,' she whispered, turning away. 'Please give me some time. I am due for Long Leave. I will go to on leave and come back to you.'

'Go where?'

'Sirglin, a beautiful small town, on the Veles mountain range here on Califra.'

'Enjoy yourself when you go there,' he said.

'"Enjoy yourself"', she thought angrily. 'A feeble, inconsequential, valueless response.' Rage swept over her. Shanaz bit her lip hoping there was blood to spit at Wynan.

His hands reached for her. She sprang up.

'Trying to enjoy yourself?' Shanaz asked.

He half rose, leaning forward to pull her towards him. She walked away towards the gully, not wanting him to see her cry. She knew he was playing a game with her. To humiliate her, to talk about her to his friends in the V Army and boast how willingly she gave herself to him. Or would he claim moral responsibility and say he virtuously rejected her advances? She would be the object of contempt and ridicule, first in V Army and then throughout the military.

Looking into the gully below her, she thanked the genius of her Mind Master Tijnar. She went through the Lesson of Effecting Immediate Emotional Mastery. She brightened, and feeling transformed, relaxed, and in control of herself, walked from the edge of the gully, masking the condemnation she felt for him.

'Do you remember what you said to me the first time you met me? You spoke of being rusty with your force-sword. Your life may depend on your skill.'

General Wynan shook his head.

'We can have force-sword practice here, now. These are the rules. If your sword drops, you lose, or if I tap your right shoulder you lose. The same applies to me. Of course if you kill me I lose. Touching anywhere else is foul. This is just a friendly contest. Friendly because you are rusty and I am not.'

'What are these rules? I have never of them before,' Wynan said

'You are correct. I just made them up.'

'I refuse to engage in any contest.'

'It is not a contest, you coward.'

General Wynan shrugged, and drew his force-sword. 'Switch the force off,' he ordered.

'No. Force on. We Saradasi are not cowards, are we?' Shanaz took four paces back, her force-sword in her left hand hanging loosely at her side.

'We may injure ourselves,' Wynan said.

'Of course! A quick death through electrocution is not a bad way to die, is it?' Shanaz swept the air in front of her with her force-sword. 'On guard, Saradasi General,' she said, advancing.

Shanaz focussed on one objective, to kill Wynan. Blade struck blade, drawing a glitter of sparks. The force-swords glowed as the electric charge intensified. Shanaz saw fear cross Wynan's face when she forced him towards the gully. She crouched when his sword swept across, above her head. He sprang back when she bent, slashing at his legs. Her right arm shot up to distract him. She saw a moment of indecision. Still crouching she sidestepped to her right, and rose, striking the hilt of his sword and saw his arm shudder. He grimaced.

'You do not love me. You never loved me,' she said, diving forwards, forgetting all her force-sword master taught her. Wynan stepped aside. Shanaz slid on a moss-covered root and fell screaming into the gully.

○

The site of the accident teemed with investigators. The Emergency Medical Craft No. 8 arrived with a medical team. Winched to the floor of the gully, the trauma specialist and the neurologist examined Shanaz, sprawled, unconscious, her hair matted with blood. They staunched the external bleeding, dressed the multiple cuts and abrasions and made her comfortable without moving her. The neurologist relayed the patient's vital signs to her military medical centre and to Lord Rasalis on Saradasi.

The neurologist, a Saradasi, watched the trauma specialist carry out a limited whole body scan with a portable scanner.

'The scan shows no fractures and in particular, the spinal cord is intact though there are extensive soft tissue injuries on her back, legs and arms,' he said replacing the scanner in its case. 'There is intracranial bleeding, but no other internal bleeding. She is lucky to be alive.'

A shadow passed over them. A Saradasi Interceptor landed on the knoll above them. A Saradasi military officer stepped out unhurriedly, arms clasped behind his head, looking down into the gully. The communicator on his wristband buzzed.

'I have a large team of neurologists and surgeons sitting here with me,' Lord Rasalis said. 'I will make the final decision.'

'You are not a medical expert. The experts should make the final decision,' the officer said. He took a step forward and leaned, watching the neurologist examining Shanaz.

He walked back and spoke into his wristband. 'This,' he said, 'is the result of a disgraceful lack of vigilance.' He watched the capsule with Shanaz winched up and transferred to the emergency medical craft. He walked across, joined the medical team, and entered the craft. He adjusted his force-sword and sat in the cramped observation area looking into the sterile treatment bay where Shanaz lay on an operating table. At a console, the neurologist adjusted the sterilising electromagnetic field within the bay and started a detailed brain scan. She looked at the serial images on the screen in front of her, and relayed them.

'I confirm there is no skull fracture. In the brain there is extensive bruising grade four, with clot formation in the left median posterior lobe,' she reported.

Lord Rasalis responded, 'Tell us your plan and we will confirm or advise an alternative.'

'We should insert a mobile scout and guide it across the blood vessels of the Circle of Silliw and reach the injured artery to deliver pulses of anticoagulant.' The neurologist leaned back on her seat, watching a second screen showing Lord Rasalis conferring with the medical advisers.

'The question is, whether to carry out the procedure immediately where you are now, or to evacuate her,' Lord Rasalis said.

'I have given you my opinion. Your experts should know the answer,' the neurologist said. 'I think time is the priority here.'

Lord Rasalis cleared his throat. 'Thank you. Your colleagues agree. They believe you would provide excellent care for her.'

'I know,' she said.

She pressed a switch, and focussed a beam of light to sterilise a portion of Shanaz's neck on the right side. The green light over the speaker glowed.

'Will you need my help?' the trauma specialist asked.

The neurologist shrugged and continued with her work, checking the continuous analysis on Shanaz's medical status. She manipulated the robotic arm inserting a pin-like mobile scout, with a fine tube, into the main artery in the neck. She threaded it up to the site of injury to inject anticoagulant into the clots in the blood vessel.

The Saradasi military officer left the emergency medical craft, his head bent, and his wristband against his ear.

'Wynan cannot speak coherently,' Lord Rasalis said. 'At his insistence, he is sedated. He did nothing to help Shanaz. His behaviour amazes me.'

'Amazes you?' the officer asked. 'You are uncharacteristically generous today. Let us not lose the Nereima Galaxy because of a coward like Wynan.'

O

Emergency Medical Craft No. 8 sped to rendezvous with a Saradasi Hunter, the *Amira*. On the flight deck of the *Amira*, a female Dost in military uniform spoke to Saradasi Space Control. She said she understood her task on board was to look after Shanaz and was aware the Saradasi Space Control computer, Keptron, would control the *Amira*, and twelve Saradasi Interceptors and a Battle Cruiser would escort her.

In the reconfigured cabin, the neurologist made Shanaz comfortable on a couch, and placed her under light sedation. The Dost joined the neurologist, smiling at Shanaz who looked at her drowsily.

'Her medication times are important,' the neurologist said. 'One medication will erase the memory of what happened to her and of the

85

time she will spend with you. If she meets you again she will not remember you.'

'Why should she forget?' the Dost asked.

'I am busy and have no time to answer your questions. When I leave, you may question Lord Rasalis, the Chancellor of Security.'

The Dost stared sullenly.

'You can contact me if you need me,' the neurologist said. 'The second medication is in three different forms. Puncturing the capsule of gas at night while she is asleep is the easiest and best. You should not inhale it yourself.'

After the neurologist disembarked, the *Amira* left, bound for Nelun Deepa, the capital of the island of Nuwara on Califra, securely guarded on land, sea and air by VIII Army troops.

Shanaz awoke, raising herself on her elbows when the *Amira* steadied a few thousand feet above the finger like island and descended over the sea lapping the white sand of the beach fringed with palms. Some distance from the shore, the land rose to central hills, and a mountain range.

A two storied building, white walled, red tiled, with fluted pillars overlooked the small harbour they were approaching. Clusters of smaller red roofed buildings dotted the coastline and the hills. The *Amira* settled with a gentle slosh on the water next to a wooden jetty. The Dost secured the *Amira* and helped Shanaz onto the pontoon and climb the wooden steps to the jetty.

Shanaz looked at her. 'Tell me again, who are you?'

'My name is Seelawathie-Ap. Lord Rasalis asked me to be with you.'

Shanaz took a few steps and stumbled. Seelawathie-Ap reached out to her, steadying her. 'I am so tired, and I feel dizzy,' Shanaz whispered squinting against the sunlight and looking at the clouds smudging the mountaintops. She leaned against the railing, staring at the *Amira* bobbing in the water and took a breath and exhaled.

'It is the wonderful smell of the sea, the salt, seaweeds, and creatures dead and alive,' Seelawathie-Ap said. She saw Shanaz staring at the red tiled white building.

'Where are we?' Shanaz asked.

'On a small island called Nuwara on Califra.'

'Why are we here?'

'Your father and Lord Rasalis wanted you to come here after your accident.'

'I remember falling into a gully. Can you tell me what happened?'

'Yes. Lord Rasalis told me you injured yourself during a military exercise. He thinks you slipped.'

'I have never been here before, yet I feel I have,' Shanaz said.

'Perhaps you were, in a past life,' Seelawathie-Ap said.

They walked towards the white building, the once resplendent palace of proud and mighty kings and queens who ruled the Dost. Seelawathie-Ap had returned to the home of her ancestors.

○

Shanaz and Seelawathie-Ap stayed on the ground floor of the palace. Army caterers prepared their food; inconspicuous Dost roamed the gardens of the palace and beyond.

On the third day of their stay Shanaz and Seelawathie-Ap walked down the broad steps from the palace veranda, through the garden onto the beach. They strolled past the jetty and left the beach, walking through woodland to a plateau above the sea. A swollen river, yellow with mud from the rains, snaked across a shallow valley. Beyond the wooded hills, mist rolled over the mountains.

They walked across the plateau, with the hills and mountains behind them, to a cove with flat rocks extending out to sea and listened to the roar of the surf and felt the spray from the waves on their faces. A faint path on the plateau led through scented thickets, which Seelawathie-Ap said were spice plants. She peeled a piece of bark from a sapling for Shanaz to smell its musky fragrance.

The path led to a building in ruins on a platform. They climbed the stone steps under an arch into a courtyard, the flagstones cracked and shattered. At each corner of the courtyard a fountain spurted a jet of water. The four fountains and a larger fountain in the centre of the courtyard worked together in a complex pattern.

A metal gate in disrepair was at the far end of the courtyard. Shanaz examined the gate, her hand tentatively on the latch. She pushed aside the stones against the bottom of the gate with her foot and opened it by lifting it off the ground.

'It is the shiny last hinge,' she remarked, 'which spoils the illusion of neglect. Careless,' she said.

The gate opened to a gravel drive bordered by shrubs, and some yards away, they saw a half completed building, its long wide windows overlooking a garden sloping to a lake below. A pair of red birds darted out of a bush, flew over the marsh beyond the lake and returned, settling on the branch of a tree, watching them.

'Notice,' Shanaz said, 'they make no sound. They are mechanical Saradasi spies. Someone, somewhere, is watching and recording all we do and say.' She looked at the large building. 'Was this the home a rich or powerful person?'

'Yes,' Seelawathie-Ap said. 'A Dost Queen started building the house for a young Saradasi female who planned to live here, on the island.'

'She never did, did she?' Shanaz asked, looking at the building.

'No. She died. She drowned. The Queen's name was Yoreciva, a Dost, like me. The Saradasi's name was Alianar.'

'Alianar,' Shanaz repeated, staring at the building again. 'This place is so familiar. I know this place, and know I have been here,' Shanaz said. They followed the path to the lake and sat beneath the shade of a tree.

'I lived on this island in a small village in the mountains as a child,' Seelawathie-Ap said. 'It was a strange place. In my village people could see into the past and the future.'

'Can you see into the future?' Shanaz asked.

'Yes, and the past. I can foretell the future,' Seelawathie-Ap replied.

Shanaz picked up a pebble. She went to the edge of the lake, held the pebble between her thumb and forefinger and sent it spinning across the water. The pebble skimmed across the water four times and sank. Shanaz sent another, bigger pebble skimming across the water, counting, 'One, two, three, four, five, six,' as it bounced.

She walked back to Seelawathie-Ap. 'I feel I have done this many times before.'

'Throwing stones across water?'

'Yes. I know I have never ever thrown a stone across water. Nor have I seen anyone else do this. Tell me again, why are you here with me? Shanaz asked.

'I am here to protect you.'

They looked over the lake at the sky. A Saradasi Battle Cruiser rose, paused and climbed into the clouds.

'How long will we stay here?' Shanaz asked.

'Lord Rasalis will decide when we should leave.'

Shanaz walked back to the edge of the lake, selected another flat stone and threw it across the water. It skimmed the surface twice. Disappointed, she joined Seelawathie-Ap.

'What can we do here?' Shanaz asked.

'We could talk about the past, the present and the future. We could talk about people trapped in all three time zones at once. We can talk about reincarnation. How, after we die we are born again.'

Shanaz gazed across the lake at a flock of birds foraging among the reeds. After a long silence she said wearily, 'I am not like other people. I am perhaps not normal.' A breeze blew across the lake, the water rippled and the rustle of reeds reached them.

Shanaz sat, her chin cupped in her hands. 'I feel angry about the injustice of my life. I believe I should not exist here. I am in the wrong place, perhaps because a great mistake occurred. In this vast universe or in the seven universes some speak of, there must be a better place for me.'

'Where is the right place?' Seelawathie-Ap asked.

'Where someone will love me,' Shanaz said, walking to a tree near the water. A gust of wind from the gardens above them carried the fragrance of flowers.

'What is your task in life?' Seelawathie-Ap asked.

'I am not sure. I must protect the Saradasi Empire, and everything else is secondary.'

'Everything?'

'Yes, everything.'

Seelawathie-Ap pointed to the lake. 'Watch,' she said. She clapped her hands twice and walked on the water to the far end of the lake.

'Come on and join me. Walk across the lake,' Seelawathie-Ap called.

'I will drown.'

'No, you will not.'

Seelawathie-Ap walked back on the surface of the lake to Shanaz.

'Why is the bottom of your trousers wet?' Shanaz asked.

'Because I walked on water not on air,' Seelawathie-Ap answered and they both laughed.

'Are you a great magician? Lighter than air?' Shanaz asked.

'I can teach you so much,' Seelawathie-Ap said. 'One day I will teach you to walk across glowing embers.'

'To incinerate me?'

'Your fate will depend on how good a pupil you are,' Seelawathie-Ap said.

'Often the success of the pupil reflects the ability of the teacher. Have we met before, somewhere?' Shanaz asked.

'Perhaps in a past life, here on this island,' Seelawathie-Ap said smiling at Shanaz. 'We will meet again and I will be beside you and you will not remember this meeting. You and I will travel to places you will not believe exist. They are not in this universe we live in.'

NINE

It was Premerdasa-Lu, Seelawathie-Ap's maternal grandfather who led her to the Saradasi, eight years before *The Prophecy* would be fulfilled. Premerdasa-Lu and his family, who belonged to the Dost race, lived on the planet, Califra, on the island of Nuwara, an inconsequential speck in the vast Saradasi Empire.

The once resplendent island of kings and queens of the Dharma Kirti dynasty lay in ruin. In days gone by, merchant ships, six-masted, with billowing sails, red halyards and blue spars, crewed by a thousand sailors, surged like rainbows into the blue waters of the harbour in the capital, Nelun Deepa. They sought precious stones, priceless minerals, and treasured spices.

'The beautiful people in this fine city are honest and gracious and treat us with great courtesy,' the sailors said. 'The females are beautiful, but sadly, their virtue exceeds their beauty.'

Nelun Deepa sat like a resplendent jewel, with green hills, and red roofed white buildings along the shore. The white palace faced the sea, its fluted pillars, supporting a single upper floor. The building boasted a thousand varieties of wood, the walls in each long corridor depicting a pictorial tale. A wide veranda faced the sea with semi-circular steps leading to the beach. At high tide, members of the royal family and their courtiers sat on the lower steps squelching the sand with their toes, the waves lapping their feet, the breeze from the northeast carrying the blended scent of fruits and flowers and a whiff of fragrant spices.

In time, the glory of the island waned. Constant invasions from the northern land of Vidara sapped the strength of the proud nation. Despite centuries of warfare, conquest eluded the enemy. A small insect triumphed where armies, war chariots, warships and generals failed. In a mighty swath of devastation, a terrible fever swept the island from north to south, from east to west and from the plains to the hills, killing men, women and children. Despite the burning fever, patients with dry swollen tongues, through cracked lips, pleaded for warmth to soothe their cold and shivering bodies. Thousands fled to the mountains to escape the insects carrying the infection.

Both trade and invasions ended. Nelun Deepa became the accursed land.

The palace lay in disrepair, the gardens choked with weeds, the ponds silted with sand. In the perfumed garden, a scraggly tree was a lonely witness to the splendour of the past and the unkind whim of fate.

In the mountain villages the people sat by open fires outside their thatched roofed homes recalling the glorious past of their land. They spoke especially of the visitors from a star their ancestors spoke about. The questions, and the answers, were the same for hundreds of years.

'Which star?' the children would ask, gazing at the sky. 'Show us! Show us!'

'We cannot. It is too far for us to see.'

'Our ancestors said they were beautiful people,' another adult would add.

'With respect, uncle,' a youth asked, 'some say they were beautiful because they wore masks. Was it to hide their ugliness?'

'Why would someone wearing a mask reveal to us what he or she looks like? It was not a good question you asked,' uncle replied.

The village herbalist coughed, as was his habit before saying what he thought was important. 'True, all this happened hundreds of years before we were born. The visitors arrived in marvellous machines flying in the air faster than the fastest bird and a thousand times faster. Their machines rose to the sky silently, up, up in a straight line, in an instant becoming dwindling specks. In a blink of an eye they disappeared. The visitors spoke through a machine attached over their throats. Our ancestors spoke to them and they replied in our language!'

'It is amazing,' another youth declared.

'How could that happen?'

'The magic of the machine,' uncle declared.

The villagers recalled the story of the teenage Queen Yoreciva and her friend from the star. They spoke of their great expectations from the visitors and their disappointment when they did not return. They forgot about our small island Nelun Deepa, they lamented.

The conversation ended when the villagers looked expectantly at the fortune-teller who foretold the future by reading palms, gazing into a flame, and casting horoscopes.

'The visitors will return,' he assured them, nodding his head and stroking his beard.

'When?'

'When the time is right.'

○

Premerdasa-Lu and his family lived in a small village called Ravithip, seventy five hundred feet above sea level, touched by clouds, tucked in a mountain valley. It was a difficult place to reach. The journey to or from the nearest town took ten days by foot along mountain trails

Vicious, bold, wild beasts roamed in the dark silence of the forest, arched like a cathedral by tall trees matted with vines and creepers, competing for life-giving sunlight. Travellers were unafraid of wild beasts. The charms written on leaves, rolled inside the amulets tied around their necks or upper arms would protect them, but they placed more faith in the charms they constantly repeated.

'Pray,' they would say, 'the animal is not deaf and cannot hear us.'

In Ravithip, Premerdasa-Lu lived narrowly between destitution and the oppression by the Headman of his village, Soo Noo. Premerdasa-Lu, his wife, his eldest daughter, her husband, and their fourteen-year-old daughter, Seelawathie-Ap, shared a mud walled house with rammed earth floors, and a thatched roof. Premerdasa-Lu's family, like one of a hundred in the village tended their small plot of grain in the valley floor. A few families grew spices or vegetables. They all worked in a communal orchard.

Unlike the villagers, who were Dost, the village Headman, Soo Noo, was from a foreign land unknown to the villagers. A fugitive from his country, he bribed his way to the job of Headman through a minor official.

Soo Noo opened a shop in the village which his frail old uncle, Saw Banh, managed for him. Premerdasa-Lu was among the first to notice old Uncle Saw Banh was a canny salesman, pretending he was absent-minded and vague about money. His stories of far off lands drew more and more people to the shop. They never left empty-handed.

Premerdasa-Lu asked his friends, his anger rising, 'Why are people buying goods of no use and of no value?' Often he would hear Saw Banh say to his indecisive customers in comforting tones, 'This debt is between friends. Why worry? It is merely money and who cares about money? Can we take it to the hereafter? Are there deep pockets in our funeral garments when we travel to the hereafter?'

The villagers bought more and more goods on credit, miring themselves deeper in debt. One day, without warning, Saw Banh stopped all credit and demanded payment within five days. If not, he said, his nephew, the Headman, would punish the debtors by confiscating their household possessions.

Amerdasa-Lu, Premerdasa-Lu's young son-in-law, also loathed old Saw Banh and his nephew, Soo Noo. One evening while in the shop with his daughter, Seelawathie-Ap, she ate a fruit from a barrel without paying for it. This was because Saw Banh urged the children to take one free fruit. Thankful children and gullible parents commented on Saw Banh's kindness.

On this occasion, Saw Banh dragged Seelawathie-Ap by her hair out of the shop, screaming, 'Why are you eating my fruit when your family owe me money?'

The Headman, Soo Noo, who also was in the shop, ran out and kicked the child. In a pantomime of what was occurring before him, Amerdasa-Lu dragged the Headman by his hair and kicked him. Terrified, Saw Banh left at a fast trot. Two large females passing by on their morning walk barred Saw Banh's flight with their bodies, one clasping him to her bosom. The other drew a long pin holding her hair and plunged it into Saw Banh's thin buttock.

Outside the shop Amerdasa-Lu sat astride the Headman ramming his face into a puddle of water with one hand, and with the other, squeezing his most private organs. It took five adult males to pull Amerdasa-Lu away from Soo Noo. Eight adult males barely succeeded in releasing Saw Banh from the embrace of the two females who resumed their interrupted stroll and conversation.

Soo Noo and his uncle fled the village.

The villagers sealed the shop and placed a guard over it saying, 'Let no one say we are thieves, though we are poor.'

Ten days later six soldiers arrived at Ravithip. They arrested Amerdasa-Lu and the two females and escorted them on the long journey to the town of Sarath. Twenty-two days later, the village rejoiced when Amerdasa-Lu and the two females returned unharmed and in good spirits. At sunset, at the feast of thanksgiving, when the fire walking ceremony ended, Amerdasa-Lu and the two females fell forward, dead.

Later, in the darkness of the night, Soo Noo and his uncle emerged with eighty soldiers. They herded the men, women and children to the village square, bright with flaming torches. Four soldiers brought Premawathie-Ap, Amerdasa-Lu's wife, to the centre of the square and pinned her to the ground. Two soldiers, wielding truncheons broke her limbs. She lay on the ground screaming until she lost consciousness. Soo Noo spat on her face. The soldiers built a scaffold and hung Premawathie-Ap by her feet.

In the glow of the flaming torches, Seelawathie-Ap watched her mother die. She kept her promise to her grandfather not to cry. 'They must not win,' he whispered, stroking her hair.

○

In the darkness before dawn, in a cave hidden by shrubs and vines Premerdasa-Lu sat in a circle with the four most holy people in the village, dressed in white, their heads covered. Seelawathie-Ap sat in the centre of the circle.

'All what happened today is written in our horoscopes,' Premerdasa-Lu said. 'Seelawathie-Ap, as it is written in your horoscope, you will begin a great journey.'

The eldest female in the cave said, 'Neither our ancestors nor we have used the power handed from one generation to the next. In each of our villages five of us have the power, which we promised to use for good purposes. At dawn, we will give you our power and with it, you can summon two spirits who were your ancestors to help you when you need them. If you use this power for good and not evil, you can change your physical form and travel with the spirits to other worlds.'

Seelawathie-Ap bowed her head.

'Memorise now, the holy sentences, written on this leaf, to invoke the spirits.' Premerdasa-Lu spread a fan shaped leaf with two groups of sentences in front of Seelawathie-Ap. 'The words must not be said aloud here. Write the words on the sand behind you with your finger until you remember them.'

They joined in a slow low-pitched chant, watching Seelawathie-Ap slip into a trance and each anointed her head with holy oil and tied two cylindrical metal amulets, each containing a written charm, each two inches long, and a third of an inch in diameter around her waist.

Premerdasa-Lu whispered, 'It is written in our holy book, your destiny is to protect a person whose name is Shanaz. Say her name thrice. You will protect her even with your life.'

'Shanaz, Shanaz, Shanaz,' Seelawathie-Ap repeated.

'The book tells us how to contact those who can help us,' Premerdasa-Lu said. 'They will come to us at noon tomorrow.'

'Are they from a star? Seelawathie-Ap asked.

'Yes.'

They left the cave, chanting, to a plateau on a mountain across the valley, far from the village.

'Grandfather,' Seelawathie-Ap whispered, 'what is it?'

A bright light enveloped Premerdasa-Lu and Seelawathie-Ap when they approached the large dome shaped silver object on the plateau. A door slid open.

Premerdasa-Lu knelt by the child. 'You will spend the next few years studying, guided by people you have not yet met. You will not like what they do or how they behave. Be patient. They are misguided. They will change in your lifetime and you will be an important person.'

'I do not want to be an important person, Grandfather. I want to stay here with you.' Seelawathie-Ap wept, clinging to Premerdasa Lu. 'What will happen to you and our family and the others in the village?'

'Even as we talk there is a great reckoning occurring. There will be many changes. We Dost will have a new role in the affairs of this and other worlds. I have something for you.'

Premerdasa-Lu tied a white metal chain with a golden circle, a red stone set in its centre, around her neck. He watched Seelawathie-Ap walk into the spaceship. The Saradasi Hunter rose into the sky.

O

For two years Seelawathie-Ap attended a secluded school in the mountains in Province 2 on Asurat, the dry, dusty planet ruled by the Great Khan. She was the single student, tutored by six unfriendly teachers, and after a year, enrolled at the Oportus Military Academy in Province 4. Principal Ansalaz of the academy said nothing concerning Seelawathie-Ap to his staff, who in turn asked him no questions.

Seelawathie-Ap arrived at the Oportus Military Academy with the Province Governor's Chief of Staff, Colonel Karolian, whose eyes bored into Principal Ansalaz like black drills. Sitting on a chair reluctantly, fidgeting constantly, Karolian looked keenly at Principal Ansalaz, sucking air through clenched teeth, in quantities exceeding normal respiratory needs. In the cathedral of the colonel's mouth, air and saliva resonated to create an odd musical sound.

Colonel Karolian rose and slid across the room, leaning against the principal. A long and slender arm gripped the principal's shoulder. The colonel's mouth lingered near Principal Ansalaz's large ear, the words clipped, 'This student interests the Saradasi. I am always near you at the Province Governor's residence to remind you if you forget what I said.'

'Why so?' Principal Ansalaz inquired looking gravely at the Califran.

The colonel sucked in more air. 'It is a nuisance for the Saradasi to replace you.'

'Thank you for telling me,' Principal Ansalaz said.

Colonel Karolian walked out, body arched backwards, head thrown back, breasts thrust out, and entered her aeromotor.

○

Principal Ansalaz heard no more from the Califran colonel. Every ten days he sent a detailed report on Seelawathie-Ap to the Province Governor. Every one hundred days the Province Governor would invite him to his residence at Koloser, the Province capital, a visit Principal Ansalaz eagerly undertook.

Eliaslaxen, the plump Province Governor of indefinite age, great charm and brilliance, enjoyed Principal Ansalaz's visits. On each visit, they started the day sampling a dozen alcoholic beverages to guess the alcohol content of each. By mid-morning they would sample delicacies brought from the surrounding provinces and the Province Governor's home planet, Merr. In the afternoon they would savour a different dozen alcoholic drinks guessing the planet and province of their origin. With the elaborate evening meal, sitting by the lake, they would consume the twelve best beverages of the twenty-four they tasted. Neither weariness, nor inebriation marred their pleasure.

'I am forbidden to read your reports,' Province Governor Eliaslaxen confided, on the principal's last visit, before Seelawathie-Ap's graduation.

'The day after your report arrives, the same Saradasi comes all the way from Saradasi to collect it. Why do they do this? I do not know.'

'It seems a strange practice,' Principal Ansalaz agreed.

'I do not know her name,' Province Governor Eliaslaxen whispered. 'She is a captain, who I suspect works in security for Lord Rasalis.'

Principal Ansalaz sipped his drink. 'I have, of course, heard of Lord Rasalis, but have never met him.' From where he sat he glimpsed Colonel Karolian listening from behind a pillar. Principal Ansalaz winked at her first with one eye and then with the other. Colonel Karolian ducked her head shyly.

○

Seelawathie-Ap studied tirelessly at the Oportus Military Academy. The academy sat on a triangular artificial island in the centre of an artificially created, unnamed lake in the southwest corner of the dreaded Kountacy desert. None dared illegally enter or leave the Oportus Academy. Large visual and loud auditory warnings declared the lake teemed with poisonous snakes specially bred for their ferocity by Saradasi herpetologists. Saradasi Space Control banned air traffic above the Kountacy Desert because it was the most inhospitable and dangerous geographical area on Asurat. Should a craft make an emergency landing its occupants, it was said, would not survive half a day.

The Kountacy Desert served as a place to commit suicide for members of a large tribe living in Province 4. Friends and relatives would escort the person who wished to die to the flat Rock of Courage at the edge of the desert and leave. They would spend months embroidering the person's name on flags in glorious colours. These flags would fly from the roof of the deceased person's home and roofs of friends and relations. The status of the deceased determined the splendour of the flag and the height of the flagpole. The poorest would have the most elaborate flags on the tallest flagpoles.

The Oportus Military Academy educated twenty non-Saradasi students. They lived singly in relative anonymity, in separate quarters, warned against talking to one another. They ate alone and were their own social companions. The kitchen catered for the tastes of individual students.

The staff except Principal Ansalaz wore facemasks and spoke InterWord through their voice-boxes, adjusted to produce identical voices. The twenty students at the academy received training in extermination

and assassination, single-handed combat, and on serving as personal pro-
tectors to important Saradasi.

The sixteen instructors became more wary of Seelawathie-Ap as
she progressed in her studies and her skills sharpened. Wariness led to
fear and fear to hatred. The instructors prevailed on Principal Ansalaz to
ask a mind master to counsel Seelawathie-Ap. After many sessions with
her, the mind master said he was not comfortable in her presence and
diagnosed a defiance-opposition disorder. He predicted she would
attack an instructor or an instructor may kill her.

When the four-year course ended Seelawathie-Ap emerged as the
best student. The Oportus Military Academy held no graduation ceremony. On the day the students graduated, a Battle Cruiser and a Hunter,
the *Sunanda* with a young Saradasi cadet officer arrived at the academy.
Under the unblinking supervision of Colonel Karolian, instructors, mess
stewards, cooks and military personnel carrying equipment, speedily
boarded the Battle Cruiser. Principal Ansalaz followed with nineteen of
the twenty students after a whispered conversation with Colonel
Karolian. During take off he received a message from his friend, Lord
Rasalis, thanking him for his work and re-assigning him to his substan-
tive post as Director, Counter-Espionage, VIII Army. Lord Rasalis
granted his request. Colonel Karolian would be an additional adjutant.

The Saradasi cadet officer boarded the *Sunanda* with Seelawathie-
Ap. They hovered above the Oportus Military Academy watching it
burn to the ground and the triangular island burst into flames, incandescent for a moment, then exploding and collapsing into the lake. The
poisonous, flammable contents of the lake ignited. With a roaring sound
like the death rattle of a great beast the lake disappeared. No snakes perished. None were there.

The *Sunanda* flew over a patch of desert littered with skeletal rem-
nants, bleached in the searing sun, and hovered over the Ravine of
Snakes with its gnarled, thorn-laden shrubs. Early that morning Saradasi
Security deposited three males with weapons, food and water in the
ravine. The Saradasi cadet officer tapped Seelawathie-Ap's arm, pointing
to the three males in the ravine on the screen in front of them. 'They are
murderers from a jail on Califra. If they kill you, they will win their
freedom and we will not execute them. Be careful of the many snakes in
the ravine.'

'I will kill the murderers and the snakes. I am an excellent fighter,'
Seelawathie-Ap said.

'You say you are, yet your instructors say you are not. Being the best among twenty counts for nothing.'

'The instructors hate me because I am better than them.'

'You can show them how good you are.'

Seelawathie-Ap rose from her seat, staring at the desert. Clusters of large rocks and a few boulders protruded from the sand. The *Sunanda* shook in a gust of wind which scooped and hurled dust, sand and rocks into the air. Rocks smashed against one another; shards of rock flew hundreds of feet across the desert.

'Seelawathie-Ap, if you reach the ravine and kill the three males, you can collect their food, water, weapons and a navigation instrument. Travel to Faramata using this. If you cannot obtain the instrument, travel in westerly direction. If you reach Faramata, enter the building there with a glass dome and a roof with living plants, and use the communication channel on the ground floor. You will receive new instructions.'

'How can you help me?'

'The ravine is seven miles from here. You should be patient and not hurry. Use all the cover available. Those waiting for you are dangerous and their freedom depends on killing you. The nineteen students in your graduating class are also trying to kill you. You are the target of twenty-two people.'

'I do not fear them.'

Seelawathie-Ap walked to a large cluster of rocks away from the Ravine of Snakes with her *kaduwa* swinging in her hand. The *Sunanda* rose above the Ravine of Snakes, signalled, and flew north.

○

Lord Rasalis sat thinking about Seelawathie-Ap in the courtyard of his two-roomed home in the Upper City in Saradas on Saradasi, at the edge of a promontory by the sea. Two years ago to the day, Seelawathie-Ap walked across the Kountacy Desert pitted against three murderers and nineteen classmates, and reached Faramata unharmed.

Since that day she served him well, living in a secluded monastery in the Veles Mountains in Califra. Three times a year she visited her prospering village, where her revered grandfather, Premerdasa-Lu, old though not feeble, was the Headman. She reported regularly to her former principal, General Ansalaz, for instructions from Lord Rasalis.

When they last met in the monastery, he saw her sit erect when he spoke about *The Prophecy* and of her important role. He explained why guards protected her and the reason he restricted her movements, and remembered her saying, 'I am not afraid,' and his reply, 'I am very afraid.'

'I trust you with my life, my Lord,' she had answered when he rose to leave with General Ansalaz.

Lord Rasalis watched the waves hurling themselves on the rocks, and felt the spray on his face. On the beach patches of fog swirled seawards. To the west the snow covered Mirellar Mountains were in the shadow of the clouds. He peered into the container on his lap with a sigh, picking up the last luscious sea brig he collected from the rocks earlier in the morning.

He watched Sub-Commander Sirrah climb the steps from the beach to the courtyard, head bowed, hunched against the wind, his cloak wrapped across his face.

'How are you, Lord?' Sirrah asked.

'I am in poor health as you well know, with a serious rhythm disorder of my heart, clinging to life.'

'Lord, I heard the tests were normal again.'

'The tests are normal because they are primitive and cannot diagnose my serious condition. Some tests do not keep pace with a new illness such as mine. You are a stone with no compassion, Sirrah!'

'A stone? Lord, you called me a blood sucking insect and a serpent the last time we spoke.'

'Insect? Serpent? Did I utter those words? Are you sure? I have no recollection. Sirrah, why are you nursing and nurturing these trivialities? Concentrate on security matters, Sirrah. Be focussed. What have you to say? Be concise and not ramble.'

'First, we have no news of the *Mithras Ennab*. I am surprised the Sound Masters have no information. We may never know what happened,' Sirrah said.

'Sirrah, give me facts, not your opinion. Time is precious for some, though squandered by others.'

'Second, I have no information on Seelawathie-Ap. How can she disappear? Where is she?' Sirrah asked.

'Think, Sirrah. Would I ask you to contact our informants throughout our Empire if I knew where she is?'

'I thought you knew where she is and wanted reassurance that no one else knew where she is,' Sirrah said, looking at the Mirellar Mountains.

'Stop babbling.'

'Lord, may I ask you a question about Seelawathie-Ap I should have asked two years ago?'

Lord Rasalis grunted.

'Why was the Oportus Academy where Seelawathie-Ap trained destroyed?'

'Which academy?'

'The Oportus Military Academy where Seelawathie-Ap trained.'

'I have never heard of such a place. Where is it?'

'Lord, you jest with me. The Oportus Military Academy on Asurat.'

'Seelawathie-Ap is an unusual name.'

'There is no record in Saradasi Security that this person with an unusual name ever existed.'

'How interesting. Are the records deleted?'

'I assume so.'

Lord Rasalis peered at Sirrah. 'If she existed, I assume very few would recognise her?'

'Yes, Lord'

'Are you sure?'

'Yes. I have another question,' Sirrah said.

'Sirrah, remind me, who is the female who works on your team? She knows perfume is a powerful weapon in the armamentarium of seduction and engages in its profligate use. Her intention is seduction.'

'Seduction? Seduce whom, my Lord?'

'I think it is me,' Lord Rasalis said gravely, heavy with mystery and went on, 'I have my admirers, Sirrah. You may not know of them because they are discreet.'

'Lord, I would like to clarify a matter about Seelawathie-Ap's disappearance.'

'Please clarify a matter about yourself, Sirrah. My memory fades. Remind me who adopted you when the Terumana killed your parents and your relatives fled abandoning you, an infant? Who persuaded the High Council to allow you, the single non-Saradasi, to live here on Saradasi?'

'You, Lord.'

They sat in the courtyard eating the elaborate lunch Lord Rasalis cooked for Sirrah.

'Early this morning I examined the visual again of Seelawathie-Ap in the Kountacy Desert. How did she escape?' Sirrah asked.

'What would I know of these matters?'

'I think she set fire to the shrubs in the ravine where the three murderers were waiting for her, and the snakes killed them.'

'And?'

'The visual ends abruptly. I do not think she poisoned the water sources as I thought she did, because her fellow students would have died. I think someone did not want her to kill innocent people. I suspect the same person arranged for her to carry a rapidly acting, temporarily disabling, chemical, which she added to the water sources. Since the person who organised all this, is compassionate and respects justice, I conclude the three in the Ravine of Snakes were robots, not living beings.'

Lord Rasalis scratched his head. 'I wonder who thought of these clever ideas and arranged for her to have this dangerous substance. These mysteries tire my mind and ailing body. Life, Sirrah, ebbs away from me.'

○

After dusk Lord Rasalis sat on a rock after his evening swim. He spoke into his wristband, waving to the two officers wading through the water.

'The sea,' Lord Rasalis said, 'is the safest place to talk. What have you learned of the *Mithras Ennab*, Seelawathie-Ap and Shanaz? Victory and power are both born of vigilance, alertness, intelligence and an obsession to detail.'

General Aricent and General Santana nodded, shivering in the water, waves crashing on the rocks beside them.

'Speak,' Lord Rasalis said.

TEN

On the *Mithras Ennab,* Fariyal lay awake in her cabin, half listening to the muffled gurgling sound that never stopped. She recalled the Quartet on Asurat, which filled her dreams and haunted her. Was it too late to atone for allowing a child and its mother to die for the sake of the Saradasi Empire? The child lurked in the darkness of her mind, pouncing on her, asking, 'Are you a good person? Have you virtue? Or are you a callous Saradasi with no respect for life especially of a child? You killed me and my mother.'

In her mind, the child would say, 'My murderer, can you ever be in the Astral Lord Gaima's team to save your Nereima Galaxy? You will never have enough goodness to triumph against the evil ones in *The Place.*'

The child laughs and continues in a small sad voice, 'Fariyal, your cousin, Shanaz, the High Chancellor and her beloved Lord Wynan, also killed children. Wynan killed thousands of adults and children with his toxin in Kersia on Califra. Shanaz refused to help rescue children lost in the Flowia Valley on Merr who drowned in a flood.'

The child warns her, 'Redeem yourself at the next opportunity.' The words were like metal-mailed fists beating on fragile glass. Was there mention of the Nereima Galaxy and its destruction and her being on a team? She was not sure.

Fariyal drew her hand across her forehead. The new insignia shone on her wristband, Commander. She propped herself on her couch and tried to read the screen on the wall opposite to check the status of the *Mithras Ennab,* but could not. She lay back, straining to hear the music she could not recognise; sweet, and soft like a velvet gloved hand caressing her mind, soothing her to sleep. She smelled scented flowers and heard summer leaves crushed underfoot and birds singing when she and Shanaz strolled through the hills, running across clear brooks when they were children at home on Saradasi.

She heard the voice of a female asking her to listen. 'Fariyal can you remember the Quartet? Can you remember Captain Lique?

Fariyal tried lifting her head.

Why is this female asking her to remember Captain Lique? A strange name, which evoked deep sadness. Fariyal moistened her lips and whispered, 'Please, you must not mention his name again.'

'Why, Fariyal?' the female asked.

'Because, my heart aches when you say, Captain Lique.'

'Why, Fariyal?'

'Because I lost love and with it my will to live.'

'Tell me why.'

'Because I valued the Saradasi Empire above someone I loved. The Empire is all that matters to me and has captured every cell in my body.'

'Do you think often of Captain Lique and how much you love him?'

'Yes. I think of him every moment of the day, and I pray I will dream of him at night, and he would hold my hand and say he loves me as much as I love him.'

'Have you told anyone about Captain Lique?'

'Yes.'

'Who?'

'Lord Medaris. He touched my cheek and said, "Listen to a song Master Glance recorded for me on the *Wave*". The song was beautiful and I cried when I heard it. Medaris said, "When you next meet Captain Lique, like the song says, you can leave the dark side of the street and walk on the bright side of the road and he will tell you he wants to wrap you in his warm and tender love. Fariyal, the Empire will change and is changing. Nothing is impossible to those who have faith. I will transfer Captain Lique under my command to the VIII Army. Be patient."'

'Don't cry, Fariyal,' the female said. 'Go to sleep.'

'Thank you. I must sleep. I feel afraid when I am awake. The child haunts me.'

'You must act with compassion when you have another opportunity to help a child. Go to sleep.'

Before she fell asleep, Fariyal repeated what she learned from childhood, 'I am Saradasi. Fear is a delusion in my mind. Succumbing to fear is weakness and weakness will grow and multiply and make me powerless and I will be a prey to the powerful. I am a powerful Saradasi. I am a powerful Saradasi. I cannot be afraid.'

She fell asleep.

○

She heard the clear voice of the female again. 'Fariyal, you have rested. Can you remember Captain Lique?'

'Yes.' She heard the sadness in her voice. 'I remember Captain Lique.'

Yes, she remembered him. She remembered the handsome young Captain, a native of Califra, a non-Saradasi. She would never forget him. The smiling eyes, the gentle hands, and the fine voice she wanted to hear again. Captain Lique who made her heart beat fast when he looked at her. She clutched the memory of his fleeting, hesitant glances at her; were they of adoration? She was never sure. Sometimes she saw his face harden. She wondered if he hated her because of the child's and its mother's death, or because she was a Saradasi or for both reasons.

Her tour of duty on Asurat working with Captain Lique ended. On the day of her departure she sat alone at the space station at Mitbara when, moments before boarding her flight home to Saradasi, she saw Captain Lique coming towards her.

Their eyes met. What did she see she asked herself? Hate, or anger because military protocol required him to her good-bye?

Half asleep on the *Mithras Ennab,* Fariyal thought about why he held her in contempt. When she heard of the child's death, her response to the accusatory stare of Captain Lique rang in her mind. 'The death of a child is of no concern to me or to the mighty Saradasi Empire I serve.'

She recalled the Quartet and what happened.

As an expert in optics she arrived as Control Officer of the Visual Assault Unit of the IX Army, on Asurat. It was the start of her rapid rise to the rank of commander. The Maranti people in Province 4, despite many years of Saradasi occupation, refused to embrace the conqueror's rule and religious beliefs. The peaceful nature of the Maranti and their belief in non-violence thwarted the Saradasi from using armed force against them, during a time the Empire experimented with guile rather than military force. Four local leaders, called the Quartet, despite Saradasi presence, governed the Maranti efficiently and secretly, upholding centuries old social and spiritual values. They politely ignored many orders issued by the Province Governor.

The anthropologist attached to her Visual Assault Unit mentioned the Maranti deeply feared and worshipped spirits, whom they believed emerge from the sky during thunder and lightning. Her propaganda teams fanned through Maranti towns and villages, assuring the people the Saradasi were more powerful than the spirits. They claimed it was the spirits who asked the Saradasi to rule the Maranti people, and, because they disobeyed the Saradasi, the spirits were angry and great harm would befall them. But, the teams insisted, the Saradasi could destroy the spirits.

The Maranti, though confused, listened carefully to the propaganda teams, and politely expressed their disbelief in Saradasi power over their spirits.

At a meeting, she and her staff explained a strategy to the Province Governor and the administrative staff. She would convert the Quartet and the Maranti to absolutely accept Saradasi rule and religion by persuasion and not force.

On her instructions the Province Governor invited the Quartet to a feast and to view Province 4 from the air on a new Saradasi aircraft. A female member of the Quartet, about to give birth to her first child, reluctantly agreed to the trip.

On the appointed day the Quartet boarded the LAC-NMP with Revenue Commissioner Melfos and his aide Orrfer.

In her command post in the Saradasi Military complex she remembered sitting in front of a large screen watching Revenue Commissioner Melfos and Orrfer on the LAC-NMP, hooting with laughter, pointing at the terrified Maranti who had not flown before, when the LAC-NMP rose with a shudder and a roar.

At the target altitude the vortex of the 'atmospheric storm' created by her Visual Assault Unit struck the LC-NMP. Lightning lit the sky and the sound of thunder swept through the craft. The Quartet gasped, watching spirits identical to those in the drawings on their temple walls, dance across the sky. The spirits clustered along the LAC-NMP glowering at the Quartet. They opened their mouths spewing bolts of lightning.

She watched the small LAC-NMP on the screen plummet several hundred feet, labouring to gain altitude. After a steep dive, the pilot shouted he could not control the craft. Even as he spoke, more spirits, baring their teeth, hurled themselves at the LAC-NMP. Screaming with terror when a cracking sound filled the craft, the Quartet cowered, their hands over their faces.

Revenue Commissioner Melfos screamed, 'I will die.' He drew Orrfer to him shouting above the noise of the thunder outside, 'The Maranti have angered the spirits. The Saradasi are right, the spirits are angry with the Quartet. Orrfer, order the pilot to eject the Quartet from this machine.'

'Cousin, you ask him,' Orrfer replied. 'You have more authority than I.'

Melfos stumbled towards the pilot. 'We have,' he said in a commanding tone, 'a solution to this problem.'

The pilot, his hands trembling asked, 'What solution?'

'Can you evict the Quartet from this aircraft? They are the cause of this problem. The spirits are angry with them, not us.'

The pilot jabbed a button. 'No. Return to your seat, you are disturbing me.' He pointed to the purple lights flashing above him. The Solid Object Warning Scanner announced: 'Danger! Danger! Terrain! Terrain! Danger! Terrain!'

The LAC-NMP cleared a hill by a few feet, lurched, stalled and climbed erratically.

'We could save ourselves,' Melfos suggested.

'How?'

'I suggest you teleport us.'

'Go back to your seat,' the pilot shouted. 'Teleport!'

Melfos lurched back to Orrfer. 'This is a Saradasi plot to kill you, the Quartet and me. That is why we are in a vehicle deliberately disabled, with a bungling pilot in command.'

'I think he is from northern Califra,' Orrfer said.

'How will that help, you fool? Be quiet and let me think.'

Outside, amid the thunder and lightning, hosts of spirits hovered, pounding the craft with their fists and feet.

The members of the Quartet sobbed in fear, cringing in their seats.

Melfos returned to the pilot. 'I order you to land this machine,' he said.

The pilot wiped his face. 'I am trying to land, but the controls are not responding. I have asked the flight controller on the ground for help but there is no response. Can you ask for help urgently?'

Melfos screamed into the communicator the pilot thrust at him. 'Flight controller, land this vehicle. I order you to land this vehicle. I am Revenue Commissioner Melfos! I say again, I am Revenue Commissioner Melfos!'

A faint voice broke through the static. 'Flight controller to LAC-NMP number 567-8956438.'

The static cleared.

'Flight controller to LAC-NMP 567-8956348,' said a crisp, clear voice, 'I cannot hear you.'

'Land this vehicle now,' Melfos screamed.

'Listen carefully, Revenue Commissioner, we cannot control this aircraft because it is not responding to our signals. Our staff are isolating the problem.'

'This is a Saradasi plot,' Melfos muttered to Orrfer. 'Who else would be so devious to kill the Quartet and us and blame these spirits?'

'Where have the spirits come from?' Orrfer asked moistening his lips.

'Be quiet, I am thinking.'

'The Saradasi want to kill both of us,' Orrfer whispered. 'You promised they would never know what we did.'

'Be quiet,' Melfos growled.

The flight controller's voice filled the LAC-NMP. 'I confirm your craft is not responding to our instructions,' she said. 'The malfunction is on the LAC-NMP you are on.'

Revenue Commissioner Melfos groaned.

'Please be calm,' she continued. 'The spirits are interfering with the controls and also with the signals we are relaying to override the controls. You are in great danger. The spirits are trying to kill you.'

Fariyal recalled sending for Captained Lique to join her. When he sat beside her, in front of the screen, she pointed to Orrfer comforting Melfos and mopping his forehead. 'Dive seventy degrees from horizontal,' she ordered the flight controller.

'Sub-Commander Fariyal, this is dangerous,' Captain Lique said looking at the screen.

The flight controller spoke, saying, 'Quartet, Revenue Commissioner, we have lost control of your craft. Directly ahead on the present flight path is the Serpent Sea. It is likely your LAC-NMP will plummet into the sea. We have ordered rescue vessels but the visibility is poor because of fog.'

'Which sea? Where is this sea?' Captain Lique asked.

'Your LAC-NMP,' the flight controller continued, 'may not reach the sea. It may hit the cliffs or collide with the slow moving vehicular traffic.'

She remembered focussing on the Quartet and saw the pregnant female moaning and slumping in her seat.

'You must stop this, please,' Captain Lique said.

She signalled the flight controller with her hand.

'This is the flight controller. May I speak with a member of the Quartet?'

Revenue Commissioner Melfos gave Orrfer the communicator and pushed him towards the Quartet. Orrfer took a few steps and stopped. 'One of the Quartet is vomiting,' he said.

'Go to them,' Melfos yelled, pushing Orrfer.

The Quartet was reciting prayers for their safety. One took the communicator from Orrfer. 'Flight controller, you must help us to land. One of our members is carrying a child and she is vomiting, and seriously ill. She will lose her child. Even as I speak she is bleeding.'

'You will kill them,' Captain Lique said.

'No. I must complete my task,' she had replied.

The storm intensified and the LAC-NMP flew more erratically, slewing sideways, plunging and levelling off a few feet above the ground.

'He is ready.' The flight controller pointed to the screen.

General Parnu, a Saradasi, the senior officer in eastern Asurat spoke, his voice echoing through the LAC-NMP, his image appearing on the huge Skyscreens installed in the cities and towns of the Maranti people.

'Quartet,' he announced, 'you will die because the spirits are angry with you. They are angry because you have not cooperated with the Saradasi who are helping you by ruling your land. The spirits are also evil because they are trying to kill you. Look at the evil and insane spirits you worship! When you die they will feast on your flesh and drink your blood.'

'What can we do? Please advise us,' a member of the Quartet wailed.

'We ask your forgiveness,' another cried.

'The time to forgive you has passed,' General Parnu replied grimly.

'We will all die,' a voice wept.

'We Saradasi,' the General said, 'are more powerful than your spirits. Therefore, we will save you. You must first tell your people they must absolutely obey us, because we wish to help you. Your people must stop worshipping spirits and must follow our religion. If you obey me I will banish these and other spirits you have not yet seen, forever. Speak now for all your Maranti people to see and hear you on the Skyscreens.'

The LAC-NMP wobbled when a burst of lightning hit it.

Melfos, speaking above the thunder and the wails of the Quartet, bellowed, 'Quartet, obey him now! If not I will kill you before I die.'

On the Skyscreens the Maranti people watched the Quartet on the LAC–NMP begging the Saradasi to rule them and promising to never worship the spirits again.

'Go, spirits! I am a Saradasi and I banish you from this land,' General Parnu commanded. 'Never again must you appear before the Maranti people. Go, I banish you in the name of the Saradasi.'

The sky cleared.

One of the Quartet said to General Parnu, 'My colleague with child is bleeding. Please help her by landing immediately.'

In the control room, Captain Lique had said to her, 'You must land the craft. The female and her unborn child are at great risk.'

'Must I abandon my mission to save an unborn child?' she had asked, surprised.

'Yes.'

'Captain Lique, I have not completed my mission. My first duty is to the Saradasi Empire and our religion.'

'So the death of a child will not concern you?'

'The death of a hundred children is not my concern. What is important is the Saradasi Empire, not the life or death of a child.'

General Parnu said 'Quartet, are you certain you want the Saradasi to rule your land?'

'Yes,' the Quartet begged.

'And you will follow our religion?'

'Yes, we will.'

'Quartet, your people are watching and listening to our conversation. I want you to speak to your people, now.'

The next morning Fariyal received a message. The Quartet member who was pregnant was struggling for her life, not expected to live. Her child died.

○

Fariyal heard a voice calling her name. She fell asleep, lulled by a sound, as if water was lapping against the hull of the *Mithras Ennab*.

ELEVEN

The message alarm sounded on the *Wave*. Breve raced to the console on the flight deck to key in the identification code of the day. The image of Sound Master Retrion came into view on the screen as Master Glance joined Breve.

'Master Glance, how is your patient?'

'The Dost guards at the space station sealed his cabin and ordered us not to enter the cabin. I am the Master of the *Wave* and I am concerned about what is happening to him on my ship. This is not a Saradasi ship for the Saradasi to act as they please. Physicians at the space station should have treated him,' Master Glance said.

'I am to inform you someone from the *Gaina* will check your patient,' Master Retrion said.

'Someone from the *Gaina*? The *Gaina* is a water carrier, not a medical ship.'

'Perhaps, Master Glance, the Saradasi have changed water into medicine,' Master Retrion laughed.

'Who gave these orders?'

'Lord Rasalis. Saradasi Space Control will give you the co-ordinates to dock with the Gaina, after which you will proceed to Asurat to deliver your patient as originally directed.'

Breve sat at the console on the flight deck, and after keying in the co-ordinates from Saradasi Space Control to rendezvous with the *Gaina,* listened to the soft hum of the new F- mercury engine installed on the *Wave*. He recalled the Saradasi engineers warning him and Master Glance, the F-Mercury engine would explode if they tampered with it.

'I cannot understand our orders about Faris,' Master Glance said to Midi78 who joined them on the flight deck. 'We left Space Station ZenFah hurriedly with him because they said he was seriously ill. Now the crew of a water carrier will assess him.'

'Perhaps,' Midi78 suggested, 'they have a physician on board.'

After an hour the *Gaina* lumbered into view on the screen and glided alongside the *Wave*. A common hatchway connected the two spacecraft.

Six Dost security guards and a bearded Califran in a red gown crossed to the *Wave* carrying breathing apparatuses and gas cylinders.

'I am the sub-commander in charge,' an unsmiling Dost said. 'The Califran is the physician. Please stay here.'

After the sub-commander and the physician wore breathing apparatus, Breve directed them to the cabin with Faris on the lower deck. From where they were, Master Glance and Breve listened to the Califran physician whisper, 'Pump gas into the cabin from the blue cylinder for ten seconds.'

'Stand back when I open the cabin door and perform your examination quickly,' the sub-commander said. 'Guards, be ready to act on my command and say nothing. We are on a sound master's craft.'

Master Glance and Breve heard the cabin door slide, the capsule snap open and the sub-commander ask, 'Is there a problem with the patient?'

'All is well,' the physician whispered. 'I will increase the flow of the hydration molecules because of mild dehydration.'

'What is the nutritional status?'

'Adequate.'

The Sub-Commander stepped out of the cabin and secured the door.

'The capsule is open. We did not hear them closing it,' Breve said.

Before Master Glance replied the sub-commander joined them. Declining the invitation for refreshments in the recreation room, he gave them a set of gas containers with written instructions and boarded the *Gaina*.

'Bizarre,' Master Glance said, shaking his head. 'Am I watching a drama on a stage?'

'Father, is it not unusual the water carrier *Gaina* carries Dost security guards, when it is from a planet not in the Saradasi Empire?'

'Life,' Master Glance yawned, 'is full of complexities.'

The *Wave* sped to Asurat on a course given by Saradasi Space Control.

○

Four days later the *Wave* skimmed above the many-domed white city of Samsara, on Asurat, settling on the shore of the warm blue Arianz Sea. On the beach, a troop of green uniformed soldiers stood in a semi-circle facing the *Wave* when Master Glance, Breve and Midi78 alighted.

114

A thickset soldier approached them. 'Master Glance, I am Ituxi, the Captain of the Guard,' he said. 'My Great Khan welcomes you and thanks you for saving the life of his friend Faris, by bringing him to us. The old summer palace is open to you. He pointed to a building, green with moss and overrun with tangled vines.

'Thank you. The Great Khan is most generous. This is my son, Breve, and our companion, Midi78,' Master Glance said. 'Where will you take Faris? Is there medical help for him here on this small island?'

'The Great Khan's own physician will attend to Faris on board your ship.'

Master Glance stared at Captain Ituxi. 'I am confused about all this,' he said.

Captain Ituxi looked towards the steps leading from the palace to the beach. 'Sound Master, here is the physician.' He pointed to a red-gowned Califran sauntering towards them along the beach.

'Father, it is the same person who came on board the *Wave* from the *Gaina*,' Breve said.

The Califran physician looked inquiringly at Master Glance who nodded and walked with him to the *Wave*. When he returned with Master Glance, he spoke in whispers to Captain Ituxi.

'You must leave immediately,' Captain Ituxi said to Master Glance.

'I will not.'

'Sound Master, please board your ship,' Captain Ituxi said gently. 'I am sure orders await you even as we speak.'

'Madness. All this is madness,' Master Glance said. 'I protest on behalf of Faris. I am ashamed of being involved in this injustice.'

Master Glance shook his head and strode to the *Wave*. When he stepped on board, the message alarm sounded and Lord Rasalis's face beamed from the communication screen.

'My dear Master Glance,' he said. 'You look well. And you too, Midi78, and Breve. It is a pleasure to see you. Your work is excellent. Excellent. I gather your passenger is stable but sadly he is in great danger. I am deeply concerned and alarmed and apprehensive. We believe he is safest on the *Wave*. Thank you for your help. Excellent. Good bye.' He added, 'I understand your anxiety about Faris and his illness. Can you trust me? I assure you Faris will be well and no harm will come to him. I value him as much as I value you.'

When Lord Rasalis signed off, Master Glance asked, 'How has he information on a passenger on the *Wave*? I resent the Saradasi monitoring us on my ship using technology I cannot detect. Nor can I understand what they are doing to Faris.'

They were leaving the flight deck when the message alarm sounded again. Grand Master Ashe was on the screen. 'Go immediately to Sea Station Xerion and dock there. I will contact you. An important Saradasi will meet you.'

'Are not all Saradasi important?' Master Glance asked.

'Listen to him carefully. Please stay awake when you are with him and please look after your health,' Grand Master Ashe advised.

◯

The *Wave* settled into Pier 2 at Sea Station Xerion, berthed next to a Daresian energy vendor from Astharia, the *Erg*. They heard the message alarm and Breve went to the flight deck followed by Master Glance.

'The Saradasi Officer you will meet is by your side,' Grand Master Ashe said. 'Not on the *Wave*. He is on the Daresian vessel the *Erg* docked next to you.'

'On the Daresian vessel?'

'Yes. You look tired, drowsy, and your eyes are congested again. Are you well?'

'I am not sure.'

'Be patient. What is the temperature there? Is it too hot for you?'

'Yes, it is hot,' Master Glance replied.

'Remember. The problem is rarely the climate. It is what you wear,' Grand Master Ashe said. 'Please remember to have your medicine as soon as Breve gives it to you.'

Master Glance watched Breve check the battle readiness of the *Wave* and went to his cabin to change into a thin grey robe. He climbed down to the pier and boarded the *Erg*, where the fat bottomed captain he met at Space Station ZenFah greeted him.

'Captain, you seem quiet today,' Master Glance murmured following her through the corridors of the *Erg*, admiring the splendour of the Daresian vessel. They reached a foyer with two Dost security guards. After the captain left, they asked him to remove his clothes and ran a hand held scanner over him. They gave him a non-flammable garment to wear, a recent Saradasi precaution since a rebel on Merr set herself alight and clasped a Province Governor in a lethal embrace. One of them

116

pointed to a door sliding open, motioning him to enter. Master Glance in the flimsy, sleeveless, knee length gown walked into a large room, the source of illumination hidden, his bare feet sinking into the thick carpet. At an oval table at the far end of the room a Saradasi in military uniform sat on a high backed chair watching him.

'Greetings, Master Glance,' he said. 'It has been too long since we met. Thank you for the music you sent me.'

'Greetings,' Master Glance replied sitting on a settee across the table. 'Have you eaten?'

Master Glance shook his head. The door opened and a Dost entered with a tray of food.

The Saradasi adjusted his firing-belt and force-sword. 'Lord Rasalis thanks you for your work and I thank you too. I heard you almost located *The Place*. However, our immediate concern is Seelawathie-Ap who we need to help save the Nereima Galaxy.'

'I cannot locate her. Other Sound Masters have also failed.'

The Saradasi placed his drink on the table, his eyes on Master Glance and pointed to the food. 'Please taste what we have prepared for you.'

Master Glance washed his hands in the bowl of water on the tray and pushed the tray away from him.

The Saradasi picked up his drink and sipped it. He looked at Master Glance and held his gaze. 'Is Lord Rasalis correct to assume no one can find her if you cannot?'

'I have not found her. Others may, but not by tracing her through the voice recording we have.'

'Why?'

'No one has better equipment than Sound Masters and we are the best at finding people by their voices and other sound characteristics. We are the best mercenaries who can track individuals by sound.'

The Saradasi moved the tray of food towards Master Glance. 'Mercenaries work for the highest paymaster,' he said.

'Not all. Some mercenaries may balance reward with survival.'

'Be more direct, Master Glance.'

'It would be foolish for a mercenary to work for the highest bidder if the opposing force held greater power. Money is of no value to a dead mercenary. We Sound Masters work for you because we honour agreements and contracts, as we have for many hundred years.'

The Saradasi smiled. 'I will remind Lord Rasalis of what you said.' He paced the room saying, 'We Saradasi and your people have some similarities. Neither seeks personal wealth. Individual Saradasi own nothing, even these clothes are not mine to sell or give away because they belong to the military.'

'We Sound Masters learned from the Maranti people on Asurat to measure the greatness of a person by the fewness of his or her possessions,' Master Glance said.

'Those who want nothing are powerful, are they not, Master Glance?'

'Dangerously so. But yet, sometimes, those not seeking power are forced into a web woven by those more powerful than them.'

'You must refer to us Saradasi who have trapped you Sound Masters in the ambition of our Empire.'

Master Glance looked at his bare chest and stared at the Saradasi. 'You have diluted my dignity. I will never undress again.'

The Saradasi left the room and returned with Master Glance's clothes, helping him to slip his robe on.

'Sound Master, I need your help again. Can you identify a beautiful tune? I am uncertain if it is from our Nereima Galaxy.'

'The tune?'

Master Glance drummed his fingers on the table listening. 'It is a religious song with three verses, each with a different melody, each sung at a higher pitch. It is in our archives and I will give you a copy.'

'Thank you. The gift is for Lord Rasalis who has many talents. He sings beautifully.'

'Lord Rasalis?'

'Yes. Master Glance, there is another matter I need your help with,' he said.

'I am happy to help.'

'I want information on the origins of a tune,' the Saradasi said and hummed the tune. Master Glance felt his pulse quicken. It was the same haunting tune he heard soon after the snatch of conversation he believed was from *The Place*. Despite the efforts of Sound Master Retrion and teams of apprentice Sound Masters, a search of the vast music libraries on Droha Major was unrewarding. He forced himself to look away from the Saradasi and decided he would not reveal where he heard the tune.

'Do you play a musical instrument?' Master Glance asked, breaking the silence.

'Yes, although I am not an accomplished player.'

'What is the instrument?' he asked. Master Glance saw and heard the changes come over the Saradasi. 'I lack the patience to play an instrument skilfully,' Master Glance said quickly and rose to leave.

The Saradasi walked with him to the door. 'When you find Seelawathie-Ap we place her in your care. Thank you. We will meet again soon.'

After disembarking, Master Glance watched the *Erg* rise in a blur of speed and disappear into the clear blue sky with Lord Medaris.

◯

'Why must they always contact me when I am asleep?' Master Glance asked Breve when he called him on to the flight deck. Looking at them anxiously from the screen, Sound Master Retrion gave a set of instructions. 'You must be cautious,' he warned. 'Danger is your close, unwanted companion. I am told the patient in your cabin is recovering. In twelve hours after to leave, turn off the gas entering the cabin. After twenty-two hours open the door.

'Is that all? Others know more about the patient on my ship than I,' Master Glance said. 'It is most odd. Please tell the Grand Master I am a sound master not a Saradasi slave.'

'You will receive your travel co-ordinates from Saradasi Space Control,' Master Retrion said smiling at his friend.

It was early evening on the next day when Saradasi Space Control contacted the *Wave* with new flight coordinates to track across the Nereima Galaxy in an easterly direction until further orders.

On a starlit night the *Wave* left Sea Station Xerion.

Breve and Master Glance worked on the sound machines, effecting minor repairs and adjusting pitch and tone sensors. The next morning Breve left the recreation room, pointing to the clock on the ceiling with its orbiting electrons.

'It is twelve hours since take off,' Breve said. 'I will turn off the gas supply in Faris's cabin.'

'I feel great responsibility towards Faris because he has been on my ship,' Master Glance said to Midi78 when Breve left. 'We took him from Space Station ZenFah and we travelled across the galaxy with him from place to place with gas being pumped into his cabin. Perhaps a gas may cure my ailment.'

'I agree with you about Faris. We are not Saradasi and therefore must follow orders,' Midi78 replied, shaking his head.

'But the orders I follow lessen my honour because I command the *Wave*.'

While Master Glance slept in his cabin, Breve spent most of the next day listening to Midi78 discussing how physicians on different planets in the Nereima Galaxy treated ailments of the body. Some, Midi78 said, used medicines in concentrations of one in a million. Others he said buried patients in special mineral mixtures up to their necks until they recovered.

While preparing the evening meal with Midi78, Breve related Terumana jokes from his collection, numbering many hundreds. When Master Glance joined them, they ate their meagre meal, with the wine, a gift from Lord Medaris.

The reminder alarm rang. They hurried to Faris. Master Glance removed the seal on the cabin door and opened it. The capsule flew above their heads, smashing on the bulkhead behind them. A figure glowered at them, fierce and furious, her arms constantly moving. One hand held the Dost sword, the *kaduwa*.

'I am Seelawathie-Ap.' The voice was deep, metallic and toneless. The blade of the sword swung threateningly. 'My duty is to protect Shanaz. Who are you?'

'If you are Seelawathie-Ap, why have you taken this form?' Master Glance asked. 'Your brain must belong to Seelawathie-Ap.'

'Yes. I have taken this form to kill you because you have captured me.'

Midi78 pushed Master Glance and Breve aside and entered the cabin. He pointed his right arm at Seelawathie-Ap his forefinger stretched out. His face was stern. 'On this ship you are a guest. You are not here to play with us.'

'Where is Faris?' Breve asked.

'He was never here,' Master Glance said. Seelawathie-Ap took a step towards Midi78.

'Revert to your normal form immediately and stop playing with us. I am a Gootamundra priest.' Midi78 said.

'That does not interest me,' Seelawathie-Ap snarled.

Midi78 placed his palms together pointing the tips of his fingers at Seelawathie-Ap. 'Learn, and learn well, to respect a Gootamundra priest, Seelawathie-Ap.'

Seelawathie-Ap opened her mouth, drawing in great, greedy, gasps of air. Her body stiffened, arching backwards, relaxing, stiffening and arching

120

again. She tried to stand but fell writhing on the floor of the cabin, her face, fingertips and toes tinged blue. Perspiration coursed down her face.

'You cannot reach your sword because you cannot move. Would you like to return to your usual form or lie on the floor?' Midi78 asked.

Seelawathie-Ap made a guttural sound. Midi78 sat on the floor, watching Seelawathie-Ap. Her breathing eased and the blue tinge left her.

'Be still. You must not move. Show us your true form Seelawathie-Ap. Quickly!' Midi78's voice cracked like a whip.

The cabin echoed with a hiss. A red mist lingered where Seelawathie-Ap lay. A female Dost, slender, lightly tanned, stood before them, her face glowing, her jet-black hair tied in a knot. A chain with a small pendant hung round her neck. Her large brown eyes swept defiantly over them.

'I am Seelawathie-Ap,' she announced, in the same harsh voice.

Breve pointed to her neck triumphantly, at the shiny, rectangular bulge on her throat.

'So you have an artificial larynx,' Master Glance said.

'Yes. Where am I?' she demanded. 'You kidnapped me from Space Station ZenFah and took me as a prisoner.' The pitch of her voice was monotonous, the tone rasping and each word clipped.

'We did not,' Master Glance explained. 'We took our sick friend, Faris who was very ill, on board, in a capsule. Those were our orders. I am Master Glance, from Droha Major, and this is my son, Breve. This is Midi78.'

'Release me to a Saradasi. If not, the Saradasi will punish you,' Seelawathie-Ap said.

'I am a sound master,' Master Glance said. 'The Saradasi ordered me to search for you but I could not find you because of your artificial larynx.'

'Her voice has changed, as I said, Father,' Breve said excitedly. 'That is why we could not find her.'

'I belong to the Saradasi military,' Seelawathie-Ap said.

'Why are you wearing a cook's uniform if you are a member of the Saradasi military?' Midi78 asked.

'Those were my orders from Lord Rasalis.'

'Lord Rasalis,' Master Glance muttered.

'As Master Glance told you,' Midi78 said, 'we assumed our friend, Faris, was in the capsule. Why were you in the capsule?'

'Is Faris the Suxt-Sux actor from Asurat?' Seelawathie-Ap asked.

'Yes,' Midi78 replied.

'You kidnapped me,' she rasped. 'I worked as a cook in Dining Room 301, punished for something I did. The night you kidnapped me, my supervisor sent me to the room of a famous Suxt-Sux actor, Faris, with his dinner. This was unusual but I said nothing. I entered his quarters and that is all I remember.'

'You went to our friend's room with food and you are here now here with us?' Midi78 asked.

'Yes.' She turned to Master Glance, ' Prove you are a sound master and a friend of the Saradasi. Prove my presence here is lawful.'

Master Glance inclined his head in acknowledgment. 'Your grand-father's name is Premerdasa-Lu.'

'Yes.'

'Seelawathie-Ap,' Master Glance said, 'we are not your enemies. We are trying to help the Saradasi save the Nereima Galaxy. We believe in *The Prophecy* and in *The Place*, which creates evil. We follow the directions Lord Rasalis gives us.'

'Lord Rasalis?' Seelawathie-Ap asked.

'Yes. Lord Rasalis, who is aware of everything but admits to nothing,' Master Glance said.

'Can you tell me how you change your form?' Breve asked.

'The change is like water changing to ice to water.' Seelawathie-Ap closed the cabin door when the others left.

In the dining room Breve asked Midi78, 'Were you able to read her mind?

'Easily. Her thoughts focus on Shanaz. She is angry she is not with her, protecting her.'

'But Seelawathie-Ap could go wherever she wants to, could she not?' Breve asked. 'Why does she not go to Shanaz?'

'Because Shanaz is on Saradasi. Seelawathie-Ap is not a Saradasi and will be executed if she goes there.'

'Why were we asked to look for her?' Breve asked.

'For Lord Rasalis to be certain no one would find where she was,' Master Glance said.

The communications screen glowed with Grand Master Ashe on the screen. 'When your passenger is asleep, re-gas the cabin using the green cylinder. Be most careful and be vigilant. Nothing seems as it is.'

○

The *Wave* docked for food supplies and water at Light Acralton South, a Saradasi space outpost staffed by a group of Astharians banished with their families by the Saradasi. They greeted Master Glance, Breve and Midi78 in the freezing building, huddling by open fires in tall metal drums. They provisioned the *Wave*, and the gaunt young storekeeper wished them goodbye, his teeth chattering, smiling when he counted the extra money Master Glance gave him.

'You are generous, Master Glance,' Midi78 said when they returned to the *Wave*.

'A few solars I gave are mine.'

'May I ask who the generous giver was?'

'Givers. Two Saradasi. They want these people to have a better life when their exile ends.'

'Can they not release them?' Midi78 asked.

'Not yet,' Master Glance said.

The *Wave* left Light Acralton South, the coldest punishment station in the Saradasi Empire. They received a message from Sound Master Retrion informing them Saradasi Space Control had not found the *Mithras Ennab*.

'Where is the *Mithras Ennab*? It is a mystery of mysteries,' he declared.

'How is it we Sound Masters have no news of the *Mithras Ennab*?' Master Glance asked.

'I have another message for you. You will travel to Asterioz on Merr where someone will contact you.'

'Contacted, contacted, contacted, always contacted,' Master Glance said when the screen was blank. He knew Asterioz well. It was a Saradasi surveillance station, desolate, with clumps of trees and patches of scrub, a haven for smugglers, their activities ignored by the Saradasi who employed them as informants.

No star shone in the sky when Breve manoeuvred the *Wave* on to a landing pad. Nearby a Saradasi Battle Cruiser loomed over them, its interior dimly lit. Master Glance and Midi78 disembarked. Gusts of wind pushed against them.

The forward hatch of the Battle Cruiser opened and a gangway, eighty feet long slid to the ground. Master Glance looked at the figure climbing down, wondering why he did not use a conveyor. The military officer reached the ground and regarded Master Glance and Midi78 silently, tucking his cloak into the firing-belt at his waist. Master Glance heard the crisp movement of the heat detecting sensors and the softer shift of the forward laser tubes. He glanced at the Saradasi's feet wondering, as many did, if the Saradasi controlled their famous firing-belt with their feet.

'Please ask Seelawathie-Ap to join us,' the Saradasi said quietly.

Master Glance spoke to Breve on the *Wave*.

When Seelawathie-Ap stepped off the short gangway, the Saradasi walked past her to the *Wave*. He unclasped his cloak, folded it lengthwise and tied it loosely on a rung of the gangway. The handle of his force-sword shone in the pale light from the *Wave*. He placed his hands on his hips.

He beckoned Seelawathie-Ap. When she came towards him, he said, 'Stop. We may need some space between us. Do you know who I am?'

'Yes. Lord Medaris,' she answered.

'I am disappointed with your behaviour on board the *Wave*. Sound Master Glance did not complain about you but we are aware of all that happens in this galaxy. You belong to the Saradasi military and the military does not tolerate bad behaviour.' His tone was casual.

'I understand.'

'You will travel aboard the *Wave* to Military Outpost Xzania and cause no trouble or annoyance.'

'Yes, Lord.'

'You must not disappoint me, Seelawathie-Ap.

'I will not, Lord.'

'Thank you.'

When Seelawathie-Ap walked back to the *Wave* he asked her to stop.

'Prove to me you are Seelawathie-Ap but not by changing your physical form as you did on the *Wave*. Never do that again,' Lord Medaris said.

Seelawathie-Ap strode into a nearby thicket, swinging her *kaduwa*. They heard her cutting branches from the shrubs. She emerged and arranged the branches in a pile and brought more wood, building the pile as high as her. Using a stick she drew a five-pointed star on the ground, twenty feet from end to end with the pile of wood in its centre. When she joined the last point of the star the temperature fell sharply. Seelawathie-Ap walked along the outline of the star seven times, her head bent, her hands clasped together in front of her forehead, the fingers pointing skywards.

She knelt by the pile of wood clapping her hands rhythmically. The wood crackled, igniting with a roar. When the flames rose a hundred feet above the ground, Seelawathie-Ap thrust her hands into the flames. She uttered a strangled cry, rolling away from the fire, lying flat on the ground, her breasts heaving.

'Is she injured?' Master Glance asked, moving towards her.

Midi78 drew him back. 'We cannot interfere, Master Glance. Look!'

Two figures stood opposite each other, on a point of the star. Their silver clothes and faces shone in the dancing flames. Their feet were bare except for the silver rings on their toes. The flames rose higher. Master Glance and Midi78 walked nearer the star to join Lord Medaris.

'It is cold despite the fire,' Midi78 said.

Lord Medaris touched Master Glance on his arm. 'Master Glance, concentrate on the two figures. What can you hear?'

Master Glance rubbed his hands, his teeth chattering. 'I hear Seelawathie-Ap's heartbeat and the other sounds created by a living being. I can hear nothing else, not even the fire crackling.'

Lord Medaris looked at Midi78. 'Who are they?'

'Lord, they are from the spirit world,' Midi78 answered. 'They mean us no harm. They are benign beings, eager to erase their past sins and enter the first astral world.'

The two figures looked intently at the fire. The red and orange flames surged across their sliver helmets and clothing. Seelawathie-Ap chanted, her body swaying, her head back, her arms open wide. The two figures went to her, held her hands in theirs and walked into the flames together. The flames engulfed them.

Master Glance whispered, 'Where are they? I cannot see them.'

'I think they have visited another world,' Midi78 said, peering at the flames.

Lord Medaris said to Master Glance and Midi78, 'Lord Rasalis tells me she can invoke these two spirits from another world using the power her ancestors conferred on her, and with them, help the Saradasi on Lord Gaima's team, whoever they are, to reach *The Place*. Midi78, do you believe she can travel from one universe to another?'

'Yes. We Gootamundra High Priests also have great power, but we cannot travel to other worlds. I believe she can.'

Master Glance jumped back when a shower of sparks erupted. 'I and other Sound Masters on Droha Major believe *The Place* is not in this world,' Master Glance said. 'What I heard on the *Wave*, "Your game, brother Red", is from another realm.'

'Where? What other realm?' Lord Medaris asked.

'I think the *Wave* entered, and was trapped in a powerful force field within a gap-hole between two universes. We were perhaps at the outer boundary of *The Place*.'

The fire sizzled with a loud hiss as if drenched with water. Dense plumes of red smoke rose above the ground.

Seelawathie-Ap, standing on the glowing embers of the fire, sang in a lilting voice, not her own, her hands clasped together and raised, looking skywards.

'She cannot sing,' Master Glance said. 'She has an artificial larynx. She cannot produce these sounds.'

Seelawathie-Ap walked towards them. Rivulets of perspiration ran down her face and bare arms. The wind blew furiously again.

'Thank you,' Lord Medaris said. 'I am grateful to you for what you showed us. Please return to the *Wave,* Seelawathie-Ap. Serve Shanaz faithfully. The time will soon come when you will have to take us to *The Place.*'

'My Lord, I promised my grandfather to serve Shanaz.'

Midi78 and Seelawathie-Ap boarded the *Wave* leaving Lord Medaris alone with Master Glance.

'Master Glance,' he said speaking above the wind, 'I have another request.' He handed Master Glance a small disc. 'I won't hum the tune. The wind is competing with me. Can you tell me where the music is from and who sings it? It is a beautiful female voice.'

'I can hear the wind dying,' Master Glance said. 'I too have a piece of music for you. May I ask Breve to play the music on the *Wave*? We Sound Masters have the best sound projection facilities in the galaxy.'

When the wind stilled, music surged from the *Wave.* They listened to two females singing in glorious harmony.

'Here it is,' Master Glance said giving a copy of the music to Lord Medaris.

'Thank you.' He untied his cloak from the gangway and boarded the Battle Cruiser.

Master Glance watched the Battle Cruiser rise into the night sky and realised why he was troubled. Why, he wondered, did Lord Medaris not mention the *Mithras Ennab*?

'Odd,' Master Glance said to himself.

TWELVE

Midi78 lay sprawled on a couch in the recreation room on the *Wave*, miserable, severely dehydrated, recovering from a disabling bout of diarrhoea. He forced himself to drink the fluids Breve gave him. Master Glance and Breve worked with the sound machines analysing and storing material and relaying important information to the Office of the Chancellor of Security, Lord Rasalis.

Late that evening Breve woke Master Glance in his cabin. 'Father, there is a message from Saradasi Space Control. They have not yet found the *Mithras Ennab* and order increased vigilance. What should we do?'

Master Glance answered drowsily, 'Remember what the Grand Master said? "Search only for *The Place*." We must obey our instructions.' He closed his eyes and fell asleep. Breve walked back to the flight deck, checked the monitors and looked in on Midi78 asleep in his cabin and went back to the recreation room to retrieve the archives to view the next day.

After breakfast, Master Glance joined Midi78 and Breve in the recreation room.

'Master Glance,' Midi78 said, 'Breve and I are looking forward to watching the archives you selected, which Breve has accessed from your sound master archive library on Droha Major. Breve tells me we may recognise some members of Lord Gaima's team in their past lives.'

'They will not have a similar physical appearance and their personality may have changed during their cycles of rebirth,' Master Glance said.

Sound Master Archive QF 72
Audiovisual
Narrator: Grand Master Belaria

The Inter Planetary Evangelistic Society thrived, controlling the life and thinking of the Saradasi Empire. On the planet Merr, the newly converted, eager Kranes, made an interesting proposition to The Society.

'May we Kranes become evangelists like you, our esteemed Saradasi teachers?' they asked piously. 'May we too gain merit to activate *our* twin in the after life, as you will activate yours after you die?' The Kranes proposed they evangelise first their small continent Krane, next the Province they lived in, and eventually their planet, Merr. 'Perhaps,' they suggested, 'after this work, we could work with Saradasi evangelists on other planets.'

Rage consumed The Inter Planetary Evangelistic Society. The Wardens angrily argued that Krane evangelists would lessen the 'availability of convertible material.' Therefore 'substantially' lessening the 'opportunities' for Saradasi evangelists to earn merit.

'It is outrageous,' a warden fumed. 'It is impertinent and dishonest of these Kranes to steal a Saradasi idea.'

'Surely,' another warden pointed out, 'because the Kranes are lesser people than us, the merit they need to ensure everlasting life by awakening their twin, would be enormous. How can they gain sufficient merit in a lifetime?'

The evangelists agreed with an elderly warden who said, 'We will gain merit by preventing the Kranes engaging in this foolish endeavour.'

The evangelistic ambitions of the zealous Kranes may have ended were it not for Meriopter, a Krane elder who lived in Oluter, a village on the eastern bank of Lake Faran. Here, on Lake Faran, he whispered to visiting Saradasi evangelists, how on moonless nights Kranes danced on the Lake.

'Dance? On the water?'

'Yes. I swear. I am your convert. Would I lie?'

Hearing of this, the First Warden of the Society who yearned to walk on water, sent for Dias, a timid and obedient evangelist. Patting Dias's head he directed him to visit Meriopter the Krane in his village, Oluter, on Merr.

'Pretend to encourage their evangelistic ambitions and learn to walk on Lake Faran. Lure the truth from them and when you return teach me how to walk on water. A promotion to Warden for meritorious work awaits you.'

'Thank you,' Dias said.

'Dear Dias, become their close friend,' the First Warden instructed.

'But they are not Saradasi!'

'Sometimes, dear Dias, we must make sacrifices for the Saradasi Empire and our Society. We have to compromise our lofty principles. Be their friend.'

In the village of Oluter, the Krane Meriopter, blue haired, and long bearded, listened attentively to Dias who said the First Warden sought more information about their plans to persuade Saradasi evangelists to accept Krane evangelists.

'A noble enterprise,' Meriopter declared.

They sat on a wooden bench under the shade of a tree on the bank of Lake Faran, fed by a waterfall. Behind them, the thirty-six houses in the village stood at the centre of a cultivated field stretching to flat-topped green hills. Meriopter pointed to the fields, talking of a glorious harvest, and Evangelist Dias reluctantly tore his gaze away from the low cut blouse of a young Krane who squatted on the sand in front of him. When he gave her a caressing gaze she drew up her skirt exposing her thighs, and bending her head she busied herself drawing on the sand with a twig. Dias stifled a gasp.

'I must teach you how to dance on the lake, though this may not interest you,' Meriopter said, watching a flock of birds flying over the lake.

'Perhaps not,' Dias said. 'I will think about it. I fear water.'

'Let us talk about another matter,' Meriopter said. 'What we propose, if you accept us as evangelists, is of greater benefit to Saradasi evangelists than to us.'

Dias leaned forwards.

Meriopter explained his *Multiplier Proposal:*

One Saradasi converts one Krane.

The Krane converts others.

They convert others who convert others.

The final merit of the many conversions will belong to the original Saradasi evangelist who converted the first Krane who became an evangelist and converted others.

'Is it like a pyramid with the Saradasi at the top?' Dias asked.

'You are clever to understand this complex suggestion which others did not grasp. Consider, how incalculably blessed is the first Saradasi evangelist?'

Dias clasped his fingers together, smiling. His long teeth shone. 'Meriopter,' he said, 'The Society will deeply value your proposal which should bear a name, yours!'

Meriopter, his family, kinsfolk and friends bowed their heads in thanks.

'Let us, Meriopter, record what you said,' Dias suggested, holding his recording pen. 'Repeat everything you said very, very slowly.'

That night, in the house provided by Meriopter, Dias relayed the *"Dias Multiplier Effect,"* to all the members of the Evangelistic Society. As dawn broke, Dias awoke to a loud noise. He ran to the front doorway. About fifty villagers were in his front yard screaming obscenities.

Dias, dishevelled and trembling, stood in the doorway. Meriopter ran to him. 'Be brave. I will save you,' he whispered.

A burly male in the crowd shook a fist at Dias. 'He has a female child inside the house,' he roared.

'Impossible,' Meriopter shouted above the crowd. 'I refuse to believe our honoured guest, Evangelist Dias, a noble Saradasi, violated our hospitality. Shame on you people. I say again, shame on you.'

'Use his manhood as bait for the fish,' another bellowed.

Evangelist Dias cowered behind Meriopter.

'Silence,' Meriopter commanded glaring at the angry crowd. Knives shone.

Evangelist Dias leaned against the doorframe and slid to the floor by Meriopter's feet. Meriopter bent over him, helping him to stand. Wailing and shrieking, a young female ran out of the house. Meriopter's eyes narrowed. The crowd roared in one voice, 'Drown him. Drown him.'

Meriopter drew Evangelist Dias aside. 'You are in great danger. Even if I can save your life, I must by law, report your crime to the Province Governor who will inform the Planet Governor who will inform your First Warden and the High Chancellor.'

'Can we,' Dias croaked, 'dispense with this matter here?'

'Yes. The punishment is drowning.'

'Drowning? Can you help me?' Dias stammered.

Meriopter scratched his head. 'Let us offer the village a small present to pacify them.'

'What present?' Dias asked,

'Money. Illegal sex is fifty thousand solars and the younger the victim the higher the penalty. The total is one hundred thousand solars.'

Evangelist Dias left the next day after arrangements were made for the payment in instalments. In two years The Inter Planetary Evangelistic Society elected Dias, famous because of the *"Dias*

Multiplier Effect," as First Warden; at a later date, he sought and won election to the High Council. The Kranes thrived.

End of Archive

'Dias reminds me of Lord Wynan,' Midi78 said.

'Yes. He is unscrupulous and like Lord Wynan had a lust he could not control. Dias changed and helped the Kranes. We should be patient. We may recognise him as someone else.'

Midi78 looked at Master Glance. 'Have you seen these archives?'

Master Glance yawned and reached for his medicine.

Saradasi Archive SQ 79
Audiovisual
Narrator: Sound Master Heizen Miyama

The evangelistic fervour of The Inter Planetary Evangelistic Society increased. Reaching Natashi, the most distant planet in the Nereima Galaxy, eluded and frustrated the Saradasi. Information on the planet was scanty and difficult to interpret. One set of data contradicted the other. When sensor satellites orbiting Natashi failed, or disappeared, Saradasi Space Control blamed solar winds and galactic storms. Others suggested unknown destructive forces.

The new High Chancellor, Lord Tirenza, a former First Warden of The Inter Planetary Evangelistic Society, decided to reach Natashi during his term of office, despite the Governing Council of Saradasi Space Control insisting it was not possible. He demanded the Council issue a statement that travel to Natashi was possible and safe. They refused.

He sent an aide to inform the members of the Governing Council of their permanent new appointments in desolate outposts on Astharia, Asurat, Califra and Merr. At the meeting, the aide said, 'The High Chancellor promises he will personally protect your families here on Saradasi during your absence by confining them to their homes. He will ban at least four generations of your family from service in the Saradasi Empire if you oppose him.'

The Governing Council issued a statement Lord Tirenza dictated to them: Travel to Natashi was possible and safe.

Lord Tirenza planned the expedition to Natashi with Moraes Gy, the silver haired First Warden of The Inter Planetary Evangelistic Society. They knew each other over a lifetime, from when they were young evangelists. On a cold, windy evening they met for dinner at Riala, an eating-house on the bank of Lake Riala in Saradas. They sat, looking across the lake with the sea rumbling in the distance, watching a grain carrier flying the flag of its homeport, Pirast, manoeuvre through the narrow entrance of the bay and lock into the magnetic anchors on the wharf.

'Are we too hasty in sending evangelists to Natashi?' Moraes Gy asked.

'No. I have four ships ready to leave. ' Lord Tirenza gazed into his bowl toying with his food. 'You too should share some of the credit,' he said, flicking aside a breadcrumb on the table.

'I will,' Moraes Gy answered. 'When the ships with the evangelists first dock at Califra, I will host a grand celebration.'

The night deepened. The illuminated fountain on the lake swayed like a rainbow in the wind. A few diners on the platform wrapped their cloaks around themselves.

'What about your senior warden, Sanath Beech, who opposes us and accuses us of risking the lives of the evangelists?' Lord Tirenza crumbled a crust of bread with his long fingers, rose, and left, returning with more wine.

'You know he hopes to succeed me as First Warden, and that is why his objections are not made public. I will take him with me to Califra. He is dangerous here on Saradasi in my absence,' Moraes Gy said.

'Will he agree to go with you?'

'Yes. He will look after the evangelists during their stay on Califra. He recognises the opportunity to make friends and lock in votes.'

Lord Tirenza grunted.

'Sanath Beech will obey me,' Moraes Gy said. 'I am one of the few who knows his secret. Many years ago he swore a vow of celibacy to show he was superior to us. But he was weak and he fathered a child.'

'Is that important?' Lord Tirenza asked, giving another diner a reluctant smile.

'It is, to one aspiring to be the next First Warden.'

'Who and where is the child?'

'Need we deal in children?' Moraes Gy asked.

'The fate of a single child,' Lord Tirenza said, 'is nothing in comparison to the destiny of the Saradasi Empire. Who is the child's mother?'

'It does not matter. Let it pass,' Moraes Gy said. 'He is expecting me tonight to discuss our preparations to meet the evangelists.'

Small ruffles of white ran across Lake Riala swelling to white peaks. A ruddy-faced youth bustled in with four braziers. Flames danced across the dining area when Moraes Gy left.

A month later First Warden Moraes Gy and Warden Sanath Beech with fifty Wardens of the Inter Planetary Evangelistic Society left for Califra, to welcome the four spacecraft with two thousand evangelists and their families on their way to Natashi.

During his welcome address, First Warden Moraes Gy slumped on the dais and died. Under the powers vested in them, the Wardens of the Inter Planetary Evangelistic Society held a speedy election to fill the post of First Warden. Their unanimous choice was Sanath Beech.

While the new First Warden was on Califra, Saradasi Space Control lost contact with the four spacecraft, *Hope, Love, Peace* and *Goodwill*. Lord Tirenza sent a message to Sanath Beech.

AUDVIS #1980
FROM: LORD TIRENZA HIGH CHANCELLOR.
TO: SANATH BEECH

The High Council, and I, your devoted High Chancellor, deeply regret that your ill-fated endeavour to spread hope, love, peace and goodwill on Natashi has failed completely. It is a shameful disaster and a catastrophic calamity.

Moraes Gy, felled by a foul and treacherous hand, who loved you like a son, as I love you, supported your disastrous mission. Thank you for your noble gesture to lend no support publicly to the expedition but to deflect the credit to me. Thank you for your generosity, which I did not need.

Though in deep and crippling grief, I and the only Warden of The Inter Planetary Evangelistic Society here on Saradasi, my son, Soman Freist, who due to ill health did not accompany the evangelists, will visit the families of every person who perished so tragically because of their unwavering, misguided loyalty to you. They fulfilled your unwise and selfish obsession too prematurely to reach Natashi against my private advice to you.

The nation and I weep for the evangelists and their families you lured from Saradasi to achieve your wishes and ambitions.

END MESSAGE

ON THE VISCREENS: FROM THE OFFICE OF THE HIGH CHANCELLOR TO THE SARADASI NATION.

Fellow citizens of the Saradasi Empire!

Our most beloved High Chancellor, Lord Tirenza has collapsed because of grief and anxiety and disappointment in a fellow Saradasi.

The High Council orders no one, Saradasi or non-Saradasi to leave or enter Califra.

Califra is now on *Purple Alert*.

A team of investigators will arrive and question Sanath Beech to dispel rumours he is the foul and callous murderer of his beloved mentor, Moraes Gy.

The High Chancellor has announced Sanath Beech resigned as First Warden and requested permission to set up *Place of Contemplation* on Califra, on an island called, Nuwara and live there.

END MESSAGE

End of Archive

Master Glance looked at Midi78.

'Breve,' Midi78 said, 'you have seen these archives before. What do you think?'

'I am not sure,' Breve said. 'Father?'

'Let us watch the next archive,' Master Glance said.

Saradasi Archive SQ 80
Audiovisual
Narrator: Sound Master Heizen Miyama

On Califra, on a hot and sunny morning on the island of Nuwara, the home of the Dost, a Saradasi Hunter settled on the water alongside the jetty in the capital, Nelun Deepa.

Two male Saradasi in blue military uniform, a young sub-commander and a heavily built commander stepped onto the jetty. They strode across the beach to the stone path leading to the large white palace with two levels surrounded by a veranda and terraced gardens. They passed a row of lily ponds, climbed to the perfumed garden, and up a flight of semicircular steps to the veranda facing the sea, where they found two males standing on either side of the entrance door. The guards, each with an upturned moustache, wearing long sleeved green jackets with silver buttons done up to their neck, studied the horizon attentively.

The commander announced, 'We have come to see the Queen.'

The guards remained silent.

'Where is the Queen?' he demanded.

In a faithful mimicry of the intonation and accent of the Saradasi who spoke in the Dost language, the older guard said, 'The Queen is not here.'

'Where is she? Is she lost?'

'We cannot tell you where she is because we have not asked her and she has not told us,' the older guard replied looking across the sea.

'Why not?'

'Because she is a Queen and we are guards. Our work is with those who want to enter the palace, not with those who go out.'

The younger Saradasi winked at the guard and drew his companion back.

'I want to wring his neck,' the commander said, his teeth clenched.

'Can we sit here till the Queen returns?' the sub-commander asked the guards politely.

The guards pointed with their feet to thick multicoloured mats on the floor of the veranda, smiling warmly at the Saradasi, relishing their act of gross discourtesy. When the Saradasi sat, one guard opened the door with great ceremony and entered the great hall of the palace. He closed the door behind him, shouting to the butler and servants, 'Two Saradasi offspring of a diseased prostitute are here. Display all courtesy to them and try not to vomit when you see them. Go find Her Majesty. Go slowly. They are perspiring and wriggling uncomfortably on the mats.'

The palace servants found the Queen and her advisers, who after evening worship at the temple, were walking through the streets talking to people, engaging in banter, listening to complaints and receiving blessings for good deeds.

The two Saradasi sat on the veranda of the palace, their blue uniforms wet. On a low table in front of them, liveried servants placed trays of food and drink. The officers were dozing when Queen Yoreciva arrived with her advisers and courtiers. She greeted them warmly, though neither responded. The Saradasi said they wanted to buy an area of land in the southern most end of the island by the sea, to build a *Place of Contemplation* for a Saradasi to live in solitude.

'Why there?' Queen Yoreciva asked. 'Why in the hottest part of the island?'

'He likes the heat,' the commander said.

The teenage Queen Yoreciva did not have the good looks of her late father but possessed her mother's cunning and analytical skills. Piling the visitors' plates with food which they did not taste, she said, 'I will sell the land to you, but, according to our custom, our priests must first bless the land.'

The commander glanced sideways at his companion. 'How long will you need?' he asked, fidgeting on the mat.

During the silence, the Saradasi followed Queen Yoreciva's gaze to the garden, sloping to the beach, well cared for with vivid flowering plants. From where they sat they saw the graceful curve of the bay and the waves frothing on the beach.

'We have not performed the ceremony of blessing the land in my lifetime,' Queen Yoreciva replied.

'When could you carry out this ceremony?' The commander asked drumming his fingers on his force-sword.

'Me? I cannot perform the ceremony. I have not taken religious orders. How can I bless the land? I am just a Queen.' She spoke to a grey haired courtier. 'Please send a runner to the temple. Pay my respects and ask the venerable priest, Vitharna, to please visit us. No. Go to the temple and take these visitors with you. Ask the priest to return with you.'

The Saradasi sprang to their feet. The younger Saradasi nudged his colleague, speaking in Saradasi. 'She is weaving a soft, ever-tightening web, thinking we are stupid.'

'Greed,' replied the other, 'is the spider we can trap in *our* web. A spider queen! She will renege on the agreement to sell the land and ask for more money.'

136

After climbing a steep flight of steps they reached the temple courtyard where four young barefooted priests welcomed them, their heads shaven, wearing saffron coloured robes. The Saradasi sat by an eight-cornered pond with pink and white lilies, waiting for the priest, Vitharna. They ate the fruits the young priests pressed on them and drank the sweet cool water from the well behind the temple. The scent of the white flowers, used as an offering in the temple, lingered in the air.

'He should be here now or he may be here later in the evening or if he has not arrived at night he will certainly come tomorrow if it does not rain in the mountains,' one of the young priests said.

In the evening, the Saradasi and the courtier left the temple.

After dusk, when the moon shone during the grand feast the Queen held for the Saradasi, the priest, Vitharna, arrived at the palace. The Saradasi, unable to eat the spicy food, looked glumly at the priest. Unlike the other priests they met in the temple, he wore a red robe.

'I am sorry I was not at the temple. I have been at a fire walking ceremony in the mountains,' he apologised, watching the Saradasi taste the sweets made with lentil flour and palm treacle, and grimace.

The priest listened to the Queen's request to bless the land the Saradasi wanted to buy.

'I am sorry. I have no knowledge of this ceremony.'

'Who else could perform the ceremony?' Queen Yoreciva asked anxiously.

'I will think about your question,' he replied.

After the priest left the palace, the Chief Adviser to the Queen, Andrase, cleared his throat. 'If I may, Your Highness?'

'Please,' the Queen answered.

'I may be able to help,' Andrase said to the Saradasi. 'My former master, the father of the Queen and I, grew up together. We would visit a priest, the Venerable Tissa, who I am sure can perform the ceremony, though I am not sure if he is alive or not. He lived on a mountain top far from here but easy to reach.'

'Why,' asked the Saradasi commander sharply, 'did the priest who was here not mention this priest you speak of?'

'I will ask him,' Andrase said.

'You should have asked him when he was here.'

'I am a servant. The conversation was between the Queen and the priest and it is impolite to interrupt. We enjoy being polite.'

The commander swore in Saradasi; the sub-commander swished his mouth with water after tasting a drink of fruit syrup and milk.

Queen Yoreciva signalled a courtier. 'Run as fast as you can. Go ask the priest about the venerable Tissa.'

The courtier returned breathless. 'He said the venerable Tissa is not alive but the ceremony must be performed, if not, bad fortune will befall all of you. He will search for a priest who can conduct the ceremony and asks us to be patient.'

Queen Yoreciva rose and the Saradasi tottered to their feet from the mats on the floor. 'Let us talk again in a few days,' she said. 'We must not hurry the priest. We regard unnecessary urgency as a weakness of the spirit.'

After the Saradasi left, great activity occurred in the middle courtyard of the palace. Two small boats loaded with equipment and passengers left by sea for the south of the island to examine the land the Saradasi were eager to buy

Two days later a Saradasi Interceptor landed on the sea opposite the palace. A smiling young Saradasi visited the Queen introducing herself as Commander Alianar. Her task, she said, was to buy the land for the *Place of Contemplation*.

She sat with the Queen on the steps leading to the beach from the palace veranda and watched the tide sweep in and cover their feet.

'How does your garden survive?' she asked.

'The plants thrive in salt,' Queen Yoreciva replied.

Queen Yoreciva made no mention of consecrating the land and that night they signed the documents for the sale. Alianar stayed in the palace with Queen Yoreciva for three days and left to inspect the land. She spent four more days with the Queen on her next visit. On the morning she was to leave for Saradasi, Alianar and the Queen strolled along the beach, barefoot, on the warm wet sand. Alianar picked up a flat stone and sent it skimming across the water the way Queen Yoreciva taught her, each guessing how many times it would skim the surface.

They walked holding hands, between glistening clumps of seaweed washed ashore. Occasionally a busy red roofed crab angled across their path.

'I will miss you,' Queen Yoreciva said. 'You are the most beautiful person I have met.' They held each other, the embrace warm and comforting, and walked on, their arms around each other. Alianar looked at the cloudless dull grey sky and stopped. She unclasped a white metal chain with a golden circle and a red stone set in its centre.

'This is a present for you. I will show you how to use it if you need urgent help from a Saradasi during a crisis. But your request must not risk the Saradasi Empire or an individual Saradasi.'

'I will remember you even without a gift.' Yoreciva gazed at the chain and the pendant. 'Someone may say I stole it from you.'

Alianar held the pendant in her hand. 'Press hard on the red stone thrice. Help will arrive as soon as possible.' She slipped the chain round Queen Yoreciva's neck. 'Every gift has a price attached to it,' she said with a light laugh.

'And the price?' Yoreciva asked teasing out strands of hair caught in the chain.

'Soon our engineers will arrive to erect a building on the land we bought from you. After that a Saradasi will come to live there. His enemies have exiled him unjustly. The plan is for a tidal wave to kill him, so his death would seem accidental. I want to save his life and I want you to help me. When I know the date of the tidal wave, I will inform you. Please send him to safety the day before. Acting earlier will arouse suspicion.'

'Though the sea is rough there, we have no tidal waves.'

'Our technicians will create one with sonic devices.'

'I promise I will send him to a place where no one will find him,' the Queen said.

'Where?'

'To a remote monastery near a village called Sirglin, in the Veles mountain range. It is a beautiful place overlooking a deep valley with a blue river running through it. He will live as a saffron robed, head shaven, barefooted priest. Six warrior priests will guard him. Does he like solitude?'

'I do not know,' Alianar said.

They paused to look at a fishing boat with an outrigger coming to shore, and continued walking to the palace.

'Are you wondering why I, the person in charge of this project to kill this person, want to save him?' Alianar said.

'Yes.'

'There are no coincidences in life,' Alianar said. 'I am in charge of this project, because I manipulated events and people. The High Chancellor of the Saradasi Empire wants to murder a good person who did no wrong, by staging an accident. The two people who hated him also hated each other, but pretended they were friends. The High Chancellor murdered Moraes Gy, the former First Warden of our Inter Planetary Evangelistic Society and spread a rumour that an innocent person was the murderer. I want you to save this innocent person.'

'Why have they not killed him before?' the Queen asked.

'Because many people believe he is innocent. The Saradasi will not accept the murder of another Saradasi, therefore, the accidental death by a tidal wave.'

'Why do you want to save him?' Yoreciva asked.

'To seek justice and also revenge,' she said, meeting her friend's gaze.

'Revenge? Revenge against whom?'

'Lord Tirenza, the High Chancellor.'

'You are pitting yourself against the High Chancellor of the Saradasi Empire?'

'I am cleverer than that murderer.' Alianar stopped walking and looked at Yoreciva. 'If you fear him, you need not help me.'

'I will help you. That is my promise.'

When they reached the jetty where Alianar's craft was moored, the communications officer ran up to them.

'There is an urgent message for you from the High Council,' she said handing Alianar the message recorder.

AUDVIS #9838
FROM: OFFICE OF HIGH CHANCELLOR.
TO: COMMANDER ALIANAR

'THANK YOU FOR PURCHASING LAND.
PLANS ALTERED.
ENGINEERS WILL CONSTRUCT PLACE OF CONTEMPLATION TOMORROW.
RETURN IMMEDIATELY TO VALONA, MERR.
TAKE CUSTODY OF SANATH BEECH.
RETURN TO PLACE OF CONTEMPLATION WITH SANATH BEECH.
LORD TIRENZA URGES YOU EXTRACT A CONFESSION FROM SANATH BEECH
REGARDING MURDER OF MORAES GY.

END MESSAGE

Alianar thanked the communications officer. 'Respond. I leave for Valona, Merr, this evening. Will obtain confession.'

That evening, before Alianar left for Merr, she sat with Yoreciva on the eastern veranda of the palace with the priest, Vitharna. He reverently placed an object at Queen Yoreciva's feet. She parted the layers of golden coloured cloth and picked up a shiny metal cylindrical amulet an inch long and a quarter of an inch wide, attached to a woven yellow thread.

'This is a gift from us to protect you,' Queen Yoreciva said, tying the amulet on Alianar's right upper arm.

Alianar embraced Yoreciva when she rose to leave. 'I feel I have been your friend for a thousand years,' she said. 'I will see you soon and before long I will live in the house you are building for me, overlooking the lake.'

She walked half way along the jetty, and walked back to Yoreciva. 'You must never eat a meal and drink wine with Lord Tirenza,' she said.

The Queen and the priest Vitharna watched the *Vanaja* speed across the sea, rise and race across a sombre sky, disappearing into dense black clouds. A beaked bird, white against the black sky, swooped down to the sea and rose with a silver fish quivering in its beak.

'Will the amulet help her?' Yoreciva asked Vitharna.

'A powerful force is aligned against her.' He looked at the dark sky. 'Death stalks her,' he said.

'Can we save the person she wants me to save? Could he be her father? '

'No. The High Chancellor has killed her father already,' the Priest said.

'When?'

'Recently. It was all foretold in the great book written by the lesser gods, thousands of years ago. One day when the time is right I will show it to you and you will believe its contents and the legend about the lesser gods and their punishment for their greed.'

The Queen wiped the sea spray off her face.

The wind rose, swirling sand on the beach and screaming through the trees. The sea frothed white as huge waves raced ashore. The sky darkened to an inky black.

'A deep karmic destiny binds your life with Alianar and Lord Tirenza,' Vitharna said. 'You three will enter many cycles of re-birth and be born again to redeem yourselves of the sins you committed in this life. You will not meet again in this lifetime. But all three of you will meet at a future time in your rebirth cycle.'

When they neared the palace, Vitharna said, 'Beware of greed. Even the gods are tempted.'

He walked away into the howling wind.

He returned and said, 'Beware especially when greed exceeds fear, for it is then that lives are destroyed and souls damned for many lifetimes.'

End of Archive

THIRTEEN

On the *Wave,* Master Glance programmed the navigation computer to retrace his steps to the sector where he believed he heard the conversation from *The Place.* Travelling in a tight grid pattern for a week, he did not hear the voice nor another laugh or the beguiling melody. His friend, Master Retrion on Droha Major, had not yet identified the music he recorded. The two teams of Sound Masters who were analysing the music said its musical form showed a similarity to Saradasi music. It contained one hundred and seventy notes. 'Could it be from another galaxy?' one asked. Some wondered if a machine played the music because of the precision, though all agreed the instrument was woodwind with a wide range of notes.

Master Glance continued his search, filing a 'random flight path' with Saradasi Space Control, but it was unrewarding. He spent his leisure time selecting music from his library for Lord Medaris. He wondered what Lord Medaris's favourite one hundred pieces of music would be from the thousands he collected and avidly listened to over the years.

Midi78 sat in the recreation room, sipping a drink when Master Glance and Breve entered. Since meeting Lord Medaris, and his cautioning her about her behaviour, Seelawathie-Ap stayed in her cabin, and ate her meals alone in the dining room. She spoke occasionally to Breve, discouraging Midi78 from speaking to her by answering him with as few words as possible.

Later that morning Master Glance told them more about the archive they watched, though evasive about the source.

'I cannot believe what you say,' Midi78 said rubbing his head.

'It is difficult to believe,' Breve exclaimed.

'It is true,' Master Glance said. 'Recall what the priest Vitharna told the Queen after Alianar left Nuwara, "A deep karmic destiny binds your life with Alianar and Lord Tirenza. You three will enter many cycles of rebirth and be born again to redeem yourselves of the sins you committed in this life. You will not meet again in this lifetime. But all three of you will meet at a future time in your rebirth cycle.'"

'Master Glance,' Midi 78 said, 'Lord Tirenza is deeply treacherous, Moraes Gy who worked with him to send the evangelists to Natashi, is treacherous. Surely Alianar and Queen Yoreciva are not treacherous.'

'Temptation and greed are powerful forces that destroy people,' Master Glance said. 'That is why Alianar bribed Chief Adviser Andrase to poison Queen Yoreciva.'

'Poison the Queen? I cannot believe that! I am amazed,' Midi78 said. 'Why?'

'Midi78,' Master Glance replied, 'even the righteous may succumb to a corrupt but irresistible offer and try preserving their virtue by justifying their actions. This is to calm their conscience. We may all piously scorn small, valueless temptations. But when a big temptation confronts us, it traps us.'

'I am confused,' Midi78 said. 'Why did Alianar who gave Yoreciva a present, have her killed?'

'Alianar obeyed Lord Tirenza's orders. He thought the Queen would reveal how *The Place of Contemplation* was destroyed by an artificial tidal wave. Lord Tirenza promised Alianar a promotion to General, working with him in the High Chancellor's Office.'

'Why?' Midi78 asked. 'What gain was there for Lord Tirenza?'

'He wanted to involve Alianar in his web, especially if she escaped the tidal wave intended to destroy *The Place of Contemplation*. He ordered her to stay there with Sanath Beech to obtain a confession from him.'

Midi78 rubbed his head. 'I cannot understand why Alianar agreed to have Queen Yoreciva poisoned. She hated Lord Tirenza. Was a promotion to General the great temptation?'

'No. I think she wanted the promotion to be close to Lord Tirenza, to fulfil the single ambition in her life: to kill Lord Tirenza. Nothing else and nobody else, even Queen Yoreciva, whom she cared about, mattered. Her rage consumed her.'

'Why was she so angry?' Midi78 said.

'She believed Sanath Beech was her father, and she, his illegitimate child whom he loved.'

'Why did she believe this?' Midi78 asked.

'Because he visited her regularly at the orphanage on Califra, and cared about her, though he never said he was her father.'

'Why did she not ask him if he was her father?' Breve asked.

'Perhaps, instead of seeking the truth, she preferred to cling to an uncertain, though comforting belief. She never asked why she was in an orphanage either. She may have thought her mother was dead and that Sanath Beech, because of his constant travels as an evangelist, could not look after her. She assumed, without any evidence, that Sanath Beech was her father.'

'Father, how do you know all this?'

'We have recordings of the conversations between Alianar and Sanath Beech at the orphanage.'

'It is a sad story,' Midi78 said. 'Who was her father?'

'First Warden Moraes Gy who asked Sanath Beech to visit her. Lord Tirenza poisoned his food and wine, and accused Sanath Beech of his murder,' Master Glance said.

'How did Alianar, an orphan, rise to her position in the Saradasi military?' Breve asked.

'Sanath Beech admired her,' Master Glance said. 'We have recordings of him urging her to achieve greatness. She joined the Saradasi military and rose to colonel.'

Master Glance looked at Midi78 and continued, 'What I now say will surprise you even more, Midi78. Queen Yoreciva knew Alianar was misinformed about the date of the tidal wave. She said nothing. She could have prevented the death of Alianar and Sanath Beech. She knew the exact time the tidal wave would destroy *The Place of Contemplation*.'

'How did the Queen know the correct date? Who told her?' Midi 78 said.

'One of the two Saradasi military officers who visited Queen Yoreciva to buy land for *The Place of Contemplation*, returned to Nuwara the night Alianar left. He told Yoreciva, Lord Tirenza offered her the Province Governorship of Province 8, which included Nuwara. In a year she would be Planet Governor of Califra.'

'How cunning and dishonourable and treacherous,' Midi78 said.

'They are Saradasi,' Master Glance replied. 'Imagine Queen Yoreciva's feelings. From being the queen of an insignificant island, she would be Planet Governor of Califra.'

'Master Glance, why was the Queen so gullible?' Midi78 wondered.

'Greedy people are gullible.'

'Father, I am confused. What did Lord Tirenza really want from the Queen?'

'He wanted Queen Yoreciva to kill Sanath Beech and Alianar if they survived the tidal wave,' Master Glance said. 'Lord Tirenza would often say, "The inevitable never happens, but the unexpected always happens." Also, Saradasi do not kill Saradasi, instead they ask others to commit their foul deeds.'

'All this is so complex,' Midi78 groaned. 'I feel the recreation room is spinning round me. Or am I spinning round the recreation room?'

'I often feel that way.' Master Glance said, drinking his medicine. 'We are dealing with the extremely complex Saradasi. Lord Tirenza's actions are not totally logical and are convoluted. Like many Saradasi, he may have the mental problem of being paranoid. Because he is paranoid, he is unnecessarily anxious and also irrationally suspicious of the thoughts and actions of others.'

'Who have these people we saw in the Archive been reborn as?' Midi78 asked. 'Is Alianar, Shanaz?

'We are puzzled about Shanaz.' Master Glance said.

'Why?'

'We have not been able to trace her past lives.'

'Whom is Lord Tirenza re-born as?' Breve asked.

'He is Lord Wynan,' Master Glance said. 'But there is a change, because Wynan has less moral coarseness than Lord Tirenza. Wynan is less treacherous though he disrespects life. Recall his brutality to the people in Kersia and being comfortable with what he did.'

'What about Evangelist Dias?' Midi78 asked.

'He was reborn as Sanath Beech. And, Sanath Beech was reborn as Lord Rasalis,' Master Glance said.

'Lord Rasalis?' Midi78 echoed.

'Are you sure father?' Breve exclaimed.

'Yes. We Sound Masters have absolute proof.'

Midi78 sat up. 'Proof? Did you say proof, Master Glance? Is there proof who was who in their past lives?'

'Yes, excellent, sophisticated proof. After his term as First Warden of The Interplanetary Evangelistic Society, Dias was elected to the High Council and subsequently elected High Chancellor of the Saradasi Empire. He held no ill will against the Kranes and often met with Meriopter by Lake Faran and sought his advice. He convinced the High Council to ban child labour in the Saradasi Empire and enact a law for Saradasi and non-Saradasi in the military to receive the same salary and eat the same food in the dining room. He tried but failed to effect other measures to improve the life of people in the vassal planets.'

'We know Sanath Beech, who Dias was born as, was also a good person,' Midi78 said. 'Are you suggesting that Lord Rasalis is a good person?'

'Yes, he is a very good person,' Master Glance declared. 'We Sound Masters have studied him closely. There is no record of Lord Rasalis having harmed anyone. He is devious, but he is compassionate and respects life. He is not ruthless. He has not sacrificed a single life for the Saradasi Empire. As Chancellor of Security he has saved many non-Saradasi.'

'But what about the Restians who Colonel Llaxem wanted drowned by Lord Rasalis when he was a general, after the mind reading experiment? You asked Midi78 and me to watch the archive, ' Breve said.

'I remember the Restians well,' Master Glance said.

'Lord Rasalis let them drown, Father.'

'He did not.'

'I will find the archive and we can view it.'

'Breve, I am familiar with this archive because I recorded it when I was Sector Sound Master. Lord Rasalis saved all fifty Restians, who Colonel Llaxem thought drowned.'

'The Restians did not drown?' Midi78 asked. 'But I saw them bound, on a platform in the sea.'

'Lord Rasalis did not let them drown,' Master Glance said. 'Like you, Colonel Llaxem also saw fifty Restians on a platform on the raging Saretosa Sea. You will recall the audiovisual transmission to Colonel Llaxem failed. That was deliberate. Llaxem presumed they drowned. A small group of Saradasi saved them'

'Was the audiovisual failure ordered by Lord Rasalis?' Midi78 said.

'Yes.'

'Who knew the truth of what happened to the Restians?' Breve asked.

'The Restians and the Saradasi involved. They were Lord Rasalis and Medaris, before the Saradasi elected them Lords, and Aricent, Santana and Nivearest, who are now General in Saradasi Security working with Lord Rasalis.'

'And of course you, Master Glance?' Midi78 asked.

'Yes.'

'Father!' Breve said. 'No one else knew what happened because you stopped recording. That is why the archive ended abruptly.'

'I am also concerned about my rebirth and my destiny,' Master Glance replied.

Midi78 rubbed his head. 'Master Glance, please explain how you are certain who the Saradasi were in their past lives.'

'I will share a Saradasi secret with you,' Master Glance said. 'Deep in the Lower City on Saradas, the Saradasi have a repository with the genetic imprint of every Saradasi who arrived on their planet and every Saradasi born thereafter. They can trace the genetic profile of each Saradasi.'

'They are clever people,' Midi78 said. 'Master Glance, you told us you were not sure who Shanaz was in her past lives. Why?'

'Her genetic material has been removed or deleted from the genetic bank. I know no more about this.'

'Master Glance, how did you learn of the genetic banks and access them?'

Master Glance yawned and rubbed his eyes.

Midi78 looked closely at Master Glance. 'I have a last question. Lord Medaris, who is he?'

'I have work to do,' Master Glance said, leaving the recreation room.

○

A purple light bathed the interior of the *Wave*, accompanied by a multi-pitched shrieking noise.

'It's the battle computer alarm. This alarm makes a hideous sound, which I cannot alter,' Master Glance complained, strolling to the flight deck with Midi78 running after him. They joined Breve, who was watching the battle computer screen.

The battle computer announced: 'I confirm I have armed the *Wave*. The *Wave* will engage seven Terumana craft attacking in spider formation. All movable objects on the *Wave* are secure, on static adhesion. Manual navigation is suspended. I am linked to our navigation computer. Saradasi Space Control master computer Keptron will intervene if we are in danger. Thank you.'

'Terumana craft attacking us? Seven? Are we not in great danger?' Midi78 gasped, grasping the arms of his seat. 'Surely Terumana would not attack us within the Nereima Galaxy?'

'Saradasi Space Control gave us a route just outside the western boundary of the Nereima Galaxy to reach Asurat quickly,' Breve explained.

'They have endangered our lives. Why?' Midi78 demanded raising his voice.

Breve gave Midi78 a reassuring smile when the individual force shields securing them in their seats were automatically activated.

'Our lives are not in danger because we are on the *Wave*,' Master Glance explained. 'The shabby, neglected appearance of the *Wave* is a subterfuge. The *Wave* is as fast as a Saradasi Interceptor and has more defensive and offensive equipment than a Saradasi Hunter or Interceptor.'

'Why?'

'The Saradasi want us alive and not dead,' Master Glance said.

'Look, Master Glance!' Midi78 screamed pointing to the screen. 'Seven Terumana craft are surrounding us and you appear calm. You and Breve smile. Why?

'We are on the *Wave and* we are safe. Watch the screen,' Master Glance replied calmly.

'Evasive action necessary,' the battle computer announced.

A noise like a hundred thunderclaps filled the *Wave*.

'Missed us,' Master Glance commented, pleased. 'What we need is better sound insulation. I must attend to it urgently.'

'Now?' Midi78 asked.

'Perhaps later,' Master Glance said.

The *Wave* spun and weaved above, below and within the Terumana spider attack formation. They watched the *Wave* destroy four Terumana Battle Daggers and the Battle Womb, the mother ship of the spider attack formation. Two slender Battle Swords persisted in the attack.

'The enemy craft are using non-Terumana equipment,' the battle computer reported.

'From where have the Terumana obtained these weapon systems?' Master Glance asked.

'Does it matter?' Midi78 groaned when a powerful laser beam with blinding intensity, half as wide as the *Wave,* passed parallel to it. Midi78 flinched. The temperature inside the *Wave* soared and reverted to its pre-set level.

'Can you flee from them?' Midi78 pleaded, his hands clenched on his lap, perspiring.

'We can, but we want to be certain the battle computer works to its specifications.'

'Specifications!'

'I wonder,' Master Glance reflected, 'where they bought such sophisticated equipment?'

On the battle computer screen, the Battle Swords lunged at the weaving *Wave*.

'Nothing will happen to the *Wave*,' Breve reassured Midi78. 'The Saradasi built and equipped this ship. Our battle computer is excellent.'

'What if it fails?' Midi78 demanded, wringing his hands.

Master Glance shook his head frowning. 'The *Wave*?'

'No. No. The battle computer.'

'Have you ever heard of a Saradasi battle computer failing?'

'How would I know? I am a priest. You may be proven wrong in a few moments.'

'Never,' Master Glance said. 'Midi78, the Saradasi built this ship.'

'Are the Saradasi gods?'

'They think they are, and at this moment, I hope they are,' Master Glance murmured into his beard, pointing to the screen. 'I regard the Saradasi as gods every time the battle computer protects us during an attack.'

The two Battle Swords collided with a shattering explosion after the *Wave* slipped out of their embrace.

'I told you the battle computer never fails,' Breve said triumphantly as Midi78 slumped in his seat.

○

In the recreation room Breve and Midi78 were talking to each other; Seelawathie-Ap sat silently and Master Glance slept in his favourite seat, his chin on his chest. Breve went to the flight deck and returned to say, 'We are fourteen hours from our destination.'

When the *Wave* landed at Military Base Xzania, Seelawathie-Ap left after thanking Master Glance, Midi78 and Breve. She adjusted the *kaduwa* slung over her left shoulder, and, surrounded by a platoon of Dost security guards, strode to the main building.

The *Wave* left. Its new orders from Sound Master Retrion were: 'Intensify your search for *The Place*. The days pass quickly for Lord Gaima's team to save the Nereima Galaxy. But beware, many seek to destroy you.'

FOURTEEN

As mysteriously as it disappeared, the *Mithras Ennab* re-entered the Nereima Galaxy. Ordered to maintain zero orbit, squadrons of Saradasi Battle Cruiser and Interceptors escorted the spacecraft to Sector 4, beyond the Exclusion Zone of the home planet. At a special meeting, the High Council decided to not board the *Mithras Ennab*. In the Lower City at Saradasi Space Control Headquarters, the chief duty officer sat bleakly in front of his screen with Lord Rasalis pushing against him.

On the *Mithras Ennab*, Lord Wynan and Fariyal sat on the flight deck staring at their screens. Fariyal wondered why the chief duty officer looked anxious, his tongue moistening his lips.

Lord Wynan shouted, scowling at the chief duty officer, 'You have no authority to stop us on our journey home. Why are we in zero orbit?'

'I must ask you a few routine questions,' the chief duty officer said. 'We have a problem which Lord Rasalis will discuss with you.'

Fariyal recognized the anxiety in his voice and decided not to voice her unease.

'Commander Fariyal, is the *Mithras Ennab* armed?' the chief duty officer asked.

'The *Mithras Ennab* carries the stipulated armaments,' Fariyal answered.

'You must follow my navigation instructions precisely,' he warned. 'Any deviation will automatically destroy you. We will navigate your craft. Therefore, do not attempt to override our actions. Satellite 9, now on your screen, is monitoring the *Mithras Ennab*. Please keep communications channels one and seven open.'

'Yes,' Fariyal answered. She understood Satellite 9 would examine the *Mithras Ennab* minutely. She glanced at the flight deck audiovisual scanner relaying sound and movement on board and ignored the questions Lord Wynan repeatedly asked her. She watched the armed Helper drones surround the *Mithras Ennab*. On board, the battle computer warned of an impending attack and reported its defence and assault functions were immobilized.

Fariyal knew if she or Lord Wynan tried to override Saradasi Space Control navigation, Sector 4 assault computers would activate the Helper drones to destroy the *Mithras Ennab*. Fed by Satellite 9, the Helpers would continuously alter their search pattern, responding to changes on board the *Mithras Ennab*.

She realized Saradasi Space Control regarded the *Mithras Ennab* with extreme suspicion. Why she wondered? What was the problem? But, being a military officer, her duty was to follow orders not demand answers to her questions. Lord Wynan sat glaring at the screen in front of him.

Why, she wondered, did Saradasi Space Control not ask them the code of the day, which the onboard computer provided when the passengers fed in confidential, personal particulars?

Why the delay? Time; they need more time, Fariyal reasoned. Time for what?

On the screen, a female officer held up her arm displaying the insignia of a colonel in Saradasi Security on her wristband. Both Lord Wynan and Fariyal recognized Colonel Wereset.

'Lord Wynan,' she said, 'I have to question you and check the answers with the database. Please state your place of birth.'

'In Tranxc, Sada IV, Precinct 18, Province 11, Asurat, where my father was posted.'

'Who is the most important person you met in Asurat?'

'I met the Planet Governor, the Great Khan once during a play the Suxt-Sux people staged.'

Colonel Wereset's image faded from the screen. Fariyal knew the interview was to confirm Lord Wynan's voice pattern and scan his eyes to match the images of his retina. Fariyal wondered why she was not questioned.

'Lord Wynan, what is your code of the day?' the chief duty officer asked.

Fariyal looked aside while Wynan entered the information. A purple glow filled the chief duty officer's work area.

'Again.'

Lord Wynan keyed in the information.

'You are wrong,' the chief duty officer said.

Lord Rasalis came on the screen. 'Wynan, what is the date today?'

'40th day of month III.'

'Fariyal, what is the date?'

'40th day of month III.'

'Fariyal, we have re-activated the navigation computer on your craft. Please use it to check the date.'

The navigation computer intoned: 'The date is 50th day of month III.'

Fariyal looked at the computer.

'Fariyal, the correct date is *not* the 40th day of month III. Where have you been?'

'Nowhere. We were travelling home from Califra after visiting the military bases there.'

'Fariyal, the journey from Califra to Saradasi does not take ten days,' Lord Rasalis said. 'Where were you?'

'I was on the *Mithras Ennab* travelling home.'

Lord Wynan shook his head.

'We will bring you in,' Lord Rasalis said. 'Leave the flight deck and go to your cabins and stay there. Do not leave your cabins unless I tell you. I do not want an accident to occur. We have a problem with the Helpers.'

The *Mithras Ennab* started its descent to an isolated landing field, which Saradasi Space Control towed to the placid Xaxias Sea, fifty seven hundred miles north of the capital.

Lord Rasalis paced a long corridor on the tenth floor of Saradasi Space Control, his mind racing, discarding possibilities and weighing probabilities. Nothing made sense. He gazed out of the window overlooking an artificial lake. He wished he were in the Upper City watching and listening to the sea and the waves and not in the claustrophobic Lower City he disliked.

He gazed at the lake recalling how he met Fariyal years ago at his friend, Cholaten's library with its musty smell and its tables and chairs piled with books. He recalled admiring her beautifully proportioned, serene face. The young cadet officer he had not met before sat engrossed in a book, her chin on her hand. She looked at him when he entered the room and bent her head again.

Was it seven years ago he first saw her? He thought of the bond that grew between them, like that of a parent and child. He returned to sit next to the chief duty officer, watching the Helpers cocooning the *Mithras Ennab* descending to the Xaxias Sea guided by the chief duty officer. He clamped a large hand on his shoulder. 'Be careful,' he said and left for his small home in the Upper City on the promontory facing the sea.

○

Heavy snow fell in the Upper City.

Shanaz walked from her home along the winding streets to the Octagon on the hill for the High Council meeting. She climbed the steps to the north garden and before entering the Octagon, watched the bay churned by the wind, the waves pounding the old wharves and sea wall.

She entered the meeting room and sat, her head bent, her eyes raised, looking at the octagonal room. Here the eight Lords of the High Council sat at the octagonal table, as had others before them for thousands of years. Here their logic, policies, decisions, beliefs, and idiosyncrasies affected the lives of billions of inhabitants of the Saradasi Empire. The first to arrive, Shanaz watched, unsmiling, as the others entered.

The meeting began when Plestrach the Inner Circle android to the High Council lit the incense burners and white vapours swirled across the room. He left the room and re-entered with the Sacred Bowl and eight green towels draped on his arms. He took the Sacred Bowl first to the youngest member, Shanaz. The other High Council members washed and dried their hands in a symbolic gesture of purification.

Lord Teras, spoke in his deep voice. 'We have no answers to three questions. How did the *Mithras Ennab* disappear? Where was it? How did it return here? Wynan, you are here at the High Council meeting as the High Chancellor's General. Tell us, where was the *Mithras Ennab?*'

'I do not know.

'You have no recollection of what happened?'

'No.'

Puzzlement dominated the meeting. Theories, conjecture, and divergent views surged across the table. Shanaz sat, her chin on her clenched hand. She saw Wynan sitting like the bewildered spectator of a perplexing drama. The faint sound of the fountain at the south end of the room reached her mind. She disciplined herself to concentrate. The brief disappearance of the *Mithras Ennab* changed many lives but Shanaz believed she suffered the most. Disturbed sleep and early morning awakening sapped her energy. On most evenings she felt as if a vice was clamping on her head, ever tighter, the pain intense, her vision blurred. Bouts of nausea were frequent.

'Lord Rasalis,' Shanaz said, her voice firm, now in control. 'I thought you were not here because you are so quiet.'

'Shanaz, I am here.'

'We must accept an unfortunate event occurred which we cannot explain,' Lord Zilva said. 'The many investigation teams have provided no information. Even the Sound Masters are silent.'

'Yes,' Lord Varsana, the former principal of the Virtan Military Academy Shanaz attended, agreed. 'The craft near the *Mithras Ennab* were the water carrier, *Gaina,* and Sound Master Glance's ship, the *Wave,* both with permission to travel to Space Station ZenFah.'

Lord Rasalis added, 'When the *Mithras Ennab* disappeared every other craft in the Nereima Galaxy travelled with our approval. Security detected no equipment error at Saradasi Space Control or on the *Mithras Ennab*. Our satellites detected no hostile forces. Our informers are silent. We at Security have nothing to report.'

Shanaz glanced round the table, ignoring Lord Wynan. 'I am fearful because of all the reasons mentioned. I am frustrated because of my ignorance. Plestrach, bring Commander Fariyal.' She stared at Lord Rasalis when he greeted Fariyal. 'Your friend is here, Lord Rasalis,' she said. 'Are you going to question her? Asking questions must be tedious when you have the answers to everything, except when we need answers.'

Fariyal gave no new information. After a short silence, she said, 'The solution to this problem is simple. We must regard the good of the Empire before all else. I volunteer to undergo the *Gwa-Halia* analysis. I am sure Lord Wynan would also agree.'

'Tell us about the *Gwa-Halia* analysis,' Shanaz asked Plestrach.

Plestrach stood erect. 'The *Gwa-Halia* analysis,' he explained, 'recovers stored auditory and visual data from the brain under hypnosis. Visual images travel from the eyes along the optic nerves to a specific part of the brain for processing and retention. Sound travels from the deep inner ear membrane by the auditory nerves to the brain. The anterior portion of the Rosa lobe stores auditory data and the Parks lobe, visual images.'

'Explain what is unique about this *Gwa-Halia* analysis,' Shanaz said.

'The *Gwa-Halia* analysis distinguishes *real* from *imaginary* information stored in the brain. The technology recovers the *real* information under hypnosis. Gwa and Halia were the neuroscientist inventors.'

The High Council thanked Fariyal for her suggestion. Lord Wynan reluctantly agreed to undergo the analysis.

○

Two days later, the *Gwa-Halia* analysis began in the hushed Octagon after a neuroscientist and four neurotechnicians from the Memory Retrieval Institute on Califra, installed and linked the equipment to the large VisScreen in the Octagon, to view the images recovered during the procedure.

Fariyal sat in the seat within the *Gwa-Halia* chamber. A blinding light flooded the room. The *Gwa-Halia* equipment glowed red and shattered. Fariyal sat, unharmed. Images appeared on the VisScreen.

Lord Wynan is asleep in his cabin on the Mithras Ennab.
The emergency alarm sounds.
Fariyal runs out of her cabin, calling out to him.
Fariyal enters the flight deck and sits on her seat. The control panel is dark. She reaches for a toggle switch above her head.
The on-board computer announces:
> *'Unidentified spacecraft on visual sensor. Unable to identify. Unable to identify planet of origin. Unable to communicate with passengers. Unable to identify weaponry.'*
> *'Why are the screens blank?' Fariyal asks.*
> *'The screens are not blank. The screen is showing the spacecraft.'*
Fariyal frowns. There is no image on the screen. She leaves the flight deck, walking quickly to Lord Wynan's cabin. She wakes him. He tells her to not disturb him.
> *'Wynan, come with me. Something is wrong. We have a problem.'*
> *'Can you not deal with it? The craft is under your command, not mine.'*
Fariyal returns to her seat on the dark flight deck.
Fariyal speaks to the computer.
> *'Give me the speed of spacecraft and directional axis.'*
> *'Spacecraft is stationary.'*
> *'Are we stationary?'*
> *'The data is confusing. Unable to answer.'*

156

'How long for contact?'

'The data is confusing. Unable to answer.'

'Give status.'

'All systems on Mithras Ennab working one hundred percent. Mithras Ennab is combat ready one hundred percent. Defence competence is fifty percent and increasing.

Seventy percent. One hundred percent.'

Lord Wynan joins Fariyal on the flight deck and frowns at her.

'Do what you have to do.'

Fariyal ignores him.

'Increase force field.'

'Confirming Mithras Ennab is one hundred percent defence ready.'

'Why is the battle computer not communicating?'

'Unknown.'

'Why is the navigation computer not responding?'

'Unknown.'

'Orbit the unidentified spacecraft at firing range.'

'Acknowledged.'

'Why are we not seeing the spacecraft on the screen?'

'Unknown.'

'Identify spacecraft from your records.'

'Unable to access records.'

'Open all communication channels. Connect to Saradasi Space Control.'

'Channels opened. Unable to contact Saradasi Space Control.'

'Check function of Keptron.'

'Keptron is inactive for Mithras Ennab.

'How is the Mithras Ennab navigated?'

'It is not.'

'How are you responding to my questions?'

'I am not.'

'Who is?'

'Unknown.'

'Check all your circuits for malfunction. '

'My circuits and all systems on board are one hundred percent functional.'

Lord Wynan looks frightened.

'Fariyal! Quick! Do something.'

'I am checking the systems.'

'You are not quick enough.'

'Go back to your cabin, Wynan.'
'I am your superior officer. I order you to act immediately.'
'I am.'
'Act faster.'
'Do you want to change places with me?'
'No! I order you to sit where you are.'
'You are not helping me.'
'Send an emergency message.'
'I cannot. All systems are non-functional.'

Lord Wynan tries to rise from his seat when the main screen on the flight deck glows.

The face of a female comes into view, her aura increasing. Her voice is gentle, pausing between each word. She speaks in Saradasi.

'Fariyal I want to talk to you. I need your help. I am on an Ashanti-Ishtana craft. We have a dying child who needs urgent medical treatment. I ask your permission to cross the Nereima Galaxy to Res-IV in the Western Galaxy to seek medical attention. You have the authority to give me permission.'

'I deny your request. The Saradasi Empire allows only authorised traffic within its boundaries.

'You are an officer of the Empire. You can give me the authority.'
'I refuse.'
'The child may die. Can I take her to Merr?'
'No. You should have obtained clearance at Space Station ZenFah.'
'You have sophisticated medical apparatus on board and you can ask for medical advice. Can you help us?'

'No. The rules forbid me to help unauthorised craft. I have to obey the laws of the Saradasi Empire. I am sorry about the child. But I must obey the rules of the Empire.'

The female smiles.

'Fariyal, do you remember me? You have not changed. Is the Saradasi Empire above life and goodness? Both you and your Empire must learn the preciousness of life.'

'I am Lord Wynan, the High Chancellor's General, the senior officer on this craft. I order you to leave Saradasi airspace.'

The Mithras Ennab shudders and the interior darkens.

The female says,

'I will try to help you and the Nereima Galaxy. Come with me.'

'Where?'

'Think, Fariyal, think. I have given you a clue.'

A male appears on the screen. He asks them to help save the child.

Lord Wynan shouts,

'The life of a child is not my concern. This is the Mithras Ennab, heavily armed. You are delaying the High Chancellor's General. I will destroy you unless you release us.'

'But how am I delaying you? Please leave.'

'We cannot,' *Wynan yells.*

'Can I help you?'

Lord Wynan leans forward.

'Dare you play with me, a Saradasi General? The High Chancellor's General?'

'Stay Saradasi, rest and learn goodness. My name is Hasiant.'

'Leave immediately. I order you.'

'Remember my name, Saradasi. Remember we are from Ashanti-Ishtana.'

Darkness engulfs the Mithras Ennab. The Mithras Ennab shakes like a small boat in an angry sea.

○

The members of the High Council looked from Fariyal to Wynan, and at Shanaz as she tried to stand, her face moist and pale. The VisScreen was blank and the *Gwa-Halia* apparatus a pile of debris.

'Fariyal, who spoke to you?' Lord Rasalis asked.

'I cannot recall her.'

'She said, *"Fariyal, do you remember me? You have not changed. Is the Saradasi Empire above life and goodness? Both you and your Empire must learn the preciousness of life."'*

Fariyal answered in a whisper. 'I remember her. I met her when I was on Asurat with the Maranti people.'

'And?' Lord Rasalis prompted.

Fariyal hesitated. 'She lost her child and she died because of an experiment.'

'What experiment,' Lord Teras asked.

'I asked her and three other local leaders, the Quartet, to travel on a LAC-NMP.'

'Why,' Lord Teras asked.

'I wanted to frighten them, using hologram. We wanted them to accept total Saradasi rule and not worship spirits.'

'What happened to her?'

'She bled to death after she aborted her foetus. I was sad about what happened but my actions were for the Saradasi Empire.'

'Fariyal,' Shanaz said, frowning. 'What are you talking about? She was speaking to me not to you, and she is *not* a Maranti. She is a Merran, an Elder from the Flowia Valley, on Merr, who asked me to help save a group of lost children.'

'And you refused, did you not?' Lord Zilva asked.

'Yes. She reminded me about the children who died in a flash flood because I refused military assistance to rescue them.'

'Wynan, who was Fariyal talking to?' Lord Rasalis asked.

'I do not know. She was talking to a blank screen.'

'Wynan, who is the male who spoke to you?' Lord Varsana said.

'He is a merchant from Kersia.'

'Kersia? Kersia, where the children died because of the toxin you introduced into the water?'

'Yes. Children and adults died because they rebelled against the Saradasi Empire. Have you forgotten? The High Council ordered me to end the rebellion.'

'Did children and adults rise against us?' Lord Rasalis asked. 'I thought it was the rebels in the mountains.'

'I saw a Saradasi female and male speaking in Saradasi to Fariyal and Wynan, asking for their help,' Lord Varsana said.

The other members of the High Council agreed with Lord Varsana. They too saw the female and male speaking to Fariyal and Wynan asking them to help a dying child. Another deep mystery engulfed the High Council as complex and bewildering and frightening as the disappearance and reappearance of the *Mithras Ennab*.

The High Council did not acquit Lord Wynan and Fariyal of misconduct.

O

The morning after the High Council meeting, Shanaz sat in the north garden of the Octagon watching the surf breaking on the beach in the bay. Sunlight lit the trees, and across the valley, she glimpsed her house alone on the hill. Beyond, on the promontory, among the sand dunes, the small white house of Lord Rasalis shone in the sun.

Plestrach placed a tray of food beside her and sat by her. Shanaz patted his soft hand. 'You may be my only friend,' she said. She bit a piece of fruit and asked, 'Tell me, have the Sound Masters reported on the recording sent them from the *Gwa-Halia* analysis last night?'

'The Grand Master Ashe himself responded. The Sound Masters heard the male speak to Lord Wynan and the female to Fariyal. Both spoke Saradasi fluently but it is not their native language.'

'The members of the High Council who heard them did not say that.'

'They are not a sound master with complex machines,' Plestrach replied. 'The Sound Masters detected a hesitation before certain words both the male and female used, they think due to phonetic unfamiliarity. Both slightly mispronounced two point three seven percent of words. One and a half percent of words showed atypical *intonation*. Zero point seven percent of words were archaic.'

'What did else did the Sound Masters say?'

'They could not hear anyone speaking to you, Shanaz.'

'I cannot understand what is happening. We may all be losing our senses. What did you see and hear?'

'I saw nothing and heard nothing.'

'Why not?' Shanaz asked, sitting up.

'I was asked to leave to retrieve a document from the repository.'

'Who asked you to leave? Let me guess. Lord Rasalis.'

'Yes.'

'Plestrach, what do you think happened in the Octagon? Fariyal saw and heard a Maranti female, and I, a village Elder from the Flowia valley; Wynan a merchant from Kersia, and the others saw Fariyal and Wynan talking to two Saradasi about a child.'

Plestrach tilted his head thoughtfully. 'I think those who set up the *Gwa-Halia* apparatus hypnotized you. Perhaps they hypnotized the others too.'

'Can we view the recording of what happened?'

'No,' Plestrach replied. 'We made one copy, which we sent to the Sound Masters.'

'Who asked you to make a recording?'

'Lord Rasalis. One of his officers from Security, the newly promoted, General Santana, collected the recording last night.'

'Was the recording sent to the Sound Masters on Droha Major or relayed to them?'

'I have no knowledge to answer you.'

Shanaz sipped her drink. 'Security could have relayed anything they wanted to the Sound Masters.'

'Yes.'

Shanaz lay on the grass with her head resting on the trunk of the tree. Plestrach went into the Octagon and brought a cushion which he placed behind her head. Shanaz patted the ground beside her. 'Come and sit near me and let me hear the murmur of your mind, active with good thoughts. What are you thinking of?'

'At this precise instant?

'Yes.'

'The lines from a poem.'

'Have you poems in your memory banks?'

'Yes. Many.'

'Poems from where?'

'Poems from many worlds which Sound Masters collect, if requested.'

'By whom?'

'By those interested in poetry. They store their favourite poem or poems in me.

'Why?'

'For others interested in poetry to listen to.'

'And the poem you thought of?'

My fairest child, I have no song to give you
No lark could pipe to skies so dull and grey:
Yet, ere we part, one lesson I can leave you
For every day.

Be good, sweet maid, and let who will be clever;
Do noble things, not dream them, all day long:
And so make life, death, and that vast forever
One grand, sweet song.

'Thank you, Plestrach. Who read the poem for you to record?

'I am not programmed to provide an answer,' he replied.

When Plestrach left, Shanaz thought of Sirglin, the small village on Califra. Soft colours, sweet scents, the rustle of autumn leaves. Peace. Contentment. This was where she wanted to live.

She remembered the valley below, tight within blue-green hills, and beyond, the seven mountain ranges. She heard the music of the blue river in the valley, the sand by the river silky to touch. She saw the house and the garden. She imagined strolling from the green roofed house through the garden crowded with bright flowers to the curvy path passing the cluster of open-air market stalls. She saw baskets piled with fresh vegetables and ripe fruit, dew clinging to them, and smelt food cooking on braziers and the perfume of fresh flowers. Happy voices rang in her ears. The voice of the blind singer, who never begged, haunted her, singing she had more than she needed. Beside her, a basket made of woven leaves sat proudly laden with fruit from her tiny garden. But not for sale. They were gifts for passers-by.

She was walking past the stables hugging the head of her favourite animal and murmuring, 'You are so beautiful and I love you.' The orchard stretched from the small grey stone meeting hall, past the funny looking tree beside a stream feeding the orchard. Here, in the orchard, in the golden evening sun, when the gentle west wind blew, the drooping leaves of the trees in shades of red, yellow and orange danced a lively arabesque.

There in Sirglin she planned to live the rest of her life. Not in years to come but in a few months. She turned her head. A tall figure left from a side door of the Octagon. Lord Wynan did not see her. In three months and four days she planned to live with him in the green roofed house in Sirglin. She watched Wynan and thought of how her love for him grew after her accident which could not recall.

She remembered a song of hopeless loneliness as she turned and saw the bay shrouded in mist. She wiped her eyes and looked again; the bay shone blue, clear and serene.

FIFTEEN

On Saradas, the days were long and sombre. The Saradasi nation felt threatened and fearful, their vulnerability exposed, their security challenged and their invincibility shattered. The High Council broadcast the *Gwa-Halia* analysis to retrieve Fariyal and Lord Wynan's memory of what occurred on the *Mithras Ennab*, throughout the home planet.

Saradasi asked, 'Where is Ashanti-Ishtana?' No one knew of such a place. But to many, of greater concern and interest, were the female and male on the Ashanti-Ishtana craft.

'The female and male Lord Wynan and Fariyal spoke with are Saradasi,' people said.

'Note,' others remarked, 'they spoke fluent, Saradasi, like any one of us. Who are they?'

The High Council ordered Lord Wynan to a Military Base on the Metros Archipelago in the desolate northeast of Saradasi, commissioning him to prepare a report on Saradasi living in two isolated settlements. He would no longer use the *Mithras Ennab* but travel on the *Fayon,* which Saradasi Space Control secretly modified.

The High Council placed Fariyal on a month's 'illness vacation,' in a 'loving, sympathetic environment'. The best location is Saradas they said, and she must not leave the Lower City. Three military physicians would check her progress thrice a day.

O

At an urgently convened High Council meeting, Shanaz told the members, 'Lord Rasalis has asked me to call you here tonight to discuss *The Prophecy* and *The Place* which we know about. As High Chancellor I am committed to saving the Nereima Galaxy. I believe in *The Prophecy* and the existence of *The Place* where the evil Prince Vira's team awaits Lord Gaima's team of five Saradasi.'

Shanaz continued, 'I want to show you a message my father left me, which Lord Rasalis gave me this morning. Please look at the VisScreen.'

They saw the solemn face of Lord Laramis who said, 'I am not aware who the new High Chancellor of the Saradasi Empire will be when you see and hear me speaking to you. It may be my daughter, Shanaz. This message is to tell you I am convinced *The Prophecy* is true. Please support your High Chancellor and Lord Rasalis.'

Lord Rasalis reminded them of *The Prophecy* and told them what Sound Master Glance heard on the *Wave*: "Your game, Brother Red". He said, 'I have with me two sentences from our archives about *The Prophecy*. "*Prepare for your journey. The Astral Lord of the East may, if he so wishes, help you reach your destination*".'

'Who wrote what you read?' Shanaz asked.

'That information is not known. This is a journey of faith, in faith,' Lord Rasalis said. ' We have no personal knowledge of Astral Lords. We must seek *The Place* in faith and I seek your approval to assemble Lord Gaima's team at the location mentioned in the archives. I cannot yet reveal the names of the five Saradasi on the team, to protect them. They are listed in the archives. I also ask permission for two non-Saradasi to help them.'

In a vote taken in secret, the High Council affirmed their belief in *The Prophecy,* and their unanimous support and confidence in Lord Rasalis and his plans to seek *The Place.*

◯

In the Upper City in her home, Shanaz slept while a gale blew. Yorens Wer shook her awake.

'Wake up,' she said shaking her arm. 'Shanaz, why are the windows open? Did you not hear the gale?'

'No, I fell asleep.'

'I have brought food for us,' she said arranging four dishes on a table.

'I am not hungry.'

'You must eat. Listen to what I say, Shanaz.'

'You enjoy ordering me like your slave,' Shanaz said, sitting up in bed.

'Shanaz, you must not eat in bed. Beds are to sleep on, not eat in. Sit at the table like I have taught you.'

'Must I? When I wake up at night I can find some food on the bed if I am hungry,' she laughed.

Yorens Wer helped her out of bed and they sat across each other at the table. 'Shanaz, you are the same troublesome child who has harassed me since you were two years old.'

Shanaz reached out and touched her cheek. 'Only Fariyal and you care about me.'

'Others do too.'

'No.'

'Shanaz, I have two messages for you from Lord Rasalis. He did not want to disturb you. He located Seelawathie-Ap at Space Station ZenFah.'

'He told me for months he could not find her. Why was she at ZenFah?'

'Perhaps Lord Rasalis sent her there as a punishment.'

'And pretended he did not know where she was. If he punished her, he was unjust,' Shanaz said. 'I visited her when she was recovering after Rensoolar Phage 67 tried to kill me, and slit her throat. She and I went to another geographical location. That is all.'

'That is all?' Yorens Wer said sharply. 'Shanaz, Seelawathie-Ap and you disappeared, and neither you nor she, or we know where you went.

'We may have been in another universe.'

'Both of you were nearly killed by aliens. That is why Lord Rasalis punished Seelawathie-Ap. But he may have also protected her by keeping her at ZenFah because he knows she has special powers which may help find *The Place*.'

'Is Seelawathie-Ap travelling with Lord Gaima's team?'

'I did not ask him, and he said nothing. I am sure he has a plan how to use her.'

'The second message is, the journey to find *The Place* has begun. Lord Rasalis has arranged for you to travel in an Interceptor to Military Base Xzania.'

'Am I on the team? Me? Are you sure? Yorens, I do not have enough goodness to be on Lord Gaima's team. It is a mistake.'

'You are on the team, Shanaz, and that is what is written in the archives.'

'I never thought I would be on the team. Perhaps I will become a better person before we find *The Place*. Who else is on the team?'

'Lord Rasalis did not tell me.'

'I am looking forward to this journey,' Shanaz said. 'And I am happy I will not see Wynan, because I hate him. I will not see Medaris either.'

'Medaris?'

'Yes, Medaris. Because he hates me.'

'Medaris hates you? He would not hate anybody. Why do you think he hates you?'

'It's the way he looks at me.'

'How does he look at you?'

'He ignores me because he hates me.'

'Shanaz, be sensible.'

'I am.'

Shanaz pushed aside her plate and packed a few clothes into her military issue backpack. She wore her firing-belt and slipped on her force-sword, tightening the belt.

'Shanaz, we must leave now for the Lower City.'

Shanaz walked to the transparent wall, looking at the Mirellar Mountains. Yorens Wer joined her.

'What is it?' Shanaz asked her voice uncertain.

'Shanaz, remember we care about you. I, more than most. I want you to think before you act, and try not to be impulsive. You should not trust everyone you meet. Look after yourself. The fate of the Nereima Galaxy depends on you and how well you lead the others. Come back home safely, Shanaz.'

The wind lashed at them when they left the house and walked along a narrow lane at the bottom of the hill into a derelict building covered by a flowering vine, with parts of the roof caved in. They stepped over fallen tiles and decaying wooden beams on the floor to reach a rectangular stone platform at the far end, merging with the colour of the floor and the walls.

Shanaz and Yorens Wer stood on the platform, facing the wall. When they raised the palms of their hands, four beams of light criss-crossed their bodies and the stone platform descended and stopped smoothly. They were in the Lower City.

Yorens Wer blinked in the brightness and muttered, 'I am glad I am not living here.' They crossed a busy pedestrian mall, a flock of artificial clouds scudding across the artificial sky, blue, with patches of red changing to shades of pink.

'Clever,' Yorens Wer said, looking at the sky. 'It even snows sometimes. Is that good?' she demanded.

'It breaks the monotony,' Shanaz said.

'I think they are mad to live here.'

'They think we are mad to live in the abandoned Upper City,' Shanaz said hailing a Disker. They climbed on the flat oval vehicle for four passengers. Shanaz entered the co-ordinates of Space Field 16 and they sped past tall buildings and residential barracks set in lush parklands. They alighted at Space Field 16 and passed through the scan gate into the Operations Centre.

The officer on duty read the screen in front of him. 'Your craft is the *Serandia*. Leave when you are ready.'

Shanaz hugged Yorens Wer and left the Operations Centre, hurrying through a winding corridor to Launch Site 13. The *Serandia,* a silver white Interceptor, gleamed on Pad 1. Shanaz ran back, calling out to Yorens Wer.

'Can you come with me?'

'No, Shanaz, this is not my destiny. The journey is yours.'

In the Operations Centre the duty officer gazed at Shanaz on his VisScreen when she sat in the flight deck of the *Serandia*.

'She is beautiful,' he said.

'She is a beautiful person,' Yorens Wer answered. 'She looks arrogant but she is not, and never admits to being beautiful. If someone says she is beautiful, she replies, "Have you seen my cousin, Fariyal? She is beautiful. I am not." She has also great inner beauty and goodness which she must show others.'

They watched the *Serandia* accelerate from the pad, reach the surface of the planet and rise into the clouds.

The duty officer spoke into his wristband. 'She has left, General.' He looked towards the door and said. 'Battle Commander Zantaq, Deputy Controller Operations of Saradasi Space Control, has joined us.'

Battle Commander Zantaq walked in and sat next to Yorens Wer facing the VisScreen. General Santana came on the screen. 'Zantaq, greetings. Copy our conversation to all Saradasi officers, general and above. Keep the channels open with each Army Commander.'

Battle Commander Zantaq bent over his wristband. 'Sir, please confirm the orders we have received. Saradasi Space Control will navigate the *Serandia* until it reaches Military Base Xzania.'

'Battle Commander Zantaq, I confirm the order verbally.'

'Saradasi Space Control will allow craft belonging to the Droha Major Sound Masters to travel within the Nereima Galaxy after authorisation from us and from you personally. The exception to this order is the *Wave* with Master Glance, his son Breve and the priest Midi78.'

'I confirm the order verbally.'

'Sir, all other craft, including Saradasi craft piloted by Saradasi military officers, will not travel within the Nereima Galaxy except on your orders.'

'I confirm the order verbally.'

General Santana's image on the screen faded.

Yorens Wer asked, 'Who is looking after Shanaz? Is the security sufficient?'

'I do not know. Lord Rasalis is responsible for her safety,' Battle Commander Zantaq said looking at the blank VisScreen.

O

In the Lower City, Lord Rasalis watched the VisScreen covering a wall in the command room in the Military Security Complex with the officers he selected to help in the battle for the Nereima Galaxy. He paced the floor and stopped in front of General Santana. 'Santana, be certain to divide the personnel we selected from VIII Army into two groups. Select an intermediary to communicate with each group. I want one group placed at a secret location but not on Saradasi. You must inform the intermediary where they are, no one else. The other group will remain here.' Lord Rasalis looked at the tired anxious faces. 'Santana, why are you gloomy?'

'Are we relying too much on the Droha Major sound master, Glance, the Suxt-Sux actor, Faris, his Great Khan and the Gootamundra priest, Midi 78, to win the battle?'

'And Seelawathie-Ap,' General Aricent added.

'Perhaps,' Lord Rasalis answered. 'But we need them all.'

They sat silently. Colonel Wereset, recently promoted, cleared her throat and coughed.

'Speak Wereset, without an introductory cacophony,' Lord Rasalis said, continuing to pace the room. 'Wereset, we need some humour to cheer us!'

General Santana groaned.

Colonel Wereset coughed again. Lord Rasalis stopped pacing and peered at her. 'You smile, Wereset?'

'Yes, Lord. I recall a joke a traveller told me.'

'Tell us,' Lord Rasalis said.

After the joke, when the laughter died, Lord Rasalis sat heavily and said, 'These are my orders, which I know you will obey. You must not compromise or seek alternatives to these orders, or obey anyone revoking these orders. Protect and watch the *Serandia* with Shanaz until it reaches Military Outpost Xzania. Another team member will meet her at there when she arrives. I have arranged this. One of you will receive instructions tomorrow morning to ask a third team member to travel on the *Mithras Ennab* to Military Outpost Xzania.'

'Are you on the team?' Wereset asked.

'Be patient. From Military Outpost Xzania the three team members will all travel on the *Mithras Ennab* to Samandrath-Bahar-Tekaya. One team member has the co-ordinates. This is where the journey begins to find *The Place*.'

'Are you on the team?' Wereset asked.

'Because we must not all travel together I will travel first to Space Station ZenFah and on to Samandrath-Bahar-Tekaya. I have arranged for this. We leave tonight.'

'We?'

'With Sirrah, Wereset. Though he lives here, remember he is not a Saradasi and he is the second non-Saradasi who will travel with the five Saradasi team members. No more questions please.'

'How will you and Sirrah go to Samandrath-Bahar-Tekaya from Space Station ZenFah?' Wereset asked.

'Who has another question?' Lord Rasalis looked round the room, poured himself a drink and paced the room again. 'In two days, signal the Great Khan on Asurat. The actors must travel speedily to their assigned locations. Guard the *Wave* with particular care.'

'We will,' General Aricent answered. He went to the wall screen showing a space map of the Nereima Galaxy. 'Lord, you told us Samandrath-Bahar-Tekaya is where the Saradasi team will start their journey to search for *The Place*. Samandrath-Bahar-Tekaya is not on our map. How will the three team members reach a location not on a map, from Military Outpost Xzania and how will you reach this place?'

'I cannot tell you all I know, because it may risk your lives,' Lord Rasalis said. 'I have learned from the archives how to reach there.'

The room was silent.

'I have another important question,' Wereset said. 'When you reach Samandrath-Bahar-Tekaya, how will you find *The Place*? Who will give you the directions? Master Glance has not yet found it.'

Lord Rasalis looked at the officers seated in front of him. 'I have knowledge I cannot share with you. My source is our archives written over two and a half thousand years ago, which only I, as Chancellor of Security, can access. Saradasi law stipulates even the High Chancellor of the Empire cannot not access these archives. When we reach Samandrath-Bahar-Tekaya, I am sure we will know our next destination on our journey. The archives also contain details on the past, the present and the future of every Saradasi. What is interesting is the archives say nothing on the future of any of us alive today. We know our past but not our future. The archives end abruptly.'

'Are we living on borrowed time, Lord?' Wereset wondered aloud. 'We may not win the battle to save the Nereima Galaxy.'

'Perhaps. *The Prophecy* says Lord Gaima's team will triumph if all five Saradasi have enough goodness. When you learn who Lord Gaima's team members are, you will ask, as I have, why these Saradasi? Why them?'

'Have you an answer, Lord?' she asked.

'I am not sure. They can all influence the destiny of the Saradasi Empire and therefore the Nereima Galaxy. Some in the team have no regard for life.'

'But not you, Lord,' General Santana said.

Lord Rasalis sat wearily. 'I may not return. If Sirrah returns home you must befriend him. You know his parents died saving my life on Merr. My debt is yet unpaid.'

'We will, Lord,' General Aricent said.

'Where is Lord Medaris?' General Santana asked.

'Medaris is busy helping us.'

An aide walked in and spoke to General Santana.

'Lord,' Santana said, 'Saradasi Space Control reports a serious security violation.'

'By Wynan?' Lord Rasalis asked.

'Yes. Lord Wynan's ship, the *Fayon,* is travelling at a dangerous speed away from Saradasi. The Space Control master computer Keptron cannot control the *Fayon.*'

'Order an urgent Empire-wide general alert.'

Lord Rasalis left the room with quick strides, smiling.

SIXTEEN

Lord Rasalis left Space Station ZenFah as an itinerant merchant with Sirrah as his assistant, for Wiox in the blue galaxy. Here they joined a group of livestock merchants on the aged *Magnificent,* its hull undergoing repairs even as they boarded.

On board, while resting in his cabin, Lord Rasalis recalled he heard the name Samandrath-Bahar-Tekaya before he learned of it in the archives. It was Wynan who mentioned the name. During a conversation about an officer he accused of not helping him, Wynan said, 'I should banish him to Samandrath-Bahar-Tekaya.'

Before he asked Wynan, 'Where is Samandrath-Bahar-Tekaya?' Wynan's adjutant interrupted them. He wondered if Wynan left with unnecessary haste. How did Wynan learn of Samandrath-Bahar-Tekaya? Had he accessed the archives illegally? If so, for what reason?

Captain Magarata and his elderly mistress, Sacriata, owned the *Magnificent.* On the first evening on board, Lord Rasalis pushed his way into the dining room and sat next to the melancholy looking Magarata, gesturing to Sirrah to sit opposite them. He watched Magarata's sobriety decrease as he ate the bright green substance on the plate in front of him and the pupils of his violet eyes dilate. He kicked Sirrah under the table, motioning to the liquor counter. Sirrah brought a decanter of wine and two glasses, which he placed on the table. Lord Rasalis pushed a glass towards Magarata and filled it.

Captain Magarata mumbled his thanks, moving aside the empty plate with a film of green on it. He drained his glass and reached for the decanter, muttering 'Thank you' to Sirrah.

'It is a pleasure to meet you, dear Captain. Delighted,' Lord Rasalis gushed, pushing the decanter closer to Captain Magarata. 'Captain, are you familiar with a game called "last man standing"?'

'No.'

'Excellent. Excellent,' Lord Rasalis said refilling Magarata's glass. 'Have you ever been to Samandrath-Bahar-Tekaya?'

'No. And I don't want to either. I have not heard of it,' Magarata said, slurring his words. 'What was it called?'

'Samandrath-Bahar-Tekaya.'

'I despise long names. I can never remember them and that is why I call myself Magarata.' He belched, and gulped more wine.

'I agree with you. It is a long name, Samandrath-Bahar-Tekaya, but it has a musical ring to it. Are we travelling close to it?' Rasalis leaned across to Sirrah, lowering his voice, and pointed to a screen at the far end of the dining room. 'Go and check our flight path on the space screen. See if Samandrath-Bahar-Tekaya is on the space map. You must not ask anyone about it. And, Sirrah, avoid endless chatter when you meet others. It wastes time and time is of the essence.'

'Lord, have we met Captain Magarata before?' Sirrah whispered. 'I think I have seen him somewhere.'

'Please, Sirrah, spare me your hallucinatory misadventures. I will think and you will act. Why are you wasting my time? Be gone!'

Lord Rasalis poured more wine for Magarata, and watched Sirrah make his way through the crowded dining room to examine the screen. When he rejoined them, Sirrah whispered, 'It is not on the map.'

'Interesting. But the archives are never wrong.' He nudged Sirrah, who filled Magarata's glass. The captain drained the glass and tried to rise to his feet. He rose with Sirrah's help, and staggered out of the dining room.

They left the table and hurried to the space map. Lord Rasalis peered at the screen. 'Sirrah, the archives are never wrong. Based on the co-ordinates I have, we are near our destination. It is fortunate, Sirrah, one of us is clear where we are going and how to get there. We must arrange to land there.'

'How?'

'How?' Lord Rasalis barked. 'Because I have the co-ordinates. Sirrah let me think and plan for both of us. Follow me.'

Lord Rasalis left the dining room pulling Sirrah by his arm. They reached the flight deck where the young Nebruscan assistant to the captain sat with Captain Magarata's elderly mistress, Sacriata, the ship's purser, twice his size, on his lap.

'I am looking for our captain. Where is he?' Lord Rasalis asked anxiously.

'He is in his cabin where I just left him,' Sacriata giggled making herself more comfortable. 'He is unconscious on his bed,' she said, winking at Lord Rasalis.

'I am so sorry,' Lord Rasalis said. 'Will he be unwell for long?'

'He may die, I hope,' Sacriata said, between nibbling the assistant to the captain's small pink ear. 'I am sure,' she said winking again at Lord Rasalis, 'we have time to conduct whatever business you have, without haste.'

'Excellent, excellent, dear Sacriata. It is a joy to see you again. We meet too infrequently. Thank you for your help, dear one. Neither I nor Saradasi Security forget our friends who help us.'

'Nor I, my Lord. Please contact the Great Khan of Asurat and he will find me. I may not be long on this wretched ship,' Sacriata said.

'I am sure greater challenges await you.' Lord Rasalis bent towards the assistant. 'You may be able to help me too,' he said. 'I will give you a set of coordinates. Please accept these Saradasi solars which are too heavy for me to carry.' He dropped a purse into Sacriata's plump hand.

'What are these coordinates for?' the assistant asked.

'To land the *Magnificent* immediately.'

Sacriata peered into the bag. 'Land the ship, you fool,' she snapped.

The *Magnificent* landed with a shudder minutes later. Lord Rasalis pushed Sirrah out of the hatch and followed him. The *Magnificent* rose with a wail.

Lord Rasalis flapped his hand at swarms of flies, after sitting on a rock with the hot sun overhead, looking at the reddish parched soil stretching to the blurred horizon. A few hundred yards away, a grove of scraggly trees drooped at the foot of a naked hill. Directly opposite, a huge triangular platform stood several feet above the ground. By the platform, six legged animals in round pens chewed their fodder, and dozen tall, lean males with matted blond hair squatted on their haunches, their clothes torn and stained with mud. A group of barefooted children walked by the platform, looking at it.

Lord Rasalis and Sirrah walked up to two females behind a wooden table in the shadow of the platform, selling food. They looked at the gleaming solars Lord Rasalis offered, laughed and served another customer who gave them a handful of coins.

'Glass. They are glass coins,' Sirrah exclaimed.

'Thank you for pointing that out, Sirrah. Why do they want glass instead of my precious solars?'

'Glass may be more valuable here than metal.'

'Try not to prattle on, Sirrah. Follow me.' Beckoning Sirrah, Lord Rasalis trudged to the hill, and the shade of the spindly trees. Here in a space between large rocks they erected their two tents and sat looking at the barren landscape.

On Samandrath-Bahar-Tekaya the temperature rose every day. Lord Rasalis and Sirrah realised they left Saradasi ill prepared, their food supplies inadequate, their currency valueless. On the morning of the fourth day Sirrah volunteered to follow a well-worn path from the triangular platform, which they thought might lead to a village.

After Sirrah left, Lord Rasalis sat on his favourite flat rock early in the afternoon, the sun burning down on him. He decided to enter his tent when he sensed the presence of someone behind him. Staring at the hill with exaggerated interest, he listened closely. He drew his force-sword and leaped off the rock. Though falling on the ground he thrust the force-sword at the intruder.

A barefooted young child, in a soiled yellow smock was looking at him. The child spoke in the melodious tonal language they heard near the platform. He beamed at the child who squatted on the ground with a long animal curled on his lap, and entered Sirrah's tent.

He returned and said, 'This is for you, from me, Lord Rasalis,' pointing to himself, offering the child a piece of dried fruit.

The child replied in his musical language when he accepted the fruit and fed it to his pet. He withdrew his hand from a deep pocket and opened his fist with a glass coin. Smiling at the child, Lord Rasalis tried reaching Saradasi once more, through the communicator on his wrist-band, hoping to relay what the child said to the Saradasi Military Language Institute, for ethno-linguists to analyse. Frustrated, he sat with the child pointing to various objects near him, naming them in Saradasi. The child repeated the Saradasi words carefully and re-named each object in his own language.

At dusk, a bell tolled. The child gathered his pet in his arms, spoke to Lord Rasalis and left. The next day he returned with a younger child. The language lessons continued. When the bell tolled in the evening, and the two children prepared to leave, he patted their heads giving each a piece of Sirrah's fruit. He watched them walk away past the hill and sat on his favourite rock.

A gust of dust-laden wind woke him. Sirrah was squatting on the ground preparing their evening meal. He called out cheerfully, 'Greetings, Lord.'

'Where were you? Who fed you? How did you survive?'

'The people in the village I went to were kind and hospitable. They wanted nothing from me.'

'Ha! Except your company?'

'Yes. Their language is difficult to learn. I tried, but it was too complex.'

'Honesty is an admirable trait, Sirrah. I admire you for recognising your limits. I have captivated two children who visit me and will return to enjoy my company. I am teaching them Saradasi. We shall both learn their language from them. With my help you will find the task much easier. Sirrah, dull minds need a nimble minded, gifted teacher such as I.'

The next day each child came carrying a sack, the six footed animal trotting ahead of them. They sang their greeting and sat, laying out the contents of the sacks in neat rows. They pointed to each object, naming it. Lord Rasalis clapped his hands, patted their heads and named the objects in their language and in Saradasi. The children repeated the same procedure with Sirrah.

'How generous they are to teach you, Sirrah. Your attempts at repeating what they are teaching you grate my ears. It is a cacophonous assault on my ears. But no matter, they will soon realize which of us to concentrate on. Sirrah, good teachers recognise good pupils.'

○

Another day passed. Where, Lord Rasalis wondered, was the *Mithras Ennab,* and the *Fayon* with Wynan? Though concerned he did not share his anxieties with Sirrah. The language lessons continued with the children who were exacting and demanding teachers. They brought a basket of fresh fruit from the village on each visit.

'I am a vegetarian, Sirrah. I know you crave for meat with the blood running down your face when you eat,' Lord Rasalis said enjoying the fruit.

'I am not a meat eater. I have been a vegetarian all my life and you know it.'

'You are vegetarian because of my influence, Sirrah. Although you dislike eating fruits, say nothing to the children. You must not offend them. I am happy to have the fruit.'

'You are very kind. I enjoy fruit,' Sirrah said.

'Perhaps not these fruits?' Lord Rasalis suggested.

'Especially these.'

The next day, at noon, the children arrived with fruit, and a bundle of twigs. Using the twigs, they laid out a large figure on the ground. The children pointed to it, repeating, 'Thwacker.'

'What is it?' Lord Rasalis asked Sirrah.

'I think it is a strange looking building, but I am confused.'

'Be patient, Sirrah. Too much sugar from eating the fruit has made you impatient,' Lord Rasalis said, helping himself to more fruit. 'Try to rest your stomach, Sirrah. A rested stomach leads to a restful brain.'

At sunrise the following morning the children woke Lord Rasalis and Sirrah, inviting them to go with them to their village. By late morning they reached the village with rows of houses with coloured conical roofs. At the centre of the village they peered into one of the deep wells. A bucket made of animal hide tied to a rope dangled from a wooden pulley on a crossbeam held by two stout poles on either side of the well.

'Be alert, Sirrah,' Lord Rasalis cautioned.

The children led them to the plantations of trees on the outskirts of the village. A trench brimming with water surrounded each tree. Two to three adults were beneath a tree. In one hand they held a long pole with large basket attached to one end and in the other grasped a similar pole with an angled blade at its tip. They cut the blue fruits at the stem, collecting them in their baskets. Occasionally, when a blue fruit fell into the water, it erupted in flames, with a plume of water spurting above the trees.

'We are seeing energy from a reaction between the fruits and water. How can this happen? Are they harnessing and storing the energy?' Lord Rasalis asked Sirrah. He wondered why the children asked them to visit the village. The villagers were neither friendly nor hostile. None except the two children spoke to them.

Later in the evening they sat outside their tents by the hill beside the grove of trees.

'Strange people,' Rasalis remarked.

'The visit did not help to improve our language skills. Why did the children want us to visit the village?' Sirrah asked.

'Perhaps for us to see what happens when the blue fruits react with water,' Rasalis suggested.

'But for what purpose?

'We will soon find out.'

At dawn the next morning, Lord Rasalis awoke to the sound of the two children and Sirrah having a lesson. He came out of the tent to join them.

'We have decided to tell you our names,' the first child who visited him said in fluent Saradasi. 'My name is Absalamara. My friend's name is Dalanagarda.'

'You look concerned,' the younger child said pointing a finger at Lord Rasalis, 'because our names are difficult for you to pronounce and remember. Our village committee has not given us names to please strangers. It is possible that the part of your brain which captures and retains new knowledge is poorly developed. You may therefore call me Absal and my friend, Dala.'

'You are rude,' Lord Rasalis said.

'I am truthful.'

Dala intervened. 'Please understand. Here, we say what we think. This habit of ours must not make you angry.'

The children strolled, singing together, towards the triangular platform below the hill.

'These children are clever to speak Saradasi so well, so quickly,' Sirrah said to Lord Rasalis, mopping the perspiration from his face.

'It is my teaching technique, Sirrah. But they are rude and disrespectful.'

Sirrah pointed to the figure in on the ground near them. 'While you were asleep, the children insisted the Thwacker is a vehicle. They said the blue fruits we saw in the village and the faeces of the six legged animals like Absal's pet, provides the energy for the Thwacker to travel. They say the Thwacker flies high above the ground.'

'Nonsense. It has no aeronautical features,' Lord Rasalis said looking at the figure on the ground. 'How can it fly?'

'I am telling you what they said.'

'They jest with you, Sirrah, but will not with me. They tease you because they know you are gullible.' He wagged a finger at Sirrah. 'You can solve the energy problems on the Sound Masters' planet, Droha Major by mixing the blue fruits with the faeces of the animals.'

'Lord, the Saradasi Empire will not want the Sound Masters to have a source of energy and not be dependant on the Empire'

'I agree with you, Sirrah,' Lord Rasalis said. 'Depending on anyone for anything lessens self-worth.'

'Lord, can the Empire change? Will it change?'

'We must be patient, Sirrah. On another matter, what, in your opinion, is the most intelligent act I have ever performed, which gives me great joy, day after day?'

'I cannot think of such an act.'

'You insensitive, ungrateful villain!'

'You saved me from the Terumana, and adopted me and persuaded the High Council, for the first time in the history of the Empire, to make me a Saradasi citizen. I am grateful for all this.'

'No, I am grateful to you, Sirrah. All my friends and I admire you. Sirrah, why am I saying all this? The heat has affected me. Perhaps my end is near. Death is near, stalking me.'

When the children ran into the camp the following morning Lord Rasalis greeted them and drew Absal aside, out of earshot of his friend, Dala. 'Come, dear child, let us sit together on this rock. We have much to talk about. Tell me, dear child, how does the Thwacker fly?'

'We have told Sirrah how it flies.'

'Yes, of course you did, but because Sirrah often becomes confused, I want to hear it myself from you.'

Absal looked solemnly at Lord Rasalis and replied, 'You must first tell me what Sirrah told you. I will tell you if it is correct.'

'Sirrah said the animal's faeces and the blue fruits power the Thwacker.'

'Are you telling me the truth?' Absal asked. 'Why did Sirrah tell you the smelly waste of these little Blombers and the fruit power the Thwacker?'

'Because that is what he said you told him.'

'Why must you believe what Sirrah said?'

'No. I did not believe him,' Lord Rasalis said. 'I do not believe you either dear Absal.

'You have made a good decision today, but not for tomorrow,' Absal said.

He looked at Absal, the pieces of a puzzle he could not put together swirling in his mind. He thanked Absal and went for a walk, grumbling about the heat.

Later in the day when the children left for their village he walked with them for a short distance.

'Dear children,' he said. 'I have a question. Dala, do you tell lies sometimes?'

'No,' Dala said.

'Good.'

'Absal, do you tell lies sometimes?'

Absal and Dala giggled. Lord Rasalis raised his eyebrows.

'We never tell the truth,' Absal said.

'Why, dear children? '

'For fun,' they chorused.

'Tomorrow your world will change. Be prepared,' Absal warned, grinning.

'It is a lie,' Dala said.

'No, it is the truth. Your world will never be the same, nor will you,' Absal insisted running towards the village, laughing.

SEVENTEEN

At dawn Absal and Dala ran into the campsite. 'The Thwacker is here,' they screamed, clapping their hands. Lord Rasalis and Sirrah came out of their tents. In the distance Absal and Dala were running towards the triangular platform. They followed the children and joined a jostling crowd near the platform, with hundreds of others running towards them. High above them a massive object loomed in the sky descending on to the platform.

'The Thwacker has arrived,' people in the crowd said reverently, the air heavy with excitement.

Lord Rasalis and Sirrah arched their necks to gaze at the Thwacker, identical to the figure the children made with the twigs. When it settled on the platform, Sirrah estimated its length as four hundred and sixty feet long and three hundred feet wide. There were two small entrances on each side, and a large transparent bubble sat at the top enclosed by a gold coloured railing. A slender gangway reached from one of the two closed entrances to the platform.

'This vehicle has no obvious means of propulsion,' Sirrah said

'I am puzzled too,' Lord Rasalis said touching the smooth surface of the Thwacker extending beyond the platform.

'Lord, this wooden platform is not strong. How is it supporting the weight of this enormous craft?'

'I am puzzled,' Lord Rasalis repeated. 'Perhaps it is not heavy.'

The adults swarming around the Thwacker lifted their arms above their head and raised their voices in song. The singing stopped when some in the crowd pointed to the sky. The silver coloured disc turned green and descended vertically, settling on the ground several hundred yards from the Thwacker near two trees.

The crowd hung back. The single door of the spacecraft slid open. Seelawathie-Ap stood at the entrance of the *Mithras Ennab,* her feet apart, her arms hanging loosely at her sides. She adjusted the scabbard on her back and the hilt of her *kaduwa* shone in the sun. She swung her eyes over the silent crowd, not wasting a glance, and stepping out onto the grass, strode by the edge of the crowd, randomly glaring at people, who shrank back. She greeted Lord Rasalis and Sirrah and walked with them to the *Mithras Ennab*. Shanaz alighted followed by Fariyal and Medaris. Ignoring Lord Rasalis and Sirrah, Shanaz walked towards the Thwacker.

'Greetings,' Lord Rasalis said to Fariyal and Medaris. 'Have you news of Wynan?'

'No. Is he on the team?' Fariyal asked.

'Yes. Wynan was travelling on the *Fayon* and he should have been here. I am very concerned he is not.'

'I am sure he will arrive soon,' Fariyal said. 'Is this where the journey to find *The Place* begins?'

'Yes. We are at Samandrath-Bahar-Tekaya. This is where the archives say our journey starts.'

'Where have you and Sirrah travelled from?'

'Fariyal, it is a long story, for another time.'

'What is this?' Fariyal said, pointing to the Thwacker.

'Two children we met call it the Thwacker and say it flies. It is a mystery, but I am sure we will learn what it is.'

Shanaz joined them with Seelawathie-Ap.

Lord Rasalis greeted her and said, 'Shanaz, the archives named Wynan as a team member. I am surprised he is not here. I spoke to him before I left and told him about *The Prophecy* and *The Place* and why he must join us. Have you news of him?'

'No. I am not clairvoyant.'

'I am certain he will be here,' Fariyal said.

'If he has not fled the Empire,' Shanaz said. Adding under her breath, 'but you are here Fariyal, and he may not leave without you.'

They watched Seelawathie-Ap mingle with the crowd, and hurry back. 'Some people can speak Saradasi,' she said.

'Lord, when we arrived here on the *Magnificent* we were not able to speak to the people here, nor at the village,' Sirrah said. 'Have the children taught a few people Saradasi?'

'I am confused,' Lord Rasalis said. 'Call the children, Sirrah.'

Sirrah brought Dala and Absal who were standing nearby, watching them, and introduced them. Shanaz ignored the boys when they smiled at her.

'Greetings visitors,' Dala said. 'We can speak your language but you cannot speak ours. Are you surprised some people speak Saradasi? We taught them after we learned your simple language in two days from your friends.' He pointed to Lord Rasalis and Sirrah.

Dala left the group and returned with a child younger than him, wearing a soiled, frayed dress. She fixed her large eyes on Lord Rasalis who patted her on her head.

'These people are unhygienic,' Shanaz remarked.

'My name is Yomaira,' she said in Saradasi. She pointed to Lord Rasalis. 'I think you are a good person. Is Sirrah your son? We know you love Sirrah, though you tease him.' She turned to Shanaz. 'When I smile at you, smile back at me. In this place, we are polite. Have you come to learn how to behave well?'

'You talk too much,' Shanaz said. 'I hate children. And I dislike you because you are filthy and you smell and you are rude. I will not listen to you.'

'Soon there will be more water because the Thwacker is here,' Yomaira said. 'We are dirty because we have very little water in our village well. Each day we collect our ration of water, but many of us share our ration with those who need more water.'

'It is stupid to share the water,' Shanaz said.

'No. It is not stupid,' Yomaira said. 'The law states each villager gets an equal share of water. But some need more, for example, mothers who breast feed their babies.'

Fariyal leaned across to Sirrah, 'Sirrah, these children speak like adults. How can they speak Saradasi so fluently? How have they learned our language so quickly?'

'Everything is strange here,' Sirrah replied. 'Nothing is what it seems.'

'Your law about water is a stupid law,' Shanaz said, her green eyes hardening.

'It is not a stupid law.'

'It is extremely stupid,' Shanaz said shaking a finger at Yomaira, 'because those who need more water should receive more water. If some need more, there should not be a law that each villager receives the same quantity. Villagers who need more water must receive more water. Others need not share their ration. It is an easy problem to solve if you are intelligent'

'But who will give them more?'

'The person who gives out the water.'

'No one gives out water. Each person, except young children, the old and the sick, draws the same amount of water from the well.'

'The village should appoint someone to draw the water and give out enough water for each one's needs.'

'There will be a problem,' Yomaira said.

'No, there will be no problem, you foolish child. I am suggesting an intelligent way to solve the problem. Why can you not understand what I am saying?'

Fariyal laid her hand on Shanaz's arm. 'Shanaz, please stop this discussion. Let us ask the children about this Thwacker.'

Shanaz shook her hand off irritably. 'No, I will not. This stupid child started this conversation. I will convince her how backward her people are.'

Dala, Absal and Yomaira sat on the ground, their hands and arms folded on their laps, talking to one another.

'Why are you speaking in that stupid language and not in Saradasi?' Shanaz demanded.

'Because we are talking about you, and our language has many more words than yours to describe you,' Dala said.

Seelawathie-Ap glared at the children.

'You say our language is stupid,' Absal said. 'Your language has fifty-nine phonemes. Our language has ninety-six. You will have difficulty learning our language because you are not as intelligent as us.'

'Nonsense,' Shanaz said. 'Go away!

'You would not know what a phoneme is! It is the smallest unit of sound in a word,' Absal said.

In the shadow of the Thwacker, Lord Medaris unbuckled his cloak, spread it on the ground and lay on it, closing his eyes. Fariyal sat next to him looking at the Thwacker.

Shanaz paced briskly in front of the children, with Seelawathie-Ap following her. 'Go away,' Shanaz said angrily to Seelawathie-Ap. She stopped in front of the children and demanded, 'So what is the problem? Why cannot someone give out the water to those who need more?'

'Because it is too much work for someone.'

'Too much work? Why, you stupid child? One person can easily give out the water in your village,' Shanaz said, her voice carrying across the crowd.

'One person cannot.'

'Why not?' Shanaz shouted.

'Because, there are three thousand and seventy people in our village.'

'In life there are no safe assumptions,' Medaris said to Fariyal.

Shanaz continued, her voice trembling, 'Well, ask more people to give out the water.'

'But who will work their fields when they draw water for others?' Yomaira asked.

'Think. Use your small brain. Who will work their fields? Those who are receiving more water should, you stupid child. '

'Are you suggesting those who cannot draw water for themselves should work in the fields?'

The people listening tittered.

'Did you speak of sharing?' Yomaira asked.

'I did. Listen when I speak,' Shanaz snapped.

'But,' said the child, 'that is what we are doing now with no problems. We are sharing the water we receive as we have for hundreds of years. I spoke of sharing, but you did not understand what I said because you are selfish.'

Shanaz strode to the *Mithras Ennab*. Fariyal joined the children, sitting with them. 'You could help us. Lord Rasalis and Sirrah may have asked you this before. We seek a friend who may have come here before us.'

'We have not seen him here at Samandrath–Bahar–Tekaya.'

On the sandy track across where they sat, four wooden carts rumbled along, piled with blue fruits, pulled by a horned animal. One of the animals stumbled and a fruit fell on the path, igniting, leaving a charred crater on the ground from which tendrils of smoke rose. A larger cart came into view, loaded with six legged animals, similar to Absal's pet.

A bell sounded. The children rose and left.

Shanaz drew Fariyal aside. Watching Lord Medaris walking round the Thwacker, she said, 'The problem with Medaris is he thinks he is the great, detached, logical general. Is he bored, or is he disinterested?'

'Shanaz, you are unnecessarily critical,' Fariyal said.

'It is always my fault, Fariyal.'

Lord Rasalis, Seelawathie-Ap and Sirrah joined them.

'Lord Rasalis,' Shanaz said, 'on the way here from Military Base Xzania, Lord Medaris ignored all of us and spoke only to Fariyal. In the sweetest tones, he would praise her, saying how well she performed her duties on the *Mithras* Ennab. Lord Rasalis, Medaris thinks Fariyal can do anything.'

'I flew with Fariyal on a Hunter and she repaired a serious sensor malfunction,' Sirrah said.

Shanaz brandished a finger in Sirrah's face. 'Sirrah, the Saradasi military has a promotion list. I am sure your name is not on it, but if it is I shall remove your name forever.' She began striding in front of them, her arms swinging, her feet deliberately raising small puffs of dust, glaring at Sirrah each time she passed him.

A child with wide blue eyes joined Shanaz, keeping pace with her.

'Go away,' Shanaz said.

'How are you?' she asked Shanaz in Saradasi.

'I am well but I think you are not, because you have a bad smell.'

'Thank you for speaking to me,' the child said. 'I am happy you are well. I am happy one of us is well and smells good. I hope your inside smells as good as your outside.

'Go away.'

'I cannot.'

'Why not?'

'I have something to tell you. You cannot leave Samandrath-Bahar-Tekaya until the correct time.'

'We can leave here whenever we want to.'

'No, you cannot.'

'Why not?'

'Because,' the child said pointing at the *Mithras Ennab*, 'nothing works on the machine you came here in. You can leave on the Thwacker, not on your spacecraft. Good-bye.' The child walked into the crowd.

'Fariyal! They have sabotaged the *Mithras Ennab*,' Shanaz said. 'Carry out a global check.'

Fariyal climbed aboard the *Mithras Ennab*. The crowd increased, thronging near the Thwacker and the *Mithras Ennab*.

'Why is Fariyal taking so long?' Shanaz asked Lord Rasalis and Sirrah. 'Why is she so slow?'

'Her work is thorough,' Lord Rasalis said.

Fariyal alighted from the *Mithras Ennab* and hurried to them. 'It is true. The craft is dead.'

'Nonsense,' Shanaz said and entered the *Mithras Ennab* with Seelawathie-Ap.

'What has happened?' Lord Rasalis asked Fariyal.

'There is no power; nothing works. This is what happened when we met the female and male on the Ashanti-Ishtana craft who asked us to help the sick child on board.'

'What should we do?' Sirrah asked.

Lord Rasalis shook his head. 'This may be part of what we have to experience. We must be patient.'

Shanaz joined them and said, 'I want to enter the Thwacker.' Adjusting her firing-belt, she walked across to the Thwacker with Seelawathie-Ap.

Eight more carts moved along the rutted track laden with blue fruits. The crowd drifted away, ignoring the visitors and the *Mithras Ennab*. A group of thirteen adults remained. Each picked up a basket which they placed on their head, and following a bronzed female, set their baskets on the ground in front of Fariyal.

'We have brought you food and drink,' one of them said.

'Thank you. You speak our language well.'

'Yes. Fluently. But we cannot stay and talk because we must visit our master and discuss your visit.' The female and her twelve companions left in separate directions.

'Shanaz, there is food and drink here for us,' Fariyal said when Shanaz and Seelawathie-Ap climbed down from the triangular platform.

'What is inside the Thwacker,' Fariyal asked.

'Nothing,' Shanaz said, avoiding her gaze.

'Were you not able to enter?'

'Don't worry about it, Fariyal,' Shanaz said impatiently. 'Lord Rasalis, how will we leave this wretched place?'

'It may not be our choice when or how to leave. We have to wait for the right time.'

'What is the right time?'

'We must be patient. We have to wait.'

'Can you secure the craft?' Sirrah asked Fariyal when they carried the baskets inside the *Mithras Ennab*.

'We have to close the hatch manually,' she said.

Shanaz snapped her fingers at Seelawathie-Ap who was seated near her observing the Thwacker. 'Lord Rasalis boasts about your powers, as if he created you. Seelawathie-Ap, what can you see which we cannot?'

'Nothing,' Seelawathie-Ap replied.

Hot, dust-laden gusts of wind blew. Shanaz wrapped her cloak around her and sat close to Fariyal. 'Fariyal, Medaris is an excellent model for a new robot for you to design. Handsome, with shiny hair and a seductive smile. Perhaps Medaris is a robot. Perhaps the motors which control his facial movements have failed. He never smiles at me. The High Council robot, Plestrach, smiled with half his mouth when three sub-motors failed.'

Shanaz picked up a small rock and flung it at a bird which cocked its head at her and flew to sit on a tree, watching her.

'Medaris spurns me,' Shanaz said.

'I think he is a shy person,' Fariyal replied.

'You are right. He is shy because he is a robot.' Shanaz wrenched out a long blade of grass, tore it into pieces of equal size and arranged them in a design in front of her. 'Tell me, Fariyal, what is wrong with Medaris?'

'Nothing.'

'Nothing? You are all the same, all of you dislike me, and you are plotting to kill Wynan and destroy my life. No one wants Wynan to love me. You want me to suffer. There may be another plot to kill me. Have you forgotten Seelawathie-Ap saved my life twice? I hate all of you and I know you hate me.'

'Shanaz,' Fariyal whispered squeezing her hand, 'what you say is not true. We love you.'

'We love you,' Shanaz mimicked. 'Nobody loves me except Wynan. Our destiny was to share our lives together. I hate this miserable job of High Chancellor and I will resign and spend my life with Wynan but not on Saradasi.'

'Would Wynan abandon his career?'

'Why are you questioning me, Fariyal? Of course he will when I ask him because Wynan loves me. I suffer constantly, but no one cares. I will end my life because nobody except Wynan loves me. Medaris hates me.' Shanaz sobbed. 'I love all of you, but you hate me.'

'The problem may be with you, Shanaz. You may love all of us, Shanaz, but not yourself,' Fariyal said, looking at the track, deserted except for a child leading two large animals tethered together, coming towards them.

'Are you seeking someone?' the child asked.

'Yes,' Fariyal answered.

'A male?'

'Yes.'

The child looked at Shanaz while toying with a strand of her hair. 'He is alive but not in your world.'

'My world? What do you mean?' Shanaz asked wiping her eyes.

'There are many worlds or universes. In Samandrath-Bahar-Tekaya, we live in two worlds and can move between each world.'

The child called out to Seelawathie-Ap sitting nearby. 'You are Seelawathie-Ap. You can travel to other worlds. You have the power to take others with you, but not anywhere.'

'Why not?' Seelawathie-Ap asked.

'Because you are arrogant. You must learn humility on the journey which starts here from Samandrath-Bahar-Tekaya.'

They heard a roar as hundreds of people ran towards the Thwacker, shouting. A blazing blue light surrounded it. The crowd hushed, staring at the Thwacker when its brightness increased, dazzling the area surrounding it.

'The Golden One is here,' they shouted, waving their arms.

'There is nothing to see,' Shanaz said. 'There is no Golden One. It's their imagination, or they are trying to trick us.'

Three females with shaved heads, their foreheads daubed in yellow and red, sat on their haunches by the *Mithras Ennab*. They drew a large circle on the sand with a stick, dividing it into twelve segments. Looking at the sky they filled each segment with circular symbols.

A few people examined the circle on the ground and shaking their heads drifted into the night.

The female child who spoke to them pointed to the circle on the ground. 'There has been a mistake. The calculations show the Golden One will appear tomorrow, not today.'

The three females covered the circle with a cloth and lay on it.

The child went to Lord Rasalis and Sirrah and held their hands. 'I will go with you to your camp by the hill where the people hid the Thwacker before it rose to the sky and came here.'

'No one hid the Thwacker,' Shanaz said. 'I refuse to believe you.'

'It is true.'

191

'Who is the Golden One and when will we see him? Shanaz asked.

'You will see her tomorrow. Come with me and your two friends, to their camp by the hill,' she said beckoning Shanaz.

When they reached the camp, the two tents swayed in the breeze.

Sirrah pointed. 'Look,' he exclaimed.

'What has happened?' Shanaz said.

'Shanaz,' Lord Rasalis said, 'the hill and the grove of trees have disappeared.'

EIGHTEEN

'My Lord, come with me,' Sirrah said, hurrying out of the tent with Lord Rasalis.

They stood staring at the luxuriant vegetation around them. The barren desert like landscape was no more and clear streams seamed the ground. A cool wind blew. The children ran into the camp, their faces shining, Absal and Dala wearing yellow and scarlet clothes, Yomaira in a flared blue dress.

'What has happened children?' Lord Rasalis asked.

'Everything has changed because the Thwacker is here and the Golden One has arrived.'

'Who is the Golden One?' Lord Rasalis asked.

'You will see her when she comes out of the Thwacker,' Absal said running ahead laughing.

Dala tugged Lord Rasalis's hand. 'Come with us. Hurry.'

They walked between streams of water, the air heavy with the scent of flowers, to the Thwacker, its colour changed from blue to gold. Lord Rasalis, Sirrah and the two children joined Fariyal, Medaris and Seelawathie-Ap seated on the ground near the *Mithras Ennab* looking at the Thwacker. Shanaz sat alone leaning against a tree.

'Look at the blessings the Thwacker has brought us. Everything has changed. See the beautiful buildings that were not here yesterday,' Yomaira said pointing.

'It is a trick,' Shanaz said.

'I should tell you of a great problem in our land,' Yomaira said. 'Five adults can speak your language. The others cannot learn Saradasi because of a disease in their brain. We too will suffer from this disease when we grow old. The cells in our brain will clump together in a tangle and not function. Our memory will be in disarray. We will remember the past but it will be impossible to retain new knowledge.'

Absal squatted on the ground facing them. 'We have another problem,' he said. 'We are all mad. Yes. Mad! Mad! Mad! Welcome, Saradasi to Samandrath-Bahar-Tekaya the land of the mad! You are here because you are mad. Part of your madness is wanting to rule billions of people who can govern themselves.'

'We are not mad,' Shanaz said.

'You are. That is why you have come here. You can be *our* High Chancellor!' Yomaira retorted.

'You stupid child, you fool, you are mad,' Shanaz shouted.

'I *am* mad. Have you forgotten what Absal said? You are losing what we call your short-term memory. Welcome to Samandrath-Bahar-Tekaya. Once you are here you can never leave.'

The pale green sky was clear when the rain fell, drumming hard on the *Mithras Ennab*. No rain fell on the Thwacker. Three adult females wearing flowing blue robes tied at the waist with a golden coloured sash sat with them. A male dressed in a purple gown joined them.

The female with plaited hair cleared her throat and held her hand over her chest. 'You must wonder, what is this Thwacker?' she said. 'No one agrees what it is, but I can tell you what my family and I believe.'

The second female with brown eyes interrupted her. 'You must not listen to her. She is a mad person who knows nothing about the Thwacker. The Thwacker is here with the Golden One who we will see today. Our world will change even more than what you see since yesterday. It will snow and Samandrath-Bahar-Tekaya will be clean and white, with children playing in the snow. Look at our beautiful clothes. After the Thwacker arrives our clothes are no longer grim and torn. When you first saw us we were filthy. This was because we had a problem with water. How we longed for the Thwacker to come with the Golden One.'

The females who drew the circle lit a wood fire at its centre and sat warming their hands over the flames. They extinguished the fire and collecting the glowing embers with their hands, scattered them over the circle. Dusting their hands, they walked along the track towards a group of buildings, each with a minaret changing colour.

The second female coughed and cleared her throat, massaging her forehead with her hand.

'My duty is to tell you about the Golden One who may speak to you because she loves all living beings, even Saradasi. She will appear at the door of the Thwacker with hands outstretched and when she does, each of us will feel her touch and her transforming love. In the presence of the Golden One we experience peace, and petty jealousies seem foolish. Feuds are of the past. Enmities become embarrassments best set aside and cast into the ocean of peace around us. They melt like snow in a warm sea. The Golden One cleanses us by her presence, healing the sick among us.'

Children threw handfuls of incense into the braziers on the ground, arranged in a circle around the Thwacker. The third female with white hair and a prominent nose, seated next to Shanaz, stretched her back, turning her head towards the track, crowded with people walking towards the Thwacker.

'The children told us people have an illness affecting their memory and that they are mad,' Shanaz said to the female with white hair. 'Why has the Golden One not healed them?'

'The illness occurred since we last saw the Golden One. That was many years ago.' She pointed to her blue eyes. 'I am blind with age and I cannot see you. The Golden One has not healed me. My sense of touch is all I need to say who you are, what you are, where you are from and where you are going. You can hold no secrets from me.

'Last night the children, little Absal, Dala and Yomaira, led me to your flying machine while two of you slept and two of you sat looking at the Thwacker, seeking understanding. No one saw me.'

'"Good mother, what is wrong with their machine?" the children asked.'

'"There is nothing wrong," I said, when I touched the machine.'

'"Will it fly in the air as it flew when the strangers came here?"'

'"No. It is no longer meant to fly. The strangers must leave on the Thwacker and start a new life. The Thwacker is the womb from which they will be born again into a life of goodness," I said. Let me touch one of you. I hear a movement and a hand is reaching out to mine.'

She bent her head towards Shanaz.

'You are the one with the greatest courage. Can I touch your face? Thank you. You are so beautiful. Your hair is thick and long, and, as my fingers weave among its strands, I can hear the song of the wind and the sadness in your heart. Let this blind old female guess. Your eyes are beautiful and large and glow when you laugh and light the world around you and set aflame the hearts of those who love you and want to hold you close to them. But often these eyes are two tombstones, cold and sad.'

The female closed her eyes and sighed when Shanaz held her hand in both of hers and bowed her head. The far off beat of drums reached them. The crowd grew around the Thwacker, its colour a hue of gold, its two entrances closed.

She spoke softly to Shanaz. 'You have asked yourself about your haunting sadness but the answer is as far as the stars hidden on a moonless night. Your many past lives burden you with sadness from memories you cannot recall. The problem about our past lives is we have no memory of them, but the sadness from the past lingers. Your sadness will die away, if, in your present life, you give joy to others.'

She continued, 'The memories of *this* lifetime also reach out to strangle your happiness. You must not dwell on what happened in the past, in this lifetime. The past must not dictate who you are, who you should be, or where you should go and who should go with you. The past will not change, but you can change. The memory of the past exists only to help you learn, to change, to give a direction for the future and bring goodness into your life. Attempt great and noble acts on behalf of the Creator. Expect great goodness and strength from the Creator. Enter the Thwacker and your life will change. All your dreams will come true.'

The sky changed from green to red and a single cloud hid the sun. On the trees near the *Mithras Ennab* the birds turned their heads towards the Thwacker. On one side, people dressed in red, blue or yellow sat in groups of ten on the ground, their heads bowed. The drums took on a faster rhythm.

Lord Medaris stepped out of the *Mithras Ennab* and sat between Sirrah and Lord Rasalis facing the female speaking to Shanaz.

The male in the purple gown who sat with them, moved his shaved head from side to side and laughed. 'I am a Thun-Mut, a sage, descended from a line of males and females who are the thinkers of our community. We prosper using our intelligence, not by ploughing fields. We preach that greed leads to poverty not wealth. Shanaz, I can read your mind. You want to ask me a riddle to test my intelligence. Here is the answer: the male with the red cross will cross the fire first.

'Listen to me. These people built the Thwacker with mud, straw, and bits of wood bonded with clay, cleverly coloured to deceive the foolish. These deranged beings, here in Samandrath-Bahar-Tekaya carried it in the darkness of the night from its hiding place, on to this flimsy triangular platform.

'It is their sacrificial chamber.

'These people receive no gifts from a Golden One. They stole the clothes they wear from Somosiato-Xyxtt medical missionaries who came

196

to treat the toxic disease of their brain, which has driven them mad. These murderous thieves worship this monstrosity they call the Thwacker.

'Why? I will explain.

'Many thousands of years ago a spacecraft arrived here with a female adult and young children. The children carried a gene with a mental disorder. The Golden One they speak of is the female adult who these people claim is alive. When it arrived the people worshipped the spacecraft. But it fell apart over the years. In this land apathy alternated with periods of fanatical worship of the Golden One and her home, the Thwacker. When people reactivated their faith, they rebuilt the Thwacker. But there were no accurate records of its original appearance. This vile monstrosity looks nothing like the beautiful original spaceship. The Golden One is a robot.'

The wind stilled and in the hush around the Thwacker, the drums sounded nearer. The birds left the trees they were on and circled the Thwacker flying by its two entrances. The smell of incense from the braziers clung in the air.

The male drew his scarlet gown over his feet and placed a five-cornered cap on his bald head. 'Saradasi, these three females and the children who spoke to you in Saradasi belong to one clan. The female who claims she is blind is their leader. The adults of this clan want to sacrifice you in the Thwacker. If you enter the Thwacker, they will seal you inside and pump in deadly vapours. The blue fruits you saw piled in carts, which ignited in the water are for your cremation. There will be a great ceremony to celebrate your death and the buildings with the minarets will broadcast the sound of your agony for thousands to hear and rejoice. Behold the Thwacker. Temple and crematorium. If you die by entering the Thwacker how will you save the Nereima Galaxy?

He sighed and closed his eyes. 'Lord Rasalis, the hill opposite your camp has disappeared because they hid the Thwacker underneath its soil. The food and drink they gave you, which you consumed, contained three sophisticated hallucinogenic agents. They lock into specific receptors in your brain, which interprets what you see and hear. Because of these agents all of you see the same illusion. A third interferes with rational thought. Logic is adrift like an unanchored boat in a wild sea.'

He held his head in his hands, sighing. 'What will become of you when I leave? The *Mithras Ennab* and your weapons are not functioning. Saradasi, seize deliverance and come with me to safety. I will take you to a Demestraaat cargo ship which will take you to the Northern Galaxy and from there you can travel to Space Station ZenFah in the Nereima Galaxy.'

He looked at the *Mithras Ennab* and at the Thwacker and laughed, pointing to the crowds. 'They are sitting patiently to celebrate your sacrifice. Who lured you here to prevent you fulfilling *The Prophecy*? Who is the deity these people worship? In Samandrath-Bahar-Tekaya, the Thwacker is their deity's home. He is Prince Vira, the evil one.'

O

As the evening turned to dusk, the Saradasi sat by the *Mithras Ennab* watching the crowds staring at them. Darkness fell and a breeze blew with flakes of snow. The crowd rose to their feet. A figure with short golden hair stood at the entrance of the Thwacker wearing a golden gown. She climbed down to the triangular platform, stepped on to the ground and walked through the crowd to the Saradasi. They stood, lit by her aura.

'I am the Golden One,' she said in Saradasi. 'I have heard what the children and the adults have told you. I invite you to come with me and start your journey to find *The Place* and save the Nereima Galaxy. Will you come with me?' she asked.

'Yes. I will come with you,' Shanaz said.

She walked with the Golden One to the Thwacker. The others followed her. In the Thwacker the Golden One led them along a passage to a room with seats and a platform at one end.

'Please sit, look and listen,' she said, leaving the room.

A young male dressed in white with loose, long, dark hair entered the room and strode onto the platform. He stood motionless, unsmiling.

'Saradasi,' he said. 'Scum of the universe!' He pointed a finger at Shanaz. 'Be quiet! I can hear what you think.'

Shanaz stood, her hand on the hilt of her force-sword, her pelvis thrust forward, the tubes of her firing-belt aimed at him.

'You would use a force-sword and a firing-belt to fight me?'

'No, to kill you,' Shanaz said.

'High Chancellor of the Saradasi Empire, who do you think I am?' he asked.

'You are Prince Vira, leader of the Forces of Evil, and I am not afraid of you.'

The light dimmed. The Thwacker rose and laughter filled the room.

NINETEEN

Shanaz woke up squinting against the bright light when she heard Fariyal whispering to Seelawathie-Ap sitting beside her.

'Are we in the Thwacker? Shanaz asked drowsily. 'Have I been asleep?'

'We have been here for a day,' Fariyal replied.

The door to the room they were in slid open and the young male in white strode in and clapped his hands while climbing to the platform. After pacing to and fro, he stopped, his expression stern and unsmiling. His eyes lingered on Medaris and settled on Shanaz. He looked again at Medaris and then at Shanaz.

'I am not Prince Vira, High Chancellor,' he said. 'I am the Astral Lord of the East. Lord Gaima, the leader of the Forces of Light who you Saradasi represent, ordered me to meet you. I am not happy because I have contempt for the Saradasi. Instead of seeking goodness and virtue, generations of you have sought power and domination and your foul Empire defiles the Nereima Galaxy.'

'Why are we here?' Shanaz asked.

'Why are you here?' His voice echoed in the room. 'You are here because I want you here.'

Shanaz looked away.

'Be silent, High Chancellor. You have nothing of value to say.'

He sat on the platform.

'I will tell you about a planet called Xetfose. I will bring to life the events on Xetfose and you will see and hear people, and be even aware of their thoughts. You need this knowledge to understand yourselves, and save the Nereima Galaxy.'

The wall behind him glowed with images.

'Listen and watch,' he said.

○

Imagine a single universe as a huge comb of honey. The hexagonal compartments of the honeycomb are like the galaxies, with a varying number of planets and other heavenly bodies. The planet Xetfose uniquely occupies a hexagon, a single planet in a vast void with its own moons and sun.

The single race on Xetfose, the Marinasi, believed a source of great evil caused misery to individuals and nations and perhaps even planets. This source of evil they called *The Place*. Its nature and location were a mystery. The Marinasi thrived, living harmoniously and placing more value on their spiritual growth than on acquiring material possessions. Each new generation gained greater spirituality than their parents.

During the reign of King Samudra-Putra, a young female visited him claiming she had visions of *The Place*. Twice he sent her away, though not unkindly. When she returned a year later, she displayed an aura so bright, none could look at her. The King, lowering his head, listened to her describing her visions of *The Place*. When she finished speaking she disappeared. No one saw her leave the Grand Room.

The next day, troubled and curious, King Samudra-Putra set out to find her. She lived on the southern face of the mighty Mahe Mountain on the island of Darath, in a small house with her parents, tending their vegetable, fruit and flower gardens. The young female, who belonged to the Ethiw clan, advised him to select twelve holy people to study *The Place*. The King chose her and eleven others, who called themselves the Scholars and decided to live on the island of Darath. Here the King built the Scholars Complex. Shortly afterwards, King Samudra-Putra married a member of the Ethiw clan, forging a strong partnership between the royal house of Xetfose and the clan.

In time the Scholars developed an aura, a pale golden sheen enveloping their bodies from head to foot. Often other Ethiw clan members developed auras, though less brilliant. The Marinasi people regarded the Scholars as the most holy people on Xetfose and called the island Darath, the 'blessed island'. Here, frequent miracles restoring health occurred.

A new impetus to studying *The Place* occurred during the reign of Queen Piara-Leela. Wanting to work closely with the Scholars she built the new capital of Xetfose, Meryan, on Darath, across two mountainsides and a valley. She asked the Scholars a question never considered before: 'How can we destroy *The Place*?'

The Queen and the leader of the Scholars began a secret plan to destroy *The Place*, which they knew needed centuries of dedicated work. The Queen accepted responsibility for one part of the plan, the leader of the Scholars for another, and the chief adviser to the monarch, called the Maithri, for the third. Each would preserve the secrecy of their work and pass it on to their successor.

Individual Scholars set out on the first of many "great voyages", travelling beyond their planet to near and far-flung galaxies. None except the Scholars knew the purpose of these voyages. The leader of the Scholars visited cities and towns on Xetfose, spending weeks with selected children, playing with them, talking to them, but mainly listening to them.

○

Clear golden sunlight shone on the gabled Scholars Complex on Mahe Mountain, and on the capital Meryan, with its tall and slender buildings and spires. The Subinara River sparkled like a skein of moulded glass through the city.

Weera-Soma 99, the leader of the Scholars, walked from her room to the garden. She sat watching the mist swirl across the five waterfalls flowing down the Mahe Mountain, forming the Subinara River on its long journey to the Sea of Hope.

'We are ready to achieve the dreams of our ancestors,' she said speaking into her audio log. 'We now know where *The Place* is, but not the extent of its power to harm us. Despite our spiritual defences, the evil in *The Place* may destroy Xetfose unless we destroy it first. I hope I am wrong, but I am becoming more concerned about our survival.'

Weera-Soma 99 returned to her living quarters and watched a recording made a century ago by the mother of the present king.

I am Queen Priya-Devi.

I have been Queen for a month. With the instructions my father gave me, I have continued the work of my ancestors. My chief adviser, Maithri, tells me nothing about his tasks and so it should be. The Scholars work secretly and travel far. They have not told me why.

I hope the Scholars see I am working hard. I think Maithri knows what I am doing, though he pretends not to know.

The spacecraft I inspected today were beautiful. Where will they travel? Who will travel in them?

I do not know. Only the Scholars know this part of the grand plan.

I'll listen to some songs and go to sleep.

Weera-Soma 99 sighed. The Queen was twelve years old.

◯

The next day when Weera-Soma 99 awoke, dark clouds hid the sun. This was the day Kings and Queens, Scholars and Maithris had prayed for, when the work of the Marinasi people over many centuries would become a reality. It may be a day of glorious triumph or catastrophic failure, Weera-Soma 99 thought. She spent the morning performing the ritual of purification.

At noon she left for the palace to meet the King, Amara-Dasa. The King rose when she entered the blue room for visitors and led her to a chair.

'My King, how blessed we are to fulfil the plans developed by our ancestors. The children we selected are ready. They understand their duty and know their journey will be long. Though young, they are eager to help build a society in the new worlds they will live in, built on love, tolerance, honesty and a lack of greed.'

Weera-Soma 99 saw white clouds, streaked black and purple, scudding across the sky through the transparent roof of the blue room.

'What is written in their horoscopes?' King Amara-Dasa asked.

'We decided not to cast their horoscopes. The future is in the hands of the Creator, not for us to delve into.'

'I have re-read my horoscope,' the King said. 'There is nothing I can change or wish to change. As you said, all is written.'

◯

In the palace garden, the King's adviser Maithri sat by the rectangular pond next to his favourite stone animal. Picking up a handful of smooth pebbles he rubbed them between the palms of his hands and on the soles of his feet. He placed the pebbles in a neat pile by his side when he heard running footsteps and shrieks of excited anticipation. Two of the three palace librarian's children raced towards him vying for his first embrace. They clambered onto his lap, pushing and shoving each other.

'So, where is Nanda?' Maithri asked smoothing his white clothes.

'He is in trouble again,' his twin, Pushpa, said. She went on hurriedly, 'I did not tell him to do anything bad. Ask her.'

'Oh, he did nothing bad,' Shanti, her younger sister said, grimacing when Pushpa's elbow jabbed her side. 'He played a trick on the milkman.'

'But his tricks are not like yours, Maithri,' Pushpa said. 'Maithri, can you please show us a trick, though you say they are not tricks? Please?'

Maithri picked up a pebble from the pile beside him and placed it on his palm, blowing gently on it. The children leaned forward. The pebble burst into flames.

'Oh!' they chorused.

He blew on it a second time. The flame rose and subsided, the pebble glowing an angry red. He blew on it a third time, clenched his hand and opened it. The children screamed when they touched the pebble, encrusted in shards of ice.

Maithri closed his hand again.

'It is your turn,' Maithri said to Shanti. He unclenched his fist.

Shanti dipped a finger into the thick, golden-brown liquid in Maithri's palm and tasted it.

'Honey' she yelled.

'Maithri,' Pushpa said, snuggling up to him. 'We love you so much and we will miss you. Tonight we and so many other children will go far, far away from our home. But I am not afraid.'

Maithri held her close to him.

'We will not come back here because we have lots of work where we are going. Maithri, where will we go?'

'It will be to a place where you will be happy.'

'Maithri!' a voice called loudly.

A group of shrieking birds in a blur of red and black flew from a bush.

An aide ran to him, breathless. 'Maithri, our lord the King has sent for you and he wants you to come to the palace with me. He says you must not use your power now. The children must go to the Scholars Complex.'

Maithri picked up another pebble.

'Please, not tonight, Sire. You must save your energy,' the aide said, staring at the sky.

Maithri dropped the pebble into the pond and looked at the black sky. The water in the pond swirled, the trees twisted in the silent wind. The figures of the four stone animals, one at each corner of the pond, cracked. The children ran to Maithri and clung to him.

'Quick,' he ordered the aide, 'take the children to the Scholars Complex. I will follow you.'

'I will never see those children again,' Maithri thought, watching them run up the steps. Bolts of lightning flew across the sky. He wondered how long the children would be in a state of induced sleep in their new home until they would be woken to live with the parents the Scholars selected.

Maithri raised his arms. '*The Place* will be no more. I curse you and damn you,' he shouted. 'We will destroy you, whoever you are!'

A fetid blast of wind tore at him. He stumbled, trying to rise, but the wind forced him to the ground.

Six palace aids ran down the steps to him.

'I will tell you who I am, you fool. I am Prince Vira,' a voice roared from the sky drowning the sound of the thunder.

'I have not long to live,' Maithri said to the aides who carried him to the palace. 'Xetfose is doomed,' he whispered.

O

The day seemed like night, the sun blanketed by darkening clouds.

Thousands of holy saman flowers festooned the roof and walls of the Scholars Complex, and holy symbols depicted with coloured flour, flowers, fruits and holy ash stretched across the gardens. Small open clay lamps with holy oil burned on the parapet wall surrounding the complex. Musicians playing the music of holy hymns walked along the perimeter of the complex between two lines of white ash, led by incense carriers dressed in red and yellow, chanting softly to the rhythm of the music.

Weera-Soma 99 looked at the designs and clay lamps, praying they would help protect the Scholars Complex from the evil from *The Place*. She entered the room of worship and performed the ritual of purification, cleansing her body and mind, providing a focus of harmony from which to draw strength.

At noon the twelve Scholars gathered in a circular room in the Complex overlooking the five waterfalls, bare except for the wooden table. A fire roared in the far end of the room. The chimes echoed from the bells in the tower. Selest, Weera-Soma 99's young aide, stood behind her. He saw her shiver and stepped out of the room, returning with a shawl, which he draped over her shoulders.

Weera-Soma 99 greeted each Scholar. 'It is time,' she said, after Selest placed a wooden bowl with a green liquid in front of each Scholar. 'The plan is complete because of the work of our Queens and Kings, the Scholars and the Maithris. Today after the King and the Maithri carry out their tasks, I will fulfil mine. I will unleash the power to destroy *The Place*. Thousands of our people are in specific positions in an east-west direction forming a holy circle around our planet. If we fail to destroy *The Place,* we Scholars especially, will die a terrible death. Before you is the bowl. You may, if you wish, end your life peacefully and I will think no less of you. Others are ready to fulfil your tasks. Whatever happens I wish you peace in our world or the next.'

Each Scholar pushed their bowl towards the centre of the table.

Weera-Soma 99 squeezed the hand of the youngest Scholar, Akila, sitting next to her. 'You must go to the King now and receive his instructions.'

After Akila left, she told the ten Scholars, 'Akila will bring you the King's instructions about your journey. Go to the garden, smell the flowers, place your feet in the ponds. After she returns, when the bells chime five times you must leave to begin your journey. Cherish the children who are waiting for you in the secret locations.'

Weera-Soma 99 left the Scholars and climbed to a knoll in the garden where she sat on the grass with Selest. 'See the small flames dancing, Selest?' she said pointing to the clay lamps. 'They are not surrendering to the wind. Instead, they stubbornly resist the wind, struggling as if in their death throes, but never dying.'

She paused when an elderly Ethiw female served them their evening meal.

'Selest, these flames are like life itself. We can surrender or triumph. Neither wind nor rain will smother these flames if the lamps have holy oil, and, of course, a new wick when it is necessary. Even if evil from *The Place* destroys us, because of the holy oil, these lamps will burn as specks in space forever. Many will wonder what they are.'

'I think,' Selest said, 'all living beings have holy oil within them and a wick.'

Weera-Soma 99 nodded pressing her fingers against her temples. For the first time since he met her, Selest saw her aura flicker.

'Are you concerned about the children who will leave Xetfose?' Selest asked.

'No. The Scholars and the children will not be in danger. We spent hundreds of years making sure we know where the children will live, and who will care for them and adopt them.'

'Is this knowledge from the children's horoscopes?'

'No. They have no horoscopes. We know their future, but not all of it. Our knowledge is from the visions Scholars have had over the ages.'

'How many children will leave Xetfose?'

'Each small spacecraft carries seventy five thousand. The two large craft carry two hundred thousand children, bound for two planets in a nearby galaxy.'

'Will *The Place* destroy Xetfose?' Selest asked.

'Possibly. Everything in the universe obeys laws. The protective force on Xetfose will decrease when the Scholars and the children leave. We will rely on the goodness of each male, female and child remaining on the planet to protect us. *The Place* may destroy us.'

The bells in the Scholars Complex chimed in rhythm with the throb of the musicians' drums and the melody of the flutes. The wind carried the smell of incense towards them.

'We face evil, often in the guise of temptation,' Weera-Soma 99 said. 'Evil will triumph if we, by choice, diminish who we are, or who we want to be. If we hold onto the goodness within us, which we all possess, evil will not triumph.'

They heard the flutes playing a mournful melody. Weera-Soma 99 listened, closing her eyes. She swept back a strand of hair, watching the clay lamps.

'Evil snares us by stealth,' she continued, 'influencing our lives and our thoughts, convincing us we are virtuous even while committing evil acts. Evil also seduces us to silence, or to inactivity. Selest, you must never become a coward. Moral cowards strangle both themselves and others struggling to uphold good and fight evil.'

Weera-Soma 99 held his arm. 'Can you remember the day when you touched my aura and felt nothing?'

'Yes,' he answered, 'and I fell into the pond.'

'Selest, come with me to the pond.'

The wind dropped. The water lay still. The auras of the two figures lit the pond. Selest looked at Weera-Soma 99 and saw his mother's smile. They listened to the bells chime five times and watched Akila walk away with the scholars.

'Go now to the King and be with him. I must stay here,' she said.

'Will we meet again?' Selest asked.

'Yes. But in another place.'

◯

In the palace, Selest entered the Grand Room and bowed to the King. 'Sire, the craft have left Xetfose with the children and the Scholars, in an induced sleep. Your Highness, Weera-Soma 99, my teacher asks your forgiveness for not coming herself. She believes we face danger earlier than she expected from *The Place*. She says the force of good on Xetfose will plummet when the Scholars and the children leave. She is at the Scholars Complex trying to strengthen the holy lines of energy protecting Xetfose but thinks she may not succeed.'

'Selest, we all have to face our destiny,' King Amara-Dasa said embracing him. 'I have known you from the day you were born. I am blessed to see the aura around you.'

Selest rose to leave. The King motioned him to stay and sat in a chair looking out at the city spread before him and fell asleep snoring. He woke up when the lights on the control panel in the room flashed. A palace duty officer came into view on the screen.

'Sire, we cannot find the Maithri,' he said. 'No one saw him leave the palace.'

The blue light on the control panel flashed again. The largest screen in the room glowed.

Maithri stood on a desolate beach in his blue and yellow ceremonial robes of office, the cape swirling in the wind. His aura glowed brightly in the dim light.

'My King,' Maithri said, 'forgive me for leaving without your permission. I am trying to protect Xetfose. We must not destroy *The Place*. If we do, it will destroy Xetfose.'

'Why?'

'*The Place* is gaining great power even as we speak.'

King Amara-Dasa shook his head. 'We cannot stop the forces generated to destroy *The Place*. I have no power to alter the plan. Maithri, how have you appeared on this screen?'

'My King, it is through the energy I have created,' Maithri said, clasping his cloak to his body.

'Why are you wasting your energy?' the King asked.

The wind drowned Maithri's words. The King and Selest watched the wind sweep up sand and stones, hurling them at Maithri as he stood staring at a cliff lashed by waves.

Selest shut his eyes. His aura increased illuminating the room with golden brightness. King Amara-Dasa shielded his eyes.

'Selest,' Maithri screamed. 'No! Please, listen to me. No!'

'My father,' Selest said to Maithri. 'Conserve your energy to save Xetfose. I will show the King what you wanted him to see.' Selest pointed to the screen. 'Behold my King, *The Place*.' He slumped forward on his chair and slid to the floor.

The room plunged into darkness. King Amara-Dasa gaped at the screen.

Two elderly figures, identical twins, frail, with broad foreheads and receding grey hair sat across a table with a green cloth over it. One wore green, the other red. They were on a cliff in the centre of a lake hemmed in by steep mountains. Lava spewed down the mountainsides into the water with a hiss.

On the table, in front of the twins were five ten-faceted dice. Each facet bore a number, +1, -2, -3, -4, +6, -7, +8, +9, or -10. The number on the tenth facet was 0.

A board stood behind each twin.

Brother Red. Total Score Now:
11235813, 31853211, 43089024, 618 03398, 73790733, 21345589, 14423337 3098236754, 57648887, 654 9872075788, 563338870910, 73890723.

Brother Green. Total Score Now:
610947155, 912345,2,6,56510626,1568759132,466436409,578123, 19286543, 56734876, 999887645, 458765, 98007865.

'Your game, Brother Green,' the figure in red announced with a laugh.

A mechanical voice rang out: 'New game. Three throws. Green to play. Pick up your dice. Throw on three. One, two, three, throw! Result is minus ten.'

'Green to play. Pick up your dice. Throw on three. One, two, three, throw. Plus eight.'

'Green to play. Pick up your dice. Throw on three. One, two, three, throw. Minus seven.'

'Green to play. Pick up your dice. Throw on three. One, two ...'

A bell rang loudly, insistently.

'End of game. Tallying total score. Note scoreboard. End of game. Thank you.'

'Red to play. Pick up your dice. Throw on three. One, two, three, throw. Zero. Penalty. Effecting rule three hundred and seven. Penalty. Removing zero in the last number group in total score. Number group 73890723 changed to 7389723. Interval.'

Brother Red and Brother Green stood, stretched their arms and strolled to the edge of the cliff.

'It is a tranquil day,' Brother Green remarked, stepping away from Brother Red.

'You are insultingly distrustful,' Brother Red objected.

'Indeed. I am in no mood for another swim.'

'You said you enjoyed it.'

'The swim, yes, you scoundrel, not the fall.'

'Must we listen to this music hour after hour, day after day, year after year?' Brother Red demanded.

'Yes,' Brother Green replied. 'The music is soothing and melodious and it is a short piece of music with just one hundred and seventy notes. The repetition of the same tune we knew so well as children is part of our punishment. Be thankful that Prince Vira let me and not you choose the music.'

'That is why I hate it.'

They sauntered back to the table.

'Your game, Brother Red,' Brother Green said when they sat.

'Red to play,' the mechanical voice bellowed. 'Pick up dice. Throw on three. One, two, three, throw. Plus one.'

'Last game for the day. Bonus game. Note well. Bonus game. Pick up your five dice, and the five in the centre of the table. Five in each hand. Both players throw on three. Both players throw on three. One, two, three, throw.'

Both Brothers leaned forwards.

'Unbelievable!' Brother Red shouted, clapping his hands and springing up from his seat.

'Brother Red, it is rude to clap at your own success,' Brother Green said.

The mechanical voice said: 'Congratulations, Brother Red! Congratulations! You have scored nine on every dice.'

'This is the first time this has happened,' Brother Red exclaimed, his lips quivering, his fingers trembling. 'I cannot believe this, after all these years!'

A voice boomed across the sky. 'Brother Red, your prize is a planet. Choose a planet for me to destroy.'

Brother Red gasped in ecstasy.

Brother Red stuttered, moistening his lips. 'I have waited for hundreds of years, for the golden dream. A planet for me to choose!' His face rapturous, he whispered, 'A dream come true. Not a wretched, petty prize of an individual, a village, town or a city, or country, or the chance to corrupt people in governments, organizations or financial institutions. A planet!'

The voice roared, 'Quick, decide before I change my mind.'

'Thank you, sir. I thank you, thank you Prince Vira, my magnificent Lord of Darkness.'

'You fool, choose a planet before I destroy you instead.'

Brother Red screamed, 'Xetfose.'

○

On Xetfose, in the Scholars Complex, Weera-Soma 99 drew her shawl over her shoulders. She saw the flowers wilt in the perimeter of the small circle she sat in, listening to the sound of the flutes die away. The chimes of the bells faltered.

A burst of light changed night into day. The holy lamps soared into the sky burning brightly.

'My Creator, into your hands I commit our spirits,' she murmured as Xetfose shattered.

TWENTY

On the Thwacker, the Lord of the East said, 'Reflect on what you have seen and heard, and think carefully why I wanted you to learn about Xetfose. The journey to seek *The Place* is not easy. You will travel to faraway places, meet strange beings and face danger.'

He turned to Shanaz with a smile. 'I hear what you are thinking, Shanaz,' he said. 'We Astral Lords cannot destroy *The Place*. That is your task. That is the agreement reached between Lord Gaima of the Forces of Light and Prince Vira. You must have enough goodness to enter and destroy *The Place* and with it, the two brothers. But first you must find *The Place*.'

He continued, 'We cannot help you except within narrow limits. Since the first conversation between Prince Vira and Lord Gaima, almost four hundred years ago, the Saradasi people have not yet worn the emblem of goodness. This has saddened Lord Gaima. However, he and the Astral Lords helping him believe you Saradasi will save the Nereima Galaxy by transforming your lives to reveal the goodness within you. If dust and grime cover a mirror, it will not reflect even the most beautiful person. When the transformation occurs, it will enrich your lives. Your lives will attract great blessings and guidance in your search for good. When you are seeking *The Place*, wherever you are, the same laws of the creation operate. In a single planetary system, one planet cannot rotate on its axis in one direction and another in the opposite direction and in each planetary system the sun sets in the same location.

'Shanaz, if you have a choice where to travel in search of *The Place*, to the north, the south, the east or the west, where will you travel to?'

'To the west, my Lord.'

'Why so?'

'My instinct.'

'Then perhaps we will meet again.'

'You must rest,' the Golden One said. 'Your journey will start when you awake. You must first seek the mountain with twin peaks where you may receive guidance to find *The Place*.'

They stepped out of the Thwacker, with a whispered blessing from the Golden One, and stood watching it rise into the sky. Before them like a yellow stain, a desert with tall dunes stretched to the horizon.

'Seek first the mountain with twin peaks. Travel to where the sun sets. Let your journey be heliocentric,' Shanaz said, repeating what the Golden One told her.

The sun hung low and hot and the air thick with heat, as they walked westwards into the desert.

Days passed. Walking ahead of the others, Shanaz wiped her face, feeling the sand and tasting the saltiness of her perspiration, trying to remember when she enjoyed a meal, slept comfortably and felt clean. She ran her dry, swollen tongue across her lips, cracked and caked with sand. Neither a blade of grass, nor an insect scurrying across her path to hide beneath a rock reassured her she would survive the desert. Thirst no longer became her concern. The possibility of her wasteful death obsessed her.

When would she die, she wondered, and how?

'I may sink gracefully on the smouldering sand, my knees buckling under me. Should I fall face down or face up? Face down with sand in my mouth and nose, with my eyes tightly shut, or face up with my eyes screwed tight against this bastard sun? A compromise? I will fall and turn on my side. But when I collapse I may not have the will to move.

'Will I hear those behind me walk past me? Who will stop to help me or throw a glance of compassion? No one! No one!'

Shanaz tried to kick a small stone and instead raised a cloud of dust.

'I will lie on the sand, fall asleep and die,' she muttered. 'A sand storm will cover me to form a nameless cenotaph. They will find me, years later, my dehydrated mummified body, a palaeontologist's treasure.'

Shanaz squinted at the sky. Taunting her, the clouds hovered purposelessly near the sun but never blotting it out; the sun, a faithful spiteful companion. She looked at the black cloud hovering stubbornly directly over them.

At dusk they sheltered within a cluster of boulders, while a drenching sandstorm whipped around them. Some hours later the wind changed direction, slewing across the desert, changing its contours. Towering sand dunes disappeared in clouds of dust, while others rose between wind-gouged valleys in the sand.

The night was hot, the sand at their feet scorching. Shanaz lay on her cloak trying to sleep, trying to ignore the grittiness in her eyes. She recalled a conversation the previous night while she lay awake. She heard Lord Medaris talking to Fariyal about his collection of vocal music and of Sound Master Glance who was helping him. The wind drowned the next few sentences and when it stilled she heard Fariyal speaking softly.

'How many will you select from the hundreds you collected?' Fariyal asked.

'I want to select the hundred I like best.'

'When?'

'Within months.'

'You must decide on a date. If not it will be a journey with no end.'

'I have set a date,' he said.

'When,' Fariyal asked again.

The wind howled again, drowning his reply. Why, Shanaz wondered, did he share this with Fariyal? Why not with her? She knew more about music than Fariyal. Musicology was one of twelve subjects she chose at the military academy and excelled in.

Shanaz realised it was her not knowing enough about Lord Medaris which annoyed her. She knew he never served on the home planet, his postings always on Merr. He never visited Saradasi on home leave, as if exiled from the planet. He rose in rank rapidly in VIII Army.

She tried falling asleep but the wind and sand kept her awake. Her mind wandered to a conversation with Lord Rasalis in Tarich's Tavern by the wharves in Saradas, before they left Saradasi.

'Tell me about Medaris,' she had said with planned unexpectedness, looking at him closely. 'You shrugged. My Merran teacher said shrugging is a gesture of defeat, but he must be wrong, because you never tire telling us you know everything.'

'Sadly, I have my limitations,' Lord Rasalis replied with a sigh. 'I have nothing to add to what I said when we spoke a few days ago. Even I know so little about Medaris. It is most frustrating.'

'But he is in your command.'

'In my command? In Security?'

'I am confused about the relationship between Security and the VIII Army,' she had said. 'Is he in your command?'

'He is a general in the VIII Army. I am Chancellor of Security not Commander of VIII Army.'

'Is the VIII Army and Saradasi Security the same organization?'

'If they are, the administrative burdens would be formidable.'

'Why is it even I, the High Chancellor, know nothing about the VIII Army.'

'Because it is a secret entity, so mandated by the High Council.'

'Who is the VIII Army Commander-in-Chief?'

'Your father. We cannot appoint another Commander-in-Chief until we are certain he is dead.'

'Is my father alive?'

'We have not found his body.'

'Tell me more about Medaris. Who were his parents?'

'You ask me his pedigree? Are you trying to buy him as a stud?'

She remembered seeing the anger in his face. He had coughed heavily and Sirrah seated nearby walked over to them and led him away.

The hot wind blew more sand towards them. Shanaz glanced across at Lord Rasalis, asleep, his arms covering his face. That morning during their first meal of the day, she asked again him where Lord Medaris was born. She saw him become wary, his jowls tightening, looking away evasively. He became silent, as if trying to staunch the conversation. She saw him calm himself, smiling to mask his annoyance. Or was it concern? He laughed throatily, and said, 'My dear, you must not let Medaris, or the irrelevant, inconsequential information you crave for, occupy you irrationally and unnecessarily.' He left, walking quickly, and sat with Medaris.

Later in the day she caught up with Sirrah and asked him the same question about Medaris. She believed him, when he said, 'I do not know,' but asked, 'Sirrah, are you telling me the truth?'

'Yes, Shanaz. Would I lie to you?'

'Never. Sirrah, you know how much I like you and respect you.'

'Yes. I respect and like you too.'

They walked in silence.

'Sirrah, you took a deep breath when I asked you about Lord Medaris. Why?'

'I am tired, Shanaz.'

'Sirrah, can you ask Lord Rasalis whether Medaris was born in the Saradasi Empire or not?' she suggested, laying her hand on his shoulder.

'Where else could he be born?'

'That is what interests me.'

'You ask Lord Rasalis, Shanaz.'

'I have and he evades the question. Is Lord Medaris's birthplace a secret?'

'Shanaz, are there secrets on Saradasi?'

'None, except those deep in the mind of Lord Rasalis. Sirrah, you say you are my friend and I swear I am your friend, though I annoy you sometimes. Please ask Lord Rasalis.'

'No. I have heard others trying to ask him about Lord Medaris. He always gives the same answer: "Medaris need not concern you."'

'Lord Rasalis seeks more and more power over us by withholding information from us. I am the High Chancellor of the Saradasi Empire but he refuses to answer my questions! He is thirsty for power.'

Sirrah laughed. 'But what power is he seeking?'

'Power over our minds.'

'Shanaz our minds are our own. I remember you telling me what the principal of your military academy told you. We are the guardians of our mind. We can control our minds by preventing both the entry and exit of whatever we want.'

'You are right and you are becoming far too clever,' Shanaz laughed.

○

Shanaz awoke to Sirrah preparing their morning meal of grains and herbs in boiling water. Fariyal thanked Sirrah, accepting her portion of the gruel and sat with Rasalis and Medaris. Seelawathie-Ap squatted on her haunches tossing her *kaduwa* spinning into the air, catching it by the handle as it descended and throwing it up again.

'This is a terrible desert,' Lord Rasalis said, staring across the desert, wiping the perspiration from his face.

'There are worse places,' Seelawathie-Ap replied.

'Such as where?'

'The Kountacy Desert.'

'The Kountacy Desert in Asurat?' he asked, raising his eyebrows. 'A terrible place, I am told.'

'Yes, Lord, it is a terrible place where many tried to kill me when I left the Oportus Military Academy.'

'To kill you? Why? It must have been a terrible experience,' Rasalis said sadly.

Seelawathie-Ap threw her *kaduwa* in the air, spun on her heels and caught it by the hilt with both hands.

'My dear Seelawathie-Ap, I am sure you terrified those villains who tried to kill you,' Lord Rasalis said. 'You are alive, while they, I presume, died. I am curious how you dealt with so many of them.'

'I carried a substance which I added to the water holes.'

'Ingenious,' Lord Rasalis said looking at the grey sky.

After the meal, they sat together and agreed they should search for the mountain with twin peaks in two groups. Lord Rasalis explained two groups would have a greater chance of gathering information. They decided when they would meet, and on the coordinates of their meeting place.

'I want you to travel with Lord Medaris,' Shanaz told Seelawathie-Ap.

'My duty is to protect you,' she said.

Shanaz drew her aside. 'I want you to go with him. Go now.'

Shanaz nudged Sirrah when Medaris and Seelawathie-Ap left. 'Sirrah, watch how arrogantly Lord Medaris walks. He marches like a king emperor. Each step he takes is precise, like a machine. He may be a machine Lord Rasalis invented. That is why Lord Rasalis says nothing about him. I think, machine or not, Medaris will desert us. But could he escape Seelawathie-Ap?'

Lord Rasalis grunted, mopping his face. 'I think it is sensible to pre-serve our energy, both physical and mental, by remaining silent,' he said.

'Energy? You speak of physical energy and mental energy. Have you a view on spiritual energy?'

'Because I want to save my physical and mental energy, I am not going to discuss spiritual energy with you.'

'Good. Neither have I the energy to listen to you. I am glad you did not answer me. Death can occur from the boredom of listening to others.'

Fariyal grasped Shanaz's hand, holding her back to let Lord Rasalis and Sirrah walk on. 'Leave me alone, Fariyal, I am hot. Don't touch me.'

'Shanaz,' Fariyal said, 'try not to think of the heat. Clear your mind.'

'It is very clear.'

'Clear your mind about the heat. Listen to me. Breathe in slowly over four steps while walking. Hold the breath for four more steps and release it through your mouth over the next four steps. Imagine the breath you draw in is cold and rising to the top of your head, then deep into your abdomen, then into your arms and legs.'

Shanaz wiped the perspiration from her face and glanced at Fariyal, her face calm and dry.

'Shanaz, hold my hands.'

'Fariyal, your hands are cold. Are you ill?' She looked at Fariyal anxiously. 'You should rest for a while and I'll stay with you. Here, have some of my water.'

'I am not ill or thirsty. I have lowered my body temperature. When your mind is very calm imagine this sand is snow. Imagine we are in a field of snow where the temperature is so low we are shivering. Our teeth are chattering. Snow is falling on you, Shanaz. We are trudging through snow up to our ankles. It is freezing, Shanaz.'

Fariyal walked ahead and when Shanaz caught up with her, she touched her cheeks.

'Shanaz, go away! Your hands are freezing.'

○

They walked westwards, their food and water dwindling. Shanaz, walking ahead of the others, stopped and waved, pointing to her right. In the distance, two objects moved across the horizon, separated by a few hundred feet, haloed in a nimbus of dust.

'What are they?' Sirrah asked, shading his eyes.

'I am not sure,' Shanaz said. 'They are travelling slowly. If we walk fast, we can intercept them.' She looked up at the dark black cloud hovering overhead.

Sirrah led the way, trudging across the sand towards the two objects, the early afternoon silent except for the clink of stones beneath their blistered feet. Shanaz listened to the rhythm of each person's footsteps, watching the clouds swirl across the sky, its orange colour changing to a deep and dirty brown. Clusters of thick leafed plants with bright flowers appeared between the rocks.

The searing day dragged on to a hot and dusty evening. The breeze from the south picked up, gathering sand, forcing them to draw their cloaks across their faces. The wind bent the tight clusters of stunted trees they came across, flattening the sparse clumps of grass growing between them.

Shanaz listened to Lord Rasalis walking smoothly along, despite his bulk, never complaining or suggesting a slower pace, or a longer rest. She admired him and felt frustrated by him. Her mental portrait of him was never complete because he constantly injected new facts about himself, complimentary and deprecatory, to surprise and confuse others.

When darkness set they sheltered in a grove of trees between tufts of weeds. Shanaz fell asleep on her cloak thick and stiff with dirt and sweat. A gnawing thirst woke her. She saw Fariyal in the pale moonlight, tranquil in sleep as in life. Lord Rasalis slept, his arms across his head. Sirrah lay on his side, his hands on his force-sword, his legs straight, his feet neatly together. Form and symmetry she thought.

Shanaz left the shelter of the trees, placed her clothes under a stone, and stood in the moonlight facing the wind. She wiped the sand off her body with her cloak and shook her head, passing her fingers through her matted hair, shaking off the sand.

She sat on her cloak, in the wind. The destination they were to reach, the top of a mountain with twin peaks seemed so distant. Where was this mountain? In which country? On which planet? Since leaving home on Saradasi, none of them recognised the star formations in the night sky. She lay down and drifted sleep.

In her dream she sat on a smooth stone in a milky white river, the foaming water lapping over her shoulders, the torments of the journey flowing with the current. On the bank across form where she sat, she heard a song from behind the trees. She knew the voice. It was Wynan, but he was not singing in Saradasi. He sang in a language she had not heard before, yet she understood the words. He sang he never loved her. He loved another.

○

The dawn sun lit the desert. Shanaz woke to a loud piercing sound, deafening in its intensity. In a well-practised motion, she activated her firing-belt and drew her force-sword. Another sound swarmed around them, higher pitched, longer and louder. The stones on the ground flew with the wind, as if in a frenzy, splintering when they struck one another. The stunted trees around them snapped like twigs, scattering in the air.

The hillocks of sand they trudged between were swept clean, as if a mighty hand smoothed the desert. The wind, laden with stones and sand, pounded against them.

'The wind changes direction in an instant,' Shanaz shouted. 'The wind blows first from the south, then the west and from the south again. How can the direction change so quickly?'

Fragments of rocks flew at them.

'We are being targeted,' Shanaz thought protecting her face with her cloak. The roar increased. Shanaz saw Lord Rasalis slump to the ground and ran to him, shielding his face with her body. She heard the voice of the Lord of the East talking to her. Her eyes were shut against the sand but she saw him smiling, no longer the stern, forbidding person she met on the Thwacker.

'Shanaz, there are great challenges you must face,' he said.

'It is difficult,' she replied, hearing the despair in her tired voice.

'It is. But nothing can stop you except the force within you, tempting you to surrender. Your weakness will defeat you, nothing else. Be the source of strength for the others. Your determination will help win the battle for the Nereima Galaxy.'

His voice became a whisper. 'Why are you so sad, Shanaz?'

'I live in a nightmare. When I awake, I hope yesterday, and the day before, was a dream. But what I dread most is that another day will dawn and I will still be alive.'

'Do you not want to live, Shanaz?'

'No.'

'Why not?'

'Because I live in the Saradasi Empire. The Empire is an evil beast with noble features, beguiling us, drawing us closer until we smell the foulness of its breath and feel the viciousness of its bite.'

'Shanaz, was not the Saradasi Empire like a protective father and mother to you?'

'Yes. It was a warm and secure womb.'

'No longer?'

'No.' The words gushed out. 'I must kill this beast and free myself and those I love to open into beautiful flowers.'

'Are you not a flower?'

'No. I am trapped by a force distorting me into a poisonous thorn.'

Shanaz shut her eyes tighter. The conversation was real, the voice clear.

'You are not a thorn and never will be one. Learn from the past and change. Learn from your lack of goodness in Flowia Valley when you refused to help the children, who died.'

'Yes. I remember the children and I think of them with each step I take. The memory haunts me every night and my heart aches.'

'Lord Gaima is cleverer than all of us. He never doubted your goodness,' the Lord of the East said.

'What is the penance for my sins?' Shanaz asked.

'There is never penance, only forgiveness. Each day, from this moment, perform at least one act of goodness to please the Creator and bring joy to you.'

'Lord, who is the Creator?'

'I have not met the Creator. But I understand why the creation is imperfect, with sorrow and suffering. I think it is perhaps imperfect so that privileged beings like you can perfect it and complete the creation.'

The Lord of the East laid a hand on her forehead. 'You must forgive yourself. Forgiving yourself is more difficult than forgiving others. When you have sufficient goodness, you will have the power of forgiveness. If you have forgotten to forgive yourself, someone will remind you in the blue city or when you reach the mountain with twin peaks.'

A deep calmness swept over her. Shanaz opened her eyes and saw a mist enveloping her like a white shroud. A blinding light engulfed her, forcing her to cover her eyes. Rain drenched her.

Lord Rasalis stood up, unsteady on his feet. They walked through the sand, helping Lord Rasalis.

'There is a sound, like a roar before anything bad happens to us,' Shanaz said.

'It is as if a monster we cannot see is following us,' Sirrah said, spitting sand from his mouth.

'An invisible monster? No. Sirrah,' Shanaz said pointing. 'See the cloud there, directly over us? The black one? It changes shape and speed, but hovers over us. It's a machine camouflaged by the clouds, trying to kill us,' Shanaz said.

TWENTY-ONE

The desert ended at a white paved road. Two huge rectangular objects stood on it and on the far side they saw a small oasis with a pool of water and a grove of trees.

'A sudden change from the desert,' Shanaz said, looking beyond the oasis at the undulating green plain stretching to blue hills.

'Another mystery,' Sirrah said. 'And what are these objects which look like giant boxes? How did they move so fast? They have no obvious means of propulsion, like the Thwacker.'

Sirrah looked down the road. Two figures sat dressed in identical clothes in the shadow of the 'boxes'.

'Twins,' Sirrah said. 'Help and perhaps food.'

The boy nearest to them sat looking at the paved road, smoothing his red and white pantaloons flapping in the wind. He looked at the Saradasi and then at the sky. He tossed his head, and swept the curls from his face.

Smiling at the boy, Sirrah approached him and sat in front of him. The facial features of the boys and their clothes gave no inkling who they were, though they looked like Saradasi, Sirrah thought. He decided to use the voice-box to communicate with them.

The boys looked at Sirrah attaching a voice-box around his throat and shook their heads.

The boy opposite Sirrah spoke in fluent Saradasi. 'Greetings,' he said. 'We will help you, but cannot be your friends because you are not good people. My name is SuoMela. The lazy one sitting with me is Haider. We will talk to you, but not answer your questions.'

'My name is Sirrah. My companions are Lord Rasalis, Fariyal and Shanaz.' Sirrah licked his swollen cracked, sand encrusted lips. The water in the oasis in front of him sparkled in the sun. SuoMela saw Sirrah looking at the pool.

'The water is sweet and safe to drink,' he said.

'Sirrah,' Shanaz called, 'we are on guard. Go to the pool.'

Sirrah stood up, his head throbbing, dizzy from dehydration. The oasis, the two boys and the road tilted around him. He walked unsteadily to the water. A cool breeze blew through the reeds, rippling across the pool. Sirrah filled his container with water, staring at his grimy reflection.

SuoMela nodded when Sirrah offered him a drink of water first, taking out a shiny metal bowl from a cloth bag slung across his shoulder. He held it out and said, 'We always purify water even though the source is safe. This bowl is made of a special metal that destroys living impurities in the water.'

He sipped the water and held the bowl out for Sirrah to refill, pointing to Shanaz, Fariyal and Lord Rasalis. Sirrah offered the bowl first to Lord Rasalis and then refilling it, to Fariyal. Shanaz declined to drink the water. 'I will have some later,' she said.

'Shanaz,' Fariyal whispered, 'are we safe? These two boys may be Terumana spies. See how innocent they look. Why are they sitting apart and what is in those enormous objects on the road?'

'I do not know, Fariyal. We may soon find out.'

'Perhaps they are plotting to kill us,' Fariyal said, tightening her grip on her force-sword. 'Sirrah, what are they saying to each other?'

Sirrah bent his head to listen. 'They are speaking in a language I do not understand.'

Sirrah glanced at Shanaz, Fariyal and Lord Rasalis, their eyes fastened on the boys.

Shanaz said to Lord Rasalis, 'Your mind must be computing, deducing and weaving smoothly through premises and deductions. Need we fear them?'

'I am not sure,' Lord Rasalis replied.

'I don't think they are dangerous,' Shanaz said. 'We can go to the pool in turn.'

'You go first,' Lord Rasalis said.

At the pool Shanaz knelt looking at the water. She saw neither fish nor insects; no plants grew and no birds sang. She drew her force-sword and watched it glow as the electric charge passed from her body. She filled SuoMela's bowl and inserted the tip of the sword into the water, moving her head back when the water bubbled. She looked around the small oasis. On a tree, on the underside of a leaf she saw a small insect.

She coaxed it onto a leaf and placed it in the puddle of water she created. After a few moments, it slithered onto the leaf she held out. She stood up and placed it back on the leaf she found it on.

Shanaz drank the water in small slow sips. Collecting more water she moved away from the pool, washing her hands, arms and face and joined the others. She sat on guard while Fariyal and Rasalis went to the pool. Sirrah sat smiling and nodding, listening to SuoMela.

Sirrah said to Shanaz, 'He wants us to share the food they have. He reminds us we must not ask any questions.'

Haider lit a fire under a metal pot on three stones and half filled it with water. When the water boiled he added spoonfuls of mixed grains, then reached for a basket. He unscrewed the tops of the twelve metal containers inside the basket and threw in a pinch from each into the pot.

When Lord Rasalis and Fariyal returned, Shanaz, sat with Sirrah.

'We have many questions we would like to ask you but we will respect your wish,' Shanaz said. 'We are poor pilgrims on a long journey.'

'Why are you poor?'

'I see your rules allow you to ask us questions,' Shanaz said smiling. 'We are poor because we have only what we wear. We have nothing to give you for the food you offer.'

SuoMela looked puzzled. 'Why must you give us anything? We expect nothing from you. You are strangers, hungry and thirsty, who we must help. Consider, what merit do we gain if our actions depend on a reward or repayment?'

'You have the wisdom of an older person,' Shanaz said.

'I am old,' SuoMela answered.

'Please, explain this to us,' Shanaz said. 'You say you seek no reward from us, perhaps because your actions will not gain merit if you receive a reward.'

'Yes.'

'You *are* seeking a reward by helping us,' Shanaz said slowly. 'Your reward is the merit you will receive for helping us.'

'But,' SuoMela faltered, 'receiving merit is different, because it has no material value.'

'It has value,' Shanaz said. 'Receiving merit may be of greater value than a material reward.'

'You speak wisely,' SuoMela said.

'I am not wise but I try to think,' Shanaz replied. 'You speak as if you address large numbers of people.'

'I speak to multitudes,' he said, tossing back his curls.

'I think,' Haider said, 'we have much to learn from you.'

'From me?'

'Yes. From you.'

'Thank you. I realise each day there is much more I need to learn than the day before.'

'You are not poor,' SuoMela said. 'You are intelligent, disciplined and dedicated. But you are also rich in useless possessions. Among these is your belief that because you are a Saradasi you are superior to other people.'

They were interrupted by the sound of a deep roar booming across the oasis. The dark cloud swept over them and out of sight.

'I agree with you. It sounds like a powerful machine,' Sirrah said following the cloud moving rapidly in the sky. When the cloud re-appeared overhead the noise sank to a soft purr, and then there was silence.

'What are these roaring noises we hear so often?' Fariyal asked Lord Rasalis, gripping the handle of her force-sword.

'Another mystery,' he said.

SuoMela looked across the road at the desert and his shoulders slumped. He shouted to Haider. 'Quick! It is our master.'

'Our master, Salamat Biswas, is coming,' SuoMela cried.

A rider galloped on the paved road, slowing to a canter when he neared them. He reined in the animal he rode, whipping it across its flank when it neighed. He sat caressing the handle of his whip. A sword and dagger hung from his belt; a trimmed black beard covered his face and his hair fell to his shoulders.

'I am unhappy,' he growled, scowling at SuoMela and Haider. Dismounting, he gave the animal a sharp blow on its neck with his fist and strode towards the boys. 'Why are you wasting your time by being idle? What have you sold?'

'We sold nothing,' SuoMela whispered, his face twitching.

'Why not? Where there are people, there is a sale. Must I feed you to waste time?'

'These people have nothing to pay us with,' Haider explained.

'Quiet!' Salamat Biswas drew his sword and pointed it at Haider.

'SuoMela, shall I cut off Haider's ear or a finger?'

'He has one ear,' SuoMela stammered. 'You cut off the other ear.'

'And, have you one or two ears, SuoMela?'

'Two.'

'I have removed none of yours?'

'No.'

'Then I may change my mind whose ear I should cut. Go, wash your ears SuoMela. I will select one.'

SuoMela ran to the pool. Salamat Biswas kicked Haider, and sat on the road, his back to the Saradasi.

His face wet, SuoMela stood, his hands over his ears.

'Sit,' Salamat Biswas snarled. 'Should I whip you both before I shed blood?' He raised his sword and leaned towards SuoMela.

Salamat Biswas's head jerked back. His sword flew from his hand as he grunted in pain. Shanaz held his hair in her right hand, her left knee thrust into his spine, the blade of her force-sword pressed against his throat.

'You two boys go and sit with the others,' she said tugging on Salamat Biswas's hair. 'I will kill you.'

'Why?' Salamat Biswas asked.

'Because I find you offensive.'

'I find all Saradasi offensive,' he spat. He grimaced when Shanaz pulled his head back further. 'Why do these orphan boys concern you?'

'Be quiet.'

'You are on a long journey, Saradasi. Let me help you.'

'How?'

He pointed to the two large rectangular objects on the road. 'You may travel in those machines to your destination.'

'The price?'

'It is inconsequential.'

'The price?'

'By law I must complete my task and punish these boys. Release me.'

'No. You will not harm them.'

'I must punish one of them. I have to obey our laws.'

'Your laws are stupid.'

Fariyal laid her hand on Shanaz's shoulder. 'Shanaz we have a mission to carry out. Millions of lives depend on our success. He will not kill the boy, release him please.'

'No. I will not.'

'Shanaz! This is not our problem or your concern. The Saradasi Empire is what we need to protect, not a child.'

'No. This is my concern.' Shanaz shook Fariyal's hand from her shoulder. 'We are trying to save the Nereima Galaxy, not the Saradasi Empire.'

'My Lord, please tell her she is wrong,' Fariyal said to Rasalis. 'Tell her the Saradasi Empire is of greater value than a boy's ear.'

Shanaz twisted Salamat Biswas's hair around her hand.

'Saradasi, you are not honourable. You attacked me from behind,' he said, wincing.

'Are you honourable to cut the ear of a child?'

'I adopted these two abandoned boys. You speak of honour to me Saradasi? I am more honourable than ten thousand of you.'

'I am honourable,' Shanaz insisted.

'You and your friend, Fariyal, were responsible for the death of children. Have you forgotten the children you refused to help in Flowia Valley? Picture Rensoolar Phange 67 pleading for your help and the elders from Extral North grieving for their lost children. You refused them, Saradasi, and the children died in a sudden flood.'

'Yes. I remember.'

'Your friend Fariyal is sick with fear. I smell her fear. She too killed a child and she killed its mother.' Salamat Biswas raised his voice. 'Fariyal! Have you forgotten the pregnant female in the Quartet?'

'Who told you these things?' Shanaz demanded.

'Told me? No one told me. Word of these crimes, not these things, has spread beyond your foul Empire, across the seven universes.'

'Where are we now? What is this place?' Shanaz asked.

'I am not your navigator. I will be your executioner.'

'And I yours.'

'Then let me test your honour, High Chancellor of the Saradasi Empire.' His voice sounded strangled, as Shanaz jerked his head back further. 'Let there be a sword fight between us. If you win, I will spare the boys and suffer shame. I will also give you a thousand of my soldiers to protect you until your next destination.'

'If I lose?'

'Where and when have the Saradasi lost a battle?' Salamat Biswas sneered. 'Saradasi always win, but not by merit. Victory is through deceit and treachery. You justify every obscene deed because it is for the Empire. If you lose, I will kill you, or I may change my mind and feed you to my pets. Or I will gift you to the Terumana who yearn for Saradasi flesh. Your friends I will take as slaves.'

'I accept your challenge,' Shanaz said.

'No don't, Shanaz!' Fariyal pleaded. 'Lord Rasalis, stop her!'

'Fariyal, destiny has already decided if we live or die,' he replied.

Shanaz released Salamat Biswas. He sauntered across the road and stood on the sand, repeatedly squatting, and rising lithely on his toes. He called out to Shanaz. 'You wear a firing-belt. You coward, will you fight me armed with a weapon I cannot defend myself against?'

'Pick up your sword. Fight or die,' Shanaz said.

'My sword fell on the road when you dishonourably attacked me from behind while I sat. May I get another? If you refuse, kill me now.'

'Get one or two or ten swords.'

Raising his right hand he clicked his fingers. 'Haider,' he shouted. 'Signal Sylat to come to me.'

Shanaz watched a black clad figure riding towards them from behind a dune. Salamat Biswas raised his arms in greeting, smiling broadly when the stocky rider trotted up to him.

'Sylat, I need a sword. This Saradasi who will fight me has sophisticated weapons. She has a force-sword and a firing-belt. Sylat, the Saradasi are cowards and bullies. They fight if the odds are in their favour.'

'You lie,' Shanaz said.

'No. Even as you speak, you prove I am right. Why fight me with a force-sword? Why not an ordinary sword?'

'I will switch the force off on the sword,' Shanaz said.

'Use one of our swords.'

'No. Your sword is different to mine. My sword is proportional to my height, arm length and strength.'

'Sylat, does it matter to me, a master swordsman, what type of sword she uses?'

Sylat shook his head. 'No. But this fight is unfair, Salamat Biswas.'

'Unfair? Why, Sylat?'

'She cannot win.'

'She agreed to fight. She chose death over life,' Salamat Biswas sighed. 'Sylat, I will not kill her. I will maim her. And, over a week, I will feed parts of her body to the birds of the sky. Sylat, I smile, thinking of carrion comfort, and as the righteous poet wrote, of darksome devouring eyes not on *my*, but *her* bruised bones.'

'I am ready,' Shanaz said.

'Remove your firing-belt.'

'No. The law forbids it. I give you my word I will switch off the force field on my sword and not use my firing-belt.'

'Your friends must not interfere by using their firing-belts.'

'They will not.'

'Can I trust you Saradasi?'

'Yes.'

Sylat dismounted and drew a line on the sand with the tip of his boot. He counted ten paces on either side and drew shorter line. He looked at Shanaz and Salamat Biswas.

'Stand on the smaller line. When I say, "advance," you will advance,' Sylat said. He gave Salamat Biswas his sword.

'Is it well honed?' Salamat Biswas asked, squinting along the sharp edge of the blade, holding it against the light.

'Wait,' Sylat said. He walked down to the pool of water and returned with a blade of grass, which he handed Salamat Biswas.

'Thank you Sylat. Two pieces or more?'

'More.'

Salamat Biswas flicked the blade of grass up in the air. His sword rose in a blur and several pieces of grass fluttered on to the sand. He laid the tip of the sword on his left shoulder.

Sylat mounted his animal and backed it. 'Stand on your line and move when I call out.' He roared, 'Advance!'

His sword raised, Salamat Biswas ran towards Shanaz. She sidestepped and bent down, his sword flashing inches from her face. Shanaz rose and spun around. His sword swung across her body striking the hilt of the force-sword. Feinting to her right, Shanaz swung her blade up, the swords clashing. Salamat Biswas parried several blows. He gasped and cried out.

'It is an old trick,' Shanaz said moving forwards, delivering a horizontal swipe aimed to open the upper abdomen. Salamat Biswas slashed his sword downwards deflecting the force-sword. He leapt aside as the force-sword sought the large arteries on the side of his neck. They fought, blade on blade, the sound echoing, circling each other near a mound of rocks.

'She is not fighting well,' Sirrah said.

'She is not. But she is a force-sword master,' Fariyal said. 'She is making too many mistakes and because of her we will all die. I have seen her fight before and she fights well. What is happening to her today?'

'She should have had a force-sword master's uniform,' Sirrah said referring to an uniform indistinguishable from the normal Saradasi military uniform, but with hidden pouches. When an opponent's sword ripped a pouch, 'blood' oozed out. The Saradasi would react with a pre-determined response to the "injury" distracting the opponent, whose vision would blur from the toxic compounds in the blood like fluid. The Saradasi would have inhaled the antidote before the fight.

Salamat Biswas advanced towards Shanaz, forcing her towards a rock. She moved back, defending herself, her back against the rock. Salamat Biswas brought his sword down with a grunt and swore when it struck her force-sword. Grasping her sword with both hands Shanaz slashed at him. The force-sword hit a rock with a shower of sparks and Salamat Biswas moved back, smiling.

Advancing, Shanaz stumbled on a loose stone underfoot and fell hard. With a bellow of rage Salamat Biswas smashed his sword across her lower legs. She lay flat on her back, moaning.

'How shall I kill you?' he asked.

In the shadow of the rock, Shanaz inched her hand under her body, reaching for her force-sword.

'My force-sword is on force, pointed at your foot and my firing-belt is aimed at you. I can fire without using my hands,' she said.

'I know you can, Saradasi. Kill me.'

Shanaz shook her head and drew her hand from under her body. 'You have won,' she said.

'You live by your word, Saradasi?'

'I try,' Shanaz replied.

Salamat Biswas bent and took Shanaz's arm, helping her to her feet. 'I hit you with the flat of my sword. You are in pain, but only badly bruised.'

'You could have killed me,' Shanaz said.

'Yes. But you must live,' he said when Sylat joined them. 'By defending these boys you have shown kindness and your desire for justice and proved you value your word. Saradasi, I am honoured to have met you. My master is right to hold you in high regard.'

'Who is your master?' Shanaz asked.

'No questions, remember?' He pointed to a line of riders behind them, dressed in black with scarlet cloaks billowing in the wind. 'My master has ordered me to see to your needs. These soldiers are the best in the land and will travel with you for two days. Thereafter you must journey alone. Hide yourselves well, hordes of Terumana seek you.' He pointed to the two large objects on the road. 'You will travel in these machines.' Salamat Biswas held up his hands. 'No questions. You must start the next stage of your journey immediately.'

Shanaz picked up her force-sword. 'This is not a question. We seek news of three friends.'

'You will meet Lord Medaris and Seelawathie-Ap soon,' Salamat Biswas said.

'And Lord Wynan?' Shanaz asked.

Salamat Biswas shrugged. Sylat looked at the dunes. Two riders rode up leading three mounts. Salamat Biswas helped SuoMela and Haider mount their animals, sprang on his and galloped into the desert.

'An interesting person. Who is he?' Shanaz said to Sylat.

'I met him for the first time yesterday night. I do not know who he is.' He led them across the road into one of the machines, entering through a hidden doorway. They looked around at the luxurious accommodation. Lord Medaris and Seelawathie-Ap were asleep in two of the beds on the upper level. While Lord Rasalis, Fariyal and Sirrah explored the machine, Sylat took Shanaz by the arm and led her outside.

'I admire your courage and sense of honour. I regret I am not allowed to show you my true face but one day I will tell you who I am, Shanaz, daughter of Lord Laramis. If it is my destiny, you will send for me and I will serve by your side when Saradasi no longer enslave others. I wish you a safe journey.'

'Who is Salamat Biswas?' Shanaz asked.

'He is an expert sword-fighter.'

'And who are you?'

'I cannot tell you.'

'Can you tell me where we are?'

'I was brought here yesterday and have no knowledge where I am. I speak the truth.'

'It is all so puzzling,' Shanaz said. 'I have learned nothing of what is happening around me.'

Sylat looked at her questioningly. 'Nothing?'

'You are right. I am learning who I am.'

'Knowing who one is a rare prize of great value. Treasure it,' Sylat said.

'I am also puzzled how well the two boys, Salamat Biswas and you speak Saradasi. There is something nagging at me about the way those we have met speaks our language. They all have the same accent.'

Sylat raised his right arm. He swung on his mount and rode along the white road alone. Shanaz's memory stirred, watching him, reminding her of a walk in the mountains, of snow, of a small child stumbling, and a gentle strong hand steadying her; her father saying, 'be with her always' and a voice answering 'as long as I live.' A blind female pressed a fruit in her hand, saying it tasted sweet like summer honey.

She knew the voice but could not remember whom it belonged to. Where she wondered, were they together during her childhood?

Shanaz climbed into a bed across from where Lord Medaris slept. She was thinking about Sylat when a sound startled her and a glow sheathed the entry door. She ran to the door trying to pull it open. When she drew her force-sword the room darkened. The force-sword slipped from her hand as she sagged to the floor.

'Go to sleep, Saradasi,' a voice said.

TWENTY-TWO

They awoke with the sun shining. The wide white paved road ended at the edge of a green plain rising to blue hills. Beyond the hills they glimpsed the blurred rim of a mountain range. A broad river with wide banks cut across the plain.

Their force-swords and firing-belts were clean and shiny. Seelawathie-Ap's *kaduwa* glowed and their backpacks were heavy with food and water. A breeze blew across the plain, warm and comforting. Lord Medaris sat alone, his arms clasped across his knees. Shanaz joined Fariyal and Lord Rasalis, Sirrah and Seelawathie-Ap.

'What is our plan?' Fariyal asked.

'To walk again to where the sun sets,' Shanaz said. 'Our first destination is the mountain with twin peaks where the Golden One said we may receive help to find *The Place.*'

'Ever westwards?' Fariyal asked.

'The Lord of the East told us to follow the sun,' Shanaz said, adjusting her firing-belt.

'We are in a strange land,' Sirrah said, 'on a planet where we cannot assume the sun will set in the west. We will have to wait till evening.'

'I think the sun will set in the west,' Shanaz said, squinting at the horizon.

They picked up their backpacks and walked westwards across the plain. When the shadows lengthened, they stopped to watch the sunlight rim the mountain range red.

'The sun sets in the west just as in our galaxy,' Sirrah said.

'We can all go west together or in two groups by different routes,' Shanaz said to Lord Rasalis. 'We would meet different people along the way and perhaps gather more information about the mountain with twin peaks. What do you think, Medaris?'

'I will follow your orders,' he said. 'You are the High Chancellor.'

After a discussion lasting several minutes, they agreed with Shanaz that Lord Medaris and Seelawathie-Ap would follow the river for a day and travel west, while the others would cross the plain westwards. They decided when and where to meet, setting the coordinates on their wristbands. After an unhurried meal they watched Medaris and Seelawathie-Ap walk along the riverbank.

○

When the light mist cleared early the next morning, after bathing in the river, Shanaz, Fariyal, Rasalis and Sirrah walked towards the blue hills below the mountain range. By evening they struck a faint trail threading through the hills.

Sirrah pointed to the ground where patches of grass and rocks were removed making the trail easier to follow. Twice they came across recently used fire pits. They stopped when they rounded a bend and saw a shred of red cloth fluttering in the breeze, snagged on a thorn.

'Intentional or accidental?' Shanaz asked.

'We will never know,' Lord Rasalis said, unhooking the piece of cloth and throwing it into a gully by the trail.

Shanaz patted Fariyal's shoulder, giving her a gentle push to keep on walking. The trail descended sharply along the edge of a deep ravine.

'We must cross the ravine to travel west,' Sirrah said, glancing at his wristband.

In the fading light they saw two logs across the ravine, many hundred feet long, tied with vines. In the darkness below they saw the glint of water swirling between rocks.

'Is it safe, Shanaz?' Fariyal asked.

Shanaz pointed to the logs, 'The leaves on some branches are green. The logs are young and strong and not decayed. They won't collapse under us.'

'Someone may have tampered with them,' Fariyal said, stepping back. 'They will give way when we walk across.'

'I will go across first,' Shanaz said.

On the opposite side of the ravine the trail continued, winding towards the mountains covered with snow, to end on a plateau. Far to the west they saw a valley with a river snaking through it.

'Is it the same river we swam across on the plain, Sirrah?' Shanaz asked.

Sirrah looked at his wristband. 'Yes. Lord Medaris and Seelawathie-Ap would be following it.'

On the fourth day since they started the journey across the plain, they camped at night in a small copse of trees, the cold wind picking up.

'Shanaz, why do we have to cross the deepest streams at the coldest time of the day?' Fariyal asked shivering, sitting by a fire, hunched against the wind.

'To test us, Fariyal. See, Lord Rasalis and Sirrah are asleep and neither complained. Remember what you taught me in the desert, how to clear my mind and not think of the heat? Try not to think of the cold.'

Fariyal shivered. 'I am trying to raise my body temperature. I feel so cold.'

'Are you tired, Fariyal?' Shanaz asked moving to sit by her. 'Are you ill?'

'I am tired, but I am not ill. I will never reach the mountain with twin peaks.'

'Of course you will. Do you remember the Golden One saying, "You wonder where you should go, but I cannot give you a route. Use nature as your friend. Trust yourselves."'

They talked about Tarich's Tavern by the sea wall and the old wharves in the Upper City in Saradas and of long walks in the Mirellar Mountains. They lay on their cloaks, and fell asleep by the fire.

The next morning the trail narrowed, clinging to the face of the mountain, a valley thousands of feet below them. They walked in single file, Shanaz with a stout stick. With each step they heard the sound of loose rocks they dislodged clattering down the mountainside. Below them the river in the valley flowed west, an ever-diminishing silver ribbon.

On the evening of the sixth day, while they were walking along the trail, Lord Rasalis stopped, wet with perspiration, leaning against a rock by a pool of water.

'I walked too quickly,' he said breathless, wiping his face. 'I will rest and then go on. It will be easier for me to walk, the trail is descending. Go ahead and find a safe place for us to camp tonight.'

'Fariyal, you go on,' Shanaz said. 'I will stay here and we will join you soon.'

Shanaz and Sirrah sat with Rasalis for awhile, filled their water containers and walked on. The trail weaved away from the face of the mountain down through groves of trees. Wisps of mist floated over the mountainside towards them.

'I can walk with Sirrah's help. Shanaz, Fariyal is alone, you should join her,' Lord Rasalis said.

Shanaz, hesitated, nodded and walked quickly along the trail. She reached a clearing beside a stand of shady trees, an ideal spot to camp and looked around calling out, 'Fariyal.' She called again and again, louder. She heard the dull echo of her voice. When she walked around the clearing again, at the far end, hidden by a bush, she saw the entrance to a narrow gorge, a trickle of water seeping from its floor. She peered inside.

'Fariyal,' she shouted. 'Fariyal, where are you?'

When she stepped out she saw Lord Rasalis and Sirrah walk into the clearing.

'Where is Fariyal?' Sirrah asked.

'I can't find her. She probably walked into the gorge,' Shanaz said, pointing. 'She should have waited for us.' She paced restlessly, adjusting her force-sword and firing-belt. 'I must follow her.'

'Shall I come with you?' Sirrah asked.

'Stay with Lord Rasalis,' Shanaz said.

Watching Shanaz enter the gorge, Lord Rasalis said, 'Sirrah, how right I am about Shanaz. All my predictions come to pass. Is it a burden for you to know I am always right?'

'Yes, but not a burden which weighs me down,' Sirrah said.

A patch of sky darkened and they hid among the trees. A growling sound swept over them as a Terumana craft passed overhead.

'Will Fariyal and Shanaz be safe, Lord?'

'Sirrah,' Lord Rasalis said, resting on the ground, his head against a tree, 'don't you worry about them. You are reverting to your old habit of talking far too much. Nourishment is what we need, Sirrah, not idle chatter.'

○

Shanaz hurried through the gorge, its soaring walls covered with stunted trees and shrubs. Rivulets of water trickled down on the smooth red floor. Ahead, she saw a blur of blue, Fariyal's cloak. Shanaz cupped her hands around her mouth but the word 'Fariyal' choked in her throat.

The words of the survival instructor at the military academy passed through her mind.

'So, what is the obvious action?' he would ask. 'Avoid it. Think, think and think again. The obvious is what the enemy expects, because most people are unintelligent. The obvious action is not the option for the intelligent person. Survival is the outcome of intelligence. Your brain is your most powerful weapon, not your force-sword, nor your firing-belt. Think and win. Think and survive.'

When the gorge darkened, Shanaz heard the rumble overhead. She rolled on the floor, slapping water on her body and ran, leaning spread–eagled against a crevice dripping with water. She glimpsed a Terumana craft flying low and knew its heat detectors would be scanning the gorge.

The Terumana craft made another slower pass over the gorge. She heard a 'plopping' sound, and smelled the foul odour. The walls of the gorge behind her trembled as if shaken by a giant fist. First flakes, then chunks of rock broke away from the sides of the gorge in a loud tumble of chaos and choking clouds of red dust. Shanaz ran, shielding her face, stumbling over uprooted trees and shrubs. When she rounded a bend, she saw Fariyal huddled by a rock, her hands over her ears.

Shanaz ran to Fariyal, hugging her. 'Fariyal, what happened? Why did you enter this gorge alone?'

'I heard a voice calling me by name, asking me for help,' Fariyal whispered. 'But I never reached the person. It sounded like a voice I knew. I am afraid, Shanaz.'

'Not any longer, because I am with you.'

'Shanaz, I feel afraid. I am a Saradasi but I feel afraid.'

'So do I.'

'I heard the noise. Were they Terumana?'

'Yes. They have left.'

'Should we rejoin Lord Rasalis and Sirrah?'

Shanaz squeezed her hand. 'We cannot. The gorged is blocked behind us. Let's find a way out and decide what we should do.' She laid a finger over Fariyal's lips. 'Shhhh! Fariyal, we must never again say we are afraid. You are a commander and I am a colonel in the Saradasi military.'

'Someone might hear us and lodge a complaint. The military will strike our names off the promotion list,' Fariyal laughed. 'They can! I am not seeking a promotion.'

'Neither am I,' Shanaz said. 'The stupid promotion list.'

Laughing together, they walked through the gorge and slept that night under a sombre sky, wrapped in their cloaks, on a ledge of rock. When they awoke the gorge shone, the sunlight reflecting off water flowing down its walls. They waded knee-deep in water, looking at the walls of the gorge changing colour as the sun rose. The floor of the gorge dropped sharply. The flow of water increased forcing them to hold on to rocks, and move forward hand in hand, each step treacherous.

'Where has this water come from?' Fariyal said.

'Fariyal, be careful,' Shanaz shouted.

A sharp noise echoed around them. A head high wave of water surged towards them, gushing from a widening crack in the floor. A second rush of water pinned them against the wall of the gorge and carried them away. Ahead of her Shanaz saw Fariyal clambering onto a rock. Fariyal grasped her arm as she swept past, helping her up.

'Where is the water from?' Fariyal asked, wiping her face.

'It is from an underground source. See, the force of the water has lessened,' Shanaz said.

'Shanaz,' Fariyal said, pointing, 'but the level is rising.'

They heard a cracking sound and a portion of the wall behind them crumbled and a torrent of water swept them out of the gorge.

They were on the bank of a river. Shanaz stood up, unbuckled her force-sword and firing-belt and massaged her sore shoulder. The river flowed in a straight line, then veered left by a clump of trees growing in the water. Rectangular white stones paved the riverbank for some distance. Set amid the white stones a row of tress swayed in the breeze, heavy with fist sized yellow fruit.

Fariyal shook the water from her hair, smiling at Shanaz. 'I thought we would drown,' she said.

'Not with a good swimmer like you helping me.'

Fariyal struggled to her feet and walked to a tree. She smelled a fruit. 'Shanaz, I am not sure if we should eat this or not. Why are there no birds? There must be something wrong with these fruits. They may be poisonous.'

'Fariyal, we have the best reason to eat them. We are hungry,' Shanaz said.

Fariyal hesitated.

'The birds may have better food to eat,' Shanaz said, joining Fariyal. She snapped a leaf, crushing it in her hand to smell it. 'It is not an artificial tree,' she said and plucked the smallest fruit on the tree. 'I'll have a bite. You can see what happens to me.'

'No. Please don't. I am sure the fruit is poisonous.'

Shanaz peeled the fruit and bit into the thick fibrous flesh. 'Delicious,' she said, bending her head forwards and wiping dribbling juice off her chin.

Fariyal plucked a fruit off the tree and sniffed it.

The fruit dropped from Shanaz's hand splattering on the white stones. Fariyal gasped as Shanaz slid to the ground, her arms extended rigidly. She lay with her back arched, her legs extended, her heels beating a convulsive tattoo on the white stones. Her eyes rolled. She stopped breathing. She breathed again sucking in deep breaths of air, moaning and thrashing her legs on the ground.

Fariyal screamed. She sat by Shanaz trying to force her mouth open to prevent her biting her tongue. Shanaz breathed more evenly when Fariyal stroked her head, cradled in her arms.

Shanaz opened her eyes and winked. 'Just being funny,' she said.

'My turn, my cousin, will come,' Fariyal said, pushing her away.

They sat eating the fruit, watching the river flow past them. Shanaz knelt at the edge of the water, washing her face, neck and arms. She dipped her head in the water washing her hair.

'Is it safe to drink?' Fariyal asked, dipping a finger into the river.

'Fariyal, taste the water.'

Fariyal dipped her finger in and out of the water quickly.

'Fariyal, be reasonable. We have survived so far. Should we die of thirst? Should we sterilize the water? Snap our fingers and catch a silver bowl like SuoMela's to kill germs?'

'I am not sure we should drink this water unless we sterilize it with our force-swords.'

'Watch me,' Shanaz said.

'No, please, you must not!'

'Watch,' Shanaz said, bending on her knees, drinking deeply from the river. She stood screaming. She thrust her fingers in her mouth, flinging something back into the water.

Fariyal ran to her. 'What is it? What happened?'

'A small snake,' Shanaz screamed. She started to retch.

Fariyal screamed louder. Shanaz held her hand across her mouth, gagging.

Fariyal pushed her into the water. When she reached the bank, she asked 'How are the snakes?' and pushed her into the water again.

They walked along the riverbank past enormous, craggy boulders and clambered down the bank when the river dropped into a series of pools fed by waterfalls from gorges, before it flowed to the valley below. They reached a plateau overlooking the valley, where they rested.

'My chest hurts,' Fariyal said. 'I wish we would reach the end of our journey,' she said.

'We are alive, Fariyal,' Shanaz said, throwing a stone over the edge of the plateau.

'We may not be alive tomorrow,' Fariyal said. 'But living or dying is becoming less important to me. How will Lord Rasalis and Sirrah find us?'

'They will travel westwards.'

Shanaz stood staring across the valley thousands of feet below and at the jagged line of mountains. She peeled a yellow fruit and offered it to Fariyal. Shanaz pointed to the west. 'See the mountain behind the others, standing alone?'

'With the funny peak?'

'Yes. If we stay till sunset, I am sure the sun will set over the mountain. That mountain may be our final destination.'

Fariyal gazed at the mountain tinged with pink.

'I have had a recurrent dream on this journey,' Shanaz said. 'My dream is for the Empire to be just to all its citizens, with no person saying we Saradasi are unjust.'

'Where a Saradasi is no greater or better than a southern Califran,' Fariyal said.

Shanaz drew Fariyal to her. 'A *southern* Califran? Why a *southern* Califran, Fariyal? Tell me about this southern Califran.'

Fariyal walked to the edge of the plateau. 'The sun is setting,' she said.

They stood together watching the sun set, first a fiery red, softening to an orange mantle behind the mountains.

'Shanaz, why do I have the feeling that I will not be by your side after this journey ends?'

Shanaz threw a stone in the air and as it descended aimed a kick at it and missed.

'Do you love Wynan?' Fariyal asked.

'I am not sure what I feel. I loved him once, more than I believe I could love anyone. I am confused about the past, the present and the future and about love and hope.'

'Perhaps we each have a written destiny,' Fariyal said. 'What we want to happen may not happen if it is not our destiny.'

'I agree,' Shanaz said. 'But I worry about Wynan's safety, and worry if we will meet Medaris and Seelawathie-Ap.'

'We may not meet Lord Rasalis and Sirrah,' Fariyal said.

'Fariyal, they will be safe and will find us.'

A sharp sound broke the silence. Fariyal motioned and Shanaz ran to a clump of trees and knelt behind a cluster of rocks. She adjusted the controls of her firing-belt and checked the charge in her force-sword. Fariyal crept to her right into a small depression. They heard the sound of snapping branches in the dense grove of trees if front of them. Shanaz checked where Fariyal was and activated her firing-belt. The multiple laser beams lanced through the trees like a flaming scythe. A breeze swept the smell of scorched wood and vegetation and a sickly sweet odour towards them.

Shanaz moved across to Fariyal, and they crawled, scanning the burning grove of trees. Six bodies lay on the ground, dismembered by laser fire.

'Terumana,' Fariyal said inspecting the bodies.

'Terumana who cannot walk quietly. Their problem is not their courage but their brains. We were lucky it was the Terumana or we may have killed innocent people.'

Fariyal sheathed her force-sword. 'Does it matter, Shanaz? Must our mistakes haunt us? We acted for the Empire, not ourselves. Remember it is the Empire we want to save and protect.'

'No, Fariyal. Our mission is to save the Nereima Galaxy and all its people. I now feel less loyalty to the Empire which enslaves billions. Who wants this great Empire except the Saradasi?'

They reclined on the cool surface of a rock, looking at the clouds moving across a pearly blue sky.

'I am worried about Lord Rasalis and Sirrah. They should be here,' Shanaz said.

'I too fear for their safety.'

'One of us should go back the way we came and search for them,' Shanaz suggested.

'The other?'

'The other should go to the valley and wait there.'

'Where?'

Shanaz pointed, sitting up. 'To the west. See the bend in the river and the heart shaped grove of trees, west of where we are?'

Fariyal sat, squinting across at the valley. 'At the far end?'

'Yes. One of us should go there and wait for the others.'

'Shall I go there and wait for you, or look for Lord Rasalis and Sirrah? Fariyal asked.

'You choose.'

Fariyal shook her head. She bent and rose with her hands clenched. 'If you pick the hand with the pebble, you go to the bend in the river.'

'Right hand.'

Fariyal opened her empty palm. 'How long shall I wait there for you and the others?'

'Two weeks.'

'So long?'

Shanaz pointed to the far end of the valley. 'We cannot gauge how long it will take to reach there. The bend in the river may be much farther than we think it is.'

'What if no one comes?'

'Fariyal, one of us will. If no one comes, follow the coordinates and join Medaris and Seelawathie-Ap. Fariyal. We can survive. We learned survival skills for a whole year in our training. We can identify which of these plants around us is edible.'

'We were not sure about the yellow fruits. But what happens after two weeks?' Fariyal asked again.

'Join Medaris and Seelawathie-Ap.'

'When will you leave?'

'Now,' Shanaz said.

'No. Though you are the High Chancellor of the Saradasi Empire, you are a colonel,' Fariyal said. 'As your military superior, my orders are that you leave at daybreak. Lord Rasalis and Sirrah may be here by then.'

○

The next morning after holding Fariyal in her arms, Shanaz walked back the way they came along the riverbank.

Fariyal watched the slight figure hurrying, her head held high.

On the crest of a rocky hill beyond the opposite bank of the river, she saw a light flicker. Friend or foe she wondered. Adjusting her backpack, she walked down into the valley. More lights flickered on the hills.

TWENTY-THREE

After spending a night on the riverbank, Fariyal woke up with the sun shining over the valley, the river and the waterfalls. She ate the last of the yellow fruits and tidied herself, mopping the patches of dirt from her uniform. She cleaned her boots with a few handfuls of grass and tested the charge of her force-sword, watching its tip burn through a fallen piece of wood. She decided she would reach the valley from the opposite side of the river where a broad meadow with groves of trees, stretched to the mountains.

At a point where the river narrowed, Fariyal unclasped her cloak, and wrapped it tightly around her waist, over the firing-belt and force-sword. She entered the water, treading between sunken rocks, and reached the opposite bank, bracing against the strong current. She crawled on to the bank, and crouched among the reeds, listening to the sound of the fast flowing river, the wind through the reeds, and the chatter of insects.

She heard the piercing call of a bird followed by another, and the sound of wings flapping. She listened to the birdcalls recalling that, as a student at the Ansara Military Academy she won a prize for identifying the calls of more than a hundred birds.

She crawled to a rock formation from where she lay. On her left a flock of birds darted in and out of a grove of trees. Patience, she reminded herself. Discipline. Do not hurry. Impatience leads to disaster, she told herself. Shutting her eyes she began a breathing exercise. She took a deep breath, held the breath counting to seven, and then exhaled over a count of seven. Her pulse no longer raced. Fariyal crept towards the trees.

The trees were heavy with pink berries. In a clearing a young boy sat humming a tune, his head tilted back watching the birds. A fire burned within a ring of rocks. His white tunic flapped in the wind and threadbare trousers reached his bare feet. Two large open baskets with their lids beside them were on the ground. An animal lay by him asleep.

Fariyal stood, drew her force-sword and walked towards him.

He tried to stand but Fariyal motioned him not to. She wondered who he thought she was, dressed in wet and muddied blue clothes, pointing a weapon at him. Fariyal raised her free hand to her throat. She remembered she was not wearing her voice-box, but knew it would not function.

'Who are you? Where are you from?' he asked.

'I am a very weary traveller. You speak Saradasi?' Fariyal asked, surprised. 'Please tell me how you learned to speak Saradasi. You speak it well. Where is this place?'

'I do not know where I live. The Saradasi punished my ancestors by sending them here long ago.'

'Did your ancestors speak Saradasi?' Fariyal asked puzzled.

'No.'

'If Saradasi was not their language, how do you speak Saradasi?' Fariyal said, turning her head when his eyes darted to the river.

'We learned Saradasi for six months from a stranger.'

'A stranger? What did he look like?'

'He was tall with long legs and arms.'

'His face?'

The boy shook his head. 'He wore a mask.'

'He wore a mask for six months?'

'Yes.'

Fariyal held the boy's gaze. His blue eyes were wide open, never leaving hers. She noticed his relaxed shoulders, his hands on his lap, still, and not fidgeting nervously.

'What was the mask like?' she asked.

The boy scratched his head. 'He wore many masks. He wore a different mask every week. He said they were in memory of those who suffered because of Saradasi injustice throughout the Empire. He told us one mask represented a million people.'

'People should be grateful to us Saradasi for what we do for them,' Fariyal said.

'The old people in the village say my ancestors were not grateful to the Saradasi for sending them here.'

'It is possible your ancestors committed a crime for which they received punishment.'

'The old ones say that our ancestors protested against Saradasi rule. Is it a crime to not want others to rule you in your own land?'

'The Saradasi may have ruled them to make them better people.'

'Better? How? I understand why good people would want to make bad people better. But how can bad people make good people better? It is a great puzzle to all of us in the village.'

'I was not there, so I would not know what happened to your ancestors,' Fariyal replied.

'But is it right to conquer people to make them better if they did nothing bad? Conquering others even to make them better is an act of evil. It is the conqueror who must be punished.'

Fariyal said, 'Many people carry out bad acts which they believe help others. They are often wrong.'

The boy leaned forward. 'Do you agree it is bad to conquer others?'

'What I used to believe is changing. Yes. It is wrong to conquer other people.'

'You are a Saradasi. Are you, better than I am?' he asked.

'No.'

The boy added wood to the fire and held his hands over it. The animal woke up and brayed.

'Tell me more about your masked teacher. What did his voice sound like?'

'I do not know. He wore a small box around his throat that spoke for him.'

Fariyal drew out her voice-box from her backpack. 'Was it like this? We call it a voice-box.'

'Yes,' the boy said.

She wondered if the teacher used the voice-box to alter his or her voice, or to transmit and seek interpretation of the language via the satellites linked to language centres. Why disguise his or her voice? Who would recognise it in this remote place? Fariyal held out the voice-box in her left hand. 'Please tie this round your neck and say three times in your language the words "interpretation requested."'

He spoke thrice in a language Fariyal did not recognise. There was no response from the voice-box. She wished Sirrah was here with her. Being a linguist, he could have perhaps identified the language.

'Now please say it again, three times in Saradasi.'

The boy followed her instructions, but there was silence. She wondered why, since their journey began, the voice-boxes were not functioning. Where was she, she thought, as the boy unbuckled the voice-box and handed it to her, and who was he? Here was another mystery. But who would provide the solution?

'Did anyone ask your teacher why he used a voice-box?'

'Yes, many of us asked him. He said it helped him to learn our language and teach us Saradasi. I do not think Saradasi was his own language.'

'Why do you think that?'

'Someone came to see him, also wearing a mask, and they spoke in another language. I listened to them when they were alone in the night, talking and laughing.'

'I think you are clever,' Fariyal said.

'I think you are also clever,' he grinned. 'You ask clever questions. Ask me another question.'

Smiling back at him Fariyal moved to sit closer to him across the fire. 'You said he wore a mask and disguised his voice. How do you know the teacher was a male?

'The person who visited him was a female and they kissed that night.'

'Are you sure?'

'Yes. Me and my friends watched them.' The boy giggled.

'Did they only kiss?'

He lowered his head.

'Did you watch them all night?'

'My friends did.' He added quickly, 'And I.'

'That's bad.'

'Not as bad as what Saradasi do. I have no weapon, why are you pointing your weapon at me?'

Fariyal smiled, sheathing her force-sword. The evening light streamed through the branches of the trees while they sat warming their hands over the fire. The animal flicked its ears.

'Why do you smile?' Fariyal asked.

'My friend, Aras, asked the stranger why he used the voice-box. Aras said a person as clever as him could have learned our language first and taught us Saradasi without wearing a voice-box.'

'If he was honest,' Fariyal said, 'he would have told your friend that it is difficult to disguise one's voice for a long time. Appearance yes, but not one's voice. That is why he used the voice-box. But I do not understand why he wanted to disguise his voice. Who would have recognised it?'

The boy stroked the animal's head. 'I think I know the reason. He did not want anyone in the village to mimic his voice. I mean, to mimic his real voice to someone who may recognise it.'

'You may be right,' Fariyal said. 'It is a clever explanation. I like the way you think.'

'Is your voice disguised?' he asked.

Fariyal shook her head.

'Your appearance?'

Fariyal shook her head again.

'Are you wearing a mask?'

'No.'

'If you are not wearing a mask, you are the most beautiful person I have seen,' the boy said shyly.

'I am sure your mother is beautiful,' Fariyal said, looking into the fire.

'I am an orphan.'

'I am sorry to hear that. You must miss her.'

The boy nodded.

'I am sorry to ask you so many questions, but I have two more. Did the stranger wear a sword?'

'Yes. And so did his female friend. Their swords were not like yours.'

'Tell me about your village,' Fariyal said.

'It is by the river. There are not many adults in our village. Years ago bandits killed many people.'

'Why were you not killed?'

'My parents hid me. Up there,' the boy pointing to the mountain slopes. 'They both died.'

'Who attacked you?'

'They were bad people. We do not know where they came from.'

'How many?'

'About a hundred.'

'Have they come since?'

'No.'

A single Saradasi, Fariyal thought, could destroy the attackers with a firing-belt and force-sword. Few knew the force-sword served beyond a primitive looking weapon for close combat. It was also a long-range laser, supplementing the multi-barrelled firing-belt.

'Who lives in the village now?' Fariyal said.

'Children and a few adults.'

Fariyal watched the green and red birds darting in and out of the trees, plucking bunches of berries and placing them on the ground by the two baskets. The boy stretched his feet, wriggling his toes. He looked at the sky and whistled thrice. The birds flew down from the

trees and entered the two baskets. He loaded the fruit into two panniers and slung them and the baskets with the birds, across the back of
the animal.

He peered into the baskets. 'I must search for two birds. I will be
back soon.' He whistled shrilly, walking between the trees.

No longer concerned about a hidden danger, Fariyal stood and
looked at the river, golden in the sun. A troubling thought came to her.
Why were Saradasi trying to make other people better? Should they
first become better people themselves?

She thought of Captain Lique, the southern Califra, who served
under her at Mitbara where she met the Quartet, when a female and
her unborn child died because of her. Memories of him crowded her
mind. She remembered each time she saw him how she wanted to hold
the memory of face in her mind forever. Once, when she bent to look
at the screen in front of him she smelled a fragrance, vague, gentle and
subdued, like Captain Lique. She remembered how he drew back as if
she was a septic impurity.

She wondered if he hated her because of what she did to the
Quartet, and the two deaths, or because she was a hated Saradasi. She
knew a gulf too wide to span lay between them, a Saradasi and Califran,
proud ruler and enraged vassal.

She heard the boy whistling again. She sat by the fire, inhaling the
pleasant smell from the twigs she threw in.

'What would my life be,' she thought, as she often did, 'if I said,
"I love you, Captain Lique"? What would he have said, a Califran, to a
Saradasi? Would I have had the courage to end my career and face exile
from the home planet if he said he loved me?'

It was during the journey to find *The Place* and fulfil *The Prophecy*,
she realised Shanaz would have cared for her and helped her. Lord
Rasalis and Medaris and Sirrah would have supported her too. The birds
fell silent in their baskets. The flames flickered. The animal brayed softly.

She remembered her last day at Mitbara. Captain Lique was at the
space station, as protocol demanded, to wish her good-bye. She stood
silently in front of him.

She knew she would never see him again. She gazed at him wanting
a perfect image of him. She remembered angrily fighting back the tears.
She searched his face for the smallest sign he loved her. He too was staring at her. Were his eyes moist? She knew she must say something to

him. She pleaded for courage to be her companion for that moment, to utter three words that would change her life forever. If he replied he loved her, nothing else would matter. The departure signal rose in pitch and the red and green lights flashed.

She heard the soft voice. 'I ask my God to be with you. I will never forget you. Fariyal, I will never love anyone as much as I love you.'

Staring at him, she knew her life had changed for ever. She took a step towards him. Frightened, Fariyal ran towards her military transport vehicle to Saradasi.

All that seemed so long ago.

The boy sat across the fire and looked at her when she wiped her eyes, pushing aside the memory of Captain Lique.

'Sometimes,' he said, 'great sadness comes before great joy.'

The sky was cloudy, the temperature dropping. The boy quenched the fire and they watched it struggling to die.

'What is your name?' Fariyal asked.

'Centar.'

He looked shyly at Fariyal. 'And what is your name?'

'Fariyal. How old are you, Centar?'

'I am nine years old.'

'I too have a nine in my age.'

'You are very young,' Centar said surprised, when she told him her age.

He checked the knots that secured the baskets with the birds and the panniers with berries. 'It will rain,' he said pointing to the sky. 'It is not safe here. When it rains, the river may flood. Where are you going?'

Fariyal remained silent.

'Where are you going?'

Fariyal saw his look of concern. 'I am not sure.'

'Are you hungry?'

'Yes, I am,' Fariyal said.

'Please have some berries. I am sorry I have no other food.' He offered her a handful of berries from a pannier.

'You have some first,' Fariyal said.

He picked a few berries and began eating them.

'How do they taste?' Fariyal asked.

'Sweet.'

'Do these berries stain the teeth?'

'Stain the teeth? I do not know. Why do you ask?'

'My teeth are sensitive to stains,' Fariyal explained. 'Can you please show me your teeth?'

Centar opened his mouth and Fariyal peered in, looking for hidden berries, not swallowed.

'Beautiful teeth,' she said, and ate the berries.

When the sky darkened, Centar said, 'Please come with me to my village. It is dangerous here.'

Fariyal thanked him, remembering the cold nights she spent in the open.

She walked with Centar through a wooded valley. The wind rose and it became colder and darker. After a long walk they reached a flight of stone steps that ended on a road.

'The village is an hour's walk from here. Do you want to rest here?'

'No. Why did we not come to the village before dark?' Fariyal asked.

Centar remained silent, walking ahead of her. Fariyal drew her cloak around her shoulders. In the dusk she saw fields on one side of the road, and near them, along the road, dark water gushed in a canal. Lights twinkled in the distance.

'We will soon reach the village,' Centar said.

Fariyal cried out in a strangled voice, 'I feel dizzy. Everything is spinning around me.' Lurching towards a tree to steady herself, she stumbled into the canal screaming. Flailing in the water, she raised her head looking at Centar.

'Centar,' she gasped, 'please help me.'

Centar reached out to her. She looked at his face and screamed before she lost consciousness.

TWENTY-FOUR

hanaz sat on the bank of the river, her feet dangling in the water. Two days had passed since she left Fariyal, retracing her steps, hoping to meet Lord Rasalis and Sirrah.

'Ho! Saradasi,' a voice called in the distance.

Shanaz climbed a mound of boulders and peered down.

'Ho! Saradasi,' the unseen voice boomed again.

'Shanaz! Fariyal!'

'Shanaz! Fariyal!' The echo made it difficult to recognize if the voice belonged to Lord Rasalis.

Shanaz drew her force-sword, setting it to long-range fire and altered the controls on her firing-belt. After an hour's wait, she climbed down to the riverbank. She heard a sharp plopping sound and stepped back from the water, looking around to identify it. She heard the sound louder and closer. Shanaz ran, clambering up the boulders when a soaring wave of water rushed towards her, reaching her shoulders. A beam of light played on the bubbling water and the river blazed, with flaming waves racing towards her and the boulders.

Dropping down on a ridge, Shanaz ran towards a gap between two boulders, pushing her way through. Behind her she heard the sound of rocks shattering and falling into the burning river. Easing her way out of the defile, she lay flat on the ground behind a shrub, looking for a route to safety. Hills, gorges and ravines spread below her; to the west a dense forest rose over a mountainside. When clods of earth and shards of rocks flew around her, she ran to a copse of trees. Behind her, she saw two figures dressed in black run across a ridge in opposite directions.

Crawling through the underbrush she reached the forest. After an hour's walk she stopped by a pool of water to wash the blood and soil from her face and arms. By evening she reached and crossed a plateau cut by deep canyons. She wondered about Fariyal, hoping Lord Rasalis and Sirrah would travel along the riverbank and detect Fariyal's direction markers to guide them to the bend by the river in the valley. Her unease about leaving Fariyal nagged her.

A blizzard struck without warning, the snow lashing at her, the wind beating against her. Shanaz walked on, her head bent against the wind and snow, shielding her face with her cloak. She entered a wood, the branches heavy with snow, and sought shelter behind a tree. The wind hushed to a whisper and there was silence around her.

In the silence, her anxiety increased when she remembered what a teacher at the military academy said about silence. "Silence is dangerous. Total silence is unnatural, invariably contrived, therefore, very dangerous. Beware. Recall the Mankunians. Their warriors are silent even when injured. Why? They consume a toxin before battle which paralyses their vocal cords, and they sever the vocal cords of their attack animals."

The silence was broken by a faint sound from within the forest. She heard the sound again, but stayed where she was behind the tree. After a while, she drew her force-sword and worked her way, sheltering behind the trees, in the direction of the sound. She stopped, peering into a clearing in the forest with snow-covered stumps of trees, cut branches and lengths of chopped wood in piles on the ground.

A moan reached her. Shanaz walked into to the clearing. A small child lay face down in the snow under a broken branch dangling from a tree. A long gash with congealed blood ran down the side of his shaven head. His saffron coloured robe was blotched with blood. Shanaz lifted the branch and turned the child over and wiped the snow from his face.

'Thank you,' he whispered. Kneeling beside him she lifted him on her back, tying him onto her with her cloak. She clasped her hands behind her, holding the child, and went deeper into the forest in search of shelter. The blizzard picked up, the snow blinding and the temperature plummeting. She knew she must act quickly to protect herself and the child. Beads of perspiration, despite the cold ran down her face. Shanaz straightened her aching back.

The child stirred. 'Leave me here,' he said. 'You go on.'

'I have nowhere to go,' she said.

'We must build a shelter,' he advised.

Shanaz squatted down and untied the cloak. The child tried to stand but Shanaz pushed him down gently. She shook the snow off her cloak and wrapped him in it.

'Thank you. I am used to the cold,' he said.

She held him close to her. 'My name is Shanaz. What is your name?'

'Pritham.' He searched her face and asked timidly, 'Who are you?'

'I am a traveller lost in the snow.'

'Don't be frightened,' he said. 'My friend, Gautham, will find us. He and I live in a monastery up on a mountain nearby. He will find us but first we must build a shelter.'

Shanaz built a crude shelter using her force-sword to cut down branches from the trees. They crawled in and Shanaz sat on the layer of leaves, trying to stay awake, while Pritham slept, his robe pulled over his head, her blue cloak over him. She woke when the shelter shook. She pointed the force-sword at the branches being parted.

A face thrust itself inside the shelter, all smiles, the shaven head covered with snow. Attentive, briskly moving eyes roamed across the shelter. A small boy wriggled in and sat on his haunches. Beaming at Shanaz, showing two rows of uneven teeth, he placed a small lantern and an axe beside him.

'Pritham. Greetings!' he said in a high-pitched voice. He raised his lantern and saw the gash on his friend's head. 'Are you injured badly?' he asked anxiously.

'You took too long, Gautham. You were playing while I almost died,' Pritham complained.

'I came to the clearing because you were not at the bridge. You forgot the axe. Can you walk?'

'Yes.'

'Thank you for helping my friend,' Gautham said to Shanaz. 'We must leave now to reach our monastery. By morning the snow may be many feet high and there are frequent avalanches. We must leave now.'

Pritham refused the offer of a litter, or for Shanaz to carry him. 'I can walk,' he insisted.

Shanaz saw the fear on their faces as they left the shelter, with Gautham leading the way carrying his small lantern. They travelled in single file through the dense forest deep with snow.

'Quick,' Gautham whispered, tugging Shanaz by her arm. They ran behind a rocky spur when a dark cloud settled over the forest. Shanaz heard the 'plopping' sound as she had on the riverbank. The forest caught fire, spreading rapidly, with sparks, and burning trees tossed into the dark sky. Gautham nudged Shanaz, pointing. She crawled behind him, with Pritham following, inching their way between rocks, the blazing forest behind them. They scrambled down an incline to a knoll of trees and reached two stout wooden pillars set in the ground on either side of narrow steps leading down into the darkness. When they reached the bottom of the steps, Gautham shouted above the wind, 'We have to cross this bridge.'

'Where is it?' Shanaz asked.

Gautham raised his lantern. She peered at a narrow bridge strung across a dark chasm, writhing in the wind, made with slender lengths of wood tied together, with two hand ropes on either side. Water roared below them.

'Pritham will go first,' Gautham said. 'When he reaches the other side you must follow. Walk quickly.'

Shanaz nodded. When Pritham stepped off the bridge Shanaz walked across grasping the soggy hand ropes, trying to adjust to its writhing motion. Gautham followed her.

After another long walk they climbed a set of steps to the monastery on a mountainside, overlooking a valley below.

'Thank you for bringing me here,' Shanaz said, watching Pritham enter the building.

'You helped my friend. Thank you,' Gautham answered.

Shanaz examined the stone pillars supporting the roof of the monastery, each carved with scenes of the birth, life and death of a person.

'He looks serene and thoughtful,' Shanaz said.

'It is his teachings we follow,' Gautham said.

She touched the carving of the figure sitting under a tree with spreading branches. A group of children sat at his feet. 'Which of his teachings do you value the most?' she asked, wiping the snow from her face.

'That desire and greed are the main causes of suffering. If you desire nothing,' Gautham replied, 'you will have all you need. Not all you want because want is different from need.'

'But I want food, shelter, protection and safety.'

'No. You *need* food, protection and safety, to survive. Seek only what you need. Also accept what you need, no more. You will then receive more than you need which you must share.'

The early morning sun beamed on the white monastery, and wisps of pale blue smoke swirled around the top of the chimney. Shanaz touched the massive bell hanging from a wooden beam on two stone pillars and wondered why no snow fell on it. She gazed across the mountains surrounding the valley, the snow pink and red in the breaking dawn and walked to the low fence enclosing the front garden and looked at the river flowing through the valley.

Shanaz caught her breath when she saw the bend in the river, searching for the grove of trees where Fariyal and she planned to meet. She looked at the direction finder on her wristband and sighed. Gautham stood by the weathered wooden door waiting for her.

She followed him into the monastery, a single long room with a stone flagged floor, stone walls and a beamed roof. At one end of the room a pot steamed on a fire, and at the other, smoke rose from an open fireplace. Gautham squatted beside Pritham near the fire, tending it to life.

'We used to argue about how to light the fire,' Gautham said, 'and in the fastest time.'

'Now we help each other and do not argue.'

The fire spurted and pungent smoke billowed into the room. Shanaz coughed.

'Sorry,' Gautham said. 'Some smoke is good.' He pointed to the beams in the roof. 'Smoke preserves wood. And, we have no insects here.'

'You may wish to wash yourself,' Pritham suggested. 'We will eat when you come back. Behind this room is a pond and by it is a shrub with red leaves which cleanse the skin.'

Shanaz nodded her thanks and walked out of the room. Outside, the sun shone in a cloudless blue sky. She saw water from a mountain stream running along a stone lined ditch to a pond. She bent down, dipped her hand in and realised the stream cooled the water from a thermal spring in the pond.

'Clever,' she said to herself, undressing. She bathed, rubbing herself with the crushed leaves from the shrub beside the pool. When she returned, Pritham handed her an earthenware bowl with boiled grain and salted vegetables, and a mug with a dark steaming drink.

The monks chanted, their bodies moving rhythmically from side to side. 'We asked for many blessings on you,' Pritham beamed at her. 'It is time to eat.'

After the meal, despite the boys protesting she was their honoured guest, Shanaz went to the pond to wash the pot, bowls and mugs. Question after question rose in her mind. Their fluency in Saradasi surprised her. Where was this monastery and who were they? She decided to respect their lack of curiosity about her and enjoy the cold mountain air and the joy of contentment. She spent the day sitting by the fire with the boy monks, listening to them and sharing in their laughter. She wished her journey ended at the monastery, with its peace and calm. After Gautham stoked the fire that night, he gave her a mat to sleep on, and a thick quilt. Before long the two monks and the High Chancellor of the Saradasi Empire were asleep on the floor of the mountain monastery.

O

She dreamed of two identical Saradasi colonels, both named Shanaz. They stood on either side of Rensoolar 67 Phange, Province Governor on Merr who tried to kill her and Seelawathie-Ap.

The Governor said, 'We have a great misfortune. These elders from Extral North tell me a group of one hundred and twenty children was on an expedition from their school into the mountains and have not returned. An extensive search by their parents and friends has not located the children. I ask you, Colonel Shanaz, as Liaison Officer, IV Army, to organise the military to help. The Saradasi military has sophisticated heat seeking equipment that could find the children.'

'Of course I will help,' one of the colonels said.

The other colonel turned her back to the Governor and examined a jewelled wall hanging. 'Provincial Governor, you can tell these people I refuse. I will not help. Neither the Saradasi military nor its equipment is here for non-military use. You have wasted my time. I will not help.'

'Please help them,' the first Colonel Shanaz begged. 'The children will die in the cold. It will snow tonight.'

The other colonel snapped back, 'Leave me alone. The lives of children are not my concern. What matters to me is the Saradasi Empire.'

'Are you sure?' the first Colonel Shanaz asked.

'No! No! No! I am confused. Leave me alone.'

Shanaz woke from the dream. What happened with the elders of Extral North and the death of the children in a flash flood seemed a long time ago, as if in another hideous lifetime.

O

Shanaz awoke the next morning to the sound of the monastery bell. The room was empty, the cooking pot stood on the fireplace. Sitting on her mat, the quilt around her shoulders, she leant against the wall behind her, watching the fire. Through the small window she saw the sun shining on the snow and the wet swathes of black rocks on the mountains.

She heard a thud, a loud shout and screams. Running to the door she pushed it open.

Pritham lay on his back, his arms and legs spread out, gasping. When she ran towards him, Gautham jumped from behind a stone bench and pushed her on to the ground. Reaching out for Gautham, she wrestled him onto the ground. When he tried to wriggle from her grasp, Pritham pushed her. Breathless, their clothes drenched, they hurled handfuls of snow at one another.

'Gautham and I sometimes play,' Pritham gasped.

'I do too,' Shanaz laughed, rubbing a handful of snow on his face with while Gautham held on to him.

Later in the day Shanaz sat on the doorstep watching the two boy monks in the garden, meditating, seated on a stone bench facing the mountains, their shaven heads shining in the sun. Shanaz stepped back inside. She went to the pot on the fireplace and peered in. Watery white gruel bubbled inside. She looked inside the earthenware grain container.

She returned and sat on the doorstep, watching Pritham and Gautham. Fresh snow began sheeting the valley below and the mountains beyond. The river flowed lazily through the valley. Her eyes closed, Shanaz sank into the calmness of a chant the monks taught her.

A small hand touched her shoulder.

'Food is ready,' Gautham announced waking her. They sat by the fire on their mats. Pritham handed her a bowl of gruel and a spoon. 'Please eat,' he said.

'Why are you not eating?' Shanaz asked, setting her bowl on the floor in front of her.

'We have already eaten, early in the morning, while you were asleep,' Gautham answered, pouring three cups of the dark drink into their mugs.

'Before your prayers?'

'Yes,' Pritham said. 'We ate before you.'

'Tomorrow will be a busy day for both of you,' Shanaz said.

'Why?' Pritham asked, crinkling his eyes.

'Because you will have to pray all day, not only in the morning.'

The boys cocked their heads, widening their eyes.

'You will have to pray for forgiveness for telling me a lie. You have not eaten,' Shanaz whispered. 'You gave me your food.' The tears ran down her face, glistening in the light through the window.

Gautham took her bowl and returned with three bowls.

After they ate, settling down on her mat, Shanaz said, 'Tell me more about your teacher.'

The fire crackled when Pritham threw in a piece of wood. 'Within each of us,' he said, 'is an inner-self, which some call an internal locus of control, labouring to protect us like a faithful friend, trying to lead us to goodness. This inner-self struggles to cast out evil, desire and greed, especially from wanting what others have. The inner-self triumphs when we are content and live in harmony, experiencing peace and happiness.'

'I understand,' Shanaz said. 'The problem arises when we genuinely mistake desire or greed for a need and harbour envy.'

'Yes. The root of much unhappiness is because we seek what we *want*, not what we *need*,' Pritham continued. 'But recognising and deciding what we need is not easy. We must therefore, in our mind, spend time thinking about our real needs.'

'*Some* sorrow arises from wanting what we do not need,' Gautham said. 'But *most* sorrow arises when we receive all we want!'

'You are so rich,' Shanaz said. 'There is nothing in the whole Saradasi Empire of any value to you. I have nothing I can give you.'

Gautham answered. 'You have already given us a great gift.'

'No. I wish I had.'

'Yes, you have. You gave us your friendship. You helped Pritham and stayed with him during a dangerous snow storm. You were happy to share what we have. You are unselfish and humble.'

'I do have something to give you,' Shanaz said. 'It's a song I learned when I was a child, but I cannot remember who taught it to me and I do not know the language of the song.'

'Sing it to us,' Pritham said.

Shanaz sang, gazing out the window framing the valley and the mountains.

'It is a beautiful song. Thank you. Have you tried finding out what the language is?' Pritham asked looking at the fireplace.

'No. I have not, because I could not share this song with anyone until this beautiful moment.'

O

A gust of cold wind from the open window woke her. Shanaz looked around for the monks and saw the two mats were bare, the quilts, a tumbled heap, the fire dead. She heard the sound of a far off bell struck repeatedly when the door flew open. The monks rushed in, each holding a staff. Shanaz stood, her force-sword glowing in her hand. They drew back.

'What has happened?' Shanaz asked, searching their faces.

Pritham looked at the floor.

'You must leave quickly,' Gautham said. 'The bell ringing is from a monastery in a valley below us. It is signalling danger.'

'You are in great danger here,' Pritham said. 'Late last night we saw two lights and we think two people are trying to reach us here. Early this morning we destroyed the bridge we crossed.'

After Shanaz gathered her few belongings, they left the monastery, climbing past the mountain spring feeding the pond, Gautham walking in front carrying a lantern enclosed in a wicker basket, shedding slivers of light. They crossed a mountain pass and reached a bluff thick with snow, the wind howling around them.

'You must reach the big rock below us,' Gautham said, showing Shanaz a spot below them. 'No one will follow you.'

Pritham handed Shanaz the coiled rope slung across his shoulder. She knelt down, staring at the rock. Gautham tied one the end of the rope to a boulder. Shanaz looped the rope across her shoulder and opposite thigh, securing the end around her waist.

'Thank you,' she said. 'I am grateful to you both for your kindness.' She scaled down the face of the bluff. Gautham and Pritham lay flat on the ground, watching at her.

Gautham drew a long knife from a pocket in his robe.

'Cut it,' Pritham said. 'Cut it quickly! We must hurry back, and complete our work before they meet us.'

TWENTY-FIVE

The smell still lingered from the rope Shanaz burnt with her force-sword and buried. It was noon, the day sunny and warm as she walked down a silent valley with shady trees, the snow piled against their trunks. She heard birds sing, but saw none. Occasionally a small furry animal darted across her path to a hidden burrow.

Three narrow valleys wound to the north, the south and the west, but she saw no river with a bend and a grove of trees where Fariyal was waiting for her. Sitting on a rock, her hunger eased when she munched the sweet berries she plucked from a tree. She turned to step down from the rock when she saw them: silent observers, sitting attentively on two rocks, their heads thrust at her. She tied her cloak round her waist and placed her hands on her hips.

'Dearly beloved,' she declared in ringing tones, 'I am pleased to see you. Silence has been my lonely companion. What shall we talk about?'

Two others joined the listeners.

'Consider my life. Will I trudge through life, joyless, tasting the despair within me since childhood?'

Shanaz held the trunk of the tree nearest to her, steadying herself while she wiped the perspiration from her face, trying to focus her eyes. She gazed at her audience, admiring their splendid attire, their slender bodies and bright intelligent eyes fixed on her. Her vision blurred.

'Is there a plan for our lives which is neither good nor bad? Can a good plan become bad? A bad plan good?' She laughed.

Her voice fell to a whisper, 'are there divine entities seeking entertainment by playing a cruel game handing out these bad life plans to us?'

She giggled after eating another handful of berries. She shivered when the wind blew, brushing her hair away from her face. The ground tilted in front of her and she held the tree beside her with both hands until her vision cleared.

'I feel strange and happy! Tell me, my dear friends, are life's events a marvellous or wretched coincidence? Who knows? No one? Is life a series of haphazard events we cannot control?'

She slipped on her backpack, fumbling with the straps. Fixing her eyes first on the listener closest to her, and the others in turn, she asked, 'Have you any questions for me? No? Good, because I have no answers.'

A mist crept across the shallow valley.

'Thank you for listening to a sad and weary traveller. The berries I ate made me talk too much. I have something to share with you.' She bent, removed her backpack, searching in it. She opened her clenched hand.

The birds were inspecting the berries on the rock when the sound reached her, exploding in her ears. Snow, rocks and uprooted trees swept down the mountainside towards her. Shanaz ran, protecting her face with her arms, and stumbled into a deep gully. Her body jarred when she hit a shrub. Flinging out her arms she grasped the shrub, wrapping her legs around its trunk. She winced from the pain across her back and shoulders. Below her she heard the roar of water. She climbed to level ground clinging onto shrubs on the wall of the gully and lay down gasping. Her backpack and water bottle were lost but her firing-belt and force-sword showed no damage. Blood oozed from her cut hands, and her back burned as if on fire. She moved her neck and spine, raised her arms, flexing them at her elbow, clenching and unclenching her fingers.

After tidying herself and checking her wristband for direction Shanaz continued her journey, westwards, down the valley. By late afternoon, the sky cleared. The mountains were behind her, white against a blue sky. She entered a meadow, quickening her pace when she smelt smoke. At the far end of the meadow, between the trees, she saw an area of brightness below, a patch of water. Hurrying down Shanaz reached the bank of a clear river, the water eddying between rocks. Across the river, beyond a cluster of trees, tendrils of smoke curled up.

Shanaz tied her cloak over her force-sword and firing-belt and swam across to the far bank. The sweet scent reached her before she entered a small orchard, the trees laden with fruit. On one fruit tree, a flock of birds watched her.

She walked through the orchard to a road with a canal running alongside. Across the road green fields flourished with mud dykes holding the water diverted from the river. The widening road led to a cracked blue stoned square where a group of children were playing. Three double storied dilapidated wooden buildings stood at the opposite side of the square. A lopsided sign in a faded script hung over the door of one building.

Shanaz crossed the square to a group of adults sitting on wooden benches outside one of the buildings. A thread of smoke hovered over its dull red chimney. They stopped talking when she approached them, turning to look at her. The four males wore thick sleeveless vests over loose shirts, and baggy trousers. The two females wore blouses and long skirts with coloured scarves covering their hair.

'Have you come to buy Zark?' a male asked in Saradasi.

'I seek a friend,' Shanaz answered.

The villagers set the clay cups they were drinking from on the bench beside them. The youngest female with a pendant hanging from the septum of her nose, entered the building and came out with a clay cup she offered Shanaz. 'Please accept a cup of Zark. We make it from berries growing in the mountains.'

'Thank you. I give you the blessings of a stranger,' Shanaz said sipping the clear white liquid.

The male who first spoke to Shanaz pointed to the two largest buildings. 'These were Zark warehouses. We sold Zark, which we made into bricks bound in leaves, to traders in large caravans. Those days have passed. A raid on the village killed most of the adults. We now make Zark for ourselves. I hope you like it.'

'Yes. Thank you. It is an unusual drink, warm and fiery.'

'The few of us left here in the village,' he continued, 'care for the children. We work in our small plots of land and think and talk about the Creator. Does the Creator love you?'

Shanaz drained her cup. 'I am not sure. Perhaps the Creator loves us all, but it is in a way I cannot understand. He or she has thousands of favourites while others suffer, often unaware of the reason. Sometimes I feel the Creator does not love me with the same love I would have for my child.'

'Why is this so?' he asked.

'Perhaps the Creator does not intervene in our affairs. Perhaps we, the creation, must care for the creation and those created.'

The villagers regarded her thoughtfully. The older female refilled their cups. They sipped their Zark in the shade of the tree they sat under. The shadows lengthened.

'Thank you for visiting us,' a younger male said. 'Your friend is here. She is seriously ill, in a deep sleep.'

'What has happened to her?' Shanaz asked.

'Your friend came here from the mountains with a village boy who was collecting berries for Zark. She reached the village but while passing the fields she fell into the canal and a serpent bit her.'

'A serpent? Here in the mountains?' Shanaz asked, staring at the villagers.

'We have loved her and cared for her as one of our own,' he said.

'Thank you. She is my friend and my cousin.'

'She is like you, beautiful,' the youngest females said.

Shanaz shook her head. 'She is more beautiful than I. She is also a better person than I.'

'Perhaps she is. But remember each of us is a flower of equal beauty and value in the Creator's garden. In a moment we will take you to your friend.' The old male sipped his Zark and wiped his lips with the back of his hand. 'If each of us is kind to others, shows compassion and kindness, we will not be confused about the Creator's love.'

'Your thoughts will help me on my long journey,' Shanaz said. 'Thank you. I realise each of us can prevent and create much suffering.'

'High Chancellor, the Saradasi Empire degrades the Creator's creation, and therefore the Creator,' the young female said. 'In the Saradasi Empire, is there suffering because the Creator is negligent? Or is it because its rulers, the Saradasi possess no goodness? Recall your actions in Flowia Valley, stubbornly refusing to save the lives of the children. Was the sorrow the Creator's fault or yours?'

'It was mine.'

'Consider on your travels, and in your future life, what changes would occur if each of us protects the creation on behalf of the Creator.'

The villagers rose and walked with Shanaz to a small stone house on the bank of the river with a courtyard, enclosed by half-walls, bright with potted plants. Fariyal lay on a bed in the courtyard, tossing her head from side to side. Lord Rasalis and Sirrah sat near her on two stools. Fariyal's swollen right leg hung from the side of the bed, her foot resting on a block of wood. A deep wound below her knee gaped; a strand of bark attached to its edge coiled to the ground. A female sat by her dabbing a liquid on the wound. A long line of small orange insects crawled along the bark to the wound, lingered a moment, and dropped dead on the floor.

Shanaz knelt by the bed and placed her head against Fariyal's cheek. 'My Fariyal. I am so sorry I left you,' she said, wiping her tears.

Fariyal opened her eyes. 'I knew you would find me, Shanaz,' she whispered. 'A child saved my life. Remember how I had no love for children?'

'Fariyal, we have all changed.'

'Have the villagers told you who they are?' she asked, her voice weak. 'The Saradasi Empire exiled their ancestors here hundreds of years ago. I am Saradasi, yet they helped me.'

A male ran into the courtyard with a bunch of leaves and a handful of roots. He gave them to the female who sat with Fariyal. 'Here is the new medicine you must prepare for her. She must drink it all when it is cold.'

A small boy, his arms laden with flowers came in and smiled at Fariyal. He placed the flowers in her hand.

'Thank you, Centar. They are beautiful and they smell sweet. Shanaz, this is Centar who saved my life,' Fariyal whispered, as she fell asleep.

Shanaz smiled at Centar and spoke to Lord Rasalis and Sirrah. 'I am so happy to see you both. I have no news of Wynan, Seelawathie-Ap, or Medaris. Have you?'

'No,' Lord Rasalis answered.

Shanaz moved a stool towards them and sat down. 'The villagers told me what happened to Fariyal. You and Sirrah should stay here with Fariyal,' Shanaz said. 'I will meet with Medaris and Seelawathie-Ap and travel with them to find the mountain with twin peaks. We will leave direction markers for you to follow us.' Shanaz looked at Rasalis. 'You look puzzled. What is it?'

'I am puzzled about Fariyal's injury,' he said.

'I am also puzzled. What is puzzling you?'

'I am not sure,' Lord Rasalis said.

A sweet smell from inside the house reached them. Shanaz gently shook Fariyal awake and helped her to drink the medicine from an earthenware cup.

'She will be well,' the villagers who sat in the courtyard said, watching Fariyal perspire.

○

Fariyal woke when the sun sank over the mountains. She heard a melody played on a flute accompanied by drums, cymbals and a stringed instrument. A bird called, and, nearer, she heard the river flowing, the sound of animals, and the chatter of children.

Sirrah joined her in the courtyard and sat with her. 'How are you?' he asked.

'I am feeling stronger, I am not drowsy, and I can move my leg. Perhaps the poison has left my body,' Fariyal said. 'Where are Shanaz and Lord Rasalis?'

'They have gone to bring us food.'

'How will they pay for the food, Sirrah? Shanaz has nothing of value to buy anything.'

'Nor has Lord Rasalis. A thief stole the bag of solars he hid in his backpack.'

'Stolen from Lord Rasalis? By whom?'

'By the captain of a tramp spacecraft, the *Magnificient*, we travelled on to Samandrath-Bahar-Tekaya, where we began our journey to find *The Place*.'

'What was Lord Rasalis's reaction?'

'He insisted he lost nothing.'

'Sirrah, where are we now? Where was Samandrath-Bahar-Tekaya?'

'Perhaps Samandrath-Bahar-Tekaya was an artificial place in space, like an enormous stage where events were manipulated,' Sirrah suggested.

'Manipulated by whom?'

'Lord Rasalis may know, but he has not confided in me.'

'Who else would know?'

'Lord Medaris, perhaps.'

'Why is Lord Rasalis doing all this?'

'He is trying to draw out the hidden goodness in the Saradasi on Lord Gaima's team. Wynan is not here and cannot benefit.'

'I hope I have become a better person,' Fariyal said.

'You are a good person. In Samandrath-Bahar-Tekaya, the blind female told Shanaz, and all of us, not to linger in the past. When you have recovered, bathe in the river and let the past flow away with the water. Listen,' he said.

They heard Lord Rasalis singing in his deep voice.

'Lord Rasalis offered to sing and relate stories in exchange for the help the villagers are giving us,' Sirrah said. 'But the villagers wanted nothing. Even so he insists on singing.'

Fariyal laughed. 'Sirrah, are these villagers and the other people we have met on this journey actors? Are they the famous Suxt-Sux actors from Asurat?'

'I do not know. But I know Lord Medaris travelled to Asurat frequently and Lord Rasalis spoke often with his friend, the Great Khan of Asurat.'

'Sirrah, if Lord Rasalis knows they are actors why does he seem very surprised when we meet them, and strange things happen? I know him well. He is not pretending to be surprised.'

'I agree. He has said nothing to me but maybe a lot of what is happening is not as he planned.'

'Do you know why?'

'No. I suspect Lord Rasalis is very confused,' Sirrah replied, draping his cloak over his shoulders. The trees rustled in the wind, the sound mingling with the hum of the river.

'Are you being evasive? Won't you confide in someone who is dying?'

'You are not dying. I think you are well enough to bully me,' Sirrah laughed giving Fariyal her evening dose of medicine.

○

They sat in the courtyard in the sunshine, enjoying the flat bread with savoury vegetables, and fruit, and sipping Zark. Fariyal sat up in bed, her leg less swollen. Shanaz sat with her, her uniform clean, washed in the river, the tears mended by the seamstress in the village. Her firing-belt and force-sword, cleaned and oiled, shone.

'If you stay here longer I can come with you,' Fariyal said.

'Fariyal, join me when you are well,' Shanaz said, embracing her.

Fariyal held Shanaz's hand. 'Shanaz, if we save our Nereima Galaxy, and if I am alive, I will not return to Saradasi. I want to make this village my home. Eighteen adults are caring for twenty-three orphans, and most of them are old. I want to help them.'

'Fariyal, first visit Califra before deciding to live here alone. I remember what you told me about a Southern Califran. Listen to your instincts. When your heart, and not your mind, speaks, listen carefully. You must never spurn true love.'

Later in the morning while Fariyal slept, Lord Rasalis, Shanaz and Sirrah, sat with the villagers in the meeting hall overlooking the river.

Shanaz told them about *The Prophecy* and the Lord of the East, and of the mountain with twin peaks, their first destination, and of *The Place,* the home of Prince Vira's team.

'A long time ago traders who bought our Zark sold it at a Grand Bazaar near a mountain with twin peaks,' a grey haired villager said. 'It may be the same mountain, but none of us have been there.'

'Who were these traders? Where were they from?' Sirrah asked.

The villagers shook their heads.

'They were not great talkers,' one of them said. 'We think they were from a mountain city, but they never told us its location.'

'How did they travel from here to their city? Is there a route?' Shanaz asked.

'The traders followed a track across the mountains to the Grand Bazaar in their city.'

A villager added, 'It is a dangerous journey. Some say those who sought the city with the Grand Bazaar never returned. Some say it is in another universe.'

O

The next day, after the morning meal, Shanaz embraced Fariyal, and wished Lord Rasalis, Sirrah and the villagers good-bye. With food and water in a backpack the village seamstress made for her, she set off with Centar and a friend to search for the track the villagers mentioned. By early afternoon, they found it. The boys wanted to go further with her, but Shanaz thanked them and sent them back to the village asking them to look after Fariyal.

Walking through green hills, Shanaz wondered why the track was easy to follow after so many years. Ahead of her, to the west, the mountain peaks stood like sawed blue steps against the sky. Though the temperature dropped as the track snaked upwards, she was warm in the heavy woollen coat, a gift from a villager. She rested by a stream and tested the tinderbox, another gift.

As evening drew, with the sun sinking behind the mountains, Shanaz increased her pace. She reached a river with broad banks, speckled with floes of ice, winding through a long valley. Walking along the bank, Shanaz reasoned that if traders and their animals carried the Zark bricks along this route, there might be places to rest. When she rounded a bend, she saw a weathered log hut on the riverbank, under a spreading tree. Shanaz unbuttoned her coat, drew her force-sword and approached the hut. Standing aside she pushed the door open and entered. The hut was empty. The floor was clean, with two circles of stones, and a blackened metal pot near one.

'One for cooking, one for warmth,' Shanaz said to herself. A pile of wood and twigs, and a mound of dry moss lay in a corner. Shanaz left the hut, cut a few branches from a nearby tree, and swept the floor.

She sat at the entrance of the hut watching the light play on the river and the drifting floes of ice. She listened to the sound of the river and the sound of ice floes snap, and the creak of branches rubbing lazily against each other.

She stood to enter the hut when she saw him, thin and stooped, walking along the bank of the river, dressed in a faded red robe with long flapping sleeves and a silver chain round his waist. A striped bag hung from his right shoulder. When Shanaz called out to him, he stopped and raised his head. He took a single tentative step towards her, and paused.

'Can you speak InterWord?' Shanaz asked.

'No,' he chuckled. 'I speak Saradasi.'

'I have food, please share it with me,' Shanaz said.

He bowed, and walked to the hut. Shanaz held the door open for him and he bowed again.

'I have nothing I can offer you,' he said. 'I am a priest collecting herbs for my temple.'

'Is it far from here?' Shanaz asked.

'It is a six month journey.'

'I am travelling westwards across the mountains,' Shanaz said.

'A difficult journey, sadly in a different direction to mine,' the priest replied.

They sat near the fire Shanaz lit and she offered a loaf of flat bread to the priest.

'No. Half is sufficient for me. Thank you. I have herbs we can drink, brewed in water.'

'Thank you.' Shanaz picked up the empty metal pot and filled it from the river.

When the water boiled, the priest dropped a handful of herbs to the pot. They sat on the floor watching the darkening water. The priest added a pinch of a white powder and the contents of the pot turned pink.

He filled Shanaz's wooden bowl and his metal container. They ate the flat bread and drank the herbal drink and sat outside the hut, below a sky scattered with stars.

Shanaz looked at the sky and said, 'The stars are beautiful, but I do not recognise any.'

'Why should you? You may be in a different universe.'

Inside the hut, Shanaz relit the fire in the larger circle of stones. Sitting across the fire with its leaping flames they smiled at each other.

'I have nothing to give you for inviting me to share your food,' the priest said.

'No. Thank you for being here with me. Your presence is a reward. I was lonely and frightened.'

'Is a Saradasi ever frightened?' the Priest asked.

'Sometimes.' Shanaz drew her knees up, leaning back against the wall of the hut and looked at the silver chain around his waist. 'Would you tell me a story to remember this moment?'

'Yes. I am happy to tell you one. In a far away kingdom, the King sentenced a poor orphan boy to death because he stole a few handfuls of grain. After the King sentenced him, the boy showed the King a glowing seed in his hand. He said it was a magic seed. In five years it would grow into a tree with fruits which will heal any illness. He told the King he would give the seed to someone who has never been dishonest. If a dishonest person planted the seed, he or she would die in a year.

'The King's Chief Minister guffawed. "You idiot," he snarled. "You should have planted the seed. You would have been rich and not a thief."

'The boy said, "If I planted the seed I would not be here today. I would have died because I am not honest."'

'"Majesty," the Chief Minister said, "this is nonsense."'

'The King scratched his chin, listening to the Queen whispering to him.

'The King asked, "Who wants this seed? Chief Minister? Army Commander? Ministers? Courtiers? Secretaries? Grand Treasurer, surely you will accept it. You decline?"'

The priest sat, his hands folded on his lap.

'What happened?' Shanaz asked.

'That,' said the priest, with a quiet laugh, 'is for you to decide.'

Shanaz and the priest wished each other a peaceful night and went to sleep on the floor of the hut.

When she awoke the next morning, the hut was empty. The fire burned brightly. Pink liquid simmered in the pot. On the floor, by her backpack, she saw a large map drawn on parchment, with the mountain with twin peaks circled, the distances marked. At the bottom of the map, a figure in Saradasi uniform, eyes closed, hands folded across the chest, lay in repose, as if in death.

TWENTY-SIX

A cold new day dawned. The mist cleared over the river with the rising sun as Shanaz walked along the riverbank. Across the river, clouds hid the upper slopes of the mountains.

The previous evening, while they sat outside the hut, the priest had asked, 'Have you learned much during your journey?'

'Yes. I am now at peace with who I am and content with what I have. I must share my possessions especially if they exceed my needs.'

'Most importantly?' the priest questioned.

'To seek what I need, and no more than I need or can use.'

His face glowed when he spoke to her. 'It is a noble goal which will transform your life, giving you great happiness. High Chancellor of the Saradasi Empire, there is much you can give by sharing your beliefs with others.'

'Despite the wealth of the Saradasi Empire, individual Saradasi own nothing,' Shanaz replied. 'The military owns even my uniform, I have so little to give.'

'Give of yourself and share your talents and beliefs of right and wrong. But first nurture your own life, and then apply what you have learned to the Saradasi Empire. Influence others to think as you think.'

'I will.'

'Avoid the trap of *thinking* about good deeds, which is satisfying but not productive. It is an evil trap. Good thoughts must have good consequences which change lives.'

'I have learned about goodness and of the power of good during this journey,' she said.

'Is the Saradasi Empire necessary?'

'No.'

'When we meet again, we will talk more.'

'Will we meet again?'

'We will. But not when you are High Chancellor of the Saradasi Empire.'

'That is my dream,' she answered.

They walked back into the hut with the staff he had cut for her, after measuring her height and the length of her arm. 'You need a good staff when you travel on foot,' he said.

Shanaz quickened her pace humming the tune of the song she taught the two boys in the monastery. A breeze fanned across the river. The day passed and at dusk, dark clouds swept across the mountaintops bringing sheets of rain and hail, forcing her to shelter under a tree. Her wariness for enemies had lessened, believing she would be safe until she reached *The Place*.

Watching the rain, her thoughts turned to Wynan. She felt a sense of loss and sadness but knew her love for him was waning. A sense of freedom and relief was replacing the joy and excitement of thinking about him.

The puzzling disappearance of the *Mithras Ennab* with Wynan and Fariyal and their return to Saradasi no longer obsessed her. She accepted not understanding what happened, how it occurred and why so many knew so little. She would not have believed in either *The Place* or *The Prophecy* were it not for the message her father left declaring his belief in them.

What occurred when the High Council met with Wynan and Fariyal lingered in her mind? The rain petered to a drizzle, the sky cleared. Watching the stars, Shanaz fell into a restful sleep.

The next morning, the day bloomed. Shanaz swam across the river and back, dried herself and set out, following the map the priest gave her. By noon she crossed the arched stone bridge marked on the map, heading west. She broke into a run when she glimpsed the motionless, blue clad figure lying on the grass by the river.

'I thought you were Wynan,' Shanaz said.

'I am not. Are you well?' Lord Medaris asked, watching a bird skim over the water.

'Yes.'

'Where are the others? Where is Fariyal?'

'Lord Rasalis and Sirrah are with Fariyal.'

'Why?' His head jerked up.

'She is sick.' Shanaz saw his face cloud.

'Is it serious?'

'No, she has recovered. I would not have left her if she was in danger.' Shanaz laid her backpack down and sat on the bank against a tree and told him what happened to Fariyal.

Lord Medaris related how Seelawathie-Ap and he travelled for four days. On the evening of the fourth day she asked his permission to search for Wynan who she said she saw in a vision. Wynan was a captive in another universe and she could free him, but must travel alone.'

'Did you believe her?' Shanaz asked.

'I am uncertain,' Medaris replied. 'Lord Rasalis told me she was with us because of the powers she possessed.'

'What did she do? Shanaz asked.

'She marked a circle on the ground with flowers and lit a fire in the centre chanting in a language I have not heard before.' Lord Medaris paused, then continued, 'Two figures appeared in the circle, standing at opposite ends.'

'The two figures,' Shanaz asked, 'were they females?'

'Yes.'

'I have seen them before,' she said. 'They wore silver clothes.'

'Yes.'

'One with the lighter skin resembled me, the other resembled Seelawathie-Ap.'

Medaris nodded. 'Who are they?

'Seelawathie-Ap said they are spirits repenting for minor sins they committed when they were alive. They are helping us, hoping to gain merit to enter the astral world.'

'Seelawathie-Ap plunged her hands into the fire,' Medaris said, ' and pulled out handfuls of embers which she laid in a line to where each silver figure stood. A huge plume of red smoke surrounded the circle.'

'Did one of them speak?' Shanaz asked.

'Yes. A single word. She said, "Yamu". When the smoke cleared they were gone.'

Lord Medaris and Shanaz sat watching the reflection of the trees rippling in the river. Shanaz pulled off her boots and shook them out. 'Will Seelawathie-Ap find Wynan?'

'I hope so. We should leave now,' Medaris said picking up his backpack and force-sword.

They followed the priest's map to a mountain ridge and across a windswept tableland hemmed in by mountains. When night fell they huddled in the shelter of a cluster of rocks, struggling to sleep in the icy wind.

At dawn they set out on a track cut into the face of a mountain and by mid-morning rested by the pool of water marked on the map. The track wound through two mountain passes and in the evening they reached the summit of the mountain marked on the map.

To the west, they saw the mountain with the twin peaks dominating the landscape. Shanaz and Medaris sat on a rock, gazing at the mountain they had travelled so far to reach.

'Unfortunately, that is not our final destination,' Medaris said. 'The Lord of the East showed us *The Place* where Prince Vira's team lives. It is a cliff surrounded by water. We have just begun our journey.'

'Medaris, there is something joining the twin peaks, below their summit. What is it?'

'I do not know,' he said shading his eyes. 'We may now start the most dangerous part of our journey.'

○

The next morning they set out to climb the mountain with twin peaks. At noon they reached a shallow valley, and around a bend of the stream they were following, they saw a small figure dressed in a green gown and a loose yellow tunic sitting by a pot on a fire. He reminded Shanaz of the two priests, Gautham and Pritham.

He called out in fluent Saradasi, 'A thousand welcomes! My father invites you to his house to rest after your long journey. You are in my father's kingdom.'

He beckoned them. 'Please join me. My name is AnXa. I have food and drink ready for you. Come.'

They crossed the stream and sat on the ground across from AnXa. On lacquered plates, he served them a portion of the steaming food from the bubbling pot.

'A drink?' AnXa asked, pouring a blue liquid into three translucent cups rimmed with a blue motif. Medaris declined the drink and toyed with his food.

After Shanaz ate her food, Medaris said, 'Thank your father for his invitation. But we must continue our journey to the west. We have many miles to travel.'

'You cannot go,' AnXa said.

'Why not?' Shanaz asked.

'Because you are very sick.'

'No, I am not,' Shanaz said. She tried to stand and sank to the ground. 'I feel dizzy and I can't see clearly,' she said, gasping.

Four males, in blue gowns ran out from behind the trees carrying a palanquin, which they placed on the ground near Shanaz. One reached for her wrist, placing two fingers over her pulse. 'You are too weak to walk because your heart rate is very slow and feeble. Your pupils are dilated and your body is cold. Someone has cast a spell on you or poisoned you.'

'In my father's house we have a famous physician who will cure you,' AnXa said. He snapped his fingers.

The four males lifted Shanaz on to the palanquin, placed the poles on their shoulders and set off, crossing the stream and entering a long canyon, which opened onto a packed earth road.

Lord Medaris walked behind them with AnXa. When they rested on the crest of a hill, Shanaz sat up and squinted against the light. She saw a three-tiered town enclosed by a wide wall with nine watchtowers, built in alternating shades of azure blue reflecting the light of the late afternoon.

They entered the town through a small metal gate, and went along winding streets with narrow three-storied houses, until they reached a large market with rows of open-air stalls, teeming with people.

'This,' AnXa said sweeping his arms, 'is the Grand Bazaar.'

They passed row after row of stalls. In one, merchants sold perfumes. In the next, ornaments made of precious metals and jewellery. A group of females, busily talking, paid no attention to customers sweeping in and out of their stalls with boxes of precious stones. In another row of stalls vendors and their armed guards watched over baskets of green flowers with long stems.

'Aphrodisiacs,' AnXa explained.

They wound their way past stalls selling grains of a hundred colours, aromatic spices and writhing fish in green baskets.

'The next market sells perfumes and perfumed plants. The next vegetables, and the last, animals for pets,' AnXa said. 'It will take one week to visit every stall in the Grand Bazaar.'

The east end of the Grand Bazaar bordered a park with flowering plants arranged in triangles and circles, which they crossed to reach AnXa's home, standing alone, set high in a large sloping garden. The garden stretched across the front of the house with water flowing across channels, down waterfalls and through wooden tubes of different sizes into ponds.

'This is a water music garden,' AnXa said. 'Listen to the music as the water flows and falls. Listen carefully, what can you hear?' he asked Lord Medaris.

'Four tunes.'

AnXa's eyes widened. He smiled and said, 'Four tunes? No one except the designer of this garden has heard four tunes. We hear three.'

They entered the house through a door emblazoned with a metal figure of an animal with a long head and tail, fire erupting from its mouth. AnXa led his guests along a cool corridor to a room opening onto a courtyard with fruit trees and a pond. Servants lifted Shanaz from the palanquin on to a soft couch.

A servant entered, opening the door for a tall female with bright red hair elaborately piled on top of her head.

'Physician,' the servant announced loudly, rolled his eyes and withdrew.

The physician swept in and swept her large sea green eyes over Medaris. She sat by Shanaz, bent and smelt her breath, pulled back her eyelids, and felt her body pulses from her neck to her feet. She ran her fingers along Shanaz's head and spine. She probed her abdomen and placed her ear on her chest and over her heart.

'Open eyes! Open eyes,' she shouted in InterWord.

Shanaz opened her eyes, trying to sit up.

'Down. Down,' she barked, pushing Shanaz back.

She wagged a finger at Lord Medaris. 'Rude to stare! Beautiful female. For sale?'

Medaris shook his head.

'What means shaking head? Yes or no? Too much shaking head and head falls off!'

'Not for sale,' Lord Medaris said.

'You for sale?'

'No.'

'I no buy you anyway. Too skinny,' she scolded.

She placed her hands on top of Shanaz 's head. 'This one sick. Many burdens in head and in heart affecting flow of life force in body. Life force instead going boom, boom, boom, is going tchak, tchak, tchak. No good. No good,' the physician yelled, scowling at Lord Medaris. 'Has burdens? True or not true?'

'I do not know,' Lord Medaris replied.

'Liar! Liar! I see from face, you understand everything, but pretend you silly. No fool me.' She strode to the door, muttering and clapped her hands.

Six servants, their backs bent, entered carrying wooden tub. Sixteen others glided in, each with a flat metal gong of a different size, suspended on a stand. Four servants lifted Shanaz into the shimmering liquid in the tub.

The physician placed her hands on Shanaz's shoulders and pushed her under the liquid. 'Better, or more press under?'

Shanaz sat up spluttering.

From a pocket in her gown, the physician drew a wooden mallet, its head wrapped in cloth. 'Can you hear me?' she asked, bending, her head close to Shanaz.

Shanaz blinked her eyes.

'I will hit gong. If you like "dinggg" sound you smile. If not, no smile. You hear?'

She struck each gong a sharp blow. Shanaz smiled when she struck the third and ninth gongs.

The physician held the mallet between her teeth and rubbed her hands. 'She carries big, big sadness and guilt in heart. Never mind. I will fix. I will fix.'

The servants lifted Shanaz from the tub, wrapped her in a perfumed sheet and laid her on the couch. One dried her hair. Another rubbed her feet with sweet scented oil. The physician sat on the floor facing Shanaz and sang to her. Her voice echoed mournfully across the room. She paused often during the song, signalling for the third and ninth gong to be struck. She sang twice, her hands stroking Shanaz's head, pressing her fingers on her temples.

She leaned forwards, her head against Shanaz. She whispered in Saradasi, 'Shanaz, the past is over and you must forgive yourself. I know it is easier to forgive others than forgive yourself. You have shown love and compassion to others. Start loving yourself without condemnation. Go to sleep, Shanaz.'

'I have met you before,' Shanaz said drowsily.

The physician shook her head. 'You have not met me before. You have seen me before. Close your eyes and listen to what I whisper to you. When you wake up the past will no longer haunt you.'

She winked at Lord Medaris. 'You not for sale, lover of music?' she demanded in InterWord drifting out of the room.

After a deep sleep Shanaz woke refreshed the next morning and joined Lord Medaris in the garden. A servant escorted them to AnXa's father, General Vo, short and plump, with his cheeks and lips painted red. He nodded when they entered an octagonal room with a mirrored table. The general's wife, daughter and AnXa joined them at the table.

'Welcome to our home. We will share the Feast for Visitors,' he said, gesturing to Lord Medaris and Shanaz to sit at the table.

'Thank you for your what you have done for us,' Lord Medaris said.

General Vo clapped his hands, his lacquered nails shining in the light. Servants streamed in and served the first of the twenty dishes of the Feast for Visitors.

'Recently, a stranger visited me,' General Vo said, 'asking me to send my son to meet you and bring you here, believing one of you was poisoned on your journey here. He gave me a gift of a thousand precious metal ingots.'

General Vo looked at his food. 'I also have sad news for you. Two people wearing blue clothes similar to yours were here some days ago. First, a male came here, and a day later, a female with dark hair. Are they your friends?'

'Yes,' Shanaz answered.

'Their names please?'

'Lord Wynan and Seelawathie-Ap.'

'Yes. After they arrived, people we have never seen before attacked us, demanding to know where your friends were. The female wanted to help us fight them. But the male declined. He showed great fear and hid during the attack. We forced the attackers to retreat.'

'What happened to our friends?' Shanaz asked.

'The attackers were unable to capture them. But we could not find them either, though we searched the town and the countryside.'

'Can you describe the people who attacked you?' Lord Medaris asked.

'I cannot. They were all masked,' General Vo replied

They finished the meal in silence. General Vo bent towards his wife and daughter and they rose from the table, smiled and left.

Shanaz wondered if Seelawathie-Ap and Lord Wynan escaped with the two silver clothed females. Who led Wynan here? Where were they now? The questions multiplied in her mind.

'The stranger you spoke of, who said one of us may be poisoned, was he tall, dressed in a red robe with a silver chain tied round his waist? A priest gathering herbs?' Shanaz said.

'He was tall but he wore no robe. Have you knowledge of this person?'

'I am not sure,' Shanaz said. 'Was he wearing a silver chain?'

'A silver chain? Interesting. We sell silver chains here in the Grand Bazaar made by craftsmen in the east.'

'The chain was unusual with the trunk of one animal holding the tail of the animal in front of it,' Shanaz said.

General Vo scratched his head. 'I do not remember.'

From the end of the table AnXa said, 'Father, I went with him to the Grand Bazaar where we visited many stalls. He said he wished to buy presents for his two friends on the ship he came here in. He bought three silver chains. He gave me one of the chains and told me to help the two Saradasi I would meet.' AnXa raised his tunic to show a silver chain wound around his gown at the waist.

AnXa handed the chain to Shanaz. 'Look, the animals are just as you described them.'

'You told us the stranger mentioned a ship he came here in. What ship was he referring to?' Shanaz asked.

'I cannot tell you,' AnXa said. 'I too wanted to ask him because we are on a mountain range and have no sea or lake or river to sail in. But something happened and I forgot to ask him.'

'How long was he here?'

'On which occasion?' General Vo inquired. 'He was here once before, for a month.'

'To teach you InterWord?' Shanaz asked.

'Yes.'

'Where is the physician with red hair from?' Shanaz asked.

'I have not asked her. She came here with the stranger who taught us InterWord. After treating you, she left last night, as she had planned.'

O

The following day before dawn, General Vo and AnXa accompanied Shanaz and Lord Medaris to the town gate.

'Beware. A perilous journey is before you,' General Vo warned.

TWENTY-SEVEN

Snow fell lightly while they climbed the mountain of twin peaks on the track marked on the priest's map.

'Medaris are you cold? We can take turns wearing my coat,' Shanaz said over the noise of the wind.

'No thank you,' he called back. 'I'll tell you when I am cold. I was posted in the southern mountains on Merr, where it is colder than this.'

'In Merr?' She sensed he regretted mentioning Merr, when she caught up with him.

'I become breathless when I talk,' he said, increasing his pace.

Shanaz fell behind. How interesting, she reflected, posted in the southern mountains of Merr, desolate, inhospitable and hard to reach. A memory tugged at her, refusing to surface. Thinking back, all his postings were away from the home planet, free from probing eyes and attentive ears. He spent his entire military career in VIII Army, the mysterious and secretive arm of the Saradasi military, which officers joined by invitation. Her father, Lord Laramis, continued to command the VIII Army after his election as High Chancellor, by a special decree of the High Council. Even as High Chancellor she was unable to penetrate its barrier of secrecy. Trudging behind Lord Medaris, far ahead of her on the track, Shanaz recalled the frustrating conversations between herself and Lord Rasalis when she sought more information on Medaris and the VIII Army.

Snow covered mountains and valleys spread into the distance to their right. The track ended at a horizontally curved bridge above a blue lake between the twin peaks. The temperature dropped; a fine drizzle fell and mist drifted over the mountaintops. The bridge swayed in the wind.

'Medaris, will this bridge carry our weight?'

He knelt at the bridge inspecting it. 'I will cross first,' he said, placing a foot on it. The bridge stopped swaying and swayed when he stepped off at the opposite end. Buttoning her heavy coat, holding her staff loosely in her hand, Shanaz walked across the bridge and joined Lord Medaris, on a rocky outcrop, the thawing snow exposing patches of green between the rocks. A single shrub, its red leaves blotched with snow, grew at the base of the steps leading to the summit. Lord Medaris bent to touch one of the octagonal steps.

'The steps are warm but not due to the sun,' Shanaz said, placing her hand on a step, spreading her coat on another. Lord Medaris sat on the step below.

'There is so much we cannot understand,' Shanaz mused aloud, pointing to the bridge. 'When it sways, it looks dangerous and fragile, but when you step on it, stationary and strong.'

'It is a clever deception to dissuade people from using it,' Medaris said as they climbed the steps.

When the wind died, they heard music. Shanaz jerked her head, looking around her frowning. She saw Medaris perspiring, his eyes bloodshot.

'Medaris, what is it?'

'Your father taught me this tune and said when I heard it, my life would change for ever.'

'Where is this tune from, Medaris?'

'I am not certain, but I think it is from the planet Xetfose which we saw destroyed hundreds of years ago, when we were on the Thwacker with the Lord of the East.'

'I know this tune too,' Shanaz said. 'I cannot recall who taught me or when or where I learned it.'

They were on the twenty first step when the music stopped, and a voice spoke in Saradasi: 'Stop when you are on the thirty-fourth step. Press your left palm on the centre of the step.'

Kneeling on the thirty-fourth step, they pressed their left palms.

'Continue climbing. When you hear the first verse of a song, stop. One of you must sing the last verse.'

They stopped on the fifty-fifth step. A child sang, but not in Saradasi.

'Sing the last verse of the song,' the voice ordered.

Shanaz sang the last verse.

'You sang the words to the tune from Xetfose your father taught me,' Medaris said. 'Are you certain it was not your father who taught you the song?'

'No. It is an old memory, too old to bring back. Who would have taught me a song in a language I cannot understand?'

'You should know the next step to place your palm on,' the female voice said.

They climbed the steps and pressed their palms on the eighty-ninth step. The statues of two adult males, two females and two children moved, three to each side revealing a recessed opening in the mountain.

'Enter,' a voice said.

When they stepped into a bright hall, the light dimmed and on their left a huge screen lit with an image.

'Medaris, look,' Shanaz whispered. 'It's the twins we saw on the Thwacker before the evil from *The Place* destroyed Xetfose.'

Brother Red and Brother Green sat across a table set on a cliff in the centre of a lake enclosed by needle like mountains. Frothing waves of lava swept down the mountainsides to the water. Near the cliff, geysers spewed spumes of steaming water.

A voice growled, echoing across the hall. 'Your game, Brother Green.

'Thank you, Brother Red.'

The Brothers sat, their scores on the boards behind them.

Brother Red. Total Score Now:

11235813, 31853211, 43089024, 618 03398, 73890723,21345589, 14423337 3098236754, 57648887, 654 987, 2075788, 563338870910, 969203, 3672020, 465534

Brother Green. Total Score Now:

610947155,   912345,2,6,565106,   261568759132,   466436409, 56601784, 73658847, 70938778, 09099, 8776345, 68774590, 54567.

A mechanical voice called: 'New game. Brother Green to play. Pick up your dice. Throw on three. One. Two. Three. Throw. Total ten.

A bell rang.

The numbers on the board behind Brother Green increased. The sound grew to a roar when a wave swept over the cliff. The Brothers sat with water and foam swirling around their waists.

'New game. New game. Brother Red to play.'

'This repetition will drive me insane,' Brother Red fumed.

'It has not, for the last hundreds of years,' Brother Green pointed out. The bell rang.

'Pick up your dice. Throw on three. One. Two. Three.

'Repetitious mechanical monstrosity,' Brother Red snarled, throwing the dice.

The voice announced: 'Zero. Confirmed, zero. Penalty for scoring zero. Effecting rule two hundred and seven. Removing zero in a number group selected randomly. Change effected. Score decreased.'

Brother Red slammed his fists on the table. Brother Green smiled.

When the images faded from the screen, a male dressed in white walked towards them. 'My name is Deva-Putra,' he said. 'The Lord of the East has shown you the life and times of the planet Xetfose, and you have seen the twins, Prince Vira's team, who live in *The Place.*'

'Yes, and we saw Xetfose destroyed,' Shanaz said.

'The Scholars on Xetfose made plans for the Marinasi race to continue if Prince Vira destroyed Xetfose,' Deva-Putra said. 'Therefore, after exploring many planets, they decided on two where the Marinasi children they selected would survive.'

Deva-Putra looked at Shanaz.

'Saradasi and Natashi.'

'Yes. The Saradasi are direct descendants of the compassionate and spiritual Marinasi. But, the Saradasi exerted power over those they regarded less good than themselves. By creating an empire to make others good, they lost their own goodness. However, the Astral Lord Gaima believed he could flux goodness into the members on his team during their cycles of re-birth. He believed they would have sufficient goodness to save the Nereima Galaxy. Shanaz, you and Fariyal needed to change, and you have. Rasalis and Medaris acquired goodness and have secretly saved many thousand lives. Lord Gaima has not yet succeeded with Wynan. But he will not admit defeat.'

'Where are we?' Shanaz asked.

'Marinasi engineers built and equipped this great hall before Prince Vira destroyed Xetfose. They wished to help others searching for *The Place* if they, the Marinasi failed to destroy it.'

'Who are Brother Red and Brother Green?' Shanaz inquired.

'They were two Marinasi scholars. During one of their journeys they met Lord Vira who imprisoned them in *The Place,* condemned to gamble their way to freedom. They betrayed Xetfose and the Scholars. When you enter *The Place,* if your goodness nullifies the evil, you will destroy *The Place* and the Brothers, but not be harmed yourselves.'

'Can you tell us how to reach *The Place*?' Shanaz asked.

'There is a problem.' Deva-Putra touched an embossed portion on a wall which slid aside, exposing a platform with the figures of Lord Gaima's team: Shanaz, Fariyal, Lord Medaris, Lord Rasalis, and Lord Wynan. At the base of each figure, a rectangle with the outline of a palm glowed.

'Lay your palm on the rectangle in your figure,' Deva-Putra said.

A voice announced, 'Shanaz, Medaris. We accept your palm print. We require the palm prints of Fariyal, Rasalis, and Wynan. We need the five prints to provide the information we have about *The Place*.'

'I understand,' Shanaz said to Deva-Putra. 'All five of us should be here.' She turned when she heard footsteps and saw Fariyal, with Lord Rasalis behind her, running towards them.

Fariyal embraced her. 'We met Seelawathie-Ap and she led us here. She is at the bottom of the steps,'

Deva-Putra took Fariyal and Lord Rasalis to the figures bearing their likeness. After the machine confirmed their palm prints, Lord Rasalis said, 'Wynan stands between us and finding *The Place*.'

'Yes,' Deva-Putra replied. 'If Wynan was here, you would receive the directions, but he must possess sufficient goodness.'

'Can you tell us where Wynan is?' Shanaz said.

'He is alive. That is all I can say. You must find Wynan quickly because you have not much time to locate *The Place* and save the Nereima Galaxy,' Deva-Putra said leading them to the entrance.

Shanaz was the last to leave. She knelt before Deva-Putra and touching his feet with her forehead, said, 'I know who you are. I am blessed to have me you and Lord Gaima is blessed to have you by his side. If we save the Nereima Galaxy, and if I am alive, one day I hope you, Lord Gaima and the Astral Lords of the East, the South and the North will say it has become a blessed galaxy.'

The entrance closed behind her. On the rocky outcrop where the steps ended, Seelawathie-Ap, Sirrah, Master Glance, Breve, and Midi 78 stood by the *Wave*.

'Master Glance, how did you find us here?' Shanaz asked.

Before Master Glance answered, Lord Rasalis said, 'Let us talk later, we must hurry on board the *Wave*.'

On the *Wave* they sat crowded in the recreation room.

'Do you know where Lord Wynan is?' Shanaz asked Seelawathie-Ap.

'I think he is with evil spirits who are preventing him from joining you and gaining goodness to enter *The Place* with you.'

'Have you seen these evil spirits?' Shanaz asked.

'No.'

'Why have they not captured Lord Rasalis, Lord Medaris, Fariyal or me?' Shanaz asked.

'Lord Wynan is most vulnerable to evil influences.' Midi78 explained. 'They would use too much energy trying to harm you. Each of you is now a powerful person because of the goodness within you.'

'Who are these evil forces?' Lord Rasalis asked. 'The archives state the agreement between Lord Gaima and Prince Vira forbids either to interfere.'

'Prince Vira is not interfering,' Midi78 said. 'There are many evil forces in the universes around us and this may be another force.'

'These evil forces,' Fariyal suggested, 'which none of us have seen, may not be supernatural. They may be living beings from another galaxy or universe, or from our own galaxy, wanting control of the Saradasi Empire for material gain. They may have promised Wynan he would rule the Saradasi Empire.'

'If we cannot destroy *The Place,* the Nereima Galaxy and the Saradasi Empire will not exist. What will Wynan rule?' Shanaz said.

'Neither he nor these forces may believe in *The Prophecy* or *The Place,*' Fariyal replied.

'Wynan never believed in supernatural forces,' Shanaz said. 'He sought power, not only for himself but also in memory of his father who he said should have been High Chancellor. He could be trying to fulfil his father's ambition.'

'Seelawathie-Ap, how could Wynan disappear from the blue city? How did he reach there and how did you follow him there?' Lord Medaris asked.

'The spirits ignore the questions I ask them. They took me to the city and I am in a trance when I travel with them.'

'I believe,' Master Glance said, 'there are portals through which we can cross into different worlds. Perhaps Seelawathie-Ap's spirit guides travel through these portals with her. They reached the blue city through a portal and left through a portal. Lord Wynan and those helping him may also know of these portals, and used them.'

'Master Glance,' Shanaz said, 'how did Medaris and I reach the blue city? We did not travel through a portal. We walked there.'

'You may not know you entered a portal,' Master Glance replied. 'It may have been through a simple door, or others may have weakened your consciousness and taken you through the portal. I am sure the blue city exists but where is it?'

'Before I left Saradasi,' Lord Rasalis said, 'I sent out a general alert to detain Wynan fearing he may not join us, but he eluded us. Where would he be now?'

'It would be somewhere he could enjoy himself and return to the Saradasi Empire conveniently if wants to be High Chancellor,' Fariyal said.

'Where is such a place?' Lord Rasalis said.

'I have a simpler explanation,' Lord Medaris said. 'Wynan is hiding from us because he is afraid of danger, because he is a coward. He has probably bribed the Great Khan to provide him a disguise and is living in a crowded metropolis in the Saradasi Empire.'

'Shanaz? What do you think?' Lord Rasalis said.

'I am not certain what he would do. His behaviour is sometimes inconsistent.'

'Seelawathie-Ap, can you take us to Lord Wynan?' Lord Rasalis asked.

'Yes, if Midi78 can tell me where Lord Wynan is hiding. The two silver spirits will help me to travel there and I can take you with me, but I must know where he is hiding. I do not think he is in our universe.'

'Wherever he is, even if we find him, he may not return with us. He may not want to leave,' Fariyal said.

'Please let me meditate for some time,' Midi78 said. 'I am certain I will see a vision with enough detail for Seelawathie-Ap to take us to Lord Wynan.' Midi78 sat on the floor in a corner of the recreation room, closed his eyes and bent his head.

Grimacing after swallowing his medicine which Breve handed him, Master Glance said, 'High Chancellor, before we boarded the *Wave*, you asked how I found you here. General Aricent who works with Lord Rasalis relayed a set of travel coordinates to me on the *Wave*.'

'I have not contacted Aricent since leaving Saradasi,' Lord Rasalis said.

'We followed the coordinates to an asteroid in the Nereima Galaxy, where we landed on a vast plain of ice with a dense fog surrounding us. None of us on the *Wave* know how we arrived here on this mountain from the asteroid. '

'I gave Aricent no such coordinates,' Lord Rasalis said. 'Where is this asteroid?'

'It is not on my space map. I have another message for you,' Master Glance said to Lord Rasalis.

'From Aricent?'

'Yes. He received an urgent enquiry from the Great Khan of Asurat. He asked General Aricent why you cancelled your plan for Faris and the actors to help you during the journey to find *The Place*.'

'I did not cancel my plan,' Lord Rasalis said. 'The plan was to help bring out our goodness before we reached *The Place*. We spent years training actors, identifying locations and building vast stages. I thought the adults and children we met on our travels were Suxt-Sux actors trained by Faris and the Great Khan. But I became confused as we travelled.'

'Lord Rasalis,' Master Glance said, 'Faris and the actors never left Asurat.'

Midi78 sprang to his feet, spreading his arms wide. 'I have seen Lord Wynan in a strange land which is neither flat nor mountainous, with rolling plains and gentle hills.'

'Why is this land strange?' Shanaz asked.

'Mist rises from hundreds of crevices in the ground. It is not a cold place but mist surrounds everything in some areas. I can see rocks on the beach of a tongue shaped bay, and islands, small and white are strung across the water like stepping-stones to hell. The islands appear and disappear in the mist.'

'Perhaps it is not mist,' Master Glance said.

'Perhaps not.'

'What can you hear?' Master Glance asked. 'I can hear the howl of the wind and the screech of angry birds and the waves of the sea and of liquid bubbling in vast pools partly hidden in the mist. In places, the ground is deeply split, and from these abysses, flames leap into the sky.' Midi78 shook his head. 'There is a foul smell'

'Of death?' Master Glance asked.

'No, not of death, Master Glance. It is a strange smell I know, but cannot recall.'

'Lord Wynan is in another universe and I can travel there with all of you,' Seelawathie-Ap said. She swayed from side to side, chanting in a sweet voice despite her artificial larynx. She arched her back placing her palms on her chest. A cocoon of pale light sheathed her body, transforming her to a lustrous silver clothed figure, two-thirds her usual size. Two silver clothed figures appeared behind her.

The *Wave* rose, disappearing within the arc of a dazzling rainbow spanning the twin peaks.

○

Faraway, in another place, Prince Vira, the leader of the Forces of Evil watched Lord Gaima and the Astral Lord of the West, looking anxiously at the soaring *Wave*.

'Are they making a mistake?' the Lord of the West asked.

'Perhaps,' Lord Gaima said.

Prince Vira laughed.